BLUEBELL WINDOWS

The Third Instalment in the story of the Rising Family

BLUEBELL WINDOWS

Susan Sallis

This first hardcover edition published in Great Britain 2000 by
SEVERN HOUSE PUBLISHERS LTD of
9–15 High Street, Sutton, Surrey SM1 1DF.
Previously published in paperback format only
in Great Britain 1987 by Transworld Publishers Ltd.
This title first published in the USA 2000 by
SEVERN HOUSE PUBLISHERS INC., of
595 Madison Avenue, New York, NY 10022.

British Library Cataloguing in Publication Data

Sallis, Susan
    Bluebell windows
    1.   Domestic fiction
    I.   Title
    823.9'14 [F]

    ISBN 0-7278-5578-6

Printed and bound in Great Britain by
MPG Books Ltd, Bodmin, Cornwall.

For the family

Chapter One

Saturday was David's busiest day at the shop and because there was no school, it was probably the day Davina missed him most. Looking at the round, milkmaid's face of her daughter that hot May Saturday of 1934, April suddenly decided that she would take both girls for a picnic. She and David had given Davina a proper two-wheeled bike for her eighth birthday and there was a wickerwork chair on the back of her own bicycle for Flora. The bluebell woods were a mere three miles from Longmeadow in Winterditch Lane where they had lived for the past two years.

Davina clapped her moist hands and her milky blue eyes widened with excitement and apprehension.

'Are we 'llowed to go there without Daddy?' she asked.

Flora sang, 'We're going on a picnic, a picnic, a picnic. We're going on a picnic 'cos it's Satur-atter-day.' She was just four and had been able to read fluently for a year. Davina could write her name and lots more words if no-one minded about spelling. April kissed the top of Flora's dark head before she answered her older daughter.

'Of course we can, Davie. And you can choose what sort of sandwiches we take.'

Flora wasn't interested in food. She went up the stairs one tread at a time to fetch her teddy, while

Davina unhesitatingly chose banana sandwiches with lots of sugar, and ginger beer to drink.

There was no traffic along Winterditch Lane. It meandered over brooks and fields and eventually divided, one spur to connect with the Tewkesbury road, the other with the road to Cheltenham. The Daker women took the left fork to Tewkesbury and pedalled lazily through the tiny hamlet of Down Hatherly where already the cow parsley leaned into the road heavy with blossom the size of dinner plates. April dismounted to show Flora the ancient village pump and to watch the big hand on the church clock jerk on another minute. Time had a weird fascination for the small girl. 'It's gone, Mummy! That's a whole minute gone! Where has it gone? What has happened to it?'

April was at a loss and it was Davie, cycling round and round the pump unwilling to dismount before their destination was reached, who said patiently, 'It's gone to God, Flo. I told you that before. Everything goes to God.'

April was not often surprised by Davina. She said, 'When did you say that to Flo, darling? About everything going to God?'

'When she asked me about Uncle Teddy and Granddad and Uncle Albert and everyone who is dead.' Davina stuck out one sandalled foot. 'Look, I can pedal with one leg. It's hard though.' She replaced her foot and bent to her task. 'Don't be long, Mummy, else I might fall off.'

April stared for another moment at the orbiting child, her pale hair silky flat over her round head, the sun glistening on the blond hairs on bare arms and legs. How much of Teddy, Albert and Will Rising was there in her? Everyone said how much like her mother's side of the family she was; obviously, since David and all the Dakers were as dark as sloes.

Flora said, 'I'm going to pick two bunches of bluebells. One for Gramma Rising and one for us.'

April twisted round and kissed her daughter's dark head again. No doubting that Flora was a Daker with her quick intelligence, brittle hair and black eyes. She laughed as she mounted the bicycle and pushed herself off. 'Onward Christian soldiers!' she rallied. They were all laughing as they turned down the rutted lane that led to the woods.

The bluebells were so dense it looked as if the trees were growing out of a mist of blue. But in spite of the week's dry weather there were boggy patches in the leaf-mould and it paid to pick the flowers nearest the path. They worked their way through the wood, pulling the flowers carefully from their sheaths so that the stems were pale white at the ends. Flora asked her usual searching questions, and for once April gave Davina time to answer first. The husky voice, with its unmistakable Gloucester burr, supplied strangely mature replies.

'You have to pull them like you pull rhubarb. Else the bit you leave in sort of chokes up the plant.' 'Well, of course it's still soggy in here 'cos the sun can't get through to dry it out, can it?' 'It's a worm, Flo. How can it be a snake in this wetness?'

April smiled at their industriously bent backs as she brought up the rear. She must remember this small exchange to recount to David tonight. And maybe her sister May would like to hear it too if she could spare time from looking after their mother, coping with her lively son and bored husband and putting in a full day at the hair salon. April's smile died as she remembered Mother, confined to her room now, waiting – indeed longing – to join poor Pa. She would doubtless make an effort to show pleasure when Davina and Flora arrived with their offerings of flowers, but bluebells were notoriously short-lived and her energy would certainly not survive the flowers. Life was cruel some-times: Pa had been dead for five years now and Mother, never strong, burdened with pernicious anaemia, had expected to be with him in less than a year. And still she lived.

April called, 'Don't hold the stems too tightly, my loves. They are so easily crushed.'

Both girls stopped and placed their bunches in the picnic basket. 'Them's for Gramma Rising,' Flora decreed. 'An' them what's squashed are for us.'

April smiled again at such a right sense of priority and said gently, '*Those* are for Gramma Rising, darling. Not them.'

At the far end of the wood there was a stile leading to an empty acre of land dotted with gorse and rabbit holes and called by the Dakers, 'the wilderness'. Here they laid out the picnic and poured the ginger beer carefully past the marble in the bottle. Davie held her sandwich in both hands and munched stolidly through it. Flora used the Bakelite picnic knife and cut hers into pieces on the plate so that she could savour each one. April was reminded of May and her best friend at school, Sibbie Luker. Sibbie, always hungry, had crammed; May had picked daintily. April said sharply, 'Eat more slowly please, Davie, you'll give yourself a tummy-ache gobbling like that.' But Davie still had her crusts and Flora had eaten every scrap of hers.

The scent of the gorse was thick and heavy and before they had finished wasps had joined the bees and were rolling drunkenly over the crumpled cloth.

'They'll sting – they'll sting—' Davie and Flora hopped around almost spilling their drinks.

'Anyway, we've finished almost.' April gathered up the remains. 'Let's go away from them if they won't leave us. How about hide and seek? You two go and hide and I'll find you.'

They ran off holding hands and squealing. April leaned back against a molehill and ran her hands through her short tawny bob and began to count loudly. The skirt of her green shantung dress was rucked above her knees showing her suspenders, and she wriggled upright and hoped the gorse thorns wouldn't ladder her pale stockings. She should have changed them or even gone without. Though, as older sister March said so firmly, ladies don't. 'Twenty-four!' she yelled loudly to drown Flora's give-away giggles, and wondered then if she was indeed a lady. She knew she was not and on an impulse she stopped combing up her hot hair and reached under her skirt to release her suspenders. Her legs felt wonderful, free of stockings, and her lowheeled strap shoes weren't uncomfortable. She stretched luxuriously. She was happy. She had been happy for nearly five years now. Ever since she had known she was expecting Flora. But she must not ever take it for granted. It was a precious gift which must be savoured piecemeal like Flora's banana sandwich. This Saturday was a special tasty morsel of happiness, even though David wasn't actually here. She let herself think of him, his darkness, his inscrutability which had opened to her and her alone. The precious moments of their love when she could still murmur 'Devil Daker', the name she had first called him when she had been not much older than Flora was now.

'Ninety-eight and coming, ready or not!' she bawled and distinctly heard Davie's hoarse whisper, 'Shut *up*, Flo!'

It was time to go home. 'Do we *have* to?' asked Flora, suddenly weak at the thought of the walk back through the wood to their waiting bikes.

'Yes, we do,' Davie replied. 'Daddy will be home and no tea ready.' She marched ahead to the stile and clambered over without grace but safely. Flora, swinging her small body over the top bar, crashed down the other side and wept bitterly. April felt her heart lurch as she gathered her up. There was no blood and all the tiny limbs seemed intact. 'Mummy will carry you, darling.' She gathered her up. 'Davie, can you manage the basket?' They staggered back through the wood, some of the joy temporarily quenched. It was quite a business loading up the bicycles, tying the flower bunches to the handlebars, coaxing weepy Flora into her scratchy basket seat. When they reached home, April had little sympathy to spare for Davie, who dismounted in her usual way by letting her machine fall between her legs. Unfortunately this time the brake handle scored a scratch down the inside of her calf.

'Here's a clean hanky.' April took an ironed one from the pile on the kitchen table. 'Hold it against the place while I settle Flo with a drink.'

It did not occur to her that she might have got her priorities wrong until Davie remarked matter-of-factly,

'It's better now. Anyway Flo is more important.'

April glanced quickly at the eight-year-old but knew already there was no jealousy in her, let alone sarcasm. She left Flora slurping milk through a straw and bent to the blood-stained handkerchief but it was too late. Guilt, shut in the darkest cupboard of her mind, burst open its doors and swamped her. She would always favour Flora because Flora was David's child and Davina was not.

Florence Rising, tempted by the glorious sunshine, had found enough strength to get out of bed and sit by the window overlooking the gasometer. The view from the back window of 33 Chichester Street was not uplifting: the strips of back yards, eroded by their wash-houses, were all overshadowed by the Coke and Gas Company's large container which, at this time of the year and in this weather, was at its full height. But to Florence Rising, her own small yard a-flutter with the laundry which May was bound to do on a Saturday because she worked during the week at Helen's Hair Salon, was beautiful indeed. There Florence had sat so often in the past, grateful for the cool shadow from the gasometer, while her children had laughed and talked and wept around her. It was that view she had seen each morning when she strip-washed at the shallow kitchen sink, frightened of catching sight of her own nakedness in the reflection of the window, hearing her darling Will riddling the range and setting the kettle on the popping gas. She smiled now in recollection. What a lucky woman she had been . . . and still was. She had had so much more than most women. Her husband, plying his tailoring business from his home, had shared everything with her, from the most menial to the truly magnificent. The times she had enjoyed the sunshine while she finished the button-holes on a suit for him. And the bitterly cold winter days when he had gone into the yard with April or young Teddy and rolled up the snow into fantastic shapes so that from the dining-room or the kitchen it seemed as if they were living in an ice grotto. Will had brought her fun. That was what people failed to realize when they covertly criticized him now. She saw her life as one of the grey prison blankets which she sometimes patched. Dull grey. Until Will arrived. Then the grey was shot with colour and lights of all hues, woven into an intricate embroidery which one day – she prayed quite soon now – would make a perfect pattern.

Her smile widened as the kitchen door burst open and May's only child, Victor, erupted into the yard. Victor was like Teddy had been, all bright reds and blues and vivid greens; ever cracking jokes which often Florence did not understand but which made her laugh anyway because Victor's brown eyes were so bright and full of mirth. He was tall at sixteen, taller than Will had been, taller than his father Monty. And very good-looking in his dark, fine-boned way. He whipped behind the wash-house and disappeared from her view; the washing flapped at his passing and then hung still again. Really, May's smalls were barely decent; the petticoats, especially, seemed made of cobwebs. And the drawers looked more like gym skirts . . . The kitchen door opened again and Albert Frederick looked through. Florence guessed at some devilment on Victor's part and leaned closer to her open window.

'Victor! Are you there?'

Albert Tomms, son of March's ridiculous first marriage to her Uncle Edwin Tomms in Bath, was seventeen and so like his Uncle Albert who had been killed at Mons, that March and her mother never ever mentioned it for fear of hurting the other. He wasn't so much fair as colourless, though his incipient moustache had the touch of gingeriness seen in the first Albert and in Will Rising. He was as tall as Victor and much more solid. He wore cricket flannels and a blazer over his white shirt. Both boys belonged to one of the lesser county teams.

'Victor! Come on, you low-down creeping little skunk! Come and take your medicine like a man.'

Albert, who did not live at Chichester Street and therefore had some difficulty in remembering that the first rule there was not to disturb Grandma Rising, raised his hoarse young voice to tones of mock outrage, and was immediately rewarded by Victor's emergence from behind the wash-house.

'Shut up, you blithering idiot! Grandma will wonder what the hell is going on!'

They were both beneath the shielding washing but in any case Florence drew back slightly, not wanting to be deprived of the scene below. There was some subdued scuffling punctuated by Victor's gasping laugh, then his voice panted, 'Pax – pax I say!' and the two heads appeared, both bent above heaving backs. Florence leaned forward.

Albert straightened and took a deep breath.

'If ever you deliberately cut me out like that again, you beastly, precocious . . . *boy* . . . I'll tell whoever it is that you draw women without any clothes on!'

Victor exploded quietly again but still managed a

Gallic shrug. 'What can I do about it? Girls cannot resist me, Albie old chap. One look and they're done for. The fact that I am an artist would probably drive them mad with desire. I beg you will keep that information to yourself.'

Albert again doubled up with laughter, but continued to spout nouns obviously intended to describe his cousin. 'Swine. Jumped-up, mouthy little would-be Valentino. Gigolo. Lounge lizard.' He grabbed Victor by his shirt collar and brought his ear close. He said something which caused Victor to fall to the ground in mock horror.

'Not that! Not that, oh great one! Forgive me—'

A third time the door opened and Sylvia Rising appeared. Sylvia had always been large and raw-boned. She still was. She clipped both boys smartly and pointed to the kitchen.

'Inside. Both of you. Any squabbling is done indoors, not where the whole world can see!'

The boys went in, hands over their heads. Sylvia cast a look toward the window and saw Florence. Her grin made her ugly weatherbeaten face beautiful.

'So you got out o' bed, our Flo! I'll be up directly with your liver.' The grin widened as Florence made a face. 'All right then, a nice cup of tea first, eh?'

Florence would have preferred May to bring her tea in a china pot with her own milk jug and cup and saucer. But her love for her sister-in-law was very deep.

'That would be lovely, Sylv,' she said in her thin voice. And she looked beyond the gasometer to where the cathedral spires must be, and her smile widened too.

The spurious quarrel between Victor Gould and

Albert Tomms was quite normal and one of their ways of keeping the love they felt for each other on an acceptable everyday level. Shorter though he was by half an inch, Albert was the physically stronger of the two and had always been able to subdue Victor without causing any real hurt. In fact when either of them felt animosity towards the other, the last resort was violence. Victor could reduce Albert to a simmering silence with his quick tongue. When he did so his remorse was instant. And Albert could break Victor's wrist with a quick twist of his own hand, but at the first wince of pain on the handsome dark face, there was an end to it.

Albert said now, dodging away from his Aunt Sylv's arm as she filled the kettle, 'You're welcome to her anyway. She made me feel I'd got a snotty nose.'

Sylvia tutted as she lit the gas, but on behalf of Florence rather than from personal disapproval. When her daughter Daisy had been small, her perpetually runny nose had defied any amount of mopping up.

Victor grinned at the gargantuan back and said provokingly, 'No. You have her, old chap. She wasn't worth drawing even nude.'

He dodged the expected swipe, but Sylvia surprised them both with her wide-eyed query: 'An' 'ow do you know that then, young Victor?'

'Wrong proportions. Breasts not big enough to balance hips.'

He got the swipe then and was told to lay up a tray like his gran liked it before *his* hips got put out of proportion. Albert passed the brown teapot, making no effort to control his delight.

'It's not fair, Aunt Sylv,' Victor complained, deliberately lowering his long black lashes at her. 'You know

I'm a proper artist and proper artists are bound to notice things like that.'

'Indecent,' she muttered, whamming a jam-jar of daisies onto the tray. 'Boy of sixteen . . . Christamighty . . .'

Albert added a teacup and saucer and said righteously, 'He's always been like it, Aunt Sylv. When he was about six years old he wanted to see Aunt April without any clothes on.'

Sylvia, bereft of speech, just stared, and Victor said swiftly, 'Wrong tea things. The white pot and cup. *If* you don't mind, cousin.'

So Florence got her thin china and the joy of hearing a tactfully expurgated version of the boys' latest conquest from Sylvia.

'That Victor's only got to blink once and the girls come runnin',' Sylvia said on a sigh of disapproval. 'Just like his mam. Just like our May in her prime.'

Florence nodded, remembering the hordes of young men who had trooped through their other house, during the war, ostensibly to discuss Haig and Ludendorff with Will, but really to watch May with blind adoration as she cut sandwiches or knitted socks with the light carefully behind her so that her fair hair looked like spun gold and her eyes turned deep violet.

'But May was never really interested. Not until she met Monty,' Florence reminded her sister-in-law gently. 'And Victor is like that too.' She sipped and thought about her grandson. 'Even more so,' she added. 'Victor has that single-mindedness from Monty as well as May.'

Sylvia pursed her lips and said nothing and Florence's clear, tea-brown eyes, weak though they were now, sharpened and stared questioningly at her sister-in-law. So many people thought that because Sylvia looked and sounded bovine, she was insensitive to the point of being stupid. Florence knew better.

She said, 'Sibbie Luker is married to Edward Williams now, Sylv. She'd be a fool if she looked elsewhere.'

Sylvia took Florence's cup and poured more tea into it. Her big liver-marked hand was rock steady and her rough voice the same when she replied.

''Course she would. There's never been any hanky panky for Monty Gould anyway, my dear. Only one woman in the world for Monty, feckless though he might be. And that's our May. You don't want to worry about that.'

Florence was still for a moment, then Sylvia's eyes flicked upward and reassured her with their country frankness.

She took the cup and sipped gratefully.

'I wouldn't like to think . . . May wouldn't understand, you see.'

Sylvia nearly said, 'Not like you understood when my daft brother wandered off with a girl young enough to be his daughter.' But because she was neither stupid nor insensitive she said nothing.

Florence replaced the small cup in its saucer and leaned back, replete.

'I often think how pleased Will would be,' she said, her gaze going out to the gasometer again. 'All the girls so very happy. After so many difficulties. But then I think happiness hard-won is appreciated more. Perhaps. Yes.'

Her lids drooped and Sylvia gathered up the tray and

planned in her mind how she would chop Flo's raw liver with a little of her beetroot chutney at supper-time. And if May cut a slice of bread and butter extra thin, between them they might get her to take more than usual.

March, the eldest of the three Rising sisters, had had a delightful Saturday afternoon. Her husband, Fred Luker, had announced just the night before that he would be bringing four people along for lunch the next day: influential people who needed buttering up. This did not please March on two counts: firstly and fore-most, to prepare lunch, even a cold buffet as Fred suggested, was hard work at such short notice; secondly, Albert, her pride and joy, was playing cricket for the county second eleven and would not be there to pass the drinks and make the sort of small talk he had been taught at Marley's school. Albert himself had disposed of the latter objection right in front of Fred.

'Jolly good job I'm out of the way. You know I can't stand your posh parties.'

'Nobody can stand them,' March snapped, as usual, when she really wanted to hug him and tell him she understood perfectly. 'But one of the reasons I paid those enormous fees for you to go to a private school was so that you could manage the sort of conversation they have at parties.'

She avoided Fred's eyes. He had paid Albert's fees long before they had married. He avenged himself by doing the very thing she disliked when Albert was around; he slid his arm around her shoulders and kissed her on the mouth. Fred knew her so well.

'Darling Marcie . . .' He kissed her again and Albert

looked away. 'Don't worry so.' She tried to free herself and could not. 'I've got a maid for us. If you like her tomorrow, she'll stay.'

'A maid? Don't be ridiculous, Fred.' When March had married her Great-uncle Edwin there had been maids in the house; they had interfered, silently criticized, known too much. 'We don't need a maid. Mrs Prosser comes in to do the rough and Aunt Sylvia helps with spring cleaning and now that I use the laundry for the linen—'

'I've engaged her for tomorrow. On trial.' Fred turned her to face him and made her look into his eyes. She felt her limbs begin to dissolve in spite of Albert's presence.

Her name was Caroline but she was known as Chattie. She was small and round with dark eyes and a look of eager interest that hovered on a smile. And she smelled nice.

She took over the 'cold buffet' as if she'd been doing parties all her life, though she had been a clergyman's skivvy until then. She loved the big house in Bedford Close; she thought the tennis court with its adjacent lawn and shrubbery was 'just like the pictures' and she adored March on sight.

'If I suit, madam, could I . . . sometimes . . . brush your hair?' March's hair, uninterestingly brown compared with May's and April's golden heads, had come into its own as theirs faded. She had steadfastly refused to have it cut in spite of fashion, and its sheer length and thickness showed up the auburn tints to perfection.

She smiled, pleased.

'We'll see,' she said.

By the time the guests had departed at four, she had well and truly seen. Chattie looked charming in a white cap and black dress and she had the knack of being everywhere at once. The visitors were the kind who could not face anything without a full glass in their hand, and the day spent with the up-and-coming Lukers made them feel they could face anything at all. They were impressed by Luker's wife, so aristocratically thin and refined, with her large clear brown eyes hiding more than they gave away, rather like that woman seen everywhere these days with the Prince of Wales – what was her name – Wallis something or other? And of course Luker himself was the sort you wanted on your side. He was astute. And he could be ruthless, very ruthless indeed. There'd been some story about him and the Portermans. Hadn't he seduced the wife and then old Captain Porterman had hung himself? The little maid who had obviously been with the family for years – and that was a good sign these days – said, 'Would you care to try some of this hock, sir? Very refreshing as the weather has turned warm.' And Mrs Luker was talking about tennis parties this summer. Yes, the Lukers were the people to know.

March said, 'Not too bad, was it?' which was tantamount to hysterical enthusiasm, coming from her.

'Marvellous. I've got the Peplows in the palm of my hand and that other chap will follow shortly. Let's go upstairs.'

'Certainly not. There's the clearing up, remember, Fred. For you it's over, for me . . .'

'Chattie will see to all that. Why do you think I hired her?'

'She hasn't stopped since she arrived at nine this morning.' March drifted down to the trestle table beneath the lilac tree and began to load a tray. 'Albert will like her I think, don't you?'

'If he's got any sense he will. Give me that and bring those bottles and let's go upstairs.'

'Fred, for goodness sake . . . and that reminds me. You spent a lot of time with that other woman. Not Clara Peplow. Tilly wotsit.'

'Tilly Adair.'

'It's her husband who owns the land, you know. Not her.'

'He's tricky. I might get to him through her.'

She walked ahead of him clutching empty wine bottles. Sometimes she hated his honesty more than his secrecy. Sometimes she hated the way he saw people: as creatures to be manipulated. Yet it was how she too had been; it was how she had *had* to be even though guilt had threatened to eat her very soul away. At least Fred now absolved her from guilt. Fred made them all happy somehow. She did not want to know how.

The kitchen was neat in spite of the mound of dishes. Chattie had filled the sink and was coping efficiently.

'You go on and have a rest, madam. This won't take me a minute, then I see there's a bit of mending in the basket. If I could sit me under that there lilac with a bit of mending I'd think I were in heaven.'

Fred answered, laughing, 'Don't keep anyone from heaven, please, March. Go on. Walk right through this kitchen and into the breakfast-room. And keep going out of there across the hall, up the stairs and into the bedroom.'

March blushed deep crimson, but Chattie said, 'A nice lie-down. Just the thing. Would you like me to bring up a tray of tea, say about six o'clock?'

Fred waited, his eyes on his wife. She swallowed. 'That would be lovely, Chattie.' She went to the door and stopped again. 'Thank you, Chattie. You've done marvels this afternoon. I think, if my husband agrees—'

'We want you if you want us,' Fred said in his precise voice that still retained some old Gloucester in spite of self-tutoring. It pleased Chattie, it sounded so sincere.

'Oh, sir. That *would* be heaven.'

April was upstairs putting Flora to bed when Albert arrived. David and Davina were 'looking at the garden'. Davina immediately linked her hand with her cousin's.

'Well, Albie?' David collapsed thankfully into a rustic chair left by the previous owners of the house. Any sudden change in the weather hurt his leg and the heat today was proving especially trying. 'How did the match go?'

Albert grinned. In the past he had been frightened of David Daker and seen the dark saturnity as a threat to beloved Aunt April. But that was long ago. David's bitterness had melted with the years and the births of Davie and Flora. Albert crouched to bring himself level with his uncle and cousin.

'Not too bad at all. We didn't expect to bring it off even though we were playing at home. Cheltenham's got a few college boys playing for them and you know how they specialize. One of 'em, chap called Adair, bowled like the Australians, straight for you. He got

Victor out lbw, so Victor pinched his young lady. Right from under his nose.' Albert forbore to mention that the young lady in question had cast eyes in his direction before Victor appeared in the pavilion. Davina looked on her cousin – and rightly so – as her own.

David smiled and Davina gave her hoarse chuckle and began to pick daisies. Talk between the two men settled around cricket generally while they both waited for April to appear. Davina told them about the picnic.

'I'm going to take some bluebells to Grandma when we see her tomorrow. I've taken daisies for ages now and they don't last.'

'I don't know about that.' Albert lowered his head to receive a chain of the flowers. 'She had a vase of them on her tea tray this afternoon.'

'Bluebells don't last either.' Davina surveyed him with her head on one side and began to arrange his hair to her satisfaction. 'Mummy's flowers are the best.'

'What are they?' Albert asked idly, closing his eyes at the touch of her fluttering fingers.

'Primroses. They come for her birthday. You know, "April brings the primrose sweet, scatters daisies at our feet." Daddy calls Mummy Primrose Sweet, don't you, Daddy?'

Albert opened his eyes and looked at David. The dark eyes smiled back at him, sharing whatever secrets they had.

'I do indeed. It suits her, don't you think, old man? The three of them – your mother, Aunt May and April, used to be known as the Daffodil girls. But I thought Primrose suited April better.'

Albert nodded doubtfully. April could still make him tremble and sweat with love which was hard to associate with the shy blossoming of the primrose. He watched as Davina skipped away for more daisies; now *she* was like a primrose, pale and . . . undiscovered. It pleased him to think that he was the one to, in fact, discover her. He rolled onto his knees and crawled after her and she was rolling about, convulsed with tickle-laughter when April emerged through the conservatory door a moment later.

'What on earth's going on? Davie, it's your bedtime. Darling, you look exhausted.' She stood behind David and studied him upside down, then kissed his forehead. It felt waxy beneath her lips. 'I've got mint tea cooling like your mother used to make. And lots of watercress and thin bread and butter.'

'Temptress.' He put up a hand and took her wrist and she felt his need of her.

'Davie's bedtime first, darling. Then plenty of rest and quiet. You shouldn't work so hard, you know.'

Albert stood up. 'I'll put Davie to bed. Is she still reading that book about trains?' In the attic at Bedford Close Albert had a magnificent model train lay-out which Davie loved. She showed her interest by choosing birthday books of erudite specialization. *Electric Locomotives: the future* was the name of the latest. She leapt up enthusiastically at Albert's offer and led the way indoors. April called weakly, 'Are you sure you can spare the time, Albert?' then collapsed by David.

He said, 'Don't worry, Primrose. They're good friends, those two.'

'Like we were.' She picked up his hand and put it to her face. 'How I loved you when I was a child, David.'

'Loved? In the past?' He looked at her sideways, his eyes full of laughter.

'It was different then. Sort of sacrificial. I knew that you belonged to May and I accepted that. I simply wanted a chance to serve you in some way. Then, when you were in disgrace with the family, I knew you were beginning to love me. Properly. And my love changed too.'

Their eyes met and the smile died from David's.

'Don't, April. Sometimes . . . I can't bear it.'

She said swiftly, 'You're tired. Don't worry, darling. Come along inside and let's be cool.'

'No hope of that. Not for us.' He kissed her and stood up with difficulty. She put his hand on her shoulder and took as much weight as he would allow. 'God. April. I wish I could do more for you.'

She said passionately, 'You do everything. Everything.'

He laughed drily. 'But not very often, darling. Admit it.'

They moved slowly through the conservatory and into the large cool dining-room. Their furniture from the flat was there: the big boxy leather armchairs, the ashtrays on their chrome stalks, the Belgian carpet.

She said, 'You're tired. That's all it is.'

He sank into a chair but would not release her.

'Admit it, April. Just between the two of us. Just this once. Admit that I cannot satisfy you often enough.'

She dropped to her knees and took him in her arms.

'Everything about you satisfies me, David. Not simply in bed – which I know is what you mean. Everything.' She drew back her head and looked at him. 'You are so much cleverer than me, darling, but in that you are stupid.'

He smiled slightly, acknowledging her greater

wisdom in this, but as she stood up his hands ran the length of her body and he closed his eyes as if in pain again.

'You see, my darling, I want you so much. That is what is so awful. In spite of this.' He glanced swiftly at his groin where they both knew the shrapnel moved and grated sluggishly when it would. 'I still want you. Practically all the time.'

Her own blue eyes darkened but she refused to pander to him. 'Good. That is very good. Kindly start to worry when you no longer want me!' She leaned swiftly and pecked at him. 'Would you prefer something stronger than mint tea? There is still some whisky in the sideboard. From Christmas.'

It showed the extent of her anxiety. Since those days at the end of the war when he had drunk himself into a stupor to get through each day and each night, she had never suggested a drink. He looked at her steadily, then shook his head.

'Mint tea will be fine,' he said.

Upstairs Albert waited for Davina to come out of the bathroom. He looked in on small sleeping Flora, so dark and like her father, and felt amused indulgence. Then Davina came into her room in an aura of clear Pears soap, trailing her summer dressing-gown behind her, her short hair damp at the ends. He forgot that April's hair would have been long and her nightdress a hand-me-down from March or May and imagined this was how she would have looked at eight years old. He lay by Davina's side and began to turn the pages of her book.

'They will use overhead cables . . .' He pointed to a photograph and replied to her immediate question:

'Too dangerous to electrify the rails, animals and so forth . . .' and he realized how much happier he was with this small female than with any of the young women he and Victor made such a fuss about meeting. Dammit, he even knelt by the bed and said her prayers with her! Then afterwards, when she was drowsy, she put her arms around his neck and kissed him trustingly.

'I love you, Albert Frederick,' she murmured. 'I love you better than anyone else in the world.' Her eyes widened, slightly surprised out of sleep for a moment. 'I love you better than Mummy. Better even than Daddy.'

Albert thought of his own adored mother – Fred did not count of course – of beautiful April before Davie was born, with her long cigarette-holders and her short shapeless dresses that showed her . . . shape.

'Yes. I think I love you better than anyone too, baby.' He put his hand to the soft cheek to settle it more comfortably on the pillow. She was beautiful; but definitely pale and undiscovered, like a primrose. He kissed her button nose. 'Dear Davie. Sleep well.'

Chapter Two

May awoke early and surveyed the day ahead without pleasure. It was her birthday month and she would be forty in two weeks' time; it was not a pleasant prospect. She knew only too well that her celebrated good looks were on the wane; her hair had lost its gold and she had made the mistake of letting Madam Helen bob it after-hours one evening. It was baby-fine and did not have the body to hold a short style. And unless she wore corsets her figure was . . . ample. She found excuses for this immediately: years of theatrical digs where land-ladies supplemented pork pies and fatty brawn with mountains of potatoes and pyramids of bread and butter; and now, when she was doing a job, looking after a son and husband and trying to nurse Mother . . . now she seized her comforts when and where she could – a chocolate biscuit with her tea at Madam's, a piece of Aunt Sylv's fatty bread with her morning bacon, and of course Mother's left-overs. Waste not want not, she always said, as she came downstairs with a tray, popping bits of cake or toast into her mouth.

She sighed and turned to look at Monty. He had worn better than she had. His likeness to her brother Teddy, which had first attracted her so greatly, was still there. Dark lashes which veiled the brown eyes lay thickly on flushed cheeks and though there were lines around the mouth and across the forehead she knew they would crease only when he laughed. She put out a long forefinger and touched his aquiline nose. He was handsome still, and until she insisted that they returned to Gloucester permanently after her father's death, his face had been his fortune. It still could be. He hated working for Tolly Hall, cataloguing old books. It was all too quiet and sedate for Monty. But the other life, racketing around the country, auditioning, always hoping for something really good . . . had that been any better?

May sighed again and turned on her back to stare at the ceiling. This had been her parents' room, and all five children had been delivered in this bed. The cracks in the plaster above her assembled themselves into a map of Scandinavia; she remembered so well when she had registered this first, it had been when April was born, and she and March had slept with Mama to 'see to things' during that first night. Pa hadn't liked that. He hadn't liked his daughters usurping his place in his bed. Had that started his trouble? No . . . she moved her head on the pillow in negation. Teddy had been born the following year, so Pa certainly did not start wandering until after then. May frowned, thinking back. There had been Hettie Luker first, of course. Then years later there had been Hetty's daughter, Sibbie.

May felt tears behind her eyes. That was another awful drawback to growing older; memories seemed to gather weight with each year. The memory of Pa with Sibbie pulled her down physically, more than the extra pounds around her middle. Sibbie Luker, her best friend, the town's scarlet woman, ostracized by everyone except her father and old Alderman Williams.

And now respectably married to the alderman's son, Edward Williams.

It was all too much and the tears overflowed onto May's pillow. It was not that she was jealous of Sibbie's security, indeed affluence. It was not that she minded any more about her liaison with Pa, because darling Mother had forgiven her so publicly a long time ago. It was not that Tolly Hall worked for Edward Williams and therefore so did Monty. It was just that she missed Sibbie so much; she missed her girlhood so much; she was . . . she was getting old.

Monty woke and pecked at her face automatically and felt her tears.

'Mummy-darling. What is it?'

Victor had long called her Mother, but Monty still used the diminutive. She had loved it at first, now it made her weep anew. Yet she couldn't say why. To admit her hankering for Sibbie's adulation and her own lost youth would be disloyal, and Monty was still very dear to her.

'I'm just tired,' she managed at last as his anxiety mounted to irritating heights.

'You do too much, Mummy, and there's no need for it. Sylvia is here to look after Florence. We could afford another house of our own now.' She saw she had given Monty a chance to get on his favourite hobby-horse: moving out of Chichester Street.

'Don't start that again. Please, darling. You know very well Mother needs me specially now. She'd die in a week if we left her.'

Monty was tempted to ask whether that wouldn't be a good thing, but he too loved Florence so he did not.

'All right then, darling. But why stay on at work in that case? We could easily manage with my regular salary at Williams'.'

Again May found it difficult to answer. There were so many reasons for staying on with Madam Helen. Monty still occasionally had the odd flutter and never put any winnings towards a rainy day. And she was extravagant too. She liked to dress well and she could no longer pick up a cheap frock to fit her fuller figure. And there were Victor's many demands . . . But besides all the financial considerations was the undeniable fact that she could not bear to stay in dreary Chichester Street all day long. It had been she who wanted to come home; it was still she who wanted to stay there to be with her mother; but to be there all day and every day trying to tempt Florence to eat more, watching her fade gently away and all the time remembering . . . it was too much.

She said almost sulkily, 'You know you hate it at Williams'.'

He withdrew some of his concern. 'Yes. Well. I've hated it for nearly five years now, darling. So I hardly think—'

'Darling Monty. I'm sorry. I didn't mean—' Her contrition was still warm and instant. They kissed lovingly. 'We should have had another baby,' she sighed. 'I was reading an article in one of the magazines at the salon. It happens to a lot of married couples when their children don't need them any more. They feel sort of . . . old.'

'Well, I don't feel old. Not in the least. And if it's a baby you want . . .' He slid her nightdress from her shoulders and nuzzled into her breasts. She stroked his gleaming dark hair, visualizing how erotic the scene would look on stage; but she sighed yet again. Monty had always liked to take the role of child to his mother and at first she had indulged him lovingly. But over the years the game had developed aspects of reality. And Monty could be an irresponsible and demanding small boy at times.

Sunday was Florence's visiting day. The ancient vicar of St Aldate's came before Matins; Victor took up his week's sketchings to show her while she ate her lunch, in the hope that she might inadvertently finish the one 'good' dinner of the week. After her nap she saw the grandchildren in relays. Little Davina came first and on her own as befitted someone of eight years old. Then Flora sat on April's lap and was encouraged to utter some of her latest sayings. And after tea came Albert, grown-up and serious, and more than ready to leave Marley's school at the end of the summer term and start a mechanical training at the garage.

'Uncle Fred says once I've got the practical knowledge, I can take over the coaches entirely,' he confided to his grandmother that Sunday in May.

Florence brought her mind to bear on everyday matters with some difficulty. She frowned, considering this.

'What about Henry Luker?' she asked. 'After all, he's been running that side of Fred's business for years now, and he is Fred's brother.'

'He's pretty dense too, Gran.' Albert made a funny face. 'Actually it's Aunty Gladys who really runs the charabanc business. She does all the bookings and routes. Uncle Henry just drives. No, I think Uncle Fred wants someone there who can – can – correlate – the mechanical side with the organization. That was why he got Mr Marley to let me take that engineering course.' He grinned. 'He said to Mother frills and feory are all right, as long as they go with nuts and know-how.'

Florence showed her incomprehension.

'Theory, Gran. He meant theory. He thinks all I learn at Marley's is good manners and bookwork.'

'Thrills and theory?'

'Never mind, Gran. The thing is, Aunty Gladys has got something wrong with her neck—'

'Goitre.'

'That's it. She's having injections and she's supposed to take it easy so she really needs someone to do—'

'The correlating and organizing.' Florence smiled mischievously as she used to when the first Albert was alive. 'You see, I'm not as "dense" as you thought, young man.'

They laughed together with what Will would have called mutual appreciation. When Albert stood up to leave, Florence said seriously, 'Your Uncle Fred is awfully kind to you, dear boy, always remember that.'

Albert met her translucent brown eyes and knew that she understood about his jealousy of 'Uncle' Fred. He lifted his shoulders slightly, acknowledging it. When she held out a hand, awaiting his reply, he said, 'I'll try, Gran. I really will try.'

Victor did not make a special visit that afternoon, so Florence was surprised when April reappeared and said there were some children hoping to see her. Tolly and Bridget Hall had brought round their five girls and wondered whether she was up to seeing some of them.

April whispered, 'Olga has improved a lot since you saw her last, darling. And Natasha isn't quite so bad. How about if those two come in with Bridie?'

Florence nodded. 'And I would like to see Tolly afterwards, April dear. On his own if possible.'

She leaned her head against the pillows, trying consciously to garner her strength against the grandchildren of her dearest friend, Kitty Hall.

Bridget Hall, née Williams, had always 'run things to death' and from the moment she had met April and Teddy Rising at their first dame school, she had been obsessed with all the family and their friends. When Teddy Rising had died aged six years old, she had fastened her devotion to Tolly Hall, his small friend, and eventually married him. That was in 1925; now, nine years later, her obsession had shifted slightly. Tolly as a suitor had been undemanding, aloof to the point of reluctance; as a husband he was ardent to the point of selfishness. They now had five daughters, four with Russian names, and the household was run like a communist collective. Bridie, indolent as ever, was the queen bee of the establishment. Her role was to produce children and she discussed her symptoms and emotions constantly. Otherwise she left the work and the constant squabbling to her overworked housekeeper, her mother-in-law, or her husband. Tolly was thin still, but the burning light of his political beliefs, kept mostly to himself, showed in his high colour and shining eyes. He lived a scholarly life, strangely apart from the zoo which was his home. Next to David Daker, he was the cleverest person Florence knew; and she trusted him more than she trusted David.

She patted the counterpane.

'Sit here, Tolly, so that I can hear you properly.' She smiled. 'Your voice is so quiet, my dear.'

Tolly did as she asked, recognizing Florence's real wish was to have him close. He knew that in some ways, for her as well as for Bridget, he had taken the place of Teddy. 'It's some months since I saw you, Mrs Rising. How are you?' he asked in his gentle, formal manner.

'I am surprisingly well, Tolly.' Her smile flickered again. 'Let me be honest with you. I am surprised because I thought I would have been with my husband by now. And here I am.'

Tolly did not try to brush this aside as her close family might have done, though she would not have said it to them.

He inclined his head. 'Because you are still needed.'

She was quiet, considering this, then she said, 'I cannot think how, Tolly. Yet I know you never speak meaninglessly.'

He gave her one of his rare smiles, acknowledging the compliment.

'Let me try to explain. This is a time of falling standards. The family is no longer sacrosanct as it was in your day.' He used long words but she understood them. Will had been a family man; in spite of Sibbie Luker he had been entirely a family man. '. . . the degeneracy in Germany. You have read things in your newspaper?'

'Not exactly. But Victor . . .'

Tolly smiled again, this time with indulgence.

'Victor was always the journalist in this house if I

remember. It is happening here too. People in high places no longer set an example. The Prince of Wales—'

'The old Prince was no better,' Florence murmured.

'But he maintained his family life. He upheld the Crown.'

Florence nodded. Will had done the same, of course; and Will had even looked like the old Prince.

Tolly went on pedantically. 'You see, you set standards. In a world where most people are unable to discipline themselves, you show them how it is done. That in fact it *can* be done.' He touched her blue and white hand in an unusual gesture of affection. 'Do you understand why you are needed?'

She understood what he said, but was unable to view the matter as objectively as he put it.

'Do you mean . . . are the girls in any difficulties? Monty is devoted to May, and though Fred and David . . . in the past . . . I'm certain that now—'

He reassured her quickly, then to show his complete sincerity he trod on difficult ground.

'No marriage is really made in heaven, is it, Mrs Rising? We have to do the best we can. That is what I meant about self-discipline. And your example.'

'Yes. Quite.' Florence sank back among her pillows. She was very tired and wondered hopefully for the hundredth time if this was the tiredness of death. But she could not die without enlisting some help for her favourite. 'It's Albert. My grandson Albert Frederick. I wanted to talk to you about him for just a moment.'

Tolly was surprised. At one time he could see that Albert Tomms might have been at risk; not now.

'Albert is a credit to you and March, Mrs Rising. Until March's marriage five years ago I know you were partially responsible for his upbringing, and in view of what I said just now, I can only reiterate, Albert is an example of the kind of family discipline—'

Florence waved her hand. She knew Tolly was a clever boy, a serious boy, a boy wrapped up in ideals, but in a moment she would fall asleep and there were things to be said.

'Tolly, I must be direct, even blunt. I rely completely on your discretion – I know I can, and that is why I chose you . . . It is Albert's character which worries me. He is so like the first Albert, and March is as close to him as she was to her brother. You were young when Albert was killed, my dear, so you wouldn't remember, but he and March were . . . inseparable. I feared for her reason when we learned of his death. And now . . . I think sometimes she sees her son as a reincarnation of her brother. You will think I am dealing in foolish fancies—'

'No. I don't think that, Mrs Rising.'

'No, perhaps you don't, Tolly. You are so quiet. You see and understand a great deal. You probably see that Fred Luker is a very . . . ruthless . . . man.'

He nodded slowly. 'I think most people who know him agree he can be ruthless.'

She too nodded. 'And he has always been in love with March. As a child, when he taught her to drive a car, he was in love with her then.'

Tolly thought back and nodded again. 'Yes. I can see that now. It makes their eventual marriage more of a blessing, surely?'

'But you see, Tolly, he had to wait so long. When he came home from the war it was a terrible shock to him to find that March was married to Edwin Tomms. He

went to Bath to visit, and brought her home. I sometimes think by force. I don't know what happened, but
he brought her home. She only returned to Bath to
nurse Edwin through his last illness. And even then,
after Edwin's death, she refused to marry Fred.'

'There was a scandal if I remember correctly.'

Florence looked sick. 'There were so many scandals
. . . but through them all Fred was determined that one
day he would marry March. And he did.'

'And they are very happy,' Tolly said firmly.

'I think so. I hope so. But all that ill-feeling . . . it
cannot disappear, not for people like Fred. Fred cannot
forgive easily.'

'But he loves March, Mrs Rising.'

'He does not love Albert. Albert is a reminder of all
the years he had to wait for March.'

Tolly considered. 'Possibly. Have you evidence that
he ill-treats the lad?'

Florence's face was ashen now. 'That is not Fred's
way. He is very good to Albert. Recently he has been
very good indeed. Promised him a slice of the business,
made sure that his education is properly . . .' Her voice
trailed off.

'Channelled. Yes, I heard from Bridie that Fred was
doing a great deal for March's son. Don't try to speak.
I understand your meaning. Albert is to be made depen-
dent on his stepfather. It is Fred Luker's way of getting
power.' Tolly leaned forward. 'You are exhausted. Let
me come back tomorrow or the next day—'

'No. That is all, Tolly. I want you to know about it.
So that you can help Albert if . . . you would help him,
wouldn't you?'

'Of course. You need not fear for Albert. March

would not let anyone harm him. And your other sons-in-law – David Daker especially—'

'I know. I wanted someone outside the family, yet someone who knows them intimately. You grew up with my children, Tolly.'

He bent his head and wondered why this frail woman had the power to move him more than any other human being in the world.

Bridget and April sat in the room on the first floor which contained the piano and Will's old banjo, so had always been called the bandy room. Here was space for Bridie to feed the baby, the toddlers to squabble on the floor with their wooden building blocks, and Olga, Natasha, Davina and Flora to sit at the piano and pick out tunes with one finger while talking.

'I think of myself as mother of all humanity some-times,' Bridget said dreamily, gazing down at the new baby apparently suffocating beneath the weight of her mother's enormous breast. 'Little did I imagine when I danced all night with Maurice Foster and taught all day at that ghastly school for snobs, that my real place in life was—' Catherine set up a howl as the two-year-old chopped at her tiny hand with a brick. Bridget interrupted herself to say languidly, 'April darling, smack Beattie really hard for me, will you? We should have brought Mrs Goodson with us, but of course we had no idea your mother would want a private chat with Daddy, did we, my little darling?' she cooed down at the feeding baby.

April took Beatrice on her knee and tried to tease her old friend.

'I too think of you as mother of all humanity at

times.' She wiped sticky hands deftly before they could plaster her linen Sunday dress, and glanced at the doting Bridget. 'You're not pregnant again, are you?' she asked apprehensively. 'The baby is only four months old.'

'And not even named yet.' Bridget lifted the infant and changed sides. Her breasts were as pendulous as old Gran Rising's had been. April averted her eyes. 'Well, I wouldn't know whether I am or not yet, would I? But I wouldn't be surprised. Daddy only has to look at me, you know. That's what I mean, April. I am . . . mother.'

'You are disgusting,' April said with the frankness that had always been possible between them. 'As for Tolly, I would never have thought he could be so utterly selfish. But if he is, why don't you *do* something, Bridie? You should read Marie Stopes. I mean it. The world is not such a wonderful place for children these days, you know.'

'I've read her. She's for people who don't know any better. Darling, can't you understand? It's my destiny. I love it.'

'But you don't actually do much, Bridie.' April was half-laughing, half-serious as she indicated the two remaining toddlers. They both needed a facecloth and their nappies were odorous. Bridget waved her hand dismissively.

'There are others who can do that sort of thing. Only I can do this.'

April gave up before she physically shook her friend. 'Well . . . anyway. How are you, apart from all this?' She swept the room with her hand again. 'Are you doing any reading? Tolly and David have got hold of one of Shaw's unpublished books. *An Unsocial Socialist.* I'm being force-fed, but I'm not enjoying it.'

'I don't read anything Daddy recommends, on principle. He wants to convert me to his political views and I simply cannot stand that Ramsay MacDonald. I've no objection to Tolly being out-and-out Labour. In fact I'm all for it because there are just too many Conservatives around for him to stand out in such a crowd. I'll support him, but I won't have anything to do with politics myself.' She kissed the baby. 'They are so utterly boring.'

April was ashamed of secretly agreeing with this, so she tried another tack.

'Have you seen anything of your father lately? You told me you had promised Tolly you would heal the breach.'

Bridget rolled her eyes. 'I did, didn't I? But the thought of Sibbie Luker being my *stepmother* – April, it's just too much. You must understand. After all, she came close to being *your* stepmother!' Bridget could be frank too and though April did not like any allusion to her father's long alliance with Sibbie, she took it as best she could.

'I don't really think so. Father would never have left Mother. I know he loved Sibbie, I accept that. But he loved Mother more.'

'Yes, but if she'd died first—'

'Well, she didn't.'

'No, but if she had. Put yourself in my place. How would you have felt about Sibbie if she'd married your father?'

April quailed at the thought. Would she and March and May have ostracized poor Father as Bridget did Edward Williams? Impossible to say.

'It's just that . . . all these granddaughters he's got and never sees. He would love them so.'

'He made his choice, April.'

'And he'd do it again, I'm sure. He is very happy with her, you know, Bridie.'

'Then he doesn't need my babies. And he must learn to do without them.'

'He still pays you an allowance, you said.'

'So he should. Mother would have left me all the money if she'd outlived him. Now Sibbie Luker will get it.'

'I rather doubt that. But in any case, don't you think you're being illogical? If you won't have anything to do with him, you should have nothing to do with his money either.'

Bridget lifted the baby onto her shoulder and proceeded to wind her. 'You sound like Daddy. Logic. What has logic got to do with anything? Is it logical to marry a whore? Is anything logical when you stop to think about it?'

April thought of herself and David, then Flora and Davie. 'No. Nothing at all,' she said.

It was a depressing conclusion, tantamount to saying that life itself had no meaning. She was glad when the door opened and March and May appeared with their boys.

'Tolly and David are organizing the country again and boring poor Monty to death,' May announced.

'And Fred has gone over to talk to Gladys and Henry about business.' March smiled fondly as Albert opened his arms and Davie ran into them. She was reminded of herself and her brother Albert. These two were cousins

44

and there were almost ten years' age difference between them, nevertheless they were easy and right together. She surveyed her sisters affectionately too and even forbore to look disapprovingly in Bridget's direction. 'Shall we all go back to Bedford Close?' she asked with unusual hospitality. 'It's nice enough for Albert and Victor to knock around on the tennis court, and the girls could play in the garden.'

May said, surprised, 'It's a lot of work, March. They'll all want lemonade or something—' She moved her eyes significantly in the direction of the Hall children.

March said, 'I've got a maid. Wait till you see her, she's an absolute treasure.'

Approval was unanimous and rowdy as far as the children were concerned. Davina asked, 'Can we go upstairs and see your train set, Albert?' Victor swung Flora onto his lap and began to thump out 'My old man said follow the van' on the piano. Olga and Natasha polka'd the length of the bandy room and managed to tread on Catherine's already painful hand, and, as she started to scream, the baby joined in.

April followed her sisters hurriedly out of the room and down the stairs. 'Will Mother be all right?' she asked.

'She'll be glad to get rid of us,' May laughed, rolling her eyes at the racket. 'She and Aunt Sylv will sit together without a word passing between them. I sometimes think they use telepathy.'

'Yes.' April thought fondly of her mother and aunt and how, over the years, the two of them, so completely different in every way, had built up a respect which had matured into love. 'Yes. They enjoy sitting together.'

*   *   *

And so they did. At eight o'clock Sylvia brought up the mandatory raw liver which had been a part of the menu at 33 Chichester Street for so long now, then went downstairs to clear up while Florence struggled with it in private and eventually gave it to the cat who appeared hopefully as usual at this time. Then Sylvia came back again and stayed with her until she went to sleep for the last time. Sylvia made no attempt to call the girls home, though one of the Lukers would have run down to Bedford Close in the car and been back with them in no time. She knew that Florence would want it this way; she had said her goodbyes that afternoon and would want no deathbed scenes. At nine she reached out a feeble hand and Sylvia took it in her large horny fingers and held it to her face and thanked her sister-in-law for over thirty years of close companionship. And then she did something she had done only four times in her long life. She wept.

And it was fitting, as Sylvia and Florence knew, that the three Rising girls should be together with all their families at this time. They spilled over the big house in Bedford Close and made the most of that Sunday evening in May 1934, when they were still daughters of Florence Rising before they were anything else. Fred took the men into the sitting-room and opened the french doors to the garden so that they could keep an eye on the children. He had had one of the new cocktail cabinets installed next to the grand piano, and he plied his brothers-in-law with drinks until they were all mellow enough to think they liked each other. Tolly steadfastly refused to join them, and viewed David

Daker with some disapproval as he downed his third brandy. He was partially reassured when David winked broadly at him during one of Fred's perorations on the ideal site for Gloucester's new estate of council housing, which, of course, was on land which Fred owned; and was finally won over when David himself gave a long description of his latest dress design: 'roomy enough in the bust to tote a Thompson', which was the gun which had been used in the recent St Valentine's Day massacre in America. Monty, the mimic, immediately improvised a scene in which he played the menacing George Raft, and Fred, tipping his head back as he drank, did not need to act any part. In different circumstances he could have been the definitive gangster.

The women settled themselves around the table in the breakfast-room. It was easier for Bridget to deal with the baby whose next feed was imminent, and May, March and April, unused to being waited on, felt less awkward next to the kitchen where plump little Chattie ran back and forth with teacups and sponge fingers. The talk was all of fashion, Bridget and May bemoaning the fact that you needed to be as thin as a rail to wear the long-waisted line still in, and April forecasting that deeper waistlines still and big shawl collars would arrive next autumn.

March said, 'I don't see how you can know that, April. David hasn't been up to the London shows since Flora was born.'

'He doesn't need to go anywhere, darling. You know he's got a natural flair that way. Remember my lampshade dress?' April had been the talk of Gloucester before Davie's birth. David had used her as his 'shop window' and her outrageous dresses, hair-styles, pointed satin shoes and long cigarette-holders had been the envy of Gloucester haute couture.

May gurgled delightedly. 'Remember our London weekend, girls? Oh, Bridie, we had such *fun*! We had practically identical tube frocks, and April absolutely vamped an Indian maharajah and we went to the Wembley funfair and rowed through the grottoes—'

'We must have been mad,' March said repressively as Albert and Davina appeared in the doorway. 'Thank goodness we got it out of our systems without any damage being done.'

Bridie remarked, 'I think baby needs changing, there's a peculiar smell.'

Albert said, 'I'm taking Davie upstairs to see my new loco, Aunt April. Won't be long.'

Bridget wrinkled her nose. 'I haven't brought anything with me. Anyway I'm not good at nappies. I'd better feed her instead.' She began to unbutton her blouse and Albert lingered. Aunt April had had to bottle-feed Flora because she hadn't been very well, and this afternoon's performance in the bandy room had intrigued him. He wondered whether he could call Victor in again.

March said, 'Off you go then, Albert. Has Davie had a drink of lemonade?'

Davie gave her placid smile. 'Chattie gave me a glass, Aunt March. With a big lump of ice in it.' March was one of the first Gloucester housewives to own a refrigerator; it was an enormous American Westinghouse which hummed away in the kitchen like a contented polar bear.

'Good. Then you can take a biscuit with you.' March handed the oak biscuit-barrel to her niece to choose for herself. It was something she would never have done for Albert or Victor, but Davie was the first girl in the family and had a special place in her heart.

'I wish you wouldn't do that in front of the children,' she said as soon as the door shut behind them.

Bridget made a face and May said placatingly, 'I don't think Albert was embarrassed, March dear. I know Victor wouldn't be.'

March thought grimly that she was quite certain Victor wouldn't be, but she said, 'I was thinking of Davie.'

April sipped her tea. 'Davie probably didn't notice.'

But May laughed. 'I bet she did. I was her age when you were born, April, and I remember Hettie Luker showing me how babies should be fed! Mother was appalled.'

'Poor Mother.' April still looked into her teacup, feeling the need not to stare at those ballooning breasts. 'How difficult it must have been for her to have the five of us and bring us up and cope with . . . everything. All that basic living wasn't really Mother's cup of tea, was it?'

March remembered her own degradation at the hands of her first husband, and shivered. 'No. She is very fastidious.'

May still giggled. 'I wonder we didn't grow up absolutely frigid. Aunt Lizzie said once that Mother should have been a nun.' She stopped giggling. 'Of course we've got Pa's blood too.'

Bridget looked across the table at the three women who, for her, would always be 'the Rising girls', and said, 'Well, I don't know how she did it, but I do know that when I got to know you first I thought yours was the most wonderful family I could ever imagine. I used to go to bed every night envious of you, praying that your mother would adopt me so that I could live with you for ever.'

March, May and April looked up, surprised, no longer put off by the proud fecundity of their friend. April smiled dewily.

'You're right, Bridie. She made a wonderful family out of us somehow. So did poor Daddy of course. But she . . . she is still doing it from that bed.'

And March and May nodded, fiercely proud.

Upstairs, Albert, prone on the floor as he fitted his new model engine to its tender, felt a tremor in the region of his chest. He sat up with difficulty and put a hand where it hurt and breathed deeply. Davina was all concern.

'Have you got a pain? Oh, Albert, what is the matter?'

'I don't know.' Albert took a last deep breath and suddenly smiled. 'I don't know, Davie. But I do know . . . I love you very much.'

He wondered what on earth had prompted him to say such a soppy thing to this small girl. But when she put her arms around his neck and held his head to hers, he did not feel shy or awkward. He too held her. And so they stayed for a long moment, very still, while their grandmother left her physical body.

With her going, probably coincidentally, the placid life which her family had enjoyed since Will's death, the 'harbour' for which she had been so thankful, was broken. Perhaps, as Tolly had said, they needed her example. Probably in any case, the Risings were not meant to live too peacefully for too long.

Chapter Three

The gentle spring weather lasted through Florence's funeral, then blossomed into full summer. Day after glorious day went by, heartbreakingly beautiful. It was the best summer yet for the lilac in Winterditch Lane and Bedford Close. The hedgerows were choked with huge pans of cow parsley, the fields were brilliant with buttercups. From one of the moss-filled gutters in the cathedral close sprouted a hollyhock. It nodded its heavy head at the passers-by and little Flora called it the Angel Gabriel. David took all the wax models out of his window and displayed a single daring one-piece swimsuit in black wool against a sand-yellow background. Fred's land-buying negotiations languished in the heat and he turned his attention to sending daily charabancs to Weston-super-Mare and Barry Island. At weekends Albert drove; in the evenings he went round to the garage which had been the Lukers' old livery stable, and lovingly serviced engines. Fred clapped him on the back and said he'd never had a season like this one, not a single breakdown. Guardedly they let their companionship expand from garage to home. March was delighted.

Surprisingly, after years of living at home with her mother, March weathered her death better than the other two. April, ramrod straight at the funeral, singing her Mother's favourite hymn, 'Eternal Father', in her clear soprano without one tremor, seemed to wilt with the bluebells. May was frankly devastated, leaning heavily on Monty and Victor as she followed the coffin from St Aldate's and finally collapsing completely by the graveside. But March was quiet and unusually philosophical. 'She did everything she wanted, can't you see that, Sis?' she said to April. 'And lately all she wanted was to make sure we were all right and then join Pa. These last four years have been hard for her.'

'I know I'm being selfish.' April stared dry-eyed at her burgeoning garden. 'I . . . just miss her so much.' She gave a small laugh. 'Everything looks different now that I know she's not seeing it. Look at that lilac. It – it's cruel, March. It's cruel.'

And March remembered how the world had looked to her after her brother Albert's death. She held April to her and started to weep. But April did not join her.

May wept constantly. She wept for the terrible sorrow in Florence's life, unable to bear it now that her mother was no longer there to reassure her of her own innate fulfilment. She wept anew for her two lost brothers and her foolish, happy father. She wept for Aunt Sylv who had borne three illegitimate children and then lost the one conceived in wedlock. She wept for Grandma Rising whose one fear had been the workhouse. She wept for herself, bereft of the secure factor in her life. Finally, it was as if she wept for the whole world.

Aunt Sylv said, 'If you go on like this, our May, I shan't be able to get you enough clean 'ankies for next Monday.'

'I can't go to work, Aunt Sylv. I can't face anyone.'

'No, well. I don't suppose salt water does them fancy shampoos very well.' Sylv's clumsy humour failed to raise a smile and she sighed deeply. 'Look 'ere, our May, you can't take no more time off from that shop of yours. You bin off three weeks now and that Mrs Helen en't going to like it.'

And that night Monty added his persuasions too.

'Mummy baby, don't you see it will help you if you go back to the salon? David is going to try to rope April back into the shop again for the same reason. Neither of you must sit around and brood like this. You've got the children to think of.'

She said again, mournfully, 'We should have had another baby, Monty. April is lucky with Flora so young. She will have to put the loss of Mother out of her mind.'

'Darling, if we'd had another baby you couldn't be working now and we couldn't afford to move.' He began pecking her face from the chin up; she tasted very salty. 'That's what you need, Mummy. A move. And your mother would want us to get out of this awful old house now with all its memories. I'll pop over to the other office tomorrow and get some leaflets about those houses at Longford. D'you remember how you loved them when they were first built? Or we could go to Winterditch Lane. You'd like living near April, wouldn't you?'

May wept anew.

'Oh, Monty. I've already thought about that. But darling, how can we? What would Aunt Sylv do? She couldn't afford to keep this place going, and anyway she'd be so terribly lonely.'

Monty was silent for a while, then he said, 'When sentenced the prisoner asked – is there any reduction for good behaviour?'

May sobbed, but the next Monday she dragged herself back to 'Mrs Helen's shop', and worked with thick fingers and red eyes.

The summer wore relentlessly on. March gave just two of her famous tennis parties and they were for the benefit of the Peplows and the Adairs. Albert beat Robin Adair in a singles match but very much preferred being beaten time after time by Victor when they played their knockabouts after school. When school finished he started to teach Davina the rules of the game. More often than not, Flora would watch them, holding Chattie's hand and jumping up and down while April went to the shop in the Northgate and helped David at the big cutting-table upstairs. Just as her mother had sewed button-holes for tailor Will, now April finished David's model dresses. There was a satisfaction in this for her: history repeating itself. In the autumn David was planning something different for the Gloucester fashion-conscious. A mannequin parade with coffee and wine and a string quartet and potted palms. April worked hard towards this end. When Tolly and David talked of the 'Nazification' of Germany, of the ninety-odd communists in prison there, of the Social Democrats trying to form a government in Prague, she hardly listened. David and Tolly always talked politics. But when David spoke of long lines or box-shapes or sailor collars or toques, then she listened and understood and smiled her willingness to co-operate.

*　　*　　*

One early evening in late August the four Rising grand-children were together on the lawn at Bedford Close. Chattie had supplied them with a 'real, proper' tea served on a card table; Davina had poured, Victor had passed, Flora had convulsed the boys by her repeated incantation 'Thank you very kindly indeed,' and Albert had cleared away with a tea-towel over one arm like the waiters in the Cadena café. March and Fred had gone to help with the final arrangements at Daker's Gowns. Without adult supervision, the occasion had become a party.

Suddenly the silver-blue sky seemed to darken.

''S going to rain,' Davina commented.

''S not,' Victor teased solemnly.

Davina put her hands to her face. 'You said snot Victor Gould! Albert, Victor said snot!'

Flora leaned forward in her deckchair so that her sandalled feet touched the grass. 'It's the Angel Gabriel,' she whispered.

'The Holy Hollyhock!' Victor pretended to cower.

'Shut up a minute, Victor,' commanded Albert.

Faintly, from the direction of the city, came a quiet, confident hum.

'Traffic?' Albert looked at Victor and they both shook their heads. Certainly motor traffic in Gloucester was on the increase, but it could never be heard at this distance. Besides, it was always intermittent. This was constant.

'It's getting darker!' There was a note of panic in Davina's voice and Albert bent down and picked her out of her chair and held her against him. Victor glanced at Flora, but she was entranced.

'I told you. It's the Angel Gabriel.'

The hum grew louder and Chattie ran from the house to join them. She crouched by Flora, her button-brown eyes aghast.

'Whatever is it? Albert, come inside, we ought to get inside!'

Then, seeming to grow out of the chimney-pots of March's big house, came a long cigar-shape, black at first against the west-sinking sun, then silvering swiftly as it glided above them.

'Christamighty!' Albert reverted to his grandfather's favourite oath. 'It's an airship!'

Chattie cowered. 'Is it going to crash? Like that other one?'

Victor gazed, awestruck by the streamlined symmetry of the huge craft. 'The R 101? No, it's perfectly all right, Chattie. Stand and get a good look. It's beautiful.'

'It's not an angel,' Flora whimpered.

Chattie responded to the child's disappointment instantly. 'Come on, baby. Let's have a good look, shall we?' She stood up and took Flora with her. Five pairs of eyes gazed upwards and other eyes stared back from the row of portholes above their heads. Hands waved. They waved back.

As the giant airship moved slowly away from the garden they could see clearly the letters painted along its side and the black hooked crosses on its fins.

'It's German,' Albert said. 'That's the new Nazi badge, it's called a swastika.'

Victor read aloud, 'L . . . Z . . . one, two, nine.' He frowned, then grinned at Albert. 'That's the Olympic Games symbol, isn't it, old man? They're going to be held in Berlin soon, aren't they?'

The airship glided around Chosen Hill and was gone. Albert set Davina on her feet and beamed at Flora and Chattie.

'Well. What did you think of that? Specially arranged by Victor and me.'

Chattie made a scornful dismissing noise, but Flora did not smile. 'It was a sort of angel, Albert, wasn't it? My daddy says the Olympic Games are one of the things to make everyone friendly and happy. So it was a peace angel, wasn't it?'

Victor laughed. 'More like an advertisement angel, Flo. You know how the aeroplanes go over with flags advertising Uncle Fred's garage? Well, that was the same. Germany want lots of people to go to Berlin to see the Games, so they are beginning to advertise them already. Not a bad idea, eh, old man?' He looked at Albert.

Albert nodded. 'Not bad at all. You couldn't miss that, could you?'

Davina wouldn't let go of his hand. 'I didn't like it. I thought it was frightening and horrible. Like a flying monster. Not an angel at all.'

Chattie dusted off her apron. 'Come on inside now. We'll have milk and biscuits and forget the silly old airship.'

Flora took her sister's other hand and swung it comfortingly. 'Tomorrow we'll ask Mother to take us to the cathedral and see the real proper angel,' she promised.

'How the Holy Hollyhock avoids getting a Horrible Headache nodding its Head up there all the time, I really cannot conceive,' Victor intoned piously. And Albert released Davina and chased him all the way up the garden while the females stood and laughed at them.

Tolly saw the incident more seriously. He called at the shop just as they were all packing up to leave.

'You realize what their game was?' he said to David, standing on the carpeted walkway which had just been carefully brushed by March.

'I realize they got plenty of attention.' David was trying to keep an eye on April who was arranging tomorrow's collection on hangers in a certain order. She had made no comment when the airship had passed over the city, but when everyone else waved and shouted hysterically from the Cross, she had stood perfectly still, her eyes almost navy-blue in her white face.

'It was a reconnaissance sortie,' Tolly said in his quiet intensive voice. 'They'd have flown up the river from the Bristol Channel. They'll have photographed all the factories and airfields the length of the country.'

At the age of sixteen Tolly had been one of a team of schoolboys who had raised money for an ambulance and gone to France in the last stages of the war. In some ways his scars were worse than David's, who at that precise moment wanted nothing more than to get his wife home.

'Nothing we can do about it, old chap. It's all above board. The airship was on a scheduled flight from America.'

'And diverted right across Britain?'

'A good advert for their country.'

'For Adolf Hitler you mean. My God, David, the man is a criminal. He's no Chancellor. He's a dictator.

And how sure he must be of his own powers if he can openly send an airship to photograph all our salient—'

David shepherded his friend off the carpet and away from March's furious dustpan.

'Look, old man, I know how you feel about the communists. How do you think I feel about the Jews? I am Jewish, you know that, don't you? We can write to our Member, we can demonstrate, but other than that, there's nothing we can do.'

'I'm going there.'

'Where?'

'I'm going to Germany.'

'Tolly. You can't afford it. And what's the point?'

'I'll go for the Olympic Games. There will be cheap trips – something. It gives me eighteen months to save. And I can talk to people, find things out. I might be able to help. I must do something, David.'

'We'll talk about it another time. Look, we're in the way here. April and I have to pick the girls up from Bedford Close. We must go.'

Tolly left Daker's Gowns and walked blindly to the Cross and then on down Southgate Street. The streets were empty at this hour, which was how Tolly liked them; he had never been keen on people. He passed the infirmary and the sharp smell of antiseptic momentarily drowned the redolence from the pickle factory. He remembered when Sibbie Luker had worked at the pickle factory and had bound her hair in a cloth each morning. And now she was the wife of his father-in-law. How strange life was. How meaningless. When Florence Rising was alive there had seemed some point to things, some mysterious point that she knew by instinct. All his life he and his parents had revolved around the Risings like satellites around a sun, and now the sun had set.

He came to the level crossing where Southgate Street divided into the Stroud and Bristol roads. A goods train chugged slowly across on its way to the docks. Tolly watched it unseeingly and then marched on down the Bristol road towards the canal. April. He should have married April and filled his life with love instead of ideologies. But April had never wanted him and Bridget had been determined to get him. He smiled bleakly; at least she had not had him entirely on her own terms; at least he had been able to obey the Party in that. A respectable marriage, an influential job which gave him the opportunity to go inside and investigate the homes of the aristocracy, the possibility of one day inheriting the firm of Williams, Auctioneers, because surely Edward Williams would salve his conscience by leaving Bridget the firm and Sibbie the house? And meanwhile, a large family brought up from the cradle by himself, taught by himself . . . He smiled again, not so bleakly.

There was a wooden footbridge over the canal at this point and to avoid the traffic he crossed it and walked along the old towpath where Gloucestrians with nautical aspirations tied their small craft. A barge was coming towards him, loaded with wood for the match factory. He stood to one side while the ancient horse plodded by. His thoughts switched to a set of barge paintings in nearby Hartpury House which he intended to buy one day. He had already bought the library and left false book-spines along the empty shelves. The pictures came next. He had a buyer for them; it was Tolly's way to line up a buyer before any purchase was mentioned. The commission would go into his 'Berlin Fund'. If the Party disapproved of his plans he would defy them and go alone. He must do something, anything, to try to help those imprisoned communists. Over ninety of them, some said. And Jews too. How David could shrug the whole issue off as he did was inconceivable.

He marched on, hardly noticing the brilliant sunset over the Bristol Channel. He came to a cluster of clap-board buildings on the canal bank. One was a teashop, another a boat store. And wasn't one of them the infamous bungalow where Sibbie had plied her trade?

He turned and walked away, suddenly sickened by the thought of the Lukers. Poor and underprivileged, they should have been companions, his comrades. But the Lukers of this world had no time for co-operative effort. Fred had clawed himself up to his present pos-ition, literally from the mud of the Dean Forest. And Sibbie . . . well, Sibbie was a chattel who did not know she was a chattel. Somehow she had used all the men who had used her, and she had won.

The thought gave him no pleasure, indeed his revul-sion was turned suddenly upon himself. Those five children in eight years, and Bridie insatiable for more . . . it was profligate. What he and his parents had admired in Florence Rising was her purity. She had mothered a large family, yet she had never lost that purity. He wished passionately she had asked some-thing of him that would take effort and endeavour. Anything. But all she had wanted was for him to keep an eye on her grandson. And Albert was doing so well now what with the garage and the driving and his new relationship with his stepfather. He did not need any protective supervision at all. He was like his grand-father, naturally happy.

Tolly stopped and turned as a voice hailed him. Coming from the direction of the wooden buildings was his friend and colleague, Monty Gould. He wore a striped blazer and light grey flannels and carried a boater. Tolly smiled in spite of himself. Monty was so open and trustful and transparent. Like a schoolboy.

'Too nice an evening to stay inside, eh, Bartholomew?'

It was Monty's whim to address his senior colleague by his full name. When May had first arranged the pos-ition for him at Williams' it might have been an embarrassment to call Tolly Mr Hall in the office and Tolly outside it. Monty had solved the problem easily, as he solved most of his problems.

Tolly said, 'I'm surprised you're not helping at the shop. Even Victor was somewhere around.'

Monty grinned, showing his perfect teeth.

'Wearing a smock and a black beret?' he asked. 'Not my side of the arts at all, old man. I looked at March working herself up into a temper and decided on a walk.'

'Very wise.' They crossed the footbridge and started back up the Bristol Road.

'You too, Bartholomew?' Monty asked, making it into a rhyme.

Tolly smiled. 'As you see.'

'Strange we should choose the same route.' Monty clasped his hands behind his back and lowered his head so that all Tolly could see of his face was a section of chin beneath the rim of the boater. 'Were you – er – looking for anyone?'

'No. Nor anything. I was just walking.'

Monty flashed a quick sideways look and gave another grin, then unlinked his hands and swung them militarily.

'Best foot forward then. Back to the little women. Eh?'

'Yes. Yes, I suppose so.'

As he spoke Tolly realized that the real purpose of his walk had been to avoid going home to his 'little women'. He lengthened his stride to keep in step with Monty and made one of his steely decisions. He could do one thing for Florence Rising. He could adopt her purity.

He had learned never to discuss anything with Bridget, simply to inform and then to act; or, in this case, not to act. Bridget did not believe him.

'I want another baby, Tolly. If David Daker has been prosing to you about over-population, I'll murder him! I want at least another six babies. My God, we haven't had a boy yet. You promised me a son and now you tell me no more babies. My God . . . it's ridiculous.'

'David has said nothing. And if he had talked to me about my personal life I certainly would not listen.'

Tolly took his discarded trousers by the ankles and fitted them carefully seam to seam. Bridget, who had been lying back on the pillows, her latest breast-feeding stint over, sat up slowly; a sure sign that she was beginning to take her husband seriously.

'Well? What bee have you got in your bonnet now? I thought you wanted an enormous family to educate to your way of thinking?'

He did not deny it. 'We have an enormous family, Bridie.'

'But all girls. If you're serious about sending out your own personal disciples, surely you need sons?'

Tolly snapped his trouser-press sharply and his voice dropped a tone when he spoke. 'Don't denigrate your own sex, Bridie. What hope is there for women if women themselves think so little of their own potential?'

'Oh, you know what I mean!' She sat bolt upright and wriggled her shoulders impatiently. 'Don't let's start all that prosing for God's sake! Just give me one good reason why you don't want any more children.'

Tolly put his collar studs carefully next to his cufflinks on the dressing-table; his collar perched on the mirror support reminded him of a halo. Then of Florence Rising.

He turned to look at his wife. She was only three years older than he was, yet in a way she had brought him up and made him hers. He had always known that in spite of all her other boyfriends, he was the one for Bridie Williams. Only very occasionally had he wondered whether she was the one for him. He said gently, 'Bridie, I don't want our family to seem like a succession of irresponsible acts. Can you understand that? I want them to be what they were, carefully planned and provided for.'

'So? As you say, that is what they are. No, Tolly, I still don't understand.' She leaned forward. 'Darling boy, I know we're not rich now, but we're comfortable. And I am convinced that Daddy will eventually provide for us.' She put out a hand that was strangely unworn considering the past eight years. 'Don't worry so much about the future, Tolly darling. Please. Come to your Bridie. Now.'

He withdrew slightly.

'No, you don't understand.' He sounded sad rather than condemning. 'It's a question of . . . discipline, Bridie. It's a question, frankly, of knowing when to stop. It's a question of keeping ourselves . . .' He hesitated to use the word 'pure' which he knew would elicit Bridie's mirth, but he chose instead a worse one. 'It's a question of keeping ourselves clean, my darling. Clean and sharp and – *tempered* – for what might come.'

She too sank back and eyed him levelly.

'You mean the revolution, don't you, Tolly?' She laughed shortly. 'When you became a radical, my dear, I saw you leading a few intelligent, clever men towards social change. I saw your quiet strength being used in leadership. Always leadership. But your politics aren't like that, are they? You . . . you're like a mole. You're digging underground.' She gave another laugh. 'And you've got the nerve to talk about keeping *clean*!'

He flushed slightly. 'I have to serve as I am told to serve, Bridie. At the moment that amounts to consolidating myself – ourselves – as serious citizens—'

She interrupted angrily. 'Were you told to get me pregnant then, Tolly Hall? And keep me pregnant? Do Olga and Natasha and Beatrice and Catherine and Svetlana owe their existence to a command from Russia? Is this what I have to understand?'

Her accusations were so near the truth that he was diverted from the real meaning behind his wish for abstinence and said quietly, 'You wanted the children more than I did, Bridie. Or so you led me to believe night after night in this bed.'

66

She stared at him, furiously silent, for a long moment. Then she turned an angry shoulder and rammed her head into the pillow. When Tolly turned out the light and climbed in beside her she was tempted to tell him to sleep elsewhere; but she did not. This was a temporary hiatus in their relationship, after all; she was determined not to make more of the rift than that. Tolly might be a mental rather than a physical being, but he was used to the marriage bed. He could not do without their love-making any more than she could. It would be all right soon, very soon. As if already asleep, she turned towards him groaning softly, arms upflung. He received the length of her body against his and did not move away, but there was no other response. She waited for ten minutes then turned back again, tears hot behind closed eyes.

Tolly allowed his purposely relaxed muscles to tighten and lay tensely, staring at his collar which gleamed in the moonlight like a real halo.

Saturday dawned already hot again. The first of the Daker mannequin parades was to begin at six o'clock that evening, and April was meeting the Paddington train at two and taking the six real live London mannequins to the flat above the shop to relax and eat sparsely until the appointed hour. The flat, where they had lived themselves for over six years, was still partially furnished and had been made ready previously, but as soon as David left for the shop, April took the girls with her and did some last-minute shopping before climbing the fire escape to their old eyrie far above Gloucester. She was tired already.

Davina said, 'Mummy, Flo is crying.'

April glanced down and saw the lowered lids beneath the straight dark fringe. The lashes looked longer than usual pearled with small-girl tears, and April felt her heart contract.

'Darling, what is it? Tell Mummy.'

Flo shook her head dumbly and trudged on up the stairs. Davina followed, her free arm encircling yet not touching the waist in front like an anxious hen. April brought up the rear for safety's sake and thought that if Flo was going to be ill she'd have to go home and forget the whole day. The thought filled her with relief.

They went straight into the big cutting-room with its dormer windows overlooking King's Square. April dropped her shopping bags and crouched by her daughter.

'Sweetheart. Have you got a pain?'

'No, Mummy.' Flora shook her perfectly shaped head and tears flew. 'It's the Angel Gabriel.'

'She means the hollyhock,' explained Davina unnecessarily.

'It's gorn,' Flora sobbed. 'It was leaning over yesty. Today it's gorn.'

April had always assumed Flora looked like David, dark with a long sensitive mouth and high cheekbones. Suddenly she saw her as a small replica of the other Flo. Her own eyes filled.

'Oh, darling. Never mind. It's been so hot and up there with no shade—'

'But it was blessing us, Mummy! All the time it was blessing us. And now it's gorn.'

April held the little body to her, at a complete loss for words. Davina took a bag of lemon caley from among the shopping. 'I'll make us some nice fizzy,' she offered, turning to the door, then added as an after-thought, 'and don't you worry about the hollyhock, Flo. You ought to know by now that it will come back next year. They always do.'

April felt Flora's tears check and withdrew far enough to look at her face.

'It's true, baby,' she said softly. 'It will grow again. Wait and see.'

'Just like Jesus at Easter?' pursued Flo relentlessly.

'Yes.'

'Like Grandma in heaven?'

April swallowed. 'Yes.'

Flora smiled. 'I love Davie. She's my very best sister,' she said.

April stood up. 'Yes,' she said.

Everyone who was anyone in Gloucester was at the show that evening. April, May and March were the dressers and peeped around the screens identifying the wives of local bigwigs, and sometimes the bigwigs themselves.

'That's Mrs Adair,' March murmured to May as a small brunette drifted through the doors trailing chiffon around her like a blue mist. 'Freddie said he'd talk her into coming. Good lord, she's brought her husband with her. I didn't imagine he was like that.'

'I really don't see why a man shouldn't come, March,' May murmured back. 'After all he will pay for anything she buys.' She peered again. 'Mrs Adair is more short than small, wouldn't you say? I wonder if I could wear chiffon.'

April finished tacking a tuck on a dress and looked at the girl who was wearing it.

'Is that all right? Eugenie, isn't it? We should have fitted this on someone a little bigger in the bust.'

Eugenie laughed without moving her facial muscles. She had completely blackened her eyelids and reminded April of an ancient Egyptian.

'Busts are absolutely out, my dear,' she said. 'If anyone has them they bind them as flat as possible.'

April shuddered. Before Flo she had had a boy's figure; now she was unmistakably a woman.

Eugenie continued speaking through slightly parted lips like a ventriloquist. 'You're April Daker, aren't you? I meant to ask you when we were eating but forgot. I have a message from a friend of yours. Mannie Stein. He sends his love.'

April stared at the darkened eyes on a level with hers and thought how tall the girl must be; April had at one time the distinction of being the tallest girl in Gloucester.

'I – er – I think I used to . . . My husband was in hospital with him. After the war, don't you know.'

The girl said carelessly, 'He's all right is Mannie. Looks after me well. He runs the model agency, calls himself Manuel now. You wouldn't have known.'

May took April's arm. 'Sis, come and look. The mayor's wife would you believe? And Madam Helen over there. And there's Bridget over there, so she managed to tear herself away from her brood. Oh my God . . . there's Sibbie.'

March came behind them. 'The celebrity has arrived and David says we're ready.'

The celebrity was none other than Violet James who wrote books that were 'after' Ethel M. Dell and broadcast quite regularly on the BBC short wave-band.

Disappointingly she proved to look very mannish, with an Eton crop and a severe coat and skirt. However, she was an expert at her task and used the electric microphone hired for the occasion with all the aplomb of a professional.

'The Daker Autumn Collection tries to combine three things,' she smiled quite charmingly at Charles Adair who saluted her familiarly. 'High fashion, comfort, and, above all, economy.' She pattered on about the lead that neighbouring Cheltenham had in the matter of fashion and how it was up to Gloucester ladies to patronize their local creator. 'Because David Daker is a creator, make no mistake about that. Just as I create stories of romance and excitement, so he creates romantic and exciting clothes. Can you imagine Dorinda Grey—' one of the Violet James heroines— 'in our first outfit. Perhaps as she meets the mysterious sheikh outside her Bedouin tent . . .' Violet swept on, publicizing her own work, while Eugenie slunk down the catwalk in the tucked dress. April watched her turn aggressively as she reached the mayor's lady, and felt that in a ghastly way she was a connection with Mannie Stein and all that he symbolized. Mannie the Predator. She shivered although she was so hot that Eugenie now appeared to be walking through a mist.

'Now something for the outdoor girl. Perhaps Dorinda might have worn this outfit as she rode her Arab steed . . .'

May whispered in April's ear, 'Highly unlikely I should think, unless he had a tennis court somewhere in the desert.' She giggled then said anxiously, 'Are you all right, Sis?'

'Of course. Nervous.'

'It's going well. The girls don't need us, they're very professional. That Louise doesn't wear knickers I'll have you know.'

This time she did raise a smile from April. May patted the hand which already showed needlemarks, just as Florence's had. 'Listen, darling. I'm going to leave you for a minute and have a word with Sibbie. It's about time we started to acknowledge her again. And Bridie is doing such a damned good job of dumb insolence I feel sorry for her.'

April managed to nod agreement though she knew that March's wrath at May's desertion would be monumental. Unwillingly she went towards Eugenie and began to unbutton her.

David coped as best he could with the caterers. There were no proper facilities for them at the back of the shop, but to use the kitchen up in the flat was completely impracticable. It was the cocktail hour so there would have to be cocktails, and the fitting-rooms had been opened out to provide a makeshift bar. He wondered gloomily what on earth he was thinking of, putting on an affair like this in workaday Gloucester. The expense could never hope to be covered by the ultimate sales. In any case the relation between the two was incalculable; how could he know whether sales in a year or even five years weren't as a result of this evening? He had a few words with the penguin-suited waiter and escaped into the yard for a breather.

This evening belonged to April and her sisters, not to him. He had lost interest in the outfits when they reached the sales stage; already he planned to have a sketching day tomorrow. They no longer visited

Chichester Street on Sundays of course, so he would sit in the garden with his sketch block and force April to sit with him. It would do her good. She was getting thin again and the way she sat over a piece of sewing with bent head reminded him painfully of Florence. They would talk about Katherine Mansfield and he would concentrate on outdoor clothes. He visualized a loose jacket, something like the old motoring dust coats, swinging from the shoulders outwards. His sketch would be gallant and brave; like April had been when he had known her first. She had faced life with . . . with a swagger. He would call his coat a swagger coat.

Sibbie, who had once been mistaken for May's sister, smiled slightly as her old friend heaved a sigh of relief and breathed something about getting the weight off her feet.

'But why here?' Sibbie could be horribly frank at times. 'There are lots of women here who are not in disgrace. Why sit by me?'

But May could be frank too. 'Because we were friends and I hoped, when you married Edward Williams, we could be again.'

'I've been married to my darling Edward for almost two years now, May,' Sibbie pointed out sweetly. 'And you know exactly where we live, because you visited the old house in Barnwood quite regularly when Bridget lived there.'

May flushed slightly. 'I haven't been invited to that house for many years, Sibbie. After all Edward employs my husband . . . besides, you still visit your mother in Chichester Street and we live just opposite if you recall.'

Sibbie took her attention away from the catwalk and

turned in her seat to survey her friend. What she saw made her suddenly sad. May still looked out from the sky-blue eyes, but the fair lashes which had been silky and thick were clogged with mascara and the peach-coloured skin faded into parchment along the hairline and under the chin. The masses of angel-fair hair were reduced to baby wisps around her ears. The nine-teen-thirties did not suit May; she was a pre-war creature.

Sibbie said, 'Don't lie to me, May. I called three times. I wanted to thank Florence for . . . many things.'

May's face contracted as if in pain. Then she sighed sharply and returned to the present. 'I didn't know. Mother didn't tell me. Perhaps she thought it was best.'

'I didn't see her. I didn't get past your Aunt Sylv. Perhaps *she* knew best.'

'Aunt Sylv? My God, how dare she! Mother wanted us to be friends again, I know it. Aunt Sylv had no right to interfere!'

'Hush, May. What's done is done.'

Both women turned back to the scene before them. Louise was showing some lounging pyjamas in black jersey-knit, which, apparently, would be admirable for Dorinda to wear as she languished in the arms of her sheikh. Sibbie put her mouth to May's ear and whis-pered, 'I shall order those. Edward adores me to languish.'

After a doubtful moment, May smiled roguishly.

Sibbie held her gloved hand out, palm upward; May placed her ungloved hand on it. They gripped hard.

The thunder began as the cocktails were taken round. The first clap was felt rather than heard; a tremor that tingled the soles of the feet. A few minutes later came a spectacular flash of lightning that coloured the darkened evening luridly and made the electric globes suspended from the ceiling flicker and dim. On its heels the second thunderclap was felt and heard, the blast arriving an infinitesimal moment before the sound. Someone spilt a drink, and small screams could be heard through the rumbling after-math. David mounted the catwalk and apologized for the lights.

'Obviously I arranged for a storm so that nobody could rush off—' There was plenty of obedient laughter. 'If anyone is in a hurry there is a taxi rank in King's Square of course. Meanwhile, do enjoy your cocktails and the music. I am delighted to present Mr Tom Ritchie on the piano.'

A young man in a boiled shirt and tails stood by the hired grand, bowing and carefully removing his white gloves, fingertip by fingertip. He flipped his tails and sat on the piano stool and the reassuring tinkle of 'Kitten on the Keys' was heard through the ensuing thunderclaps. It made the evening suddenly intimate, everyone drawn together by the storm outside.

Eugenie slunk up to April holding two White Ladies.

'My dear, you're going to do well. It couldn't be better. Mannie will be so pleased.' She drank the contents of one glass, put it down and started on the other.

April said, 'I think I must go. I find the closeness rather oppressive.'

'Oh, don't leave yet. I thought we could chew Mannie over. He's so good at it, isn't he?'

'At it?'

'In bed.' She giggled. 'Don't pretend you don't know.

He's told me all.' She fiddled in her bag and extracted a jade cigarette-holder, almost a replica of the one April had once used. 'Darling, have you got a cigarette? Mannie said you smoke like a trooper so I know I can rely on you.'

April put a hand on the back of a chair. 'I don't any more. Not since my daughter was born.'

'Oh, is that the one that belongs to Mannie? He said something about your husband not being quite up to it.' She surveyed David coolly. 'Must say he looks all right to me. Very all right indeed. And if we've shared one man, why shouldn't we share another?'

April knew she should walk away but her feet would not move. She said faintly, 'He's perfectly all right, thank you.'

'Oh . . .' The Egyptian eyes glazed with sudden boredom. She said, 'Darling, do excuse me, I simply must have a cigarette and another drink. There's a lone man there, I'll try him.' She slunk off in the direction of Charles Adair and April stood alone, leaning heavily on a chair.

Young Tom Ritchie went into 'Love is the Sweetest Thing' and she looked round and saw David still on the catwalk surrounded by a bevy of women. She began to move from chair to chair, stumbling over handbags and scarves, halting at each clap of thunder as if it were gunfire.

'. . . no power on earth can ever bring such happiness to anything . . .'

She released her last handhold and held out her arms to David and he looked over the many marcelled heads and saw her there, her face chalky-white and shining with sweat. He brushed past people and things and took the outstretched hands.

'What is it, my Primrose?' he asked in a low voice.

'Oh, David. The Angel Gabriel has gone,' she said. And she fell down in a dead faint.

Chapter Four

At first everyone said it was the heat and the fact that
April had worked too hard towards the mannequin
parade. David, cursing himself because it had been his
idea to involve April wholeheartedly, insisted on calling
in young Dr Green on Monday. Old Dr Green had
brought April into the world thirty-two years previously and his son felt a special kinship with her and
spent almost an hour examining her. David had taken
the afternoon off and hovered anxiously in the background; Davina took Flora into the front room and
taught her to play Chopsticks on the piano. The unnatural silence, concentrated on stethoscope and pulse,
was broken by the single staccato notes heard faintly
through the wall. April badly wanted to sing the words
she had learned in the playground at Chichester Street
Elementary: 'Oh will you wash my father's socks and
will you wash them clean . . .'

Young Dr Green folded his stethoscope at last and
began putting everything away in his father's old
Gladstone bag.

'Well?' David changed his weight from one foot to
the other; he felt an urge to shake this man who was
supposed to be an expert but knew nothing of the
precious being that was April.

'Nothing too serious.' Dr Green smiled and sat down
again. 'I think you're very run-down, Mrs Daker. You

haven't been eating properly perhaps? You're suffering from the same complaint as your mother. Anaemia. But I think we can treat the condition more easily—'

'Raw liver!' April said and made a comical face because she could see that this was like a nightmare for David. History repeating itself might be a comfort to her; to him it was not.

'No. Iron pills. And a very careful diet.' He smiled again. 'Lots of greens. Watercress. You're going to enjoy it, I assure you.'

'Of course I am. Nothing to worry about, you see, darling?' She reached out a hand. 'I felt better immediately the rain started. See how the grass is reviving already.'

David did not look through the window at the rain which had fallen incessantly since Saturday evening; he refused to smile back either, but he took her hand.

'I'm going to make absolutely certain you don't neglect yourself in future, April. Let's be clear about that. Make up your mind that I shall watch you like a hawk and worry you like a shrew.' He pushed her gently down. 'No, don't get up. I have the tray laid for tea and I was about to offer Dr Green some.'

But the offer was declined. The long heatwave had incubated a crop of bilious patients the doctor had to see. He left his prescription behind the clock and advised April to cultivate an interest in the wireless which was a less tiring entertainment than reading. He left his thermometer behind, also some germs from his bilious patients, and April went down with violent sickness that same night. March came round and looked after the small household for two days, then Fred protested, and she sent Chattie in her place. Everyone except April preferred Chattie: she was a kindly nurse and loved the girls, and she was less of a strain for David.

May, visiting her sister a week later, pretended to be envious.

'A lady of leisure!' she exclaimed as she arranged the fruit she had brought from Eastgate market. 'Nothing to do all day but read and look forward to Henry Hall in the evening!'

April smiled and declined a grape. 'How is Monty? And Victor? What about the scholarship to the art school?'

May sat on the end of the bed and ate the rejected grape, then many more. 'He's got it, my dear. Isn't it marvellous? And he's borrowed a fiver from me and bought himself a beret and a smock! Monty will be tickled pink – I could have murdered him!'

'Nonsense. You love it all.'

'Yes, I know. Can you imagine March's face though? It will take pounds to provide all the paints, canvases and so on. The scholarship covers the fees, nothing else. March's face will be as long as a horse's when I tell her he spent all that money on what she will call a ridiculous get-up.'

'Albert will help her understand.'

'What? Albert doesn't understand anything except car engines! He's never understood my Victor.'

'He loves him though. So he's willing to accept all his eccentricities.'

'You've always had a soft spot for Albert.'

April detected a hint of pique in May's voice and smiled placatingly. 'There was a time when he seemed to need a bit of extra love. Victor has so much. You and

Monty – you're such marvellous parents.'

'We used to be awful actually. Lugging the poor old chap around the country like we did.' May leaned forward and kissed April fondly. 'You're so sweet, April. And you're so like Mother sometimes.'

'No I'm not.' April sounded very definite.

'Well, you're as gorgeously thin as she was, anyway. Oh, darling, what am I going to do about my figure? When I think I was thinner than any of you . . . and now just look at me.'

April cupped the plump face in her hands and gazed at it. 'You look exactly the same as when you danced at the Corn Exchange all those years ago.'

May turned her face and kissed the palm of her sister's hand, then to cover sudden emotion, she sang in a high falsetto, 'I'm a dainty dancing fairy . . .' She laughed and said, 'D'you know that concert was in aid of missionaries or something, and you loved it and when Pa asked you what you wanted to be when you grew up, you said – a misery! You were only about three so you wouldn't remember.'

'Oh but I do. And I remember Mother being worried because you were pale and peaky and had to have wintergreen on your chest when the weather was cold.'

The girls laughed sentimentally and May finished the last of the grapes and stood up to leave.

'Even so, I must do something about myself. Perhaps one of these new permanent waves.'

She had the permanent wave, fifty curlers all over her head, each one connected to an electric lead which plugged into an overhead umbrella and was switched on. In spite of protective cotton wool, one of her ears was quite badly burned and the wave did not suit her at all. As she said to Monty that night, 'I look like a nigger minstrel!'

It seemed that Madam Helen might have agreed with her because a month later, when the frizz was at last lying flat again, she said that she really felt she would 'have to let our darling Miss May go'.

May, who was just sliding into her new fur-collared coat, felt as if a knife had been slipped between her ribs. She was frozen in mid-shrug and stared at her employer in disbelief.

'Do you mean . . . am I being dismissed, Madam?'

Madam was appalled and threw up her hands in a Gallic gesture that had taken years to acquire.

'Never. Nevaire! My dear May – you are like a daughter to me. Weren't you apprenticed here before the war? Was it not me – I – who begged you to return from London and work here again, although you know well that it is not my policy to take on married women?'

'But you just said—'

'May. My child. My loss is so much greater than yours. There is no question of dismissal. It has been hard for you, I know that. All work and no play. Now, with so little money around for the small luxuries of life – clients dropping off like flies—'

'But now that my mother has gone I have so much more time, Madam.' May considered being cooped up in the house all day with Aunt Sylv and shuddered inwardly.

'Ah, May. I would do so much for you. So much. But this is beyond my power. You will understand. You know the state of the business better than I know it myself.' Madam Helen had never allowed anyone else, even her husband, to look at her books. However, it was true that May did not have the clients she used to have.

She could not beg. She buttoned her coat, eyes down, feeling very near tears. There had been long breaks in her working life, but on and off she had been here since the age of fourteen, and she was now forty.

Monty, who should have been a comfort, a mainstay, who incessantly nagged her to leave work, was unexpectedly affronted.

'First of all, we can't leave this hole because of your mother.' He raised his voice although Victor slept across the landing and the bedroom door was open. 'Then we couldn't leave Sylvia. Now, if Sylvia dropped dead tomorrow we couldn't afford to leave! You've settled our hash nicely, haven't you?'

'For God's sake, Monty! Aunt Sylv could be coming upstairs at any moment!' May hastily closed the door then pulled the blind over the rain-streaming window. 'And I wish you wouldn't take off your shirt in front of the window like that. We're exactly opposite the Lukers' bedroom and they can see right in!'

'I'm sure poor old Hettie Luker wouldn't turn a hair if I stood there stark naked! She must have seen your father often enough!'

May flushed angrily. 'Well, Sibbie could be visiting her mother.' She wished the words back and waited for him to repeat his gibe about her father. But he did not and she was suitably grateful.

'Darling, don't be horrid.' She came behind him and wound her arms around him. 'I can assure you the thought of being here all day with Aunt Sylv doesn't exactly enthral me.'

But he wasn't to be won over. 'I bet you didn't ask her to keep you on part-time though, did you?'

'No. I didn't think of it. I was so . . . well, taken aback really.'

He caught hold of her hands and turned to face her.

'Well, you could do that. Go back tomorrow and suggest to her that you go in on their busiest days.'

'Monty, I couldn't possibly. You know what she's like – rather a common woman under all that French nonsense. I'm not going to ask her favours.'

'No, I thought you wouldn't.'

She was shocked at his bitter tone and looked into the familiar brown eyes which had always reminded her of her brother Teddy, and saw unfriendliness. It was like a physical blow.

'Monty! Baby! Come to Mamma now . . .' She tried to release her hands so that she could take him in her arms. She could win him round so easily whenever she wanted to. She closed her eyes and made kissing noises. He continued to look at her.

'Honestly, May, that perm. I think it might have damaged your hair. Good job if it has, then you can sue your beastly Madam Helen for ruining your looks.'

She opened her eyes quickly and very wide.

'You think my looks are ruined?'

'I didn't say that. I said we could take that blasted woman to court and make her pay for sacking you!'

'You said for ruining my looks!' May pulled suddenly and freed herself. She felt as if her darling Monty had turned into a python. 'And she didn't sack me! She didn't want me to leave! Because of all this damned political nonsense—' she waved her hands frantically, 'Mr MacDonald instead of Mr Baldwin and a National Government instead of a proper one, nobody can afford to have their hair done and she had to let me go! I can understand that even if you can't! I can feel sorry for her even if—'

It was his turn to protest. 'May, keep your voice down. Never mind the Lukers seeing me without my shirt, they'll hear you without yours!'

'Don't you tell me what to do! My God, Monty Gould, when I remember that ghastly day you told me you'd sold our lovely house in Bushey Park to pay your beastly gambling debts – and you've got the sheer nerve to criticize me now for losing my job through no fault of my own—'

Too late he tried to hold her. 'Mamma . . . Mamma . . . calm down now. You promised you'd never bring that up again. Come to baby now and—'

'Get away from me!' May was beside herself. She could bemoan the state of her hair and figure, but that Monty should do so was the absolute end. 'Go for one of your walks or something! Go on – I mean it – go now! I don't want to have you near me!'

He was still.

'Do you mean that, May?'

'Of course I mean it! I'm absolutely shattered, my nerves are raw!'

'Very well. I will go for a walk.'

He began to pull his shirt back over his head. The back collar stud was still in it and he pocketed the other one and went out with his collar flapping around his ears like a small pair of wings. Across the landing Victor's door closed hastily. Monty pulled a face and went towards it, then changed his mind and swung around the newel post and downstairs. The boy knew almost all there was to know about his parents anyway; a little more was educational.

Victor, who had clawed his father's naked body once in defence of his mother, stood just inside the door with his ear to it. He was fully dressed. As soon as he heard the front door close below, he went onto the landing. From Florence's old room came the sound of sobbing; he hesitated, then heard Aunt Sylv creaking about in the attic. He went quickly downstairs and out into the darkness. The weather was still so hot the rain felt almost warm. He lifted his face to it and let it soak him, surrendering to it unconditionally. Then, acclimatized like a fish, he padded off down Chichester Street. He was practically certain where his father was going, but he had to know for sure.

Bridget went through her dressing-table drawers with great care. Somewhere she had a nightgown and matching negligée bought for her next confinement and very décolleté. She had got it at the beginning of the summer in a tiny shop behind the Promenade in Cheltenham, and it had cost the earth. She had imagined wearing it in the Brunswick Square Nursing Home and telling her nurse about her five other confinements with a sweet insouciance that would have everyone falling backwards with sheer amazement. And she was still determined all that should happen. But the nightdress need not be absolutely new.

She found it and slipped it over her naked body with satisfaction, if not relief. She hadn't gone to pieces like

May Rising but after five babies her figure was definitely not what it had been. The nightgown's shadowy chiffon was most flattering. She turned and twisted before the long pier glass. It was a dusky rose colour and emphasized her blue eyes and fair hair. She knew that her likeness to the Rising girls had been one of her attractions for Tolly, and had never resented the fact. She went back to the dressing-table and found some slaty blue eye-shadow to help her eyes to look darker. Like April's.

Tolly did not appear. The rain drummed on the leaded roof of the big bay window, which meant she couldn't open it to get any air. She lay on top of the bed and the humidity made the chiffon cling horribly here and there; and was she the tiniest bit smelly under her arms? She scrambled off the bed and went to the dressing-table a third time for cologne.

It was almost eleven when Tolly opened the door quietly and came into the big room. Upstairs in the four rooms called, collectively, the nursery, someone started to cry, and Mrs Goodson's voice could be heard. Tolly closed the door.

'You shouldn't have stayed awake, Bridie, you knew I wanted to finish my reading.' He went to his chest of drawers, stifling yawns, and began to strip off his tie. 'It's the Wolstoneholme again. You should try it, my dear.'

'I'm not interested in all that stuff, Tolly.'

'You used to be. Before we were married you were very avant garde. You read Marie Stopes before anyone else in Gloucester!' He smiled at her in the mirror and saw the nightgown. He lowered his eyes.

'Marie Stopes!' She laughed. 'That *was* before we

were married, darling! Before you got me into trouble!'

She roughened her voice into a servant's whine. 'You told me it would be all right, sir! And I trusted you! And now look where it's got me.'

He snorted a small laugh in reply, though he knew full well it was no joke.

She said suddenly, 'Come on now, confess, Tolly. You did it quite deliberately, didn't you? Made me pregnant.'

He clipped his trousers into their press and pulled on his pyjamas. He said, 'If it's confessions you want, Bridie, I'll confess that you seduced me. When I was sixteen I think it was.' He looked at her deliberately. 'You said you'd done it before and it was very nice.'

'Was I wrong?' she asked, lifting her chin.

His eyes went past her, trying to remember. It had always been such a desperate business coming up to Bridget's expectations. There were moments of high ecstasy; but had he enjoyed it? He really did not know.

He replied obediently, 'Of course you weren't wrong.' But his hesitation had been too long.

She said, 'Now come on, one more confession. That last time before our wedding, did you deliberately make me pregnant?'

He could remember that all right. The instructions from Moscow about a respectable marriage and a large family and an impregnable entrenchment in Gloucester middleclass society; and then Bridie's capricious dithering about an actual date because she was having such a marvellous time with Maurice Foster.

He said, 'All right. I'll confess. Yes, I hoped I had made you pregnant that day. I wanted us to be married that summer and you shilly-shallied and put me off. So

I left off those ghastly things you used to bring.'

He waited. She had always guessed as much of course, but it had never been admitted between them before. She would lose her temper and there would be a scene which he would hate, but he owed her something and he would put up with it.

She sat up in bed very slowly. The chiffon clung to her breasts. She said in a low voice, 'That was a dirty trick, Tolly Hall.'

'It was. I should have tried to talk to you.'

She put her hands on his neck and slid them under the collar of his pyjama jacket to his shoulders.

'No. You talk too much, Tolly. You think too much. You are better when you act. Like you acted then.'

'You mean I did the right thing?' He was amazed. Bridget enjoyed a good row and this had been a wonderful opportunity for one.

'Yes. Yes. Oh yes, my darling, you did the right thing.' Her hands slid to his back and she began to pull him towards her.   He drew back sharply.

'Bridget. Stop it. I told you the other night how I feel.'

'And I am telling you how I feel, darling. Come to bed, Tolly.'

He tensed himself against her but his voice was gentle. 'No, Bridie.'

It was the gentleness that convinced her. She gripped his bare shoulders; his bones, so close to the surface, were heartbreakingly familiar to her. She said in a high voice, 'I should think you owe me something, Tolly Hall! By your own admission you tricked me into marrying you! You made me what I am – a mother! I want another baby, Tolly, d'you hear me? There's no point in my life otherwise!'

He lowered his head and closed his eyes. 'Darling girl. You've got five children. Five. That is admirable. Any more would be . . . indulgent. Can't you understand that?'

'I can't understand anything except my need for a baby!'

'Bridget, try to be reasonable. For your own sake. It cannot possibly do you any good physically to produce children endlessly. The care of the girls is a full-time job—'

'Mrs Goodson sees to the little ones. And Olga and Natasha are your girls. Once they're off the breast I lose them – I lose them, Tolly!' She shook him but though her nails were hurting he would not look up at her.

'It need not be like that. You can change things.'

'I don't want to – I don't want to change anything!'

She was still, breathing quickly. Suddenly she lunged down at his face with hers, found his mouth and forced her own against it. They clung for perhaps six seconds, then she withdrew.

'Is this because of new instructions from the communists?' she asked in a low voice.

'No.'

'It is your own idea? That we have no more children? Your own idea absolutely?'

'My own. I promise.'

'And the other? Don't we sleep together any more?'

'Of course. We are husband and wife.'

'But sex. Am I so repellent to you now?' She tried to get her wrists beneath his chin and lift his head but could not. Something told her that if she released his shoulders he would move away.

He said very quietly, 'I would prefer . . . Bridie, I am

looking for some kind of purity. Will you – can you – bear with me for a while?'

She coughed a laugh. 'You cannot do it, Tolly. Your five daughters prove that you enjoy sex.' But they both knew that she always instigated it. 'You cannot *do* this, Tolly!' Her voice rose with incipient hysteria.

He made no reply. His bowed head seemed to be inviting castigation; it was infuriating that he would not resist her. She could have inflamed an angry outburst into passion.

She dropped her hands and immediately he stood up. Above them Mrs Goodson's heavy tread crossed to the night nursery. Bridget thought bitterly: I should be doing that – I'm useless.

She whispered, 'I cannot live like a nun, Tolly. I cannot do it. There were men before our marriage – other men – you know that.'

He did not speak.

She went on, unable to stop. 'I'm going to go out. Now. Like this. In the rain. I'm going to ask the first man I meet to do what my husband should do.'

The silence stifled her words.

'I'm going to do it, Tolly! You think I won't, but I'm going to. Now.'

She scrambled off the bed and thrust her feet into her summer slippers. She wanted to weep but would not permit herself to show weakness.

'I can understand Sibbie Luker now! She always said it wasn't only for money, and I believe her at last! Some women can be nuns – like Florence Rising – she was a nun even when she was pregnant! Poor Will Rising, no wonder he turned to Sibbie – I can understand all of that now—' She thrust her arms into the sleeves of the negligée and opened the bedroom door. 'Life is so unfair, so unbalanced, and – and . . .' she waited, halfway onto the landing '. . . I'm going, Tolly.'

He spoke at last. 'Please don't hurt yourself like this, Bridie. I know it's my fault. Try to forgive me.'

But it was the wrong thing to say. He should have protested, or been coldly angry, or begged her to come back. His submissiveness was impenetrable.

She slammed the door.

It was strange how the disreputable Luker family had kept its strong links with the respectable Risings through the years. Fred, the same age as dead Albert, had at last married March Rising; Gladys, the same age as April, still visited her and was Flora's godmother; Henry, common and loutish though he undoubtedly was, visited Teddy Rising's grave every February on the anniversary of the death and stood staring at the stone and shifting uncomfortably from one foot to the other. And Sibbie . . . Sibbie had always been conscious of her links and had sought to forge them stronger. First May. Then May's childhood sweetheart, David Daker. Then, when David was disgraced and she was too, she had won the biggest prize of all, her surrogate father, Will Rising himself. With Will's death, there had been a hiatus. She had married Edward Williams and had found that wealth and position were pleasant and Edward's love very rewarding. And she loved him too. But of course he wasn't a Rising.

At the beginning of that halcyon summer of 1934, she had taken to walking along the canal bank and sitting on the verandah of her old bungalow. Edward had wanted her to sell it, but it was the first thing that had belonged to her completely and at last he understood this; and her need to go there occasionally.

It had happened as she hoped. Someone who needed her had walked along the canal bank and looked longingly at the bungalow. Someone who had been lured there years ago, had been unwillingly seduced, and had run from her frantically as far as he could. In fact to theatrical digs.

Now on this rain-drenched evening in September, he was no longer unwilling, and he sought to drown his shame with repeated justification. Sibbie stifled a yawn, began to plait the hairs on his chest, and decided he had gone far enough.

'Darling Monty. It's not a bit of good you telling me that May drove you to it. She might have driven you out, but our meeting was arranged a fortnight ago and you know that very well. Every other Friday, isn't that our arrangement? Now come on, be honest for once in your life.'

He was cut to the quick. 'You can accuse me of what you like, Sib, but not dishonesty. I am honest as the day.'

She raised herself on one elbow and gazed down at him. She could understand what May saw in him; she was really fond of him herself.

'Yes. Yes, you really are, my darling boy. You're honest in the part you're playing at the time, aren't you?' She kissed him. 'The trouble is, you never stay in the same role for long enough, sweetheart.' She kissed him again very slowly. 'And you're not a sum total of your parts, are you?' She kissed him a third time and he groaned and rolled away from her.

'You keep on about my "parts", Sibbie Luker.

You've got an absolutely one-track mind.' He tried to get off the bed as she made a grab at him. 'Stop it, darling. I have to go. It must be gone eleven and May won't go to sleep till I get back. We never let the sun go down on our wrath.'

'Baby boy, the sun went down hours ago.' She grabbed successfully. 'Come on, darling. Come to Mummy now.' She laughed at his protests and put him to her breast. He nuzzled obediently, half-laughing, half-angry. She was so like May used to be years ago, the perfect foil to his constant acting. But May hadn't really been like that since the awful business about the house. And it was obvious she still blamed him for that. Sibbie blamed him for nothing. Absolutely nothing.

He went up the Bristol road and then Southgate Street at a jog trot, between roles, smitten with a terrible remorse, longing for May and knowing that nothing would have changed between them. Under his breath he sobbed, 'My life is ruined. I cannot go on living,' and at the same time he wondered whether there would be any cheese under the china cover in the larder, because Sibbie was hard work and there was no food in the canal bungalow. This was his third visit there, and each time he had intended it to be the last. Sibbie had been quite wrong in saying he had meant to keep his assignation with her tonight: if May hadn't told him to go for a walk, he would still be at home with her now. It *was* her fault, after all.

He ran over the Cross into Northgate Street and was coming alongside Daker's Gowns at a stumbling trot when something caught his eye. He slowed, then stopped. At this hour of the night Gloucester was well and truly deserted and any human movement was suspect. In the time it took him to look over his shoulder, he had built up a completely new scenario. Monty Gould, hero of the hour, apprehending burglars as they entered the new premises of the county bank . . . uncaring of personal injury . . .

It was a woman, looking remarkably like Greta Garbo in *The Temptress*. She was, of course, soaking wet, but she seemed to be in a gauzy evening dress with no raincoat or umbrella. It was a situation with instant appeal for Monty. Especially as she was face to wall and weeping.

'Madam,' he deepened his voice. 'May I be of assistance?'

She looked up. It was Bridget Williams.

Chattie came back to Bedford Close that evening because Fred and March gave a dinner party for the Adairs. The long hot summer seemed to be drawing to a close and the time for business was coming again: the soft Peplows had succumbed almost immediately to Fred's bid for their land; the Adairs were more astute. Chattie removed the bowls of broth, known in these circles as clear consommé, and carried in the salmon.

'I say, old man, a fine specimen.' Charles Adair groped for his monocle and screwed it into his right eye. 'I had no idea you fished.'

Fred smiled at Mrs Adair. 'I don't, old man. Other people do it for me. Nothing like Severn salmon. The river feeds us well in Gloucester. Salmon in the autumn, elvers in the spring.'

Mrs Adair wrinkled her nose; elvers were the poor man's feast. 'They have always revolted me,' she said.

'They do look disgusting.' March glanced at Chattie.

95

It was wonderful to have her back. She served without fuss and very efficiently.

Charles Adair let his monocle fall the length of its ribbon. "Fraid I've never tasted the things. Must admit they look rather like worms – young eels, aren't they?'

Albert felt his mother's eyes on him and made a real effort to stop thinking about the internal combustion engine.

'Yes. They're eel fry. My grandfather used to cook them really well, didn't he, Mother?' He noticed the young Adair lift a scornful lip.

Fred said bluffly, 'We were brought up on them. They're a very powerful food.' He kept looking at Mrs Adair; she blushed.   'Not for me, thank you.' Robin Adair shook his head at Chattie, then stared again through the window, making his utter boredom completely clear.

'Oh dear.' March's glow was dimmed. 'It really is fresh, Robin. Is it all this talk of elvers?'

'Not at all. I'm really not hungry.'

Mrs Adair rushed in. 'Fish of all kinds have a bad effect on Robin's skin,' she explained. Everyone stared at the boy and he darted a furious glance at his mother, his studied ennui spoiled at last. 'Well, it does, darling,' she insisted. 'Don't you remember when you had that crab last year? And when we were at Cannes those moules marinières?'

'For goodness sake, Mother.'

Albert sucked in his cheeks against a smile, then said, 'Those are shellfish. I think you'll find salmon will help skin – er – complaints.'

'I haven't got a skin complaint thank you, Tomms,' snapped Robin. 'I am not hungry.'

'Oh, come on, old man. If you really won't try the salmon, Chattie will boil you an egg, won't you, Chattie?'

'Of course I will, Master Albert.' Chattie came forward, all concern. 'Or would you like it poached? A nice poached egg with some plain bread and butter is just the thing for delicate stomachs.'

'I have not got a delicate stomach either.' Robin seemed to be speaking through clenched teeth and Albert could no longer restrain his smile. He was no master of sarcasm and had shot his bolt, but he was well satisfied. He had had to put up with supercilious condescension from Robin Adair most of the summer.

Fred realized he had lost Mrs Adair; he frowned repressively at Albert. 'Leave the boy alone, Chattie. He said he's not hungry. Adair – the hollandaise sauce?' He had gone to some pains to discover Charles Adair's favourite food: it was salmon with hollandaise sauce.

'I say, old man. Marvellous. Tilly – it's hollandaise.'

Mrs Adair tore herself away from her fledgling and beamed at March. 'You couldn't have known, Mrs Luker. But this is Charles's favourite meal.'

Albert found one more shot in his locker.

'Ah well, we can't please everyone.'

Fred said smoothly, 'Potatoes? Albert, perhaps you'd go with Chattie and bring back some more potatoes.'

It was Albert's turn to glance at his mother, but he got no help there. March was as anxious as Fred to 'land' the wealthy Adairs. However, Chattie was suitably consoling.

'Spoilt. That's what he is. You're worth a dozen of him, Master Albert.' She tapped chopped parsley from the board straight onto the potatoes. 'Delicate stomach indeed. As if my salmon was poison or something.'

'Delicate skin actually.' Albert picked up the vegetable dish, grinning again.

'Skin? Don't be daft, Master Albert. He isn't going to rub fish on his skin, now is he?'

Albert burst out laughing and went back to the dining-room followed by a smiling Chattie. It was obvious they had been laughing about Robin Adair, and he stiffened defensively.

March was talking about Bath.

'A beautiful city.' Her normally pale face was flushed with enthusiasm and wine. 'I'll never forget when I saw it first. I must have been nine or ten. The station is set by the river and Bath appeared in a perfect bowl-shape – it was lit by the evening sun. April wasn't a year old and we took it in turns to push the pram up to the Royal Crescent.' She laughed reminiscently.

'April? Ah, that must be Mrs Daker. It's her husband who has Daker's Gowns, I believe?' Mrs Adair found the topic of Bath very dull, but she had thoroughly enjoyed Daker's mannequin parade. March nodded and took the vegetable dish from Albert. 'After the death of my first husband, April stayed with me in Bath for a long time. She loved it too.' She meandered on about the gardens and the hot springs and the Pump Rooms until the cheese. It gave Robin Adair time to relapse into affected boredom again; Albert time to return to his reverie on the insides of the Morris Oxford which he had on the work-bench at the garage; Fred and Mrs Adair time to resume their covert glances, their silent challenges.

Charles Adair chose Stilton and decided it was time to move away from the glories of England.

'We heard that Mrs Daker fainted after that do at the shop the other night. Is she all right now?'

March smiled. 'Yes. A little frail perhaps. She takes after our mother.'

Fred laughed. 'Not a bit of it. April is more like her father than her mother. You take after Florence, my dear.'

March smiled, pleased. She modelled herself on Florence whenever she could. At the moment with life so easy and pleasant, she knew she had perfected the art and was glad it was so apparent. She had inherited Florence's dark, narrow, aristocratic good looks; but she needed that beautiful soul too.

'Mrs Daker takes after Will Rising – that was the tailor, wasn't it?' Charles Adair had screwed in his monocle again, suddenly very interested. The way he referred to Will as 'the tailor' made it obvious he knew some of the scandal.

March said quickly, 'Shall we leave the men to it now, Mrs Adair? I understand you are a pianist? We have rather a fine Bechstein in the sitting-room which I'd be glad if you'd try.'

The two ladies stood up and the boys raced each other to get to the door first. Robin won. He smiled and thanked March charmingly for his dinner, or at any rate the bits of it he had eaten. She gave him one of her special smiles. Albert glowered.

Charles Adair accepted the port from Fred.

'Hope I didn't put my foot in it, old man. All that old business – water under the bridge, of course.'

'Exactly.' Fred wondered which water and which bridge. There had been so many tales told about poor old Will.

Adair grunted. 'I like a red-blooded man myself. One of the reasons we get on so well, old man. Now Peplow . . . hard to know how to talk to him. Bit of a Bible-thumper, isn't he?'

'Could be,' Fred said judiciously. If he was, it could be the reason he'd practically given away sixty of his acres. 'Listen, why don't you two lads take that new Rover of mine for a spin? You must be bored stiff listening to us for over two hours.'

'It's still pouring with rain,' Albert objected, though his heart leapt at the prospect of driving the Rover. He glanced at Robin.

'It's all right, Mr Luker, don't worry about the conversation. I'm a red-blooded man too.'

Adair laughed uproariously, filled his glass a third time and pushed the bottle towards his son. 'You don't mind, old man? He's been drinking port since he was twelve!' He watched approvingly as Robin filled his glass and drank. 'I believe in educating them young. Took him up to London with me last year. He thoroughly enjoyed it, didn't you, old man?'

'Yes.' Robin stared straight at Albert who turned pink.

Fred forced a grin and topped up the young pup's glass; the sooner he was under the table the better. Albert might have behaved childishly tonight but at least he was normally bearable.

Adair leaned forward confidently.

'Matter of fact, I went to that dress show last month myself. I like to see what girls are wearing.' He sniggered. 'Or not wearing. As the case may be.'

Fred said smoothly, 'What did you think of it? I've never had much time for Daker myself, but he's a good designer I believe. Not much of a business head on him.'

'Fellow called Stein used to do all the selling apparently. Jew-boy of course. If he and Daker had stayed together, the sky would have been the limit. According to my information.' He sniggered again, drank, and refilled.

'Oh?' Fred remembered Mannie Stein. He'd been the cause of the bust-up between April and David. And indirectly the cause of Davie's conception. He said smoothly, 'Best man at April's wedding. He disappeared some years later.'

'Ended up in London, old man. Doing very well indeed there. Daker booted him out it seems. For handling his wife.'

Albert sat bolt upright.

Fred said easily, 'He probably did blot his copybook. April was the toast of the town in those days. But she only ever had eyes for Daker.'

Robin started to laugh. A small drop of port appeared on his lower lip and ran down his chin. He hiccupped loudly.

'Hold your drink, old man . . . hold your drink,' his father reproved. He jerked his head confidentially. 'Robin was still around the night I took Eugenie home with me.' He began to laugh too. 'The fuss your mother made over that! I took her in for a nightcap, that was all . . .' His look turned lugubrious. 'Have to toe the line now and then, old man. Tilly holds the purse-strings, don't you know.'

'Really?' Fred salted that away for the future and passed the port.

'Lovely girl. Looked after by Mannie Stein . . . if you get my meaning.'

'I think so.'

Robin looked at Albert. 'They live together, old man. In sin.'

Charles shook his head. 'Stein's never got over your sister-in-law. Hates Daker it seems. Reckons he's a bit of a queen. Shrapnel in his groin . . . can't do his duty . . .' He sniggered and drank. Robin appeared to be having difficulty in holding his head on his shoulders.

Fred said casually, 'Sounds as if Stein is a bit of an old woman himself.' He glanced at Albert warningly; the boy was puce.

'Well, don't know about that . . .'

Robin blurted, 'Can't be. He got the first kid. Christ knows who got the second.'

Fred tried to hold Albert. He was amazed at the boy's strength. In spite of restraining hands he shot out of his chair and grabbed Robin Adair by the throat. The next instant his spare fist slammed into the wet chin and Robin Adair was out for the count.

Somehow Albert blamed Fred for the whole incident. His loyalty to April had been one of the standards of his life and that Fred did not support him finished the tentative companionship he had experienced with his stepfather.

'Whether I punched Charles Adair or not makes no difference,' Fred tried to explain after the fiasco of the dinner party. 'Anyone who knows April, knows it's a pack of lies.'

'That's not the point.' Albert still looked sick an hour after the Adairs had left in disarray. 'You don't stop to think about it when someone you love is being vilely slandered.'

'You do when you want something from the slanderers.' Fred sighed heavily. 'The Adairs are fools in many ways, but when it comes to striking a bargain they know what to do. They've got the edge on me now, Albert.'

'You're surely not still after their land, are you?'

'Naturally. The council will be planning a by-pass through to the Bristol road before long, and whoever owns that land will be a millionaire.'

'How do you know the council are planning a new road?'

'They're not. Yet. It's quite simple. When I have the necessary land, then the proposal for the by-pass will be made.'

Albert said angrily, 'It sounds dishonest to me.'

'Well, it's not. It's good business. And in good business you have to keep control of the game . . . all the time. By letting that story about April get your goat, you lost control.'

'I don't want anything to do with business. I happen to know that Aunt April is as honest and straightforward and – and – wonderful as anyone in the country. And I don't intend to sit still and listen to—'

'I know that too, Albert,' Fred said heavily. 'I know that better – far better – than you do.'

They went to bed, Albert still fermenting with indignation, Fred sliding into his mood of withdrawn concentration.

March watched him undress; she was still smiling.

'It was a success in spite of Mr Adair and Robin getting drunk, wasn't it, Fred?' she asked. 'I suppose you helped them on their way?'

'I suppose I did.' Fred got into bed and put the flat of his hand on her abdomen. She still shivered when he did that. 'Did you get anything out of Silly Tilly?'

'Oh, Fred . . . d'you remember how Albert called that awful old midwife Snotty Lottie? Oh, Fred . . .'

He pressed harder. 'Well, did you?'

'Her father's an honourable.' She reached up and touched his hair: it was so very like her brother Albert's gingery fair locks. She whispered, 'She was very immodest. She wanted to know if you were a good lover. I was shocked.'

He kissed her. 'I expect you were, Marcie.'

But as he proved that he was in fact a very good lover, he smiled into the rain-drumming darkness. Silly Tilly held the purse-strings and wanted him. She knew her husband was a lecherous bounder, so she would have no loyalties there. Maybe he could get that land and pay the Adairs back for the insults they had thrown at April tonight. Then, as thoughts of April came into his mind, he felt his throat thicken almost as if he were going to weep. He bent his head and kissed March tenderly.

'I love you, Marcie,' he whispered.

'Oh, Fred. I love you too.'

He thought: that's one good thing I've done. I've made March Rising happy. I might even get into heaven on that.

*　　　*　　　*

And Monty, regaling May with the full story of the drowned rat who had turned out to be Bridget Hall, forgot that he had been consumed with shame only two hours previously.

'She needed someone to talk to, May,' he said, towelling himself vigorously, while May, propped on his pillows as well as her own, let the discontents of the day sublimate themselves in concern for this new unfortunate. Besides, May loved to gossip with Monty; it was the perfect way to patch up their quarrel.

'I always thought that she'd have to pay a price for all those babies. So quickly.' Her voice held a note of satisfaction; she had frequently envied Bridget her enormous family.

'Obviously it must be that.' Monty rolled up his underwear. The rain, soaking through everything, was the perfect cover for his evening's recreation; he had already convinced himself anyway that it had been innocent. 'Funnily enough though, she kept on and on that she wanted another child. Perhaps it's poor old Tolly who's had enough.'

'Poor old Tolly, my sainted aunt!' May was scornful now. 'If ever there was a wolf in sheep's clothing it's Tolly Hall. When I think of that meek and mild little boy tagging around with Teddy and April. Next thing we know he's off to France with that ambulance, and when he comes back he's chasing Bridget as if she's the last woman on earth!'

'Like I chased you, darling?' Monty sat on the edge of the bed. He had to be up and ready for work in seven hours flat, and he was tired already. But in for a penny, in for a pound.

May dimpled deliciously; her plumpness had done wonders for her dimples.

'Not quite, darling. We did not sleep together until after we were married.' She wanted to lean forward and touch him; he was still such an Adonis sitting there, naked and beautiful. But she was terribly tired and it was well past midnight. She murmured, 'We're so much more than lovers, Monty. Friends and companions . . .'

'Bridget said that. She said we were lucky we could talk together like friends.'

'Did she? Poor Bridie, it's hard to imagine Tolly ever coming down from the clouds to talk to her.' She stared dreamily past him. 'How strange life is, Monty darling. If I hadn't lost my job we wouldn't have quarrelled. And if we hadn't quarrelled you wouldn't have gone for a walk. And heaven knows what might have happened to poor Bridie. She could have been murdered.'

'Yes. Poor Bridie. I'm glad I was around to take her home and patch things up for her. Tolly didn't like it of course, but it might make him a bit more approachable in the office in future.'

'He should thank you. He should give you a rise.'

'May, you're such a darling girl.' He was filled with wonderful gratitude to her for taking the last shreds of his guilt and making them into a shining virtue. 'Monty loves his May. Monty is May's little boy—' He reached for her.

'Oh darling boy, d'you mind awfully if we don't? I'm so wretchedly tired. But I do love you.'

He was even more grateful. 'Darling, we don't

need to prove anything. Of course I don't mind. I love you too.'

'Oh, Monty. We're perfect together. Don't let's forget that. Ever.'

Chapter Five

The winter of '34–'35 was mild but long and dreary. Flora Daker started school with Davina and found the half-mile trek across two muddy fields so arduous that Davina piggy-backed her for the last few yards. When April got out of bed one afternoon from one of her enforced rests, she was horrified to see the nine-year-old tottering up the drive bent double beneath her burden.

'Darling, you mustn't do that,' she admonished her as she made a nursery tea in the kitchen. 'You will hurt your back. You know poor Olga Hall has to wear a brace because of her round shoulders.'

'But Flo gets so tired, Mummy,' Davina explained.

Flora said, 'I don't like going to school, Mummy. My toes hurt and I can't hold those funny pencils.'

April smiled. 'Do you try to hold them with your toes then, sweetheart?'

But it was one more thing to blame on her foolish anaemia.

'I used to take Davina along to Christchurch in the pushchair,' she reminded David that night. 'And I really think the fresh air would do me good.'

'Like it did when you got the coal in by yourself last week?' He was still angry with himself for forgetting that chore. 'And when you hung the washing out that very frosty day?' On both occasions she had been ill afterwards.

She sighed. 'Darling, there are certain things I have to do. You simply don't understand.'

'I'm beginning to.' He took her hand tenderly. 'April, I knew you were wonderful, but I didn't know how wonderful. You have looked after the children and the house and the garden, and helped me with my finishing . . . yes, you're wonderful.' He put her hand to his lips. 'But now we've got to do something about it, my love. We can't borrow Chattie every other week, it's not fair. We need someone all the time.'

'We can't afford it, David. There's that big family down at the farm. One of those girls might consider coming to do the rough and the washing.'

David said nothing. The Byards on the farm were shiftless and dirty and they threw stones at Davie and Flora.

'I'll make a few other enquiries first,' he said when he had washed up. He was hopeless in the house and knew it. His mother had done everything and when they moved out of the shop in the Barton and into the flat above Daker's Gowns, April had taken over. He went out to the coal shed for the next day's supply of fuel and tried not to limp as he returned with the buckets.

It was May who solved that problem. All three Rising girls, trained by fastidious Florence and practical Will, were excellent and unobtrusive housekeepers, and May made the long trip out to Winterditch twice a week to give April some company and help out where she could.

'This won't do,' she decreed when she too discovered Davina's latest chore. 'Honestly, if only you'd stayed in the flat, March and I could have kept things going between us. This place is the back of beyond.'

'But lovely in the summer, and so close to the bluebell woods.' April gave the patient smile that had become her hallmark over the last few months. 'Spring will soon be here, May.'

'I'm not so sure. This lane wasn't called Winterditch for nothing.' May fetched a chair so that Flora could stand and cut out the gingerbread men her aunt had made for her. 'Dear little maid.' She snuffled into the baby neck. 'Aunt May will help you with those nasty tables. I've got a lovely song to go with them. All about cherries on a plate.' She looked at April mournfully. 'You're so lucky. Two of them. I should have daughters. Three or four or even five like Bridget.'

'You always used to criticize Bridie.'

'Ah well. One grows older and wiser. Put them on the tray, darling, and make them hold hands.' She opened the oven door and tested the blast of hot air against her cheek. 'We're ready for the gingerbread men, Flo. How many? Eight? Two . . . four . . . six . . . eight . . . see how easy tables are?'

'Have you seen her recently then?'

'Who? Oh, Bridie. Yes. Actually I see quite a bit of her. She's rather down lately, so I go along Wednesdays to keep her company.' She glanced at April apologetically. 'I'm at such a loose end with no job, you see, darling, and Brunswick Square is so close.' She closed the oven door and took Flo to the sink to wash her hands. 'As a matter of fact we do our shopping together. Saturday mornings. She's very generous.'

'Generous?'

'She's always buying me things. She knows how hard up we are and she'll buy two of something and give me . . . well, that new vanishing cream, have you seen it? She gave me a pot of that. And hand cream. She's terribly lonely you know, April.'

'Lonely? With five children not to mention Tolly?'

'I know. It's crazy, isn't it? But she's got Mrs Goodson and of course Kitty Hall is always round there helping with the little ones. She doesn't get on with Kitty.'

'Poor Kitty. She's so lost now that Mother's gone.'

'I know. It's not fair, is it? Bridie's got too much help and you've not got any.' May thought fondly but bitterly too of Aunt Sylv, who insisted on continuing to cook for the small household and produced vast quantities of watery potatoes and hard pastry. And suddenly the idea was born.

'April, be quite honest about this, would Aunt Sylv be of any help to you here?'

Davina, sitting next to her mother with some knitting in her lap, lost count of her stitches and gazed from May to April with dawning excitement. Flora stopped paddling her fingers in the sink and turned round too. Aunt Sylv was like an ancient carthorse to the children, slow, amazingly strong, eternally secure. April was caught in that breathless moment and stared out and in as she considered possibilities. Finally she said, 'D'you think she would?'

'I think she'd be thrilled.'

'She's never suggested it though.'

'It hasn't occurred to her that she could be useful. She thinks she's past it since Mother died. She'd *love* it!

She adores the girls. And you. And David.'

'I'm not sure about David.' April smiled fleetingly because of course Aunt Sylv knew all there was to know about David . . . about everything. Or nearly everything. 'What about you, May? Could you bear to be in that big house on your own?'

'Darling, I'd love it. Aunt Sylv never *says* a word, but if she disapproves of anything she glowers.'

April's smile turned into a laugh and it was as good as settled. May took the long walk home down Oxstalls Lane in a lightened frame of mind. If she had the house to herself all day long she could do things. Paint everything white. Hang Victor's pictures – the naughty ones. Even invite Sibbie round . . . perhaps. Certainly Bridie could come to lunch without fear of having to face boiled sheep's head, which was what Aunt Sylv had prepared for her last time as a special treat. And Victor could bring all his art school friends. The house would be full of laughter again, just as it had been in the old days.

At the end of September, Edward Williams, now nearly sixty years old, received the first of a series of anonymous letters concerning his wife. He burned each one carefully and never asked Sibbie where she went every other Friday evening, but suddenly the years caught up with him. He had looked to be in his mid-forties ever since the war, when he made many female hearts throb as he walked around in his captain's khaki, but now he looked elderly. Sibbie told him he was like wine, better as the years went on.

'Am I, Sib?' He watched her fondly and very closely. 'The trouble with vintage wine, you have to sip it so slowly and you were always a fast girl.'

She gurgled her pleasure at this remark and then kissed him hard. 'But after one sip, everything else tastes like rubbish,' she said slowly.

He looked at her then nodded. 'All right, darling, all right.'

He continued to burn the letters as they arrived.

At the end of November, when Aunt Sylv took up residence at Longmeadow, Fred Luker – Filthy Luker to his adversaries – met Tilly Adair for the third time. The first meeting had been a carefully arranged accident; Fred had discovered that on the fourth Thursday in the month, Mrs Adair had a taxi from her large house at Quedgeley to Barton Street, and enjoyed a Turkish bath. He walked past the entrance to the bath house just as she emerged, pink, full of well-being, and thoroughly – as her masseuse said – 'limbered'. Fred expressed amazement at his good fortune, dismissed her waiting taxi, and insisted on taking her out to lunch. The second and third meetings were arranged and were acknowledged to be clandestine.

'I feel so terribly naughty!' she told him when he collected her in a remote country lane. 'Did anyone see you?'

'No.' He stifled a yawn of boredom as he bundled her dog onto the prepared blanket in the back. 'Though it would hardly have mattered. I drive all over the countryside looking at prospective building sites.'

'I suppose you do. Oh, Freddie, you're so powerful. Quiet and powerful. D'you remember what you said about elvers that night we dined with you? That they were a powerful food? I knew what you meant of course, though no-one else did. And you are a powerful man.' She giggled and leaned slightly sideways so that their shoulders touched.

He sighed inanely. 'And I know what you mean.' But it seemed the right thing to say because she giggled again and pressed closer. Something wet nibbled his ear and he thought for a moment it was her until the dog-smell reached his nostrils. That really did it, she couldn't stop laughing till they started to climb towards Stroud.

'Oh, Freddie. Where are we going? We could have a lovely walk over Nymphsfield if you like.' She put lots of significance into the name of the hilltop village and he growled obediently in his throat. The dog growled too and there was a moment of chaos while she kneeled on the seat and pushed him back.

Then he told her, 'I want to give you lunch again. You're too thin, you need feeding up. And when you said last time that we mustn't be seen together, I thought I'd better take a private room. At the Unicorn. They're very discreet there: they'll serve lunch then go away and leave us in peace.'

'Oh, Freddie. That will be nice.'

He drove on in silence, letting her babble her way through Adair's blunders since they'd met last. She must know what his intentions were in taking a private room for lunch, and he realized she was condemning her husband in an effort to justify her imminent infidelity. It must be a trait of these shallow, easy types. Sister Sibbie told him that Monty Gould, May's husband, was just the same.

He braked hard outside the ivy-smothered walls of the Unicorn so that the gravel clattered beneath the huge arched mudguards. She produced smoked glasses which she had the devil of a job to ram on because of her deep cloche hat. She turned the fur collar of her coat up to meet the hat, then made certain no-one would overlook them by taking the dog. Fred hid a smile. The first woman he had seduced for what she could give him had pulled the curtains wide and switched on the light, wanting to play the scene publicly. This one imagined she was being frightfully discreet, but he wondered whether she was so different when it came down to it.

Lunch arrived on a trolley with champagne in an ice bucket. She squealed and clapped her hands, then reached for the plate of chicken breasts. He stopped her.

'First things first,' he said bluntly.

She was almost affronted. 'But, Freddie, everything will get cold.'

He pulled her to him and took off the glasses.

'That's exactly what I'm afraid of.' He kissed her as he had done last time, sedately and with what she called 'respect'. She came up for breath, giggling and protesting, and he threw her hat after the glasses and kissed her again, this time with less respect. She began to back away, stammering, his mouth still on hers; after a moment he let her go.

'What's the matter?' he asked curtly.

'Freddie . . . two wrongs don't make a right. This is what Charles must do. Oh, Freddie.'

He wanted to kill her. 'Wrongs . . . rights . . .' He practically tore off her coat. 'What have they got to do with this? Is it wrong to eat when you're hungry if food is there?' He kissed her deeply and pushed her back on the bed and said, 'If there is any wrong, it is mine, Tilly. Not yours. You have no choice now.'

She giggled and lay lifeless. 'Oh, Freddie . . . are you going to rape me?'

'Yes.'

He remembered how he had taken March's guilt on his shoulders years ago. Did all women require to be absolved similarly? No . . . there had been one, just one, who had accepted damnation freely. Just one.

He dealt with Tilly Adair efficiently. She was the sort of woman who would now become enslaved to him. But his shoulders were broad, and after all he must have that land. The dog was the worst problem. In the end when Tilly lay moaning and the dog started to whine, Fred leaned from the bed and knocked the plate of chicken onto the floor. They heard no more from him.

In the late spring of 1935, Gloucester City Council discussed the controversial new plan for a by-pass which would link the west and east of the city. It was discovered that at one end of the site the land was owned by one-time Councillor Edward Williams. Though he had disgraced himself by marrying Gloucester's scarlet woman, nevertheless his father had been a respected alderman, and it was considered only right and proper that he should receive a good offer for his land. At the other end of the site, the relevant land had recently come into the hands of Mr Fred Luker of Luker Transport. The Council Chamber was split in half about what it should offer for this land. Many councillors knew of Fred's doubtful connections with the coal industry in the Forest of Dean; his acquisition of several productive surface mines there had been very suspect. They suggested that alternative routes for the new road should be found. However, enquiries proved that this was impossible; farms would have to be split or were owned by large families who could not agree on a sale. Reluctantly it was decided that the Luker land should be bought but at a cut price. The other half of the Chamber, who were strangely for Fred Luker although many of them had been worsted in previous deals, pointed out that a good offer had been made to Edward Williams, therefore a similar offer must be made to Mr Luker. They carried the day.

Fred was not unduly grateful. As he pointed out, had the land still belonged to two families, the Adairs and the Peplows, there would have been an extra bill to foot. He took champagne with him and visited his sister and brother-in-law at their big old house in Barnwood.

'Now I'm no longer on the council, who have you got there, Fred?' Edward enquired without malice. He had never allowed himself to be manipulated by Fred, but most of the schemes Luker put forward were sheer common sense as well as beneficial to himself.

'Dalloway. Smith. They carry others with them.' Fred grinned. 'I have to watch Dalloway. He's nearly as fly as I am. If I'd told him too much he'd have had that land off Peplow before I could have looked round.'

Sibbie lifted her glass. 'And Adair? What about the Adair land?' Her voice was sly.

'I don't think he'd have been so successful there.'

Fred grinned back at her. Ossie Dalloway was fat and florid. Sib must have twigged how he managed the Adair purchase.

Edward did too. 'Be careful, Fred. Remember what happened over the Leonie Porterman affair.'

Fred turned a blank stare on him. He liked and respected his brother-in-law, but he would discuss the

Portermans with no-one. Edward shrugged and lifted his glass and the talk turned to investments. They were all very rich.

However, Sibbie pressed the matter again as she walked down the long gravel drive with her brother.

'Fred, do be careful with Tilly Adair. I know you. You'll want to be rid of her now, and she will cling.'

Fred breathed deeply of the country air. Summer was coming. He would take March away; abroad somewhere. She had always had a hankering to go abroad. It would free him from Tilly and perhaps when he came back she would have found another diversion.

Sibbie said, 'I mean it, Fred. You've got more to lose now than you had when Leonie was around. March wouldn't forgive you a second time.'   He stopped in his tracks.

'Is that a threat, Sibbie?'

'Don't be ridiculous, why should I threaten you?'

'You did before. And you carried out your threat. You betrayed me to March.'

'That's all in the past, Fred. I didn't think you and March could ever be happy. Besides, I thought I might marry Will Rising—'

Fred flung back his head and laughed. 'Oh yes, I remember now. It rather worried you that you might end up as my stepmother!'

She flushed. 'It wasn't funny at the time, Fred. I loved Will Rising.'

'You've never loved anyone in your life, my dear. And you killed Will Rising. Don't forget that.'

She gasped and flinched as if from a physical blow. Then she said, 'Just as you killed Marcus Porterman! Don't forget that either, Fred!'

They faced each other angrily for a moment, then Fred relaxed and laughed again.

'We've always had to have an edge on each other, Sis. Well . . . nothing has changed. You blab to March about Silly Tilly, and I'll blab to Edward about Monty Gould.'

She said with a certain dignity, 'I'll never tell March anything to make her unhappy. I've always done everything I could to make the Risings happy, you know that. As for Edward – he already knows all there is to know about me.'

Fred frowned. 'How?'

She shrugged. 'Talk, I suppose.'

They walked on and reached Fred's car before he spoke again. Then it was with untypical hesitancy.

'Why don't you forget Monty Gould? Why don't you keep away from everyone connected with the Risings?'

She laughed and put her foot on the running-board.

'You'll never understand, Fred. If it wasn't me it would be someone else. Or something else. Gambling probably. Monty needs something now he is no longer an actor. I'm that something. I make that marriage work.'

'So you're a philanthropist?' Fred pulled the new self starter and the engine caught first time. Sibbie slammed the door.

'No need to be sarcastic, brother dear. One of the ways you keep March happy is to increase her bank balance. Ergo . . . Tilly Adair.'

'Ergo? Latin? You've lived with Edward Williams too long.'

Fred moved slowly away and into the Barnwood road. She was right, of course, and she was probably the only one to realize it. The reason for his existence now was making March happy.

But Victor knew nothing of 'ergo's'; the delicate balance of human marriage was a mystery to him in spite of studying his parents' union since the age of four when he first became aware of it. He loved his mother better than he loved his father, and thought this was probably the norm. Certainly Albert had loathed his old father, Edwin Tomms, and thoroughly disliked his stepfather, Fred Luker. And if Davina and Flora did not love April very much more than David Daker then they must be crazy. So when his father's lonely walks continued on every other Friday evening, he had to think of another way of stopping them. Obviously Edward Williams was too old or too stupid to do anything at his end. The alternative was obvious.

He wrote his first letter with his left hand on Izal lavatory paper filched from the art school. Now that Aunt Sylv lived with the Dakers, it was easy to make certain it came through the letter-box when Monty was in the house on his own. He wrote the second letter when he began to wonder whether his father might think the Izal paper and childish hand represented a joke. This time he used the typewriter at the art school and some paper he stole from Monty's office.

The next Friday he waited down by the canal. He had to be careful because the evenings were now light, and the last thing he wanted at this stage was for his father to see him. He waited till ten thirty and the light in the bungalow was lit. He saw Sibbie come out onto the verandah and peer along the towpath, and when she went back inside he left for home. His parents were both sitting in the front parlour, May doing her embroidery, Monty reading aloud to her from Bernard Shaw's *Saint Joan*. They looked the archetypal happy couple and Victor went to bed well satisfied. He had no way of knowing that his father's nerves were at screaming point and his mother was bored to tears.

Monty was convinced that the letter came from his immediate superior, Tolly Hall. All type looked the same to him, but he recognized the stationery all right. He had never trusted Tolly, and, in a strange contrary way, resented him for finding a niche in his office when Will Rising had died. Now he saw his reserve as 'closeness' and his political ideas as anarchy. When Stanley Baldwin came into office again, all sensible Englishmen breathed a sigh of relief, because anyone who smoked a pipe and looked so ordinary must be a good man. Tolly Hall went around with a face as long as a fiddle and talked about the victory of capitalism and wondered how the working man could ever trust Baldwin after he had broken the strike of '26 with his plus-four boys. And of course Monty knew first hand that Tolly couldn't make poor old Bridie happy. Probably he had sent the damned letter because he resented the fact that Bridie had been able to pour her heart out to Monty that rainy night last September. And how had he found out anyway? There had been that time he had been walking along the towpath just after one of Monty's visits to Sibbie. Had he put two and two together then? If so, he'd kept mightily quiet about it. Another example of his blasted closeness.

So Monty, who had been happy for almost a year, was discontented again. And frightened. He might be able to fool himself, but evidently he could not fool Tolly Hall.

Another, possibly more serious effect of the anonymous letters was that Monty never told Sibbie why their Friday nights finished so abruptly, and when, after two further abortive trips to the bungalow, she realized they had, she did not know the reason. And she suspected her brother of being behind it.

That autumn, Fred took March to Italy. It was at the time that Mussolini bombed Addis Ababa and the tiny Emperor Haile Selassie appeared in person before the League of Nations to plead help for his people. Back home, April and May were terrified that March was in the middle of what the papers called 'Europe's melting-pot' but Fred and March were not interested in politics and had never heard of Abyssinia. They knew nothing of Haile Selassie until they returned home and saw him on the Movietone news-reels at the Hippodrome Picture Palace. But March was very taken with the Bersaglieri and she assured her sisters that the black-shirts were impeccably polite and had stopped all the goings-on for which Italy was so infamous. Fred told David and Tolly, quite curtly, that Benito Mussolini was the saviour of Italy and had started life as a communist anyway, so what were they howling about. April asked doubtfully about the incident in the Bay of Naples when some blackshirts had swum to a yacht and blown it up. Fred said there would always be hotheads in every party – look at the Bolsheviks in Russia. May, who had been nodding most of the time, told how she had seen a gathering of British blackshirts in Hyde Park on her last trip to London. Their leader, Sir Oswald Mosley, was some kind of British duelling champion too, so it must all be very patriotic. Monty chipped in and asked whether Tolly was aware that the new Nazi salute was also the one the Greeks used at the Olympic Games. Before Tolly could reply, March swept on enthusiastically.

'You must go, April. David, it would do her the world of good, she still looks so peaky. Why don't you start saving right now and plan to go next year?'

David smiled at March with unusual affection.

'Why not indeed? April, we will do it!'

'But, darling, the girls are so very young. And it's not a healthy country for children.'

March laughed. 'You say the most ridiculous things, April. Italy is far cleaner than England, I assure you of that – it's one of the things Signor Mussolini has done. Besides, you won't take the children. They shall come to me. They both adore Chattie, and Albert will love having them.'

May said, 'It sounds marvellous. Monty, d'you think we might go too?'

'Don't be stupid, May. How could we afford it on what I earn?' Monty shot a resentful look at Tolly, who had let it be known that he was taking two months' special leave next year to attend the Berlin Games.

May objected to being called stupid in front of her sisters and flushed, but March saved the day again.

'Darlings, you'll go one day, I'm sure. But be fair. You've roamed the length and breadth of this country and had your fill of travelling. April didn't even come to Weymouth that time in the war.'

May was immediately repentant. 'April, I'm sorry.

I'm not a bit jealous really. You deserve to go and you'll tell us all about it so that we shall feel we've been too.'

'I'm trying to tell you all about it now, May,' March said tartly. And did so at such length that April was exhausted by the time they'd gone. Aunt Sylv tutted her disapproval at so many visitors all at once and took the girls into the kitchen for one of her 'proper' teas which consisted of boiled eggs and heavy dough cake.

April said apprehensively to David, 'What's for supper, darling?'

'Cauliflower,' he reassured her. 'I picked a beauty before I went to the shop this morning.'

'You're becoming a gardener,' April teased, leaning back on the sofa and wishing she could do more. Was it only last year she and the girls had cycled to the blue-bell woods? It seemed aeons ago.

'Yes.' He smiled at her. 'Yes, I find the garden something. . . real.'

'Aren't we real? The girls and me? And certainly Aunt Sylv!'

'Of course. But other things, outside things, they are so petty, April. I need to see my real life – you and Flo and Davie – in a real setting.' He shook his head. 'Sorry, darling, I shouldn't be talking like this. Shall I get you a cup of tea?'

'No.' She patted the sofa by her side. 'Please talk to me, David. You've been finding topics – making conversation – for ages now. And it's not natural.' She made her smile into a grin. 'All right, I never really understood what you were saying, but I miss it now!'

'Cheeky wench.' But he sat by her obediently and patted her hand. 'If you didn't understand, how was it you always argued the toss so vehemently?'

'Did I?' She thought back. 'I suppose that I thought you were condemning some people. Ordinary people. People like Pa. And Monty. I had to try to put their point of view.'

He laughed. 'You mean the people who think that Stanley Baldwin cares about them?' He dived a kiss at her nose. 'Sorry, darling. I couldn't resist that.' He looped a friendly arm round her shoulders. 'All right, I'll talk to you. I've put another row of winter greens where the bean sticks were. And Sylv says to give the roses cold tea to drink so I've been doing that.'

She said nothing, just looked at him with a tight mouth. He kissed it.

'All right, all right. I'll try to explain. D'you remember the end of *War and Peace*? All through the book Pierre has been trying to find some truth through politics. Where does he find his truth in the end?'

'By the bedside of his children,' April said slowly.

'I've always known that was where my truth lay. And where did Pierre find that his truth made sense?'

'In the fields. Working side by side with the peasants.'

'Exactly.' He lifted her bodily onto his lap, not without some difficulty, and held her close. 'Primrose. My April Primrose. I enjoy designing still, though you are no longer modelling the things I design. But the world of business, of commerce, of politics, of power . . . it's not real. I'm no farmer and never shall be with my gammy leg. But I'm glad you talked me into buying this old house in the country. We're putting down roots, darling, and that is real.'

She put her face against his and did not try to stop the tears of weakness that ran between their touching cheeks. After a while she whispered, 'Nothing is ever wasted, David, is it? I have thought that this last year has been useless. Just keeping everything going and waiting for me to grow strong again. Nothing happening. And all the time we were putting down these roots.' She turned her face and kissed him, tasting her own tears. 'Thank you for talking to me, David. Thank you for everything.'

She could have told him then about the shadow that had hung over her during that year; the shadow of Mannie Stein. But the sun was shining through the french doors from the garden, and there were no shadows anywhere.

Monty's desertion damaged far more than Sibbie Williams' pride, though that stung and smarted like a raw place every morning when she woke up before she could marshal her defences against it. But underneath that was something much more. Most of her life she had managed to maintain her links with the Risings; and when she had lost contact for a time she had always known why. Now she did not know.

She took to visiting her parents, Hettie and Alf Luker, practically every day, and she insisted on sitting in their front room which they never used so that she could watch number thirty-three opposite. Over a period of time she built up an accurate picture of the Goulds' routine: the only time that May was definitely alone was on Mondays after the weekly wash. She then drew the curtains in the front bedroom and rested from two till four; as Hettie said, 'Er sleeps off the starch.' Hettie was not a fussy laundress and had small patience for May's careful soaking, blueing and starching.

So, on a Monday in late October when summer seemed to return for a day, Sibbie donned her most modest dress and coat, pulled on an old-fashioned cloche, and crossed the road from number seventeen to number thirty-three.

May had risen early from her post-laundry rest that day. She wanted to get herself dressed up before Monty came in because they were going to the theatre in Cheltenham that night. The Opera House was real theatre with red plush seats and golden cupids, and Monty had promised to take Victor backstage to meet the scene-painter after the show. It all warranted the dress which Bridie had helped her to buy last Saturday. Not a cost-price from Daker's this time, but a grey slipper-satin, very sleek, that made her look like a well-fed Persian cat. She surveyed her reflection and wondered whether it made her look like an over-fed cat. It had been so expensive that she must like it. In fact she must adore it. She turned sideways and breathed in. The sun glowed off all the protuberances: naturally her breasts, of which she was quite proud, never having had any until after Victor's birth – that was all right. But then beneath the breasts there were two large pads which obscured her ribs. Then her abdomen and rear. And her thighs showed too; surely she didn't have thighs, not in quite that way?

The door-knocker thumped below and her frown changed to one of puzzlement because no callers came on Mondays, it was a day dedicated throughout Gloucester to laundering. She fluffed at her hair, breathed in again and went downstairs.

The first thought that came into her head when she saw Sibbie was: thank God I'm decently dressed, better dressed than she is for once. She ran over her outfit besides the dress. Her stockings were silk, her shoes kid with cuban heels.

Beneath, she had her best underwear. Her hair was as good as it ever would be, and she had already applied discreet makeup. She smiled uncertainly. 'Sibbie. What brings you here? Is anything wrong?'

Sibbie smiled. And her first thought was: thank God she doesn't know about Monty and me. Her second was: she looks all right. And her third: if she'd let me help her she could be beautiful again. And suddenly there was her mission. She would make May beautiful again; she would introduce her to people; people that Edward knew, important people. And people she knew too. She would introduce beautiful May Rising to other men. She would show Monty Gould.

She said, 'Nothing wrong at all, May. I called on Ma and she wants to sleep after doing her washing and I was at a loose end for an hour, so I thought I'd call on you. I heard Sylvia wasn't here any longer!' She smiled roguishly as if their estrangement was all poor Sylv's doing.

May smiled too. She had meant to see something of Sibbie before this but between April and Bridget . . . Aunt Sylv was a useful excuse.

'How nice. Come in and have a cup of tea with me. I was just going to make some.'

The two women walked down the long passage and into the kitchen. Since Sibbie's last visit which had been in old Gran Rising's day, the house had changed out of all recognition. The drugget was replaced by shining linoleum, and the stairs were carpeted. At Victor's behest, the old dark dado had been stripped away and everything painted stark white. Through the open door into the front sitting-room where Will had cut out his suits, one of Victor's paintings dominated a whole wall. It was a nude. Sibbie swallowed; May and Monty might still live in the awful old Chichester Street Terrace, but they had style.

She watched May gather tea-things onto a tray: Florence's plain white bone china and the silver spoons that had belonged to her family. Her own china and cutlery were superior to this, but there was something about the way May laid it out . . . possession. She belonged to her things as well as them belonging to her.

Sibbie said simply, as she had said so often long ago, 'May, you look superb.' And May flushed with pleasure, no longer taking such praise for granted. 'That dress,' Sibbie followed up. 'It does things for you.'

'Does it?' May was genuinely surprised, confirming the fact that she had by no means 'adored' the dress.

'It certainly does. I should think it must drive Monty mad.'

May laughed but not with wholehearted amusement. 'I hope so.' She bit off further words and substituted, 'He hasn't seen it yet. We're going to the Opera House tonight.'

'How exciting. I mustn't delay you.'

'Oh, I've plenty of time. I'm glad to see you. I'd have filled in the time with eating, I always do.'

They both laughed, remembering May's fastidious appetite in the old days. Then Sibbie asked, 'And how's Victor?'

'Fine. Loving art school. And Edward?'

'Oh . . . fine. He rests a great deal.'

'Yes. Well, he's . . .' May stoppered her words again and resorted to her teacup. Sibbie laughed.

'May, if we can't talk about Edward and Monty, what can we talk about? You were going to say that Edward is getting old, weren't you? It's true, he is almost sixty and he has become elderly all of a sudden. But I love him still.'

May looked at her friend who had always been able to match her own frankness. She smiled into the eyes that were as blue as her own, and again they clasped hands as they'd done at Daker's Gowns last summer.

'You're right, Sib. And before that I was going to tell you that I don't drive Monty mad – like that – any more. But I still love him too.'

'And he loves you.' Sibbie made it a statement also.

'And Edward you?'

'Completely. So now we can talk. Darling, I want you to help me with my dining-room. We give these stodgy parties for Edward's old colleagues, and the room looks like them – stodgy. Will you come and look at it and tell me what to do?'

May's eyes sparkled. 'No expense spared?'

'None whatever.'

'Oh, Sib. What fun.'

'I'll pay you. Interior decorators cost the earth in London.'

'You certainly will not. We're friends.'

'Are we? We always were, I know. Oh, May, could we be friends again?'

May leaned back in her chair and said definitely, 'Yes.'

'What about Bridget? You see a lot of her and she won't stomach me.'

'How do you know I see a lot of Bridget? Sib, you've been spying on me!' May laughed delightedly. 'And don't worry about Bridget. I can manage her.'

'You'll probably have to choose between us, May.'

'We'll see.' May smiled. 'Mother welcomed you back – don't you remember? And when you married Edward it was all right again.'

'You mean I became respectable?' Sibbie too was laughing. It did seem hilarious; the past few years a silly fuss about nothing.

'You could never be respectable, Sibbie Luker! Oh, Sib, it will be marvellous to see something of you again.'

'Yes. Yes, it will. Darling, that dress.' Sibbie stood up to go and put a long forefinger on the slippery satin shoulder and moved it along May's arm. 'It is so very touchable.'

May felt warm all over and very beautiful.

That evening was the best they'd spent since they returned to Gloucester. Victor had a marvellous time and decided to specialize in set designing. And Monty . . . May knew that she was driving Monty quite mad.

Chapter Six

The year 1936 proved an eventful year for the Rising girls and their families. So often before, their domestic affairs had run parallel with international ones, and again, as events arose, blossomed and burst in Europe and at home, so they were reflected in the microcosm of life in Gloucester. The city itself seemed to fester that summer, the winter floods rivalled those of 1908; the Severn invaded the water meadows around Westgate Street and the causeway itself which led into the Forest of Dean was impassable. The gypsy encampments which clung odorously around old Llantony Abbey were under water much of February, and the crones who sold their pegs from door to door swayed along the streets, their rheumaticky hips moving like wallowing tugs. Vegetables rotted in the ground and when the first new potatoes appeared in the shops, they commanded the ridiculous price of threepence a pound. David dug his own with some smugness.

On 20 January the new king acceded to the throne. He was an even more romantic figure than his grandfather, the seventh Edward, and it was fitting he should take that name and become the eighth Teddy on the throne of England. He was a modern king, good-looking and essentially young. It was difficult now to remember George or his father looking anything but the patriarchs they became; and before them had been the mother figure of Albion herself, Victoria. Edward the eighth, or 'David' as his family called him, symbolized the young spirit of Britain: high hopes and aspirations as always, certainly, but fun as well. The outrageous flapperdom of the twenties had gone, but because of it people now knew how to enjoy themselves. They could dance to the wireless, drive to inaccessible beauty spots, swim without bathing machines, and make love without having babies.

During the euphoria of the accession, April and David planned their trip to Italy, and Tolly was in communication with the British Communist Party regarding his trip to Berlin for the Games. On 7 March when Germany repudiated the Locarno Treaty, Tolly received instructions that he must make his trip as an observer only; individual action could not be tolerated by the Party. Tolly had been prepared to protest if necessary to Herr Hitler himself, and felt as rebuffed as the Locarno countries.

Just before the Italians finally occupied Addis Ababa in May, Sibbie Edwards, née Luker, took a new friend to her canal bungalow: his name was Charles Adair. She pampered and flattered him; she groomed him for May. Meanwhile she watched with sardonic amusement as Tilly Adair refused to be dumped by her brother Fred. The small, rather ineffectual woman made no secret of her enslavement and waited quite openly for him outside his office in King's Street. Gladys Luker, who ran the day-to-day business so admirably, had managed to keep any rumours from reaching March so far, but with a bit of luck Sibbie need not soil her soul by tale-bearing; March would hear anyway. And serve Fred right.

Before the year had closed, the abdication of the young king, and the sense of bewilderment that went with it, were to have their echoes in Gloucester too.

In spite of the outbreak of civil war in Spain during July, Tolly's plans went forward. Sometimes Bridget felt she could not bear it; the Berlin trip was the last straw; if he really went she would have to do something about it.

'Why can't I come?' she asked petulantly. 'Not that I want to – boring old Olympic Games. But why do you have to go on your own?'

'I'm not going for pleasure, darling, you know that. There will be thousands there – I'll melt into the background – take photographs – find things out for myself. Besides, it's rather expensive.'

'I could afford my own ticket out of my allowance.'

He looked at her. 'Could you? You've been spending rather freely lately.'

'Are you criticizing that too now? My God, surely I can spend my own money how I like?'

'Certainly. Then you have enough to buy a ticket? I'm not sure about the hotel booking but I could try—'

'Oh, don't bother! I know when I'm not wanted. My God . . . I was free until I married you. Free to choose my own friends and do what I wanted to do. Now, after ten years of bearing your children, you've given me my freedom back and I don't know what to do with it any more!'

His conscience was smitten. He put out a propitiating hand. 'Oh, Bridie – come with me – let's forge new links – let's be friends, Bridie – can't we be friends?'

'No. A woman can never have a man friend. It's not possible.'

'Rubbish. You don't believe that, surely?'

'I do. And so do you. When Monty brought me home last year after that row, you hated it. Yet he was being just friendly.'

'Was he? Or was he pleased to know something about our private affairs?'

'I confided in him as I would confide in a friend. He sympathized as a friend sympathizes. I'm not going to probe deeper than that.'

He sighed. 'All right, Bridie. Leave it at that. Come with me and let us try to be friends.'

She stared at him, smouldering with a resentment newly fired by May's resuming her old friendship with the hated Sibbie.

She snapped, 'No. No, I'll stay at home like you want me to do, Tolly. I might find a friend, you never know. But it certainly won't be you. You are my husband and as far as I am concerned you can never be anything else.'

Tolly looked at her for a long moment more, then said quietly, 'So be it, my dear.'

And Bridie put her mind to how she could make him pay in full for this last insult.

May said, 'You really like it, do you?'

They were standing in the dining-room at the house in Barnwood. The decorators had moved out a week previously and the ancient Belgian carpet had been removed so that the polishers could finish their work. The oak boards gleamed against white walls; and the ornate cornice was picked out in blue.

'It's like a piece of Wedgwood.' Sibbie was genuinely delighted. The brown wallpaper had been copied from the Gentlemen's Club in Cheltenham and had thoroughly depressed her. 'I adore it, May. I can't thank you enough.'

Edward came in from the hall after tipping the workmen. 'It really is marvellous, May. So clean and austere.'

May dimpled. 'I'm thrilled, you're thrilled. What could be nicer?'

They went back into the sitting-room, where tea was laid on a trolley. After it, Edward went to lie down and the two women strolled in the garden.

Sibbie said tentatively, 'May, you're marvellous with houses. I'm quite good with clothes. People. Would you be terribly offended if I suggested one or two . . . things . . . for you?'

May hesitated then said, 'No. But I simply cannot have another permanent wave, Sib. And I don't like peroxide. And the long-waisted dresses don't do much for me.'

Sibbie laughed. 'I'm glad you realize it, darling.' She took her friend's arm. 'You see, your strong point is your other-worldliness.'

'Oh, *Sibbie*! You sound like Mother. I'm as strong as a horse!'

'I don't mean that kind of other-worldliness!' She smiled. 'I mean, you belong to another world. You're Edwardian. You always were. When you tried to be a flapper it didn't work. The biggest mistake you made was having your long hair cut.'

May sighed. 'I know. I've let it grow since the perm but it's taking ages.'

'We can help that along. Hairpieces piled on top. And dresses modelled on the lines of your new one. The satin.'

'It – it's too moulded, Sib.'

'That's how they were. Moulded. Very sensual. Now listen, this is what we'll do . . .' They walked between the lavender hedges and May did indeed listen, very intrigued indeed.

Tolly Hall was the complete theorist, and National Socialism, as seen in Berlin that August, was complete pragmatism. The fact that it seemed to work excellently chilled Tolly to the marrow. Like Fred and March in Fascist Italy, he could see that the Germans fed well and were all industrious, that the tottering Reichsmark was stable at last at 11¾d, that trams and trains kept time and were sterile-clean, and that practically everyone went around as if they had a purpose in life. After France in 1918 he could not believe that a country could be entirely without beggars; in Gloucester every street corner had its wounded war hero, its blind match-seller. The Berlin of brothels and transvestites was invisible beneath the enamel veneer of that Olympic summer. For the first time, the Olympic torch was ignited by the rays of the sun and brought from Greece by 3,000 relay runners through Bulgaria, Yugoslavia, Hungary, Austria, Czechoslovakia and into the Olympic Stadium itself. Tolly, isolated in the midst of the 120,000 cramming the stands, watched with a frown the sheer efficiency of the opening ceremony. Fifty-two nations took part without a single hitch.

Adolf Hitler, in his subdued khaki uniform, also watched. Tolly found his binoculars straying often to the slight figure on the bedecked rostrum; he could not help but notice their physical similarities. Average height, dark silky hair, dark eyes, and that look which Tolly knew also belonged to him: alone-ness. As the

American contingent passed beneath him, the Stars and Stripes curving above the heads of the coloured competitors, Herr Hitler lifted his own binoculars and looked at the renowned Jesse Owens. Tolly switched his own lens from one to the other, registering that the German Chancellor saw Owens as a threat to his ambition that Germany would beat America for the first time to top position.

As the raucous anthem faded, to be replaced by the sombre notes of God Save the King, Tolly focused again on Hitler. And as if his concentrated gaze was magnetized, the German's glasses swung in his direction. For a long instant it seemed to Tolly that the two pairs of glasses stared directly at each other. He felt a small tremor in his own uplifted elbows. Was this man, this dictator, noting the similarities between them too? Had he an inkling that he was studying an Englishman, not only Germany's traditional enemy but a sworn personal opposer of all that the National Socialism stood for? It could not be, of course. The look meant nothing. But Tolly held it doggedly all the same, and only when the glasses moved away did he lower his arms and look around him to check whether the object of Herr Hitler's attention might have lain elsewhere. He saw nothing of special interest.

He drew a deep breath and held it for a moment. For the first time he began to understand how this man could have conquered a country, albeit his own, in three short years. He remembered the way the German airship had slipped up the Severn estuary two years ago and knew that he had been right in his suspicions then. He gripped the rail in front of him, refusing to allow the tremor in his arms to develop further.

April, May and March sat in the garden at Longmeadow and talked about hair.

'It's not a wig, darling,' May protested again to March. 'It's a hairpiece. Just until my own hair grows again. I've decided that as I can't be all straight and narrow like you and April –' she made one of her comic faces '– I'll go back to the way I was after Victor was born. I'm not going to feel guilty every time I eat anything.' Defiantly she picked up one of April's queen cakes and popped it into her mouth. 'That is my fourth – I know, March—' crumbs spattered everywhere and all three women were engulfed in silly giggles.

April wiped her eyes and glanced at the trellis gate which led to the front of the house. Aunt Sylv had gone to collect the girls from a friend's house and was rather late.

'I have to admit I like it, May, whatever it's called. And David can copy those two dresses you bought in wool for the winter.'

'That would be marvellous. I feel so much better, girls – I can't tell you.'

'So do I.' April nodded. 'Guilty too, of course.'

'Guilty?' May showed her incomprehension.

'Well, you know. This awful business in Spain and poor little Haile Selassie. And the Rhineland and everything.'

March shrugged. 'It's got nothing to do with us, darling. People will always fight and quarrel. Don't let it get you down.'

'But it could stop you and David going to Italy – is that it?' May asked, looking at the queen cakes and deciding on another cup of tea instead. She lifted the teapot, discovered it empty and couldn't be bothered to go indoors to refill it. April stood up.

'Perhaps. I don't think so. David is very keen to see things for himself. I didn't mean that it affected us personally. It's just that when people are being gassed and bombed it seems awful to worry about the shop and what we're going to have for supper.'

May shook her head. 'The League of Nations are supposed to see to all that out there. Edward Williams says they are ineffectual, but Monty thinks they are simply being practical.'

March said, 'April, sit down. If May wants more tea she is perfectly capable of—'

'Honestly, I don't want any more, April dear. I'll have another of your delicious little cakes instead.'

April did not sit down. 'I want to go inside a moment. Aunt Sylv is taking such a long time fetching the girls.'

May said, 'Oh well, if you're going anyway . . .' She handed the teapot to her sister and watched her go across the lawn and into the house. 'She's still beautiful. And she is looking much better.'

March snapped, 'No thanks to you, May. You're impossible sometimes. You've almost finished the cakes. Now April will have to make more for the children.'

'Oh darling, don't start. She's got Sylvia after all.'

'Since when could Sylvia make edible cakes? And she's also got David and two children besides Sylvia.' Seeing her words were not penetrating May's summer content, she attacked elsewhere. 'And what is all this about Edward Williams? Have you been seeing Sibbie Luker?'

May finished her cake and dabbed at her mouth with one of April's napkins. She had known for some time that her recent association with Sibbie would have to be admitted, but that made the moment no easier.

'Mother wanted us to be friends again. At your wedding she said—'

'I know what Mother said, thank you, May. I was there if you recall. And for Mother's sake I thanked the wretched girl for coming. But we both know what she has done in the past and any kind of association with her is unthinkable.'

'Oh, March. Sometimes you are so hard. I've seen Sibbie perhaps half-a-dozen times since last winter I suppose. She hasn't changed.'

'Exactly.' March sighed noisily. 'What does Bridie think about it? She's been good to you, May, taking you out and about.'

'So has Sibbie. And Bridie makes me feel like a poor relation. Whereas Sib—'

'So you've dropped Bridie in favour of Sibbie Luker?'

'Not at all. Please stop being so hateful, March. As a matter of fact I'm seeing Bridie tomorrow.'

March thinned her lips. 'I see.'

There was a short silence. Filtering around the side of the house came the sound of the girls arriving home with Aunt Sylv.

'As a matter of fact,' May said brightly, 'I've met one or two very nice people at the Williams'. Someone you know too. A Charles Adair.'

'Charles Adair?' March was thunderstruck. 'Do you mean to tell me that Sibbie has got that poor man in tow now?'

'It's not like that, Sis.' May felt her eyes fill up at the

sheer injustice of it all. '*Edward* introduced us. It's perfectly above-board.' She eyed the last two cakes. 'If you really want to know, he seemed more interested in me than in Sibbie.'

March was not reassured. Fred had described Charles Adair as 'a wrong 'un' and Fred knew about wrong 'uns. She removed the cake stand to the far side of the table, compressing her lips again. Then she said, 'Not a word of this to April please, May. All that old business between Sibbie and David . . . we don't want her thinking about that again.'

'Oh, all right. But April always understood about that. Such a fuss about nothing. We're all *older* now, March.'

At that moment April emerged from the house again closely followed by Victor, Albert, and her two daughters. Aunt Sylv propped herself against the door jamb and watched them all, a small smile on her face.

'They were cycling out to Marley to see the Baxters!' April explained the appearance of the boys. 'So they're going to have tea with us first.'

'We thought we'd go through the bluebell woods.' Victor came to May and kissed her hairpiece.

Davina treated everyone to her solemn smile. 'Victor's going to sketch me,' she announced.

Flora leaned against May's knee. 'Victor says I'm too little to be a decent model,' she confided.

May picked her up and hugged her. Flora was her favourite, dark like David, but like Florence had been too. 'Aunt May has eaten all the cakes,' she confessed. 'Shall we go and cut some bread and butter for you, darling?'

'I'll do it,' March said resignedly. She went back

inside. Victor had never been a favourite of hers and she found her two nieces fairly hard work.

Albert Tomms was a non-political animal, as most of Gloucester's citizens were; but, fired by Victor's glowing accounts of the social life to be found in political clubs, he had recently joined the local branch of the League of Nations Union. Victor, adept at playing both sides at the same time, also belonged to the Imperial League and was now advocating immediate enrolment for Albert so that they could both attend a dance that night.

Albert lay supine on the daisy-dotted grass and watched Victor 'place' Davina. She took the project very seriously and would not move her pose to drink the milk April brought for her.

'I suppose you want to go to the Imps dance because that Beryl Langham will be there,' Albert said idly, not very interested in anything because he was so utterly content.

'Beryl Langham. Jocelyn Pitt. Judy Peplow. To name but a few.' Victor propped his sketch block on his knees and narrowed his eyes at Davina. 'Don't move, Davie. That's perfect.'

'She has to breathe, remember,' Albert said, propping his head more comfortably and smiling at April as she held the glass of milk to her daughter's lips. She was such a sport, was Aunt April. If that had been Mother she would have interrupted Victor on principle. And if it had been Aunt May she would have been too lazy to see that Davie had her drink. Albert was still in love with April. It was a wonderful feeling because it required no effort on his part. And some of it spilled over to Davie, of course.

Victor measured with his thumb against his extended pencil. 'No she hasn't. If I see her take a breath I shall mummify her.'

Davie tried to stifle incipient giggles.

Victor said, 'Well? Will you come? You can have two dances with Beryl if you do. I promise.'

'My God, you're insufferable,' Albert commented lazily. 'I might let *you* have two dances with Beryl. If you're a good boy.'

'So you'll come.'

'No. I'm not an Imp at heart.'

'You mean you don't believe in Toryism? But you uphold it, man. Your parents are bloated capitalists.'

'Fred is not my father.'

Victor looked round apprehensively and saw that March was still in the house. 'Not that again. You know what I mean.'

'You talked me into the League. That must be enough.' Albert stretched luxuriously. 'Hurry up with the sketch. Davie and I want our tea.'

Victor measured again and drew. 'You listen to Uncle Tolly too much,' he grumbled. 'You don't have to believe in these things to belong to them. Look at him. He lives like a lord and belongs to the Communist Party.'

'Uncle Tolly's all right.' Albert rolled onto his stomach and surveyed Davie's knees. They were slightly grassstained and very vulnerable. 'D'you know . . .' He looked away from them to her small square hands so like his own. '. . . d'you know, Uncle Tolly told me once that if ever I needed any help I was

144

to ask him first. He promised Gran he'd keep an eye on me. I thought that was pretty tophole of him.'

Victor was surprised but not enough to stop work.

'Keep an eye on you? You don't need anyone to do that, do you?' He glanced round again to check on March's whereabouts. 'What did Gran mean? Uncle Fred?'

Albert flushed. 'Don't know. Shouldn't think so.' He rarely talked about the man who was his mother's husband. 'Do come on, Victor. Davie's starved.'

Victor frowned as he worked. Then he said, 'But will you come tonight? You don't have to join the Imperials. Just come as my guest.'

'Oh, all right. Anything to shut you up.' Albert got to his knees and held out a hand to Davie. She ran to him. 'As soon as you're old enough I'll take you dancing. Will you like that, Davie?'

'Oh, yes please.' Davina hugged her big cousin adoringly. 'I'd like to do anything with you, Albie.'

Albert laughed as he piggy-backed her to the tea table; but Victor frowned again. He joined the others and passed his sketch block around for the admiration he always got from his mother and aunts. But it did not please as much as usual. Victor was quick and intelligent and knew his own faults well: was he jealous of little Davina?

Tolly ate his dinner slowly, relishing the foreignness of the food, while he studied a map of Berlin. The Bahnhofstrasse was not, as he had imagined, in the vicinity of the railway station, but appeared to be tucked into a maze of sidings and shunting yards to the east of the city. He wondered whether he would be more noticeable finding his way by tram and foot, or whether he should take a taxi. His instructions had been very clear about complete anonymity.

He folded the map to the relevant three square inches and tucked it into his inside pocket. His clothes felt tight already and he had been here only three days. It must be the beer and sausages.

The dining-room in which he sat seemed saturated in the odour of food. It was impossible to imagine it had ever been anything else but a room for eating. Even before the hotel was built this particular air pocket must have been redolent of food. Here and there, at random, the ceiling was supported by thin pillars, cream-painted to head height, then gradually discolouring on the way up until, out of reach of the longest arms, they became dark brown. The thickness of the atmosphere in that indeterminate ceiling space must be tangible; Tolly let his mind dwell on it for a moment. Everything would be smoked of course, from sausages to kippers. He wondered whether it was possible to put on weight from just smelling vast quantities of cooked food.

From the hot murk a figure materialized. Tolly had made a conscious effort to recognize his fellow guests in case they might be useful to him in the future, but this one was new. New, but not strange. He had seen him before. The man, dressed in street clothes, linen jacket, straw hat and immaculate dark trousers, removed one of his chamois gloves and held out a long hirsute hand. He spoke in only slightly accented English.

'By all that's holy. I can't remember the name, but

you are from Gloucester. Am I right? Gloucester in England. You were at the Daker wedding.'

Immediately Tolly remembered him. David's best man; then David's partner for a time. Then suddenly not David's partner. He took the outstretched hand.

'We went to a tea-dance once. At the Cadena.' He indicated the chair opposite his. 'Do sit down. I'm Hall. Bartholomew Hall. And you are Emmanuel Stein.'

'I am indeed.' He sat down. 'This is a very fortunate meeting. Very fortunate indeed.' He glanced significantly at Tolly. 'I am looking for an hotel. I wish to attend the Games.'

'They're all full? I'm not surprised. I booked this one nearly two years ago.'

A waiter appeared. Tolly said, 'Will you join me for coffee? Or perhaps schnapps?'

'That is most kind of you.' Stein glanced at the waiter. '*Kaffee bitte.*'

The waiter still hovered. Tolly nodded. '*Auch für mich.*'

Stein said, 'You speak German?'

'Schoolboy stuff. But you – your accent is perfect.'

'I am German Jew. My parents lived in Berlin. I have cousins here still.' He kept his small black eyes on Tolly's and lowered his voice. 'You noticed perhaps that the waiter would have liked to ignore me.'

'No. I know that German policy is very antagonistic to the Jews at the moment, but surely you have a British passport?'

'Naturally. I fought for the British in the last war. But they all know I am a Jew. That is why I cannot get a room.'

'Oh, surely . . .'

Stein smiled. 'It's true, Mr Hall.'

'Can you find a bed with your relatives?'

Stein's smile widened. 'I am here to get them out. To find a bed with them would be to put myself at risk also.'

Tolly was startled. It had been his dream: to help refugees out of Germany. He knew of the concentration camps; the communist press had informed their readers of the full horrors of Belsen since the Reichstag fire three years previously. Yet when he had requested to be used as a courier on an escape route, he had been told to 'retain anonymity'. Now here was someone without obvious political affiliations, who was proposing to organize some kind of escape route – presumably single-handedly.

'Um . . .' Tolly wondered how much secrecy was required. Stein's frankness had been surprising in the circumstances. 'You mean, you intend to take some of your relatives back to England with you?'

Stein shrugged. 'Why not? As you probably recall I am engaged in what is known as the rag trade. There is always room for another good Jewish tailor in London.'

'But passports? Papers?'

Stein smiled again. 'I can arrange those. They are not the problem. At the moment the problem is accommodation.'

'But . . .' Tolly saw his chance to be of use. 'Perhaps I can help you there?'

Mannie Stein's eyes narrowed in a way April would have remembered very well. But he replied cautiously, 'There is simply no room at the inn, Mr Hall.'

The evocative words strengthened Tolly's determination.

'But there is room in my room for a friend,' he said. 'Wait here and I will fix it.'

He went to the foyer immediately, fired with enthusiasm, and punched the bell for the clerk with unnecessary force.

'Herr Knopfel—' Luckily the man spoke some English. 'Unexpectedly a friend has arrived from England to see the Games. Not a single bed in the whole city . . . perhaps the couch in my room . . . extra blankets . . . ?'

He felt a glow of triumph as he rejoined David's old partner. At last he had struck some kind of a blow. The waiter brought the coffee and poured.

'It's all fixed, Mr Stein.'

'Please call me Mannie. It is how David and April called me.'

'I remember now.' Tolly felt a small doubt. He remembered Bridie gossiping about Mannie Stein and how he had made a pass at April and David had sent him packing. But that had been a long time ago and David had always been so sensitive. 'Well . . . it's just a couch in my room, Mannie. But it will be somewhere to lay your head.'

Mannie shook Tolly's hand across the coffee cups and talked about the generosity of all his friends in Gloucester. Then he asked about old Mrs Daker and expressed sorrow that she was dead.

'And David? You realize probably that we had to split our partnership when I had the chance to work in London? I'm afraid I've lost touch with him now.' The eyes watched narrowly.

Tolly felt relief. Naturally it was a business split; typical of Bridie to embroider it.

'David is holding his own. He still designs, so his clothes are expensive. But he's doing well enough.'

'And his wife?'

'April is recovering now. It's a slow business of course, but she is definitely stronger.'

'I did not know she was ill.'

'She became ill two years ago, soon after Mrs Rising died.'

Mannie hooded his eyes. 'I am sorry. I really must look you all up when we get home.'

Tolly slid his watch from his waistcoat pocket.

'I have to go out, Mannie. Shall I take you upstairs – perhaps you would like to collect your luggage first? I take it you left it at the station?'

'No. It is in the lobby. I took it with me all round everywhere.' Mannie stood up. He was taller than Tolly remembered, and there was a stoop to his shoulders. If he was David's contemporary he was in his mid-forties, but he looked older than David. His luggage consisted of a Gladstone bag and a black umbrella and a pearl-grey overcoat. Herr Knopfel stared silently as the two of them climbed the stairs; Mannie Stein was so obviously Jewish.

Tolly's room overlooked one of the many side streets leading onto Friedrichstrasse, its long casement windows open and admitting a slightly fresher smell of cooking. Mannie immediately crossed the square of carpet and closed them gently.

'Everywhere . . . food,' he said, wrinkling his nose humorously. He looked around. 'It is spacious enough, yes. But you do not object – really?'

'Of course not.' Tolly smiled quickly. He knew that without the undoubted lure of Mannie's refugee relatives, he might well object. Mannie's acceptance of his allegiance was a little too quick. He wondered fleetingly whether this astute man had timed his visit specifically to coincide with Tolly's own. The coincidence had too long an arm otherwise. He shrugged. 'Though I have to sleep with the windows open, Mannie. I'm not used to such heat.'

'Ah, I apologize.' But Mannie made no attempt to reopen the casement at this stage. Instead he sat on the edge of the bed and began to remove his shoes. They were soft leather and suede, almost the variety known as 'co-respondent'.

He glanced up. 'You do not mind? If you go out now I will rest on the bed.'

Tolly felt dismissed. For the first time since he left England a week ago, he felt a need for Bridie and the girls. He consciously summoned into his mind the sense of his large household, with Mrs Goodson and his mother bustling around and Bridget nursing a baby. Not that there was a baby for her to nurse now, but the picture would remain always. That was what gave him identity: his family, his wife, his work among the marvellous old libraries of Gloucestershire.

He said, 'Of course I don't mind. You must be completely done up after slogging around the hotels in this heat.'

Mannie smiled down at his shoes. 'Yes,' he said.

Beryl Langham had her brown hair shingled at the back and leaping forward onto her cheeks in the front in two large question marks. She smoked Turkish cigarettes in a jade holder just as April had done before Flora's birth and her lower lip jutted slightly in the most adorable pout. Besides those attributes, she had dimples, very large brown eyes fringed with even larger black lashes, and her skirt was well above her knee displaying lavender-silk-covered thighs that made Albert's palms sweat. And it was all too obvious that although Victor wasn't quite seventeen yet and still at school, even if it was art school, she was completely ga-ga about him. Albert resigned himself to trying to tango with Judy Peplow and talking about the aims of the Imperial League which seemed to involve nothing more than the new word 'non-intervention'. Later they changed the subject to Robin Adair which was rather more interesting. There was a rumour abroad that Robin had got a girl into trouble. This had probably happened before, but the Adair money had always hushed the whole thing up. This girl was from the Forest of Dean and Forest people did not allow themselves to be hushed up that easily.

Beryl, while keeping Victor at the prescribed stiff arms' length for the tango, held him close in her intense gaze and pouted as provocatively as she knew how.

Victor said, 'I loathe dancing.'

Beryl smiled slightly, and directed their next charge towards the doors of the Corn Exchange. Her eyes did not waver from his.

Victor said, 'I see. We're going to stand on the steps and look at the moon, are we?'

If he hoped to insult her into speech he was disappointed. She turned her body and fell onto his right arm, and as he scooped her up again on the required beat, she managed to touch his lips with hers.

'Wicked,' she murmured. 'Especially in one so young.'

'Ah, she speaks. The old crone has a voice.'

Beryl made a moue; she knew it made her look very like Pola Negri.

'So you admit my superior years, and therefore my superior wisdom, child?'

'Oh, shut up, Beryl. Why can't you be honest and say let's go outside and kiss each other.'

She half closed her eyes. 'Let's go outside and kiss each other, my little one,' she suggested.

They did so. The city had its late-night feel; the sky was pale with stars and the steps of the Exchange, where people had bartered for so many years, could have been in Greece.

Victor said, 'Look. Albert's dotty about you. Why d'you have to make a dead set at me in front of him?'

'I don't make a dead set at you, little one. You interest me. I see talent. Perhaps real talent. I wish to encourage that.'

'Beryl, I'm not in the mood. Anyway I don't joke about art.'

'Ah. Art. So much bigger than both of us. Art, wonderful art.' She did a small Fred Astaire dance up and down the steps, showing even more of her beautiful thighs. Victor leaned against a colonnade and watched.

'Victor, dearest.' She stopped by him, breathing quickly, not meeting his eyes any more. 'I've decided. I've been thinking about it ever since you told me. And now I've decided. After all, you are only a schoolboy so there's nothing . . . like that . . . about it. And if you're going to be a proper artist I suppose you need someone to help you. And it's going to be me.' She dimpled suddenly. 'So when you're famous I want you to remember that it was Beryl Langham who was your very first model.'

She looked down at her feet and was silent, and for a long moment so was he. Then joy began to dawn. He gripped her by the elbows.

'Beryl, do you mean you'll pose for me?'

'That's what I've been saying, isn't it?'

'Darling Beryl. A life model?'

'If that's what you simply have to have then I suppose—'

'You know I can't pay you anything?'

She jerked away. 'My God! If you offered me money I wouldn't do it in a million years!'

He grabbed her back. 'Beryl. Darling, wonderful Beryl. I love you.'

Her dimples returned. 'No you don't. You're soulless. All you care about is your art.'

'But next to art . . . oh, Beryl, what a peach you are!'

He put his arms around her and kissed her exuberantly and then she made him do it again less exuberantly.

He murmured into her ear. 'One more favour, dear Beryl. Could you – would you – please, please, go and dance with my cousin Albert?'

She withdrew and looked into his face.

'Sometimes I don't know whether to kill you or love you for your selflessness,' she confessed. 'Kiss me again and I'll consider it.'

The room in the Bahnhofstrasse was surely too bourgeois to be the Berlin headquarters of the Communist Party. The sofa and chairs, box-shaped, reminded him of the Dakers' living-room, and the lampshades were all painted with Japanese patterns in the very latest style. There were two other men in the room when he was ushered in by a German hausfrau; they stood up and shook his hand in turn, but as they spoke nothing but German he was unable to talk to them. The hausfrau brought him a tiny cup of coffee and a bowl of sugar crystals. She indicated one of the chairs and sat by him.

'In one moment or two, I will translate,' she told him. 'We know that you are Herr Hall from England and that you are here to – to *ausgesichten*—'

'Observe,' he offered. 'But I wish to do more than merely observe, Frau . . .'

'You will be instructed in one moment or two on how to observe.' She did not give him her name and she did not smile. 'What you must look for. How you must report when you return to England.'

He shook his head at the sugar crystals and said firmly, 'I would like you to tell these gentlemen that I am offering to take back with me at least one member. I can provide shelter and possibly work.'

'This is not possible,' the woman replied shortly. She looked at the two men and cut across their low conversation with some curt sentences. They both looked at Tolly, then away. She said, 'They say do you fully understand the role chosen for you by the Party? That you must conform completely? Infiltrate the society in which you live?'

Tolly put his cup down with a click. 'Madam, excuse me but they did not say that. They did not speak.'

She repeated, 'Do you fully understand the role chosen for you by the Party?'

He looked at her and took a deep breath. 'Yes, I understand that.'

'Then you know you cannot introduce a refugee into your way of life.'

'Madam, in the present emergency, I consider it essential to declare my true allegiance.'

She spoke without emphasis or emotion. 'You consider it essential. Do you not know that the first tenet of our credo is the submergence of the individual?'

Tolly remained silent. He had been discreet in the past, but many people at home knew his political beliefs. He did not mention this. After a few moments the two men began to speak again. Tolly picked up his coffee cup and drank. The talk continued; the woman did not appear to be listening.

Suddenly she spoke.

'We wish you to observe injustice. There will be a happening of extreme injustice at the Tiergarten tomorrow afternoon. Three o'clock exactly. You will observe that and report it to your press when you return to England. On Thursday there will be another such incident—'

'You mean these incidents are prearranged?'

'They happen all the time.'

'But these two particularly . . . they are arranged?'

One of the men spoke and the woman stood up.

'I have work to do, comrade.' She bobbed her head at Tolly and put out a hand for the cup he was still holding. 'You will prepare yourself for the day of the revolution in your country. The reports you send to the press must be neutral. Meanwhile, you are working at present in a large house near Chelt . . . en . . . ham?'

'Crabtree Hall. Yes, I am adding to the library there.'

'We have information that Crabtree Hall will be used

to make munitions in the war. We would like a plan of the ground floor.'

'The war? A Russian war?'

For the first time the woman showed emotion: impatience. '*Nein*. The war between our two countries.'

'But—'

'The Party would like a plan of the ground floor of this Crabtree Hall.'

'Would that be the Russian or German Party?' Tolly asked.

'The Party is international. You should know that.'

'I'm sorry. I don't think I can do what you ask.'

The two men stopped talking. Tolly knew suddenly that they understood English. He swallowed.

The woman said levelly, 'Can you report on the Tiergarten incident?'

'I . . . er . . . yes. I don't see why not.'

'The other. You object on moral grounds? Or practical ones?'

'Neither. I would prefer written instructions.' There was a long silence. Then one of the men stood up.

'You are courageous, Herr Hall. We need courageous men. You will receive written instructions.'

His voice was accentless and as he turned his face into the light, he was smiling with great charm. The woman turned and led the way outside. Tolly followed. When the door of the small villa closed on him, he stood in the moonshine, staring at the rest of the dark terrace, lost and full of doubt. Wanting Bridget again.

That afternoon Bridget and May met by accident in the town and did some desultory shopping together. The coolness between them, which had grown up with

May's attachment to Sibbie, seemed to disappear in the August heat. Bridie was angry, hurt, lonely; May was happy again, expansive and generous. She suggested they should have tea in the palm lounge of the Bon Marché. Bridie agreed eagerly. The girls took the lift to the third floor and wandered along the gallery looking at the local café society and smiling at the orchestral trio playing in a corner. It was delightful to recognize Mr and Mrs Adair at a table beneath one of the luxuriant palms. May made the introductions with a touch of smugness: let Bridie know that she met really nice people at Sibbie's.

Both Charles and Tilly enjoyed a personal sense of intrigue at the meeting. Tilly knew that May was Fred's sister-in-law; Charles gathered that Bridget Hall was related to Sibbie somehow. He eyed her covertly. She was as plump as May but with an extra piquancy; hadn't she got a very big family? The four of them ordered the Bon Marché's special Summer Tea of raspberries and cream, followed by scones, followed by éclairs.

'You still have a good appetite I see, Mrs Gould,' Charles Adair said in a tone that left May in no doubt he was complimenting her.

'Charles thinks I am much too skinny,' Tilly commented to Bridget, rolling her eyes. 'Luckily there are still some men who admire small dainty women.'

Bridget felt challenged. She smiled at Charles.

'It's as well there are others who don't object to larger models.' She fluttered her fingers above her heart. 'There's not much I can do about it. Five children. And I fed them all myself.'

May glanced round in surprise. At one time Bridie

had been adept at the outrageously provocative remark, but not since the children started arriving. Charles Adair thoroughly enjoyed it.

'Five? You have a wonderful figure, Mrs Hall. Five children or not. Wonderful.'

May felt his interest leave her and centre on Bridie. She shook her head at the three-tiered cake stand.

Tilly took a second éclair. 'How marvellous for you to be free at last, Mrs Hall. You must have done nothing but produce children since you left school.'

'You make me sound so boring!' Bridie looked round at May. 'Am I boring, May?'

May said resignedly, 'Not a bit.' She leaned across to Tilly. 'Bridget taught for a year or two after she left teachers' training college. She used to tear around Gloucester in a racing car. Whatever she puts her hand to, she does. So when she decided to have a family . . . she did!'

They all laughed and Bridget protested, 'I still have my car, May!'

Charles Adair leaned back, smiling. He had liked May Gould and knew that Sibbie hoped he would like her even more as time went on, but this new one was better. He was a snob and he recognized that Bridget was in his own class.

'What car have you got, Mrs Hall?' he enquired.

'A Morgan.' She returned his smile. 'They're fast.'

'Yes. Yes, I can imagine that,' he said. They both laughed. Bridget felt all her old powers returning. Tolly had never been any good at flirting. This man so obviously was.

May glanced at Tilly and saw a flush on the childish face. She said quickly, 'Have you heard from Tolly yet?'

She ignored Charles and explained to Tilly, 'Bridie's husband is at the Olympic Games. In Berlin, don't you know.'

'No, I haven't,' Bridget said shortly.

'Do you mean to tell me your husband has left you on your own, my dear Mrs Hall?' Charles practically sparkled at the thought.

Bridget looked at him through her lashes. 'Hardly. I have five children, remember, Mr Adair. Also a nanny and a mother-in-law who is never far away.'

'Poor child,' he mocked.

'Tolly particularly wished to see the conditions in Germany,' May enlarged. 'And the Games seemed to be such a good opportunity. He is probably far lonelier out there on his own than Bridie is here.'

Tilly stifled a yawn and Bridget arched her brows at Charles Adair.

'Actually he's not alone, May dear,' she said. 'D'you remember Mannie Stein, David's old partner? He telephoned just after Tolly left and asked where he was staying. Said he'd look him up.'

'Oh.' May succumbed to another éclair and gave up. Charles opened his eyes wide; this was becoming more intriguing by the minute.

'Mannie Stein. That was the chap—' He glanced at his wife and stopped. Then went on, 'No, I'm thinking of someone else.' He kept looking right at Bridget and one of his eyelids drooped significantly.

Monty was at work that afternoon as usual, and while May had her weekly shopping expedition, Victor took Beryl into one of the unused attics at number thirty-three and began his painting of the unclothed human figure. Beryl, her sleek shingle a little rufffled by the removal of her dress and petticoat, was bright red all over and insisted on turning her face to look at the wall. She had wanted the blind pulled over the window, but when Victor was adamant that he needed every scrap of light, she had adjusted the Nottingham lace curtain with great care. She felt her body must be radiating heat across the room to the young artist, but he made no comment to put her at her ease. His frown was intense, his silence more so. After five minutes she snapped, 'Haven't you finished yet? How much longer am I supposed to stand here like a complete lemon?'

'My God. I've only just started. What's the matter with you, girl? Surely you don't need to fidget for at least another hour?'

'How dare you speak to me like that, Victor Gould!' But she did not move.

'Well . . .' His voice petered out as concentration took over. Silence settled on the room thickly once more. She stuck it for another two minutes, then tried again.

'I danced with Albert last night. Like you said.'

'Good.' He spoke without interest, his charcoal filling in the white gap of the cartridge paper with satisfying strokes. If only he could get a good sketch he could work on canvas from it. If only. 'I promised you'd give him two dances.'

She kept her pose, but her body visibly stiffened. 'You what? You promised I'd give him two dances? How could you make promises on my behalf?'

'Well, you know how he is. He wouldn't have come to the dance if I hadn't said something.' Victor made a huge curve of her buttocks à la van Gogh. 'I say, old girl, could you take a deep breath and relax? The abdomen muscles are unnaturally tight.'

She exploded out of her rigidity. 'You mean, it was that important for Albert to come to the dance? I was a sort of carrot for the donkey?'

Victor had his mother's frankness. 'Well, I wouldn't have gone without him.' He would have to change that buttock. It was making the thigh too thick. 'Hold still Beryl, you moved then.'

She said furiously, 'So I owe this – this – relaxing afternoon – to Albert Tomms! Is that what you're saying?'

'Oh, Beryl, do shut up. How can I work when you keep talking?' She was silent. She was still. But his concentration on the sketch was less fierce now and he knew she was unhappy. 'Anyway,' he said after a while, 'you told me you'd been thinking of modelling for me for some time. So if you hadn't done it this afternoon you'd have done it eventually.'

The silence lengthened again. Her thighs were really marvellous and he couldn't get them. He left them and returned to the long length of the spine and then from beneath her upraised arm, the curve of her right breast. She was very beautiful.

He said humorously, 'Have you sent me to Coventry, Beryl? You've not spoken for at least ten minutes.'

She did not reply.

'Oh, all right. I suppose I must be grateful you've stayed put.' He sighed. 'You take offence at such odd things, beautiful Beryl.'

Still she was mute and he began to talk nonsense as he sketched furiously. He was getting her. Ensnaring her in the cartoon before him. If only he could transfer it onto canvas he knew it would be all right. She would be his for ever then. Even when she was old and hideous. Even when she was dead.

'Can't you see this is more important than anything else, sweetheart? Can't you see that the human form is the most miraculous creation . . .' He quoted his art teacher at some length, working furiously, conscious that he was holding her there with his flow of words, at last unembarrassed.

But when he had finished she became coquettish and difficult again. She snatched at the silk counterpane he handed her and pulled it beneath her armpits as if she expected him to attack her on the spot. And when he moved away to give her space to dress, she appeared to resent that too.

'You don't care, Victor . . . you just don't care. It's the very last time . . . I was a fool. Cheapening myself . . .'

Victor had always been precocious and he knew now what to do by instinct. After all, if a kiss now and then meant she would sit for him, it was a small price to pay. But the kiss got out of hand. Somehow the bedspread slipped and she was holding his head and going at him like a hen at corn. He found those marvellous breasts in his hands and knew suddenly how Albert felt every time she came near.

And, as if he'd summoned his cousin to him by the power of thought, the dull pounding which he'd assumed to be his heart stopped just outside the attic door and the next instant Albert himself, breathless from taking the stairs two at a time, was with them.

Mannie Stein stood close to Tolly during the closing ceremony, possibly in an effort to conceal his tall, stooped figure, more likely so that Tolly would not miss any of his frequent comments.

'Germany might be the top nation,' he murmured as the eighty-seven medal winners saluted fanatically towards the victorious Führer. 'But the prize still goes to America for Jesse Owens.'

Tolly did not even nod. The thought that tomorrow he would be returning home had sustained him for some days now. He had 'observed' the injustice outside the Tiergarten when a man had handed out Party pamphlets and then started to spout some kind of jargon. His arrest had followed swiftly. But most of the onlookers had appeared to be there by appointment, like Tolly himself. He had felt even more sickened when, returning to the hotel, he had witnessed a more impromptu scene outside a house whose door was painted with the yellow Star of David. A lorry, engine revving furiously, was being loaded with human freight. As the last passenger, a woman, was shoved over the tailboard, a child arrived swinging its satchel, presumably home from school. The woman had held desperate arms towards the child; there had been tears and screams. Someone had emerged from another house, scooped the child up and disappeared. The woman's sobbing had been audible above the note of the lorry's engine as it lumbered out of sight.

'Also the judges were biased.' Mannie's mouth was close to Tolly's ear. 'They should permit the new film finish to decide the issue.'

Tolly wondered why Mannie had insisted on coming to this closing ceremony. Every day he attended one event or another, then disappeared for hours on end. He explained to Tolly that he was fixing papers and train tickets. He took his Gladstone bag with him wherever he went; sometimes it bulged, sometimes it appeared flabby and empty. Tolly was beginning to think Mannie Stein was another Monty, playing the role he might have seen in the cinema. What with him and the rigged scene outside the Tiergarten, Tolly could not wait to get home to Bridie's down-to-earth resentment. Perhaps they should have another baby. Perhaps it was the only real and sensible thing to do in this crazy world . . . But the sobbing woman and the screaming child and the yellow star painted on the door, they were real enough.

As the German hymn rang out for the last time in the huge stadium, Mannie tapped Tolly's arm.

'We will leave now,' he said in a low voice.

'We can't. Not till after the anthem.'

'Now. Come. We have to meet my relatives.'

Tolly looked round, startled. Mannie's face was as impassive as ever, but a small nerve twitched above his right eye. His voice was suddenly pleading. 'Please, Tolly. Will you go first? You are so obviously English, they will let you through.'

'What is happening? I don't understand.'

Mannie flashed a sideways look at the forest of upstretched saluting arms, and nudged Tolly along the stand. Tolly smiled apologetically, 'Excuse me. Would you mind? I am so sorry . . .' They were on the steps and climbing down. Black uniformed guards were here and there, but the atmosphere was one of festival and the sight of the casually dressed Englishman helping an elderly man down the steps did not excite much attention. Mannie came to the bottom and turned into the grass alleyway which led to an exit in the distance. They came to a door in the side of the stand; he pushed Tolly ahead of him, though the officials at the gate seemed to be arguing with a photographer. Tolly heard Mannie rap hard three times on the door; the next moment he was being dragged through, banging his head on the low planked ceiling, landing on his knees while someone banged the door shut behind him.

He looked up and around, bewildered and alarmed. It was like being inside a drum; sound was everywhere, muffled yet enormous. The area was wedge-shaped, partitioned from the next wedge by a plank wall. Where he and Mannie crouched the roof was only four feet away, but beyond that it rose steeply, almost out of sight. Someone, presumably whoever had unlocked then relocked the door, was behind them and to the side. In front, standing clear of the roof, were six other men. They were dressed in the shorts and singlets of the British athletes; but they were not athletes.

Mannie moved away from the low roof and turned to the seventh man.

'In sack,' he said briefly.

The man took the Gladstone bag, opened it and upended it in one movement. Shorts, singlet, running shoes, socks, fell onto the grass. He began to strip off the clothes he was wearing.

'*Mein Englisch Freund*. Tolly Hall.'

Tolly stood up as far as he could and walked slowly forward. The men eyed him. They were younger than him, their bare arms and knees proclaiming that they might be clerks, doctors, lawyers; anything but athletes.

Mannie said a string of names. Tolly heard 'Wilhelm' and 'Franze' and remembered them because they were the names of kings. He looked at Mannie who lifted his shoulders.

'Sorry, old man. I stole a kit each time we came. Or bought it. It had to be done slowly. If I'd taken them all at once and been discovered, it would have given everything away.' He spread his hands. 'And if I'd told you, it would have spoiled my cover.'

Tolly said, 'I am not what I seem, Mannie. I could be a dangerous cover for you.'

Mannie smiled. 'They know you are a communist and that you are here to observe. They are very suspicious of you, but their suspicions are in the wrong direction.' His smile widened. 'I think you wanted danger, my boy. You have it now. You are what your English friends would call a sprat. A sprat to catch a mackerel.'

Tolly had never felt so confounded in his life. He wanted to ask a million questions but they seemed paltry in the face of this . . . action. Whatever Mannie Stein knew, whatever the authorities knew, still the carefully planned stages of this escape had piled up and up until now. And Tolly, who had thought he was going home with stale dreams, was somehow involved. A sprat to catch a mackerel.

He was still staring at Mannie when the seventh man presented himself, dressed, his other clothes already in the Gladstone bag.

Mannie handed the bag to Tolly. 'This is your spare suit, my friend. I have your passport here. If you come with us you must leave everything else at the Count Bismarck.'

Tolly took the bag, transferred his stare to the passport, then took it numbly.

'I don't see . . . you've done it. You won't get away with it, but you've done it. How can I help?'

'You can come with us. You are obviously English. Our manager . . . coach . . . what you think. The others—' He gestured behind him. 'They have drunk too much and insist on having a few nights in Paris before returning home. You are doing your best to control them.'

'You won't be allowed on board the train. Not in that gear.'

'We might be if you are in charge.' Mannie gestured again helplessly. 'I cannot do it, no. But if you keep talking – if you are angry with them . . . At the station there is a large bag containing English clothes and much drink. We shall continue to carouse on the journey through Germany in spite of your loud protests. I think it might be done.'

'If we are caught . . .'

'We have genuine British passports. I think we should get away with it. A joke . . . a dare . . . yes, a typical British dare I think.'

'They—' Tolly nodded briefly at the assembled men. 'They would stand no chance.'

'They stand no chance if they stay here. I do assure you of that, Tolly.'

Tolly stared down at his passport. It was all somehow ridiculous, like a Ruritanian romance by Anthony Hope. Yet it was happening.

He said, 'If I don't come with you, what then?'

'You return to the Bismarck. Use up the rest of your time. And leave on your reserved ticket as planned. Nothing else.'

'And you?'

'I shall be no worse off than I was before I ran into you three weeks ago.'

Tolly looked at the waiting men. They understood some of what had been said; they returned his look with hope.

He said, 'I'd better go first and try to get two cabs. Yes?'

Mannie clapped his arm. 'Good man. We'll do it, you see.'

Tolly felt a fierce joy like heartburn. At last he was striking a blow against the ultimate in capitalism. Not through the idealistic troop with whom he had allied himself, but through this unlikeable, cunning man who seemed to represent an element of which Tolly also disapproved. He was reminded of his stint in France at the end of the war. He had been sixteen, a pacifist, and with a team of youngsters from his school he had taken a private ambulance to France and there discovered the terrible gap between theory and pragmatism.

Outside the stadium he secured two taxis without difficulty and stood by them waiting. The refugees would come out with the crowds, well protected by noise and acclamation. He had accomplished the first part. He thought of his luggage at the Hotel Bismarck and especially of the presents he had bought for the girls. He might be able to arrange something later through Thomas Cook; now it did not matter.

Bridie was dining with Charles Adair for the third time. Discreetly they visited different restaurants, and this evening it was the long dining-room of the County

Hotel in Southgate Street. Bridie had blossomed in the warmth of Charles's admiration, and everything about her shone: her hair, her full mouth, her large grey-blue eyes; even her small nose was unfashionably bright. She was creating an aura for herself of sheer desirability. When Charles had told her the gossip about April and Mannie Stein, the whole affair had somehow become perfectly legitimate and justified. April had always been in touch with God about things like right and wrong, and April was basically good.

Charles said persuasively, 'We're friends surely? I thought we were anyway. We get on so well.'

'Friends don't sleep together, Charles.'

'Why not?' he demanded with pseudo-innocence.

'Anyway I don't believe in friendship between men and women.'

'Thank God for that. You've demolished your own argument.'

'I know.' She showed gleaming teeth. 'Aren't I clever?'

He breathed heavily through his nose. 'I could eat you, Bridie Hall. Here and now I could lean across and take great chunks out of your body with my teeth.'

She offered him her hand and he took it and put her wrist to his mouth. The waiter came with solid thick slices of roast beef. Charles continued to nibble the back of her hand and she smiled delightedly. Tolly would have expected her to tuck her hands on her lap to make room for the waiter. He was the complete conformist.

When Charles released her and they began to eat, he spoke of his plans.

'We can leave separately about eleven o'clock. You can go first if you like. Tilly won't know if I'm home or not, and it doesn't matter if she does.'

Bridie smiled. 'Same applies. Let's be real devils and stay all night and have breakfast in bed tomorrow morning.'

He looked slightly startled. 'Darling, do you mean it?'

'Why not? Tolly's away – you say Tilly doesn't care.'

'Well, I don't think she cares. But your children and – and the household—'

'I'm never permitted to do anything. Let them get on with it. Perhaps I shall be a little more welcome next time I offer to do something.'

'You're incredible. I love you.' He hesitated, chewing hard on the Gloucester beef. 'Er . . . what about your things? Most women need God knows what before they can go to bed.'

'I've put a little bag in the cloakroom. I've got a rather special nightdress waiting for you.'

He stopped chewing. 'Darling. How did you know?'

She smiled dazzlingly at him. 'I didn't. I've had the case with me each time we've gone out. I knew you'd arrange something sooner or later.'

'My God.' He stared at her blankly, then began to smile. 'Darling Bridie. You really are the most marvellous girl I've ever met.'

She gurgled. 'Charles darling. Do you realize that my encumbrance is called Tolly and yours Tilly?'

They both began to laugh.

Then he said, 'Yes, but of course mine is really Mathilda.'

She pulled a face. 'And mine is Bartholomew.'

They bent over their plates, convulsed with laughter. It must have given them wind or something, because neither of them could manage the cabinet pudding which was the County's speciality that night. Still laughing, she asked the waiter to arrange for her case to be sent up to her husband's room. Charles looked startled again, and then laughed more. The waiter thought they must be drunk. On two sherries and half a bottle of burgundy.

They had no reservations on the Paris train. Their story was that they had celebrated too well and to avoid trouble with their manager, they were leaving ahead of the others. Tolly explained largely and in English to anyone who might understand that they wanted an extra day in Paris anyway. Mannie had train tickets in his inside pocket and they boarded without fuss, but in the unreserved coaches, space was cramped, and they were scattered between three compartments. They lolled against each other, pretending to sleep. By the time the train reached Köln, they had survived three ticket inspections, and the other occupants from one of the compartments had departed, either to disembark or to remove themselves from the smell of whisky.

They gathered together, silent and tense. Mannie pulled the curtains across the windows and looked at Tolly. 'The frontier soon, my friend. Then you come into your own. Here are all the passports, put your own on top, mine next, they are the genuine ones. Try to get the guards into the corridor, explain that they—' he jerked his head at his companions '—are exhausted after the Games.'

'It will be all right.' Tolly felt strangely confident; this was his destiny after all. 'Pull back the curtains, we have nothing to hide, remember.'

Mannie smiled wanly. 'Well done, old man. You're getting the hang of it now.'

Tolly nodded, tied back the curtains and sat next to the corridor. He closed his eyes and relaxed. It was so easy now that the die was cast. He remembered the feeling from eighteen years ago; the complete detachment which amounted to disembodiment. You simply shut away part of yourself and let the rest do what it did step by step. Presumably this was how people like Fred Luker operated all the time.

Charles Adair stood helplessly in the bathroom of the County Hotel, while Bridie kissed him passionately time and time again.

'Darling. You really are the most marvellous girl. But I can't risk anything. We're having a terrible time with my son just at the moment because some girl . . . not that I'm thinking you're like that, darling—'

She giggled against his face. 'Oh, Charles . . . Charlie . . . Charlie boy. You're safe with me. Quite, quite safe. Throw that nasty thing away and come to bed now.'

She plucked the cardboard packet from his hand and let it fall into the water closet. Then she took his hand and led him back into the bedroom. She was a demanding lover and unnecessarily aggressive. Her joy was like Tolly's, fierce and indigestible. Afterwards she did not experience Tolly's relaxation. She lay by Charles Adair, hating the smell of him, wanting to go for a bath and afraid she would wake him. Tears made the dark shapes of the unfamiliar room swim, and she blinked angrily and whispered, 'I'll show him. If he won't give me babies there are others who will. I'll show him.' And when those words brought her no comfort, she whimpered, 'If April Rising can do it, then so can I!'

Chapter Seven

That September Fred Luker bought new premises in London Road to accommodate his charabancs; there was a showroom facing the road and he became an agent for Vauxhall cars. Above the garage and showroom were extensive offices. He took Albert and March with him when he visited the solicitors to register his limited company in the name of Luker and Rising.

'I don't see why I have to come,' Albert objected. 'It's nothing to do with me.'

'It's a family concern. You'll be a director with your mother,' Fred told him briefly.

'Well, her name hasn't been Rising for a long time. It was the same as my name. Tomms.'

March snapped, 'What *is* the matter with you, Albert? For the past two or three weeks all you've done is to be awkward about something or other.'

'No I haven't. I'm just saying that Luker and Rising is silly. It doesn't make sense.'

Fred gave him his fishy blue stare. 'I want to have your grandfather's name above a business again. All right?'

Albert was glumly silent. It made him happy to think of the name Rising being 'up' again, but he had no intention of admitting as much to Fred. March tucked her arm in his as they went up to the Dickensian offices of Whitecross and Marsh.

'Tell you what. After we've done all this, let's go round to Chichester Street and you can tell Victor about it.'

'No thank you, Mother. Anyway Victor is going on a week's sketching holiday with some of the other students.'

'Oh, really? May didn't say. Not that I see much of her these days what with all her other engagements.'

Fred led the way into the waiting-room and began to talk to the clerk. March frowned at her tall fair son.

'Darling, you're not ill are you?' she asked suddenly.

'Oh *Mother*.'

'Well, you should be pleased about this. It's as much your business as Fred's, you know. He's awfully good the way he's had the papers drawn up so that you're not tied to him for the future.'

'Yes. Yes, I suppose so.'

March put her finger on the trouble. 'You've had a row with Victor, haven't you?'

'How did you know? Has he been round talking to you?'

'Of course not. But you don't get like this unless there's trouble with Victor or Davie. And we haven't seen Davie since that day we had tea at Longmeadow all together.'

He shuffled, looked out of the window into the cathedral close and muttered something.

March said resignedly, 'Well, if Victor's gone away you can't make it up. Anyway I think you're too close to him, and he's not a good influence. There's always been something . . . underhand about Victor.'

'I agree,' Albert said, fervently.

March's frown deepened, but she did not pursue the

176

subject. 'Listen, darling. Aunt April is coming to the house tomorrow to sort out the girls' bedroom. You could help her – move furniture and things like that. Then we could go back with her and collect Davie and Flo and go to the pictures. What do you think?'

'Davie would be tickled pink.' He turned from the window and grinned at his mother. 'There's a Mickey Mouse at the Picturedrome.'

She wrinkled her nose. 'It's not terribly clean down there,' she objected.

'But Davie will love Mickey Mouse.'

'Oh, all right.'

Fred called, 'Mr Whitecross is all ready, March.'

They went into the inner sanctum.

Tolly, with his usual reticence, gave no explanation to his family for returning home earlier than expected. He had to admit to his missing luggage, but told Bridget he would get in touch with Thomas Cook's to instigate enquiries, and he did so. They wrote off to their Berlin agent stating that Mr B. Hall of Gloucester had been called away suddenly and had left his luggage at the Hotel Count Bismarck in Kellernstrasse. In due course the luggage arrived in Brunswick Square, perfectly packed, all his presents safe and intact.

Tolly's silence on the subject of his holiday fuelled Bridget's fires of resentment still further. She was terribly tempted to tell him about Charles Adair, but restrained herself somehow.

She had the most marvellous plans for enlightening her husband on that subject. She refused to see Charles again alone. His bewilderment was pitiful, but she was quite heartless. Two weeks after their stay at the

County she was practically certain she was pregnant, and she stayed very quietly at home, knitting contentedly and simply waiting. Tolly was so grateful to be home again, happy that she appeared happy.

At the end of the summer he received written instructions about Crabtree Hall; the letter came from London; even so he tore it up carefully and threw it on the back of the boiler in the office. He confided in David at this time and David's reaction confirmed his own feeling. 'Get out of the whole thing,' he advised. 'But hold on to your own beliefs; they are real and good.' He looked at the receipt which one of the escaping Jews had handed to Tolly in all innocence. 'So . . . Mannie Stein's charges for services rendered were . . . high.' Tolly explained the enormous coincidence of Mannie's arrival at the Bismarck and David nodded. 'He must have heard of your plan to go to Berlin from that mannequin right back in 1934. He laid his own plans accordingly. Mannie Stein is very . . . devious.'

The next day Tolly sent his resignation to the British Communist Party. He felt lighter afterwards. And very close to his family.

Meanwhile David and April packed for their trip to Italy. Davie and Flora had already gone to March's and Aunt Sylv was back with May for a while. The Winterditch house was unnaturally empty and quiet. April was trying to smother the feeling that she no longer wanted to take this holiday. She itemized the contents of David's case aloud.

'Just one change I think, don't you, darling? We must keep the weight right down. In case we can't get a porter or something.'

David said absently, 'Yes, all right. But these books must go in.'

'Books? Oh, David, why on earth? They weigh a ton!'

'I'll carry them, don't worry.'

'You will *not*!'

'April, stop fussing. My leg is so much better this summer. It must be the gardening. Why don't we join the Whiteway Colony?'

Recently a group of people had set up a self-supporting community in the Cotswolds; they were the joke of Gloucester.

April said, 'David, you are not taking anything seriously. Leave the packing to me.'

'How can I be serious when I'm going away with the most beautiful woman in Gloucester? Come here, woman.'

April surrendered with laughing exasperation, then said as she returned to her dressing-case, 'Not long ago you would have called me a girl, now a woman.'

David was in an unusually flippant mood. He came behind her and began to tickle. 'All right. Girl. The most beautiful girl in Gloucester. Is that any better?' He undid the sash that loosely defined her hips and began on the long row of buttons along her spine.

'David! There's a lot to do before the taxi arrives tomorrow morning. Will you stop it!'

He slid his hands inside her dress.

'There's something so seducible about a busy woman – sorry, girl. Is there such a word as seducible, April?' He kissed the back of her neck. 'If there is, then you are it. So very very, it.'

April clutched helplessly at her drooping dress and

then quite suddenly remembered the times she had deliberately let it fall, with her other clothes, to provoke some of the excesses of passion between them. They were older now, more staid, and her illness had made David very careful. It was a long time since they had made their particular form of love. She let the dress go and turned into his arms, and this time it was all right. Her joy knew no bounds. She held him to her as if she could weld them together, feeling as she always did at these times, the sheer fragility of their relationship.

'It's all right, darling . . . all right, Primrose,' he murmured. 'I know. Weep if you must.'

'It's so perfect, David. Like a delicate piece of porcelain. So – so delicate.'

'Would it be less delicate if it happened more often, my darling?'

'Of course not. I don't mean – I'm not talking about when – when—'

He said steadily, 'When I impregnate you.'

'Oh, David, that horrid word.'

'Why horrid?'

She did not tell him that the word was always associated in her mind with Mannie Stein's sneering accusation of David's impotence many years ago.

Instead she said, 'I'm talking about us. We've built everything – all our lives – from the wrong way round somehow.'

His steady voice itemized events as she had itemized the packing. 'Age difference. My engagement to May. My ghastly involvement with Sibbie Luker. My impotence.'

'You're not impotent!' she denied quickly. 'What about Davie. And Flora. And just then?'

'And weren't there two or three other times as well?'

She was still, listening for bitterness in his voice; he laughed at her and kissed beneath her chin.

'Strange. All these things frighten you, my darling. They make me thankful. I have been so lucky, Primrose. Somehow I have snatched happiness from all the messes and muddles I create. Or rather, you have snatched it for me.' He kissed her again with a kind of reverence. Then propped himself up and took her on his shoulder to stroke her short hair. 'I was thinking of that just now. Tolly was telling me the most extraordinary story the other night. About Mannie Stein.' He held her head as she flinched. 'All right, I know you don't like to hear his name mentioned, but I am telling you so that you will understand that Mannie Stein is no bogey-man to me. And I wish he wasn't to you.' He kissed the top of her head and recommenced his rhythmical stroking. 'He turned up a couple of months ago in Berlin when Tolly was there. It was obviously planned. He organized an escape route for some fellow Jews – commercially of course. He needed someone like Tolly. He used Tolly, yet he didn't trust him. He did not tell him what was happening.' David dropped a kiss on the deep golden head. 'It made me remember how nearly I came to losing you, Primrose. Because of Mannie Stein.'

She did not speak and after a while he leaned down so that he could look into her face.

'Do you understand what I am saying, Primrose?' he asked in a low voice.

'I think so,' she whispered back.

She thought he was listing one more danger-spot in their relationship; she thought his love-making might have been a plea for reassurance. Breathing quickly, she reached up and moved his hand to her breast, then put her mouth to his. He hesitated again, then obediently began the well-remembered techniques that had aroused her in the past.

The Italian trip was an unqualified success. They loved Florence and Rome, but it was Venice which really captured their hearts. They stayed at an hotel called La Paloma which had once been a small palazzo and just might have sheltered Robert Browning. It was off the Grand Canal, within easy reach of San Marco and the Rialto, and breakfast was served beneath striped umbrellas on the wide steps which led down to the Riva. April tried out her phrase-book Italian and managed to order '*caffee* and *toastato*'. David walked around museums and galleries with a guide-book open in his hand. He whispered to April, 'If my jaw hangs for too long, will you close it for me, darling?'

They were not seasoned travellers. There had been France for David and that had killed any desire he might have had for exploring the Continent. There had been Scarborough for their honeymoon and visits to London to see May and Monty. There were frequent day outings: Rodley, Weston-super-Mare, the Malverns, but mostly they had been earning a living in Gloucester and there had been no time nor money for holidays. Now they shared the delights of discovery together. That October, Venice was golden and warm; the horrors of the Fascist bombing of Addis Ababa had nothing to do with this ancient city, and news of the formation of the International Brigade to fight in Spain sounded like one of Tolly's theories rather than hard fact. Strangely it was in Venice that they first learned a piece of domestic news that was still unknown to the people at home.

They were in one of the lesser-known churches, a tiny Byzantine edifice lit only by the ruby-red sanctuary lamp, dark even at midday, dark too with the redolence of frankincense. April's natural elegance was enhanced by a dress which David had made specially for the holiday; the silken material was swathed towards her left hip where a large medallion appeared to hold the whole creation together. The dress was the object of some admiration from another sightseer, probably surfeited with relics and much more interested in the contemporary scene.

April was saying to David in a low voice, 'I'm not terribly keen, are you? I mean I know they were Christians, but there's a sort of barbaric feeling about the place.'

David rested his leg, nodding agreement. 'Christians were the worst kind of barbarians. Think of the terrible crimes committed in the name of the Cross by the Crusaders.'

'Golly, yes.' April noted his tiredness and sat down, patting the seat next to her. 'Thank goodness we live in more enlightened times.'

'Do we?' He subsided gratefully. 'I'm not so sure.'

'No.' She turned down her mouth. 'No, I suppose the men who drop those awful gas bombs pray each Sunday in churches like this.'

A voice said behind them, 'Say . . . you're English! Gee, what a relief. English words . . . Henry, come over here a second, will you?'

April and David looked round. The woman who moved into the pew behind them was very smart;

March would have called her 'up-together', May, 'chic'. She was probably in her late forties. She wore a lime-green linen suit and a straw saucer-shaped hat.

'I'm Miranda Morrell. This is my husband Henry. Please excuse me – *accosting* – you like this!' Her laugh was infectious. 'To tell you the truth, I'm sick of old churches and monuments! But what you said just then . . . well, it kinda made sense. Nothing much has changed, I guess.'

April glanced at David and saw he was smiling. There was something irresistible about this woman.

'Well . . . at least they fought with swords and not gas bombs,' she said tentatively, and was rewarded by a full throated laugh.

The man with her – Henry Morrell – looked at David and April humorously.

'She is a Philistine. She has ignored the statues and the murals. But your wife's dress really interested her.'

'It's all right for you, Henry. It's your city. He is first-generation American, you know. Morrelli was his name and he lived here until he was fourteen.' She smiled at April. 'You understand, I know. I can't help loving your dress. Is it a model?'

'Yes.' April introduced David and proudly explained his work. Miranda Morrell was very impressed and asked if she could order one like it. David was taken aback.

'This is the first holiday my wife and I have had since our honeymoon,' he demurred.

'But, darling. If you take Mrs Morrell's measurements you could send her the dress, surely? She doesn't expect you to produce a sewing-machine here and now!' April looked at him meaningly; he twitched his mouth at her and agreed as graciously as he could.

An unlikely friendship flowered in the forcing-house of Venice. They met the Americans the next day for a trip to the Rialto market, then dined with them in their opulent hotel actually on the Grand Canal. Miranda needed no gradual introduction anyway; she decided she adored April and worshipped David for being a typical Englishman. Henry, urged by her, spoke of the Venice he had left forty years before. Then he had carried painting materials for the many foreign artists and had starved with his mamma and the other bambinos in a garret near the Bridge of Sighs. Then an uncle in Michigan had sent the single fare for one. Mamma could not leave her children. Papa could not leave Mamma. The eldest child, Enrico, had been chosen to go to the land of plenty and make their fortune. He had done his best, but until his marriage to Miranda, he had had a hard time.

She eased his path for him, and now he owned a factory which made cars – Morrell Motors – and he could afford to take his wife on a world tour and buy her couture clothes whenever she wanted them. They had nothing else on which to spend their considerable wealth. There were no children. Papa and Mamma were dead and the bambinos either killed in the war or scattered heaven alone knew where. Henry expressed no regrets. He was a different man now; Enrico had gone with the others and Henry was very content with his Motors and his Miranda. Miranda a little less so.

'Aw gee, honey, how I envy you these two,' she exclaimed, looking at blurred snapshots of Davina and Flora in the garden. 'And your sisters' kids too – you're lucky.'

'I know,' said April. 'I don't take anything for granted.'

Miranda nodded. 'That's the good thing about having to fight for what you want,' she said. 'You never do take it for granted.'

It was Henry who burst the bombshell.

'Hey, what's cooking with your new king?' he asked suddenly, obviously searching for a contribution to the conversation. 'Will he or won't he? Everyone back home says he won't give her up. But I know these old families – he won't be allowed to marry her, will he?'

Both April and David showed their complete incomprehension. Miranda was agog.

'Surely you must know about it? Your David and our Wallis? The papers are full of pictures of them together. Everywhere. Cannes and Paris. Everywhere.'

'Do you mean Wallis Simpson?' April asked. 'Yes, I've seen photographs of them too. But she's just another guest at parties he attends. There's nothing in it.'

'Ho – oh!' Miranda rolled her eyes at Henry.

'Well, there couldn't be,' April explained. 'It's Mrs Simpson, isn't it? She's already married.'

'Twice,' Henry put in.

'Well then,' said April.

Miranda shook her head. 'You're so old-fashioned in England. My God, back home everyone gets divorced and remarried all the time.'

David smiled. 'What about you two?'

Henry said vigorously, 'We're Catholic. We don't believe in divorce.'

'No, but we're unusual.' Miranda smiled lovingly across the table. 'Henry is almost as old-fashioned as

186

you Britishers.' She turned back to April. 'Honestly, honey, this story is bound to break in your country pretty soon. Then you'll remember what we said. Your king has been courting our Wallis for some time now – everybody knows about it.'

'Everyone except his own people,' David said wryly. 'Well, that's not surprising I suppose.'

Flora and Davina were in the attic room at Bedford Close where Albert kept his train set. Flat on their stomachs they watched as a replica of the George the Fifth chugged through a tunnel which actually dipped under the floorboards by the door. Real smoke emerged from the tunnel's mouth and the chuffing of the locomotive became laboured as it took the incline. It was hot in this room at the top of the house, and the girls, dressed in their hand-knitted swimming costumes, still showed the imprint of grass on their plump arms. Chattie had given them a 'real proper picnic' outside for their lunch.

Albert said, 'Operate the home signal, can you, Davie? I'll bring through the goods train then. It's been in the siding overnight.'

'What's it carrying?' Davie asked knowledgeably.

'Not sure. Perishables though.'

Flora said, 'What's peshables? Are they like potatoes?'

Davie rolled her eyes. 'Oh, *Flora*!' But Albert said, 'Almost. They go rotten quicker though.'

Davie just managed to flick the necessary lever before rolling on her back in a paroxysm of laughter. Flora sat up and crossed her legs in hurt withdrawal. The door opened and Victor came in.

'Hello, everyone. Chattie said you were up here.'

187

Victor wore the clothes he affected all the time now. His flannels were paint-smeared and innocent of creases or turnups; his shirt was open at the neck, and he wore no jacket. Flora stood up and flung herself on him.

'Victor. Where have you been? You said you'd come and see us at Aunt March's, and this is the first time! Davie is laughing at me, Victor.'

He sat down with her on the floor, folding himself with conscious grace, looking at her so that he need not meet Albert's angry stare.

'I'm sure she's not. You both look very beautiful in your bathing costumes. May I draw you?'

Albert snapped, 'You may not.' He leaned across and switched off the train set. 'What do you want anyway?'

Victor reddened slightly. 'Surely you mean – to what do I owe the honour of this visit?' He smiled at Flora. 'I'm glad someone's pleased to see me anyway.'

Davina glanced uncertainly at Albert and said nothing. There was a small silence. Flora frowned and then asked, 'Why can't Victor draw us, Albert? He often does.'

Albert made an effort. 'I meant, not at this moment. You need to get dressed first. Shall we go downstairs now and find your clothes?'

Victor gave a deliberate guffaw of laughter, and Davie said, 'It's too hot, Albert. And Chattie says St Martin's summers don't last. So we must make the most of it.'

Victor said in a low voice, 'For God's sake, Albert, pull yourself together.'

'You took the name of the Lord in vain—' Flora looked at him, startled.

Albert began to put rolling stock into an engine shed. 'Disgusting. That's what I call it. Disgusting.'

'What's disgusting, Albert?' Davina got to her knees and began to carry some of the coaches across to the siding. Irritably he waved her back.

'Those don't go here. Leave them alone, Davie!'

She stopped as if he'd struck her and Flora began to cry. Victor tried to comfort her but she would have none of it.

'Look what you've done now!' He was on his knees and glared up at Albert furiously. 'They don't understand. Why don't you tell them what I've done? Go on – tell them.'

'Shut up, you fool.' Albert opened the door. 'Come on, Davie. Flora. Let's go downstairs now.'

Flora went immediately to him and took his outstretched hand. Davie did not move.

Albert said angrily, 'Davie, come here! I'm going downstairs.'

'Don't you trust me with her?' Victor forced another laugh and turned to his small cousin. 'Davie, you know I'm an artist, don't you? Part of my job is to paint people without any clothes on. So that I can see their bodies properly and draw them properly. Do you understand?' Flora was immobile. Davie nodded dumbly. 'Good. That's all right then. So we're still friends?'

Again Davie nodded but she still kept one shoulder between herself and Albert's outstretched hand. He shrugged.

'Come down when you're ready then,' he said stiffly. 'Flo and I will be on the swing in the garden.' They went out and clattered down the lino-covered stairs. Victor laughed more naturally.

'Storm in a tea-cup, Davie. Sorry about it.'

She sat down where she was and held on to her knees. 'I'm nearly eleven, Victor,' she said.

He was perplexed. 'Yes. Yes, I suppose you are.' He grinned. 'Gosh, I remember when I was eleven. That was when I found out about Grampa and Sibbie.'

She said, 'What? What about them? Sibbie is Uncle Fred's sister, isn't she?'

'Yes.' He stood up and went to the window. Far below in the garden Albert was pushing Flora on the swing. He clenched his hands in exasperation. Was the silly idiot waiting to hear Davie scream for help or something? He said, 'Grampa and Sibbie used to be friends.' He turned. 'I was eleven when you had your fourth birthday party at Grandma's and Grampa's. D'you remember? It was snowing. Grampa made you a fairy dress and we danced the polka in the bandy room.'

Davie clapped her hands. 'Yes, I remember that. And Albert danced with Mummy. And Mummy asked him to look after me.' She too came to the window and looked out. 'He told me that once. When he read me a bedtime story. He said it was his mission to look after me.' She looked up at Victor very levelly. 'I love Albert.'

He felt again that twinge of jealousy and quelled it quickly. 'So do I. That's why I'm here. I don't like being bad friends with him.' He flung away impatiently. 'He's so damned narrow-minded – that's what's the matter with him. Oh, he wouldn't mind seeing a few naked women, he's told me so – but he just can't believe anyone can look at the human form objectively.'

Davie eyed him. 'Is that all it is? Really?'

'Really.'

She said matter-of-factly, 'I'll talk to him. Don't worry. I'll tell him how you feel. He'll listen to me.' She pursed her mouth consideringly. 'You see, Victor, Albert is a little . . . old-fashioned.'

He couldn't stop laughing. He found a chair and collapsed on it, leaning over his knees ecstatically.

'You're marvellous, Davie. If he won't marry you later on, could you look at me, d'you think?'

But that was going too far. 'I'm very fond of you, Victor dear, but you see I *love* Albert,' she explained.

He swallowed his laughter. 'Yes, I do see. He's a lucky man. A very lucky man indeed.'

'You could marry Flo,' she offered generously.

He shook his head. 'I'm never going to marry anyone, Davie. Artists are better living alone.'

'Oh.' She put a finger to her lip. 'Oh, Victor, how sad. You will be lonely.' She thought, chewing on her nail. 'I tell you what. Would you like to draw me now? Without any clothes on?'

He stared at her.

'You mean in your bathing costume?'

'No. I'll take it off. Then you can see my chest and my tummy and all round my bottom.'

He said, 'But . . . but Albert wouldn't like it.'

'I know. But you see I'm going to marry Albert, so he'll have me all the time.' She slid unselfconsciously out of her shoulder straps. 'I don't mind in front of you.'

Somehow he could not turn her down. She was so much like his own mother, frank and down to earth at the most unexpected times. Slowly he reached inside his haversack and removed his sketch block, watching her as she kicked her legs free of the costume and looked around the cluttered attic for somewhere to stand.

'Here. Sit down here.' He got up. 'It . . . it's awfully kind of you, Davina.' There was nothing of her. Flat chested, small-rumped, not even a proper belly. Flora would have been more interesting with her baby curves. He began to draw without much interest. She sat on the chair and put out a toe.

'I saw a picture like this. A lady testing the bath-water. You could put in a bath after, couldn't you?'

'Where did you see a picture like that?'

'In Uncle Fred's little room downstairs.'

Victor tightened his mouth against a grin. He length-ened her short hair and swept a ringlet over one of the bare shoulders. She'd like that. He'd make her into something very romantic.

She said, 'I think they're coming back upstairs.'

He was flummoxed and dropped his charcoal. 'Quick, get into your costume – I'll stand against the door!' He suited action to word. She stayed where she was.

'You said there was nothing wrong.'

'For God's sake, Davie! Albert will have a fit—' The door opened against his back and he shoved it shut.

'Then let him,' she said calmly.

The door thudded against him. He spluttered, 'You little minx! You're not in the least interested in me drawing you! You're getting your own back on Albert for chalking you off just now!'

Albert's voice roared on the other side of the panels. 'What's going on? Let me in – Victor, is that you – let me in NOW!'

Victor shouted, 'It's not what you think. Davie suggested – insisted on – modelling for me and now she won't – she won't—' The door crashed sickeningly against his spine. 'Albert, for God's sake, listen!'

Davie said, 'You might as well let him in. It'll all be over quickly, then you can be friends again.'

Albert was roaring like a bull outside, and below there was the sound of a car arriving. Victor felt beleaguered. He stepped away from the door.

Albert's entry consequently was not dignified. He landed on his knees in front of Davie's naked form, having tripped over and broken at least two of his track pieces. He stared up at her for a long two seconds, while behind him Victor babbled something and Flora kept saying, 'What's happening? Where is your costume, Davie?' Then he leapt back up, turned, grabbed Victor by the front of his floppy shirt and drove a fist into his still-talking face. Victor, Flora and Davie all screamed very loudly, Victor went reeling backwards, destroying more of Albert's lay-out before sitting heavily on a farmyard; Davie then rushed forward, sobbing, 'I didn't mean . . . oh, Victor, I'm sorry . . . honestly I didn't mean . . .' Flora covered her face with both hands and fled from the wrecked room, and Albert coughed, flexed his bruised hand, then picked Davie up bodily and said, 'It's all right, don't worry. Everything is all right now.'

Victor put a hand to his nose and surveyed the result. 'All right for you two of course.' He met the combined gaze of his cousins: Albert's distinctly worried, Davie's full of remorse. A grin twitched at his mouth. 'You're welcome to each other,' he said. The next minute all three were laughing. Relief, genuine amusement, and their old companionship compounded to form a gale force hysteria that would not stop. Albert and Davie

193

clutched each other helplessly. 'It was so funny when Victor moved away from the door and you shot in—' gasped Davie. 'You look absolutely ridiculous with your nose pumping blood like that,' Albert spluttered at Victor. And Victor, lying back, surrendering to the joy of his renewed friendship with his beloved cousin, mumbled through blood and pain, 'Narrow-minded so-and-so . . . pea-brained nincompoop—'

But the drama was not over. Alerted by a frantic Flora, March arrived first on the scene. She never cared for mess or muddle in any case, so the state of the attic and its train lay-out did nothing to help the crux of the matter; which was the sight of her son clutching his naked cousin, while Victor – a bad influence if ever there was one – lay on the floor streaming blood. She stifled a scream, turned to her giggling son and fetched him a resounding slap across the face. He staggered back, but did not release Davie whose laughter immediately turned to tears.

Fred, following behind, misconstrued the situation even more than March did. He had long noted, with extreme disquiet, Albert's propensity for his girl cousin. Now he knew he would have to do something about it. He cut across the babble of sound with a single quiet command.

'Out!'

Davie slithered down from Albert's hold, picked up her costume and led the way, hiccupping on her own sobs. Victor pulled his shirt away from his trousers and staunched the blood from his nose with its tail as he staggered after her. Albert tried to speak, then was silenced by the furious agony on his mother's face. They trooped down the narrow attic stairs to the broad landing where Chattie waited with Flora to take Davie away.

April took on the job of measuring Miranda; David had not actually measured a customer since their marriage when April had been his right hand in the small shop in the Barton.

'Now, honey, I want an exact copy,' Miranda stipulated. 'No-one will know of course, I'm hardly likely to wear it next time we come to little old Britain. That shade – eau-de-nil – is just right, and the silk has a sheen to it.'

'Right you are.' April knelt to measure the gap from hem to floor. 'We could choose the material here if you like. I'm going to look around the lace shops tomorrow – I want summer shawls for my sisters. David's not in the least interested, so if you want to come with me and have a look—'

'That would be fine. We're booked on a trip to the Lido in the afternoon, but the morning is free.' She lifted April to her feet and they went to join the men on the balcony. 'Your David seems quiet this morning, honey. Is it that wound of his?'

April looked at David, nodding at something Henry Morrell was telling him. She knew his leg would always pain him, but she was inclined to believe him when he said it was improving. She had heard of other cases where embedded shrapnel moved away from nerve-ends and ceased to give trouble. She smiled; he had purposely avoided calling this holiday a second honeymoon, but in many ways it was much better than their first one.

She turned her smile on Miranda.

'I don't think so. He was worried about the news of

the king. You see, David is quite certain that we shall be at war with Germany soon, and we need to be strong at home. Our monarchy is important to us.'

'Well . . . yeah. But he's wrong about war. Germany couldn't afford another war.'

April shrugged. 'We have a friend who went there for the Olympic Games. There is no shortage of money for the army.'

Miranda looked over the heads of the men, at the wide view before them. She said, 'That's just terrible, April. If it came to another big European war, it's possible that Italy might be on the other side this time. Poor Henry.'

'I hadn't thought of that.' April looked back over the years. 'I had my hair cut off at an Italian barber's in 1917. For the war effort.' She shook her head as if to banish ghosts. 'Then I worked in a munitions factory and it turned orange!' She laughed. 'Don't worry, Miranda. Henry is American now.'

Miranda said briskly, 'Of course he is. And anyway no-one would let it happen again. There's the League of Nations. And it's nothing to do with the States . . .' She took April's arm. 'You could come and live with us. Bring your little girls and live with us in Detroit!' She sat down between the two men. 'How about that, Henry honey? How about David and April bringing their girls and coming to Detroit?'

'Why not?' he said largely. He liked David Daker, he didn't spout a lot of nonsense like most Britishers; he was deep, but straight too.

A week later when all the fuss and bother was over and Albert and Victor had played in the last cricket game of the season, Fred collected Albert from the garage behind the showroom in London Road and took him upstairs to discuss office furnishings.

'I want it to be your choice, old man.' Fred flipped a couple of catalogues onto the desk which Gladys had brought with her from the King Street office. 'Choose what you like and go up to London and order it. If there's nothing there you fancy, go anyway and see what they've got in stock.'

Albert, cautious of Fred, thought this was an olive branch. Fred had been surprisingly reasonable when Victor had eventually explained the awful business of the life modelling; in fact he had smoothed down March's ruffled feathers and even made a joke of the ghastly calendar he kept in his small study, where every month the clothing of the model diminished. The next day he had gone to the public library – an unprecedented visit in itself – and borrowed a book of famous paintings. He had taken Davie on his knee that evening and talked about art and painting and shown her the book. She had seen through the ruse and hugged him consolingly.

'Uncle Fred, you think I'm ashamed of taking off my costume, don't you? But I'm *not* – honestly. You see, Victor is a real proper artist, so it's not the same, is it? It's like when you go to the doctor. Victor doesn't see *me*. He just sees a human being.'

Fred laughed uproariously and kissed his small niece and told her she was a chip off the old block. Albert had no idea whether he meant the old block to be April or David; but of course they were both pretty avant garde, so it could be either. He had been surprised at Fred's concern for Davie, and touched too. Fred was a surprising person.

So Albert let down some of his usual guard and picked up the first catalogue.

'This new chrome stuff looks impressive,' he said, trying to sound really interested. As if it mattered what you had in the office; it was the garage that mattered. 'Look at this, it's like a hammock.' He laughed. 'Get the Adairs down in that and you'd never get them up again.'

He stopped and wished he'd kept a still tongue in his head. He was not aware of the methods Fred had used to purchase the Adairs' land, but he knew there had been some kind of sharp practice.

Fred narrowed his eyes slightly but kept to the subject in hand.

'Carpeting too, Albert. Perhaps two or three quotations wouldn't come amiss at first.'

'Yes, all right. When did you want me to go?'

'As soon as you like. Tomorrow.'

'Tomorrow?' Albert frowned. 'Aunt April and David aren't back till Sunday.'

'So? You'll be back by then if you're thinking they'll give a party.'

'No, it's not that. But Mother likes me to take over the girls in the evening. Give Chattie a break.'

'Yes, well, in view of last week I think perhaps the less you see of Davina, the better, don't you agree?'

Albert was jerked out of his complacence and stared across the catalogue at his stepfather.

'We – Victor – explained about that. I thought you understood.'

'I understood very well, old man. Better than anyone else, I dare say.' Fred went to the ancient desk, pulled out the chair in its knee-hole, and sat down. He spread his hands across the leather top as if feeling his way. 'Let's change the subject. There's an engineering course being run. Sort of apprenticeship. At Longbridge – that's not far from Birmingham.' He grinned upwards. 'They'll snap you up, Albert. It's a three-year course. You come out fully qualified. Letters after your name. How does it sound to you?'

Albert gripped the catalogue tightly.

'It sounds to me as if you're trying to get rid of me.' He watched Fred's expressionless face, and, after a moment of silence which was as good as an admission, he said, 'My God. You don't trust me with Davie. That's it, isn't it?'

'It's a wonderful opportunity, Albert. I've discussed it with your mother and she agrees. The firm can stand it.'

'For God's sake. She's ten years old and my cousin.'

'I know. Exactly.'

Albert threw the catalogue onto the desk. 'I could kill you!' he shouted.

'Like you tried to kill Victor? No-one else can touch her except you?'

'You filthy . . . no wonder they call you Filthy Luker! Your mind is like a cess-pit and you think everyone else is the same as you!'

Fred picked up the catalogue and pressed it flat. He kept his voice very low.

'Albert, listen to me. You're eighteen. A man. Whether you know it or not, you have feelings for that girl – that child. I saw it coming. Why d'you think I got Chattie?'

'Chattie? What's Chattie got to do with anything?'

'Chattie is a good, clean, attractive young woman

and she lives under the same roof as you. I know you won't get your experience like that young pup Adair gets his – thank God for that. But—'

Albert gave a cry halfway between a groan and a scream. He pushed his fists onto the desk just in front of Fred's own hands.

'Be quiet! Everything you say – everything you have dealings with . . . *I hate* you! To think you are married to my mother! You are obscene and beastly and – and—' Albert could think of nothing bad enough to add. 'And utterly beyond the pale!' he concluded inadequately.

Fred was obediently silent and unmoved for perhaps a whole minute. During that time the sound of Albert's breathing filled the large empty office. As it quietened and he began to straighten from his crouched attitude, Fred spoke again.

'All you have done is call me names, Albert. You have not contradicted me. We will not speak of this again, but on your way up to London tomorrow, perhaps you will think over my proposition about Birmingham and let me know what you decide later.'

He stood up, placed the smoothed catalogue carefully by his stepson and left the office. Albert crouched again over his hands. His body felt sore, as if it had been beaten. He could not stay in the same house with Fred Luker. He could not sleep along the landing knowing what went on in the front bedroom between that man and his mother. But what else could he do?

He lifted his head and looked through the window with red-rimmed eyes. The late summer had gone and the plane trees in London Road were splotched yellow and orange. He thought of Christmas and Davie's birthday and Victor and he going to the dances again at the Corn Exchange and laughing about nothing. He thought of April and her love for David Daker which had started when she was four years old. And he thought of Davina and wondered if Fred were right . . . he couldn't be right. He couldn't. Albert had been in love with April . . . and a little bit with Beryl Langham. But his love for Davina was absolutely pure. Wasn't it? He lowered his head again and squeezed his eyes shut to contain the tears.

Albert was not the only one to go into exile like the young king was so soon to do. Just before Armistice Day that year, Bridget and Tolly Hall gave a party. It took place in the late afternoon so that all the children could attend, and it was in the tradition of the old Rising parties, with music and dancing and party games galore. The Adairs came with Robin. The Lukers without Albert. Tilly Adair made a dead set at Fred, but Charles danced with May Gould and seemed to avoid his hostess. April had recently received some photographs from Michigan and was delighted to show everyone a picture of her new friend, Miranda, wearing one of David's dresses. Olga, Natasha and Beatrice Hall initiated a game of hide and seek as darkness fell, and David Daker proved a great success with them, hiding in the darkest corners and jumping out at unsuspecting passers-by so that they screamed and ran and became enjoyably frantic. April said to Olga, 'D'you know, he did that to me when I was younger than you. I called him Devil Daker!'

'Devil Daker!' Olga yelled at the top of her voice,

knowing Mrs Goodson could not object in the circumstances. 'Devil Taker, Devil Daker!' The stupid rhyme caught on. The two little Daker girls enjoyed it most of all.

The party was an unqualified success. It was capped after supper when Bridget held up her hand to make an announcement.

'Ladies and gentlemen!' She was mock-serious, holding her head up, pursing her mouth. 'This party was for April and David because we missed them so much when they were away.' There was cheering and clapping. 'But for another reason too. Will you rejoice with me, please. In six months there will be another baby in this house. And you all know how very much pleasure that gives me!'

April hugged her. 'Bridie, we had no idea, how marvellous!'

May sought Monty's eyes. 'You are so lucky, Bridie.'

Charles did some quick calculations. Three months ago. It could be him. But then why should she disown him so completely? It couldn't be him. She must have discovered she was pregnant and that was why she gave him the cold shoulder.

He lifted his glass with everyone else. For some reason Bridget was laughing her head off; she must be tiddly already. She and her husband couldn't stop looking at each other . . . natural enough. Yes, it must be all right. She was already pregnant that night. Charles turned away somewhat regretfully. She had been such a cracker; he'd never forget her. It made him feel quite ardent and he asked Mrs Gould for another dance.

Bridget said to Tolly, 'Dance with me, darling. I

could dance all night. I always feel so wonderful when I'm pregnant. It suits me, don't you think?'

Tolly manoeuvred her around the floor. Now that he knew, it all seemed so obvious. Her contentment, her knitting, her thickened waistline beneath the bloused dresses she wore. He should have known before now.

He avoided her mouth and said into her ear, 'Oh, Bridie, what have you done? We didn't have much, but there was always something. Always. And now—'

'What on earth d'you mean, darling? I thought you'd be pleased. You were worried about me – I could tell. And this way you can keep your precious purity and I can have my baby. Don't spoil it for me, darling. That would be . . . petty. In the circumstances.'

He wondered if this was her idea of revenge. Not once did he wonder who might be the father of this child. He knew that that was the least of the matter.

It was sheer coincidence that he joined the International Brigade on 10 December. His application took that long to be accepted.

It was on 10 December that King Edward the Eighth of England chose to leave his homeland also.

Chapter Eight

By the end of June 1937, there was no news of Tolly Hall. He did not write home, not even to his mother, not even to David Daker, certainly not to his wife. After the first flush of vengefulness had spent itself, Bridget was oddly hurt and affronted by his disappearance. Charles Adair was pushed so far to the back of her mind that she had to remind herself he was the father of the child she was carrying. She said often to April and May, 'You'd think Tolly could write to me, if only for the sake of this new baby.'

The baby was born as easily as all her girls, and it was a boy. She wept then.

'If only my darling Tolly were here to see him. Five girls and now a boy. He should at least have written.'

April, privately convinced that Tolly was one of the many unidentified casualties in Madrid, said brightly, 'Now, darling, be sensible. Tolly has no idea he's got a son. And even if he did I doubt whether he would be allowed—'

But Kitty Hall, destitute since the death of Florence, rocked back and forth in a sudden paroxysm of grief.

'She's right, April. He would have written. He has only to work out . . . He's gone. That's what it is. He's gone. My only child. I suckled him and Teddy Rising together – I'll never forget Teddy, he was half mine. Your dear mother trusted him to me, April. And now he and my Tolly are together again. Together in death!'

Her wailing was taken up by Bridget. The luxurious room in the Brunswick Nursing Home, almost next door to her tall house, was filled with women's keening. April stood up hastily.

'Now, Mrs Hall, come away now, dear. We mustn't upset Bridget just after the delivery.'

'Don't leave me,' sobbed Bridget. 'I've no husband to visit me – must everyone desert me?'

So the two visitors settled down again and Kitty tried to control her grief while April patted and dabbed at Bridie and told her to think of her milk.

'I've never had any trouble with my milk,' Bridie snapped with some pride. 'I'm the perfect mother and Tolly knows it. He's utterly selfish – utterly – you've no idea, Mother, so don't defend him. You spoiled him as a child and I've spoiled him as a man and now we both have to put up with it.'

Kitty set up another wail and April decided the time had come for a firm line.

'Now look, both of you, just stop it.' She stood up and put an encouraging arm under Kitty's. 'Why don't you go and tell Olga and her sisters what a lovely little brother they've got. My goodness—' even to herself she sounded unbearably false. 'He's Bartholomew Hall the third!' She forced a laugh and Mrs Hall obediently echoed it through her snuffles. Leaning heavily on April, she got to the door and turned to blow Bridget a kiss. Bridget did not return it.

April went back to the bed.

'Honestly, Bridie, you're awful to Kitty. Can't you see she's worried sick—'

'I suppose you think I'm not?' Bridget was red in the

face and her voice sawed aggrievedly. 'My God, April, you don't know what I've gone through for this baby! You just don't know. And now Tolly, deserting me.'

April refused to soften. 'Hardly desertion, darling.' She bustled around the room, moving vases of flowers and adjusting the window blind. 'Tolly has always had strong political beliefs, you know that—'

'Oh, come off it, April. Not one letter, not one solitary letter or wire or – anything!'

April turned and stared at her friend, two dead carnations in her hand. This was a cry she had heard often during the last six months, and as time went on and there was still no word from Tolly, she wondered whether Bridget was deliberately fooling herself.

Bridget said defensively, 'Well? Why are you looking at me like that?'

April reminded herself that Bridget had given birth only yesterday; she turned to the waste-bin and disposed of the flowers. 'No reason. Nothing.'

'You know, don't you?' Bridget's voice climbed a register. 'You know – you blame me – you always did stick up for Tolly! You were jealous when he married me, weren't you? Have you heard from him – have you? Tell me the truth, April!'

April said impatiently, 'Of course I haven't heard, you idiot! No-one has heard, have they? That's why we're all so worried.'

'Don't give me all that again, April, for God's sake!' Suddenly Bridget's colour faded and she looked terribly tired. 'Nobody need worry. Tolly left me. Whether he will come back I don't know. Possibly he will after the Spanish business is over, possibly he won't.'

April sat down on the edge of the bed.

'How can you know that, Bridie dear? Why do you keep talking like this when you know that Tolly would not keep us in suspense if he was able to contact us?'

Bridget hunched a silken shoulder.

'He wouldn't give me any more babies. After your mother died he had some crazy idea that he must stay celibate. He said no more babies. That was that.'

April was silent, frowning. Bridget stared defiantly through the window.

'It was May's fault. She introduced me to Charles Adair, and he made a dead set at me. Ask her if you don't believe me. An absolute dead set. Tolly was in Berlin. He wouldn't take me there – had some crazy idea about helping the communists who had been dumped in gaol . . . I don't know. He just wouldn't take me anyway. And he told me to . . . to . . . go ahead. Have a man friend. He *told* me. So it was his fault too.' She flicked a look at April who was still gazing steadily at her. 'You need not look at me like that either, April Rising! My God, when Charles told me about you I was shocked. Absolutely shocked. You'd always been my shining example – oh yes you had. I know you're younger than me, but ever since that day I met you and Teddy at Miss Midwinter's school, I've tried to be like you. So in a way it was all your fault!'

April said through stiff lips, 'What do you mean, Bridie? What are you talking about?'

'You, of course. You and that friend of David's – that Jew who was his best man!'

'Mannie Stein?' April's voice also went up a notch, but with sheer incredulity.

'He was the one who sent those mannequins down to the parade. And Charles took one of the mannequins out to supper. And she told him. Mannie Stein had told her all about it. How David couldn't have children and he – he'd – *obliged*!' She tried to laugh and croaked on a cough. Then she looked again at April and clapped her hands to her face. 'I didn't believe him, April, not afterwards. Not when I thought about it. But when he said it first . . . I mean, it was such a shock. And I did so want another baby. And Tolly – Tolly wouldn't – and I thought if you'd had to do it, I wouldn't blame you. So I thought you wouldn't blame me either.'

There was another silence, then April said strongly, 'Mannie Stein. Mannie Stein. Did you really believe that I would let Mannie Stein . . .' She paused, then asked deliberately, 'Did you really think I would let that man impregnate me?' She leaned forward and pulled Bridget's hands from her face. 'Look at me!' Her voice was stern. 'Remember Mannie Stein – just remember him for a moment, please, Bridie. Very dark, wasn't he? Sharp cheekbones and chin. Enormous hands and feet. Do you remember?' Bridie stared, a sick look in her blue eyes. 'Yes, you remember. Now think of my little Davie. Is there anything . . . anything at all of Mannie Stein in Davina?'

Bridget whimpered some kind of negative.

'Quite.' April held the imprisoned hands hard on the bed cover. 'Let me put things straight with you. And perhaps you will pass the information on to whomever gossips with you next. Mannie Stein was jealous of David. Right from when they first met in the hospital after they were wounded. He wanted to be like David. What David had, he wanted. If David had married you, or May, or anyone, Mannie Stein would have coveted you or May or anyone. He coveted me. Because I was

David's. And that is why he is putting about this filthy tale. When David threw him out, he started hurling accusations – accusations of – of impotence. And obviously he is still doing it.' She flung away suddenly. 'One relies on one's friends to deny such accusations.'

Bridget began to weep. 'April, I'm sorry. I'm sorry.'

'Yes. Now you are sorry. But when you heard the tale first, you believed it.'

'Oh Christ. Oh God. What have I done?' Bridget bent slowly forward, groans coming from her. 'I've lost Tolly and now I've lost you. I wish I were dead.'

April kept her back to her friend, lowered her head, squeezed her eyes shut and breathed very carefully. Bridget continued to weep behind her.

At last she said levelly, 'Bridie. I don't blame you for what you did. I don't blame you for – for – accepting Charles Adair's offer – I mean, in the circumstances, Tolly feeling as he did, I think you had some – some – right on your side.'

Bridget lifted the sheet and dabbed at her eyes. 'You don't mean that. You're just saying it so that I won't upset myself any more and harm my milk.'

'No. I'm trying to be – objective – about it. Sensible and objective. You are . . . you find it . . . necessary . . . to have babies. And Tolly knew that. So therefore to deny you was . . . cruel.' She turned with some determination, her head up, her hands clasped in front of her. 'I think he will come back to you, my dear. He's used to thinking things out for himself. And I expect he went away to do that. And he'll realize – he'll see – that there was some justification for doing what you did.'

Bridget sniffed hopefully. She was not convinced by April's halting words, but the fact that she was making the effort to say them was something.

She said, 'Will you forgive me for believing for one moment that awful tale of Charles Adair's?'

'You wanted to believe it. Because it helped you to do . . . what you did.'

'Yes, that was it exactly. Oh, April. Dear April. As if you could ever be unfaithful to your David.'

April turned and made for the door.

'I really must go, Bridie. Please try to stay calm now. I'll come to see you again.'

'When?'

'Soon. Very soon.'

April walked down Brunswick Road and into the Eastgate, and on an impulse she turned right and went on down to the Barton and past the first small Daker shop. It was sold now and the window was full of sweet jars and peppermint walking-sticks, but even as she went past it a customer emerged and the familiar clang of the overhead bell echoed into the street. April remembered her visits here with her father, when her fascination with the dark David Daker had sprouted into love. She remembered David returning from the war, tortured and twisted; his romantic love for May turning sour in the face of her disinterest, and venting itself on the willing Sibbie. She remembered her father ordering them all to ostracize David Daker because he was 'unnatural' and her own angry reaction to such an edict. And she remembered how she had worn down David's bitter rejection, brought him flowers and poems and poured her love on him until he had been forced to take her seriously. And had married her.

She went over the level crossing and turned parallel

with the railway until she came to the private school run by the Misses Midwinter, where she herself had been a pupil teacher. Miss Midwinter and her sister Miss Alicia were both dead, and someone else ran the school on modern lines. The children were in the playground now in vests and knickers, doing Swedish drill. A very small girl on the end of the line reminded April of Flora, dark with a straight fringe like a nun's coif, her eyes large and full of dreams. Flora . . . unmistakably David Daker's daughter. Davina . . . unmistakably a Luker.

April turned sharply at the thought and walked quickly down Faulkner Street and back into the Barton as if she could leave the whole problem in the playground behind her. But she could not. The gossip must be rife if Bridie had it. It was wrong, of course; gossip was nearly always wrong when it showed above ground, but the roots . . . the roots were there. No smoke without fire.

April fussed in her handbag and found a scrap of a handkerchief. She must get back to King's Square and catch her bus. Aunt Sylv would bring the children home from school and she must be there when they arrived. She stopped by the baths and blew her nose fiercely, then looked around her nervously as if her reaction might have called attention to herself. A group of women came out of the Turkish bath house, laughing, fluffing their damp hair in the June sunshine. They glanced at her; one of them half smiled. April walked on, panic-stricken. She did not know them, yet they knew her. Just as everyone in Gloucester had known Sibbie Luker at one time. Oh God. Oh God. It would kill David . . . kill him. And she had done it for him.

She had done it in cold blood, knowing she was damning her immortal soul, believing that it would save his. And it had done, Davie's birth had been a rebirth for David. It had, it had.

She reached the Cross and looked about her, bewildered, not knowing which way to go. She should have turned into King's Road to reach King's Square; now she would have to go down past Daker's Gowns and David might see her. She hung onto a buttress of Saint Nicholas's church, where, on Armistice night, David had kissed her as if she were a woman of twenty-six rather than a girl of sixteen. Memory would not be held back now; it crowded in on her, forcing her to recall their many nights of unfulfilled passion, when gradually David's frustration had built into crazy jealousy of Mannie Stein and he had given voice to the devils that tormented him: 'I want to give you a baby.' And she remembered Fred Luker; kind Fred Luker; who had rescued her when David turned her out, had listened like a doctor, and had talked objectively of artificial insemination. Fred, who had suffered in the war just as David had, so understood more than anyone else.

But it had been wrong.

Tears filled her eyes again and her tiny handkerchief was soaked. It had been wrong. No amount of talk could alter that fact. Fred had been hurt . . . she had hurt him by cold-shouldering him mercilessly, as if she could forget how Davie had been conceived. Thank God he had eventually married March and they were happy together. At least that wasn't on her conscience. And herself – it didn't matter that she had hurt herself. She had done it consciously in one of her crazy bargains with God. Her soul for David's happiness. And God had kept His part of the bargain: David was happy, wonderfully happy.

Then God had inserted a clause into the agreement, a clause which had seemed marvellous at first, like a blessing, like the Holy Hollyhock. He had given them Flora.

April turned her face into the gritty grey stone and used the sleeve of her summer cardigan. She wondered when she had started to realize that Flora's presence was God's reminder of her first sin. Was it when they'd picnicked in the bluebell woods three years ago, and Davie had accepted so sweetly that she came second to Flora in April's affections? Or was it when that mannequin, Eugenie, had first passed on Mannie Stein's slander? Sometime during that summer when she had once again justified Davie's conception, God had quite clearly said to her, 'But you see, if you'd waited, you would have had Flora in any case.' And the Holy Hollyhock had died.

Tilly Adair waited on the steps of the Turkish bath house while the other women went into town. She felt furious with April Daker for cutting her so obviously in front of everyone just now. She had been introduced to her at that lavish party the Halls had given last November, so this frigid behaviour must be because she'd heard something about Freddie. Those three sisters were closer than clams and Tilly, like her son, loathed shellfish. May was the best of the bunch, with her unfashionable Queen Alexandra hair-do and her matronly figure; Freddie's wife and this April Daker thought they were something special, tall and skinny as beanpoles, stunning in the long-waisted dresses David Daker made for them.

Tilly spotted Freddie cruising discreetly in an anony-mous Morris, and ran after him waving and calling loudly, half hoping that April might have stopped to window-shop and would see her. Freddie spoiled every-thing by speeding around the corner before he drew into the kerb, and then he didn't get out to open the door for her.

'You're late,' she said petulantly, curling her neat little figure onto the front seat like a small girl. 'I've been hanging about for ages on the steps looking for you.'

'Sorry.' Fred drove on round the park and back into Southgate Street. 'Busy at the garage.'

'No you weren't. I telephoned there before I had my massage. You hadn't been in all day. So don't be a Fibbing Freddie.'

She giggled and rubbed her cheek against his shoulder. His muscles were knotted beneath his linen jacket.

'Tilly.' His voice was very level. 'Once and for all, you are not to telephone me. Anywhere at all. Is that clear?'

She pouted. 'How can I get in touch with you?'

'You can't.'

'*Freddie!*'

'We'll go on meeting after your Turkish. Anything more is dangerous.'

'But I go to the baths only once a month!'

'I know.'

'Freddie, I must see you oftener than that. I can't live without you – I mean it – I love you. I *love* you, Freddie! Can't you understand that you are my whole life? Freddie—' She started to weep theatrically onto his jacket, trying in between wails to bite his arm. He came to the Cross and stuck his hand out of his window to turn right and into the Eastgate again. He'd take her home immediately. He could pretend concern at her hysteria, tell her she wasn't well – she believed anything he said. He couldn't face a whole evening with her. He jerked his shoulder to dislodge her.

'I've got to change the bloody gear, Tilly, for Christ's sake—'

She rolled away from him dramatically, and crashed her head against the other window. A coal cart, piled high with hundredweight sacks, turned from the Northgate in front of them; he cursed again and went into neutral. Through his open window came the strong odour of shire horse; he glanced through momentarily calmed by an instant memory of his own coal-hauling days. His eyes took in the huge rump of the horse, the plaited tail, the leather blinkers, then went on around the familiar scene: Eastgate market, Fearis's, Saint Nicholas's church . . . and April. He sat up. April, with her back to the traffic, apparently leaning against the ancient stone.

He pulled out from the coal cart and roared down the Eastgate to Brunswick Road and pulled in.

'Get out,' he said curtly.

'What?'

'I said, get out.'

Her tears, which had already dried, began again in earnest. 'Oh, Freddie – darling – you are so unkind—'

'Look, Tilly. I cannot drive around the town with an hysterical woman by me. For one thing it's not safe, for another, I can't stand it. Get out.'

'Freddie, I'm not hysterical.' She sat up straight and

forced a smile. 'Look. I'm all right now. I promise I'll be a good girl. Really. Promise.'

He got out of his side, went round to hers, opened the door and took her arm.

'Freddie! Oh God . . .' She scrambled out and would have fallen if it hadn't been for his powerful grip. She sobbed with shock and outrage. 'Freddie, what the hell have I *done*? Let me go – how dare you—' She shook herself free and held the car for support. Quiet Brunswick Road seemed to absorb and deaden the awfulness of the ejection. She panted, looking up at him with a curious mixture of fury and begging.

He said, 'Get yourself a cab and go home. Go to bed. I'll telephone you tomorrow.'

'You need not. If you leave me now you need not get in touch again.'

He shrugged. 'All right. If that's what you want.' He swung back round the car, slid into the driver's seat, leaned over and slammed the passenger door. She scooted after him.

'Freddie, it's not what I want. I'm going to your house now – I'll wait for you there. March won't suspect – I'll think of an excuse—'

'If you ever go to my house . . . if you ever try to contact me . . . we're finished.'

'Then ring me. Oh God, what's happened – what's gone wrong? Ring me, Freddie – promise you'll ring me.'

His eyes were colder than winter. 'I've said I will. Pull yourself together, Tilly, you look demented.'

He accelerated, signalled, turned down Parliament Street to complete the circuit again. She was standing in the middle of the road staring after him, her hair flopping all over her face. He forgot her.

Sylvia Turpin, still known to her family as Sylvia Rising in spite of her ill-fated marriage, walked slowly to Winterditch Junior School, knowing that she was old. The ponderous, ox-like strength which had enabled her to work all her life, was somehow disappearing through the soles of her calloused feet and the tips of her even more calloused fingers. She could date the beginning of its decline quite easily. When her sister-in-law Florence had died on that May evening in 1934, Sylvia Rising had begun to lose her strength. After all she was nearly seventy, so it wasn't surprising. But she knew without any doubt at all that if Florence had lived, her strength would have lasted. It had been for a purpose, and when the purpose went the strength went too.

She thought of her husband, 'Dick' Turpin, as she did every day, and wondered without curiosity what had become of him. She had heard nothing since the day in 1917 when he had been arrested as a deserter, and it had never once occurred to her or any of her family to try to find out whether he was alive or dead. But Dick Turpin had married her and made her a proud woman, and the dumb devotion they had shared had never died for her. She remembered him now as he had been twenty years before, old before his time after prison, but still stronger than she, with that oddly innocent blue gaze that could never deal with the complexities of living with other people. There must have been gypsy in his blood. He was different. If their child had lived he would have been with her still; but he did not know what to do about Sylvia's oddly demented grief, and had left her to be nursed back to health by her mother and her sister-in-law.

She sighed again and scrunched her way along the narrow cinder path to the school gates. Dick had respected Florence. Of all the Risings, he had taken to Florence better than anyone. She wished he knew that Florence was dead. Perhaps if he were alive himself – he would come back to her if he knew that the mainspring of her life had gone.

Then her leathern face cracked into a hideous grin of pure pleasure, as the bell sounded in the red brick building and little Flora burst out of the door, the first as usual.

'Aunt Sylv!'

The piercing shriek was a second ahead of fifty others, her pounding sandals a step in front. Sylvia got inside the gates and bent to gather the flying child into her brawny arms. She was an undemonstrative great-aunt, but there was no stopping Flora; she pursed her mouth and bounced it off Sylvia's face energetically, then drew back and said something that was completely lost in the surrounding babble. Sylvia walked to one side of the playground to wait for Davina.

'Miss Walker said . . .' Flora wriggled to the ground and took one of Sylvia's fingers. 'Miss Walker asked me what was the matter with Davie. What *is* the matter with her, Aunt Sylv?'

Sylvia frowned. 'I don't know, child. Has she had belly-ache?'

'No. I don't know. She just went home.'

Sylvia looked at the face that was so like Florence's and bent her back creakingly.

'Tell me what has happened, Flo. When did Davie go 'ome?'

'After prayers. She went up to her teacher and said something. Then she went home.'

Sylvia stayed where she was, doubled up, for three long seconds, then she straightened and took Flora's hand in hers and marched into the school.

Davie had complained of a pain in her chest, she had told the teacher that her mother had said she must come home if it did not improve, and she had walked out. Sylvia, incredulous, asked if it was usual for children to leave school by themselves. Mr Banwell, the headmaster, tried to support his young teacher.

'Not at all usual. But in the case of your two nieces, Mrs Turpin . . . they are absolutely straightforward and truthful.'

Sylvia was a dirty grey colour. She breathed deeply and carefully.

'If owt 'as 'appened to that child, master, the blame will lie on your doorstep,' she said with monumental dignity.

Mr Banwell was rattled. 'I'm sure . . . let me run you home in my car. I'll see Miss Meadows first and ask her to stay on here in case . . . yes.'

But Sylvia put the bewildered Flora in the car and refused to enter it herself. 'I shall walk the way we allus do,' she decreed. 'If she went 'ome this morning and – and—' she glanced at Flora '—and lawst 'er way, then I'll find 'er.'

'Davie wouldn't lose her way, Aunt Sylv, she knows it better 'n what you do.'

'Ah,' said Sylvia heavily, and turned back down the cinder path again.

Fred said, 'Take it steady, old girl. The girls will be all

right with Aunt Sylv. Just relax and try to see everything rationally.'

They were sitting in the nave of the empty church, he and April, the June sunlight strained through the coloured windows and lying in broad bands of purple and orange across the pews. April's hands, clenched in her lap, were pale mauve. He covered them with his own and tried to dispel his strong sense of déjà vu. It hadn't happened like this before. He had found her weeping in Westgate Street then, and had taken her down to Dean Forest, to the cottage there. But the atmosphere had been the same . . . holy.

She said for the umpteenth time, 'I'm sorry, Fred. I've burdened you enough. I'm sorry.'

'Shut up. We're in this together.'

'No. No, it's nothing to do with you.'

'Dammit, she's my daughter.'

'*No!*'

It was a cry of outraged protest. She snapped out of her misery long enough to look up at him, then repeated vehemently, 'No, Fred. We said all along that you were – were—'

'The donor,' he supplied clinically.

'Helper,' she corrected him and turned her hand so that she held his. 'You accused me once of pushing you away, Fred, but you mustn't think that. I simply don't want you to feel . . . responsible.'

He said woodenly, 'I talked you into it.'

'You couldn't have talked me into it if I hadn't wanted to do it. It was what I wanted more than anything then. To give David a child.' She gripped his hand hard. 'If he finds out . . . if he finds out . . . it will kill him.'

'You're flying off the handle again, girl. Why should he find out?'

'Oh, Fred. If Bridie knows—'

'Bridie doesn't know.'

'She's heard that Davie wasn't fathered by David. That's enough. Don't you see? The fact that she thinks it's Mannie Stein doesn't matter. If . . . when David hears—'

'Which he won't.'

'Of course he will. In his business people talk. Women order their dresses and . . . women talk.'

'Listen, April Daker. I hear every bit of gossip in Gloucester. That is no idle boast. I make it my business to hear everything that goes on.' He remembered the dinner party of three years ago and Albert smashing his fist into Robin Adair's face. He smiled directly at April. 'I've heard not a whisper of this. Not a whisper.'

She searched his face, wanting to believe him.

'Tell you what.' He patted her knuckles as Aunt Sylv might have done. 'I'll see Adair. He hangs around your May a lot lately. I'll have a word with him.'

'Hangs around May? What d'you mean?'

'There you go again, flying off the handle. I mean he squires the girls to the Cadena tea-dances sometimes, that's all. But it will give me a reason for having a word with him, and if there's anything else he knows, I'll find out. If not, then obviously he said it to make an impression on Bridget Hall.'

'It – it's so devious.'

'Quite.'

There was a long silence during which April kept her head down. Then at last she straightened and looked about her.

221

'Oh, Fred. People . . . we're so stupid.'

'We weren't stupid, April. Think back, my dear. Doesn't it seem inevitable to you now? Part of a pattern?' Fred often reviewed his machinations thus, with a cynically retrospective eye. 'David and you wanting a child so badly. Stein provoking that shocking row you had. You running wild down Westgate Street and me driving past to the Forest. It wasn't just coincidence, April, surely?'

'I don't know.' She sounded unutterably weary. 'We still had our own choices, Fred. Our free will. We chose, quite coolly if I remember, to conceive Davina. And then, four years later, came Flora. So all that – all this – was quite unnecessary.' She smiled sadly and Fred realized with a sense of shock that she was no longer young. She shook her head as if to clear it and said, 'Never mind all that. So long as David never knows.' She fixed her eyes on the red sanctuary lamp as if addressing herself to it. 'Just so long as David doesn't know.'

Fred put his hand on her arm and urged her out of the pew.

'He'll never know,' he said. And added suddenly, 'I can promise you that, April. He will never know.'

Davina Daker, like her mother before her, was tall for her age and saw the doubt in the booking clerk's eyes when she asked for half fare.

'No train till midday, miss. Then it's a stopper via Worcester,' he said with satisfaction.

'I want a stopper. I have to get off before Birmingham. At a place called Northfield.'

'Then you're all right on that one.' He used the

automatic dating machine with aplomb to cover his disappointment. If there was one type of customer he couldn't stand it was snooty schoolgirls. Then he looked through the glass partition and saw Davina's eyes. They weren't snooty, they were very anxious. 'You'll enjoy the trip, miss,' he said suddenly. 'They put a tank engine on at Bromsgrove to get her up the Lickeys. Then you're almost there.'

Davina smiled her wide painful smile and took the ticket in her ungloved hand. She should have remembered to put gloves in her blazer pocket; white gloves with the panama school hat made you look like a High School girl, which she would be anyway in three months' time. She walked through the ticket barrier and crossed the bridge to the down platform, wishing there was an earlier train. Miss Meadows was young and trusting, but there was always a chance she would mention Davina's painful chest to Mr Banwell, then it wouldn't be long before her absence was discovered. She went into the waiting-room, knelt on the horsehair sofa and kept watch through the window. The station was almost empty and somnolent in the June sunshine. She began to relax as midday drew nearer; she thought of Albert, lonely still after nine months away from home. He would be so *surprised*.

The journey, under two hours, seemed endless. Davina, inconsolable after Albert's banishment, had cajoled her father into a detailed explanation of his whereabouts. David had shown her a map of Warwickshire and Worcestershire, and had recounted the main towns between Gloucester and Birmingham. Even so, after Cheltenham, she felt on foreign territory. She remembered her father joking about a place called

Redditch which might indeed have a red ditch just as Winterditch ditches only filled up during the winter. And she herself had laboriously worked out a pun about Bromsgrove. 'What is a brom, Daddy?'

It was some comfort to grind to a halt at the bottom of the bank and take on the small, puffing tanker. She dropped the window in her compartment and peered anxiously through. Albert had written in his letters of the Lickey Hills. He belonged to the rambling club which the students had formed, and they came here on Sundays. She could see nothing except the steep sides of the railway cutting filled with steam from the frantic engines.

The guard spoke from behind, making her jump. 'I should pull that window up if I was you, missie. You'll be getting your eyes full of smuts else.'

They came to the top at last. Northfield. It was ten past two by the station clock. Albert finished early on a Friday; he would be back in his digs soon after three thirty. The guard saw her in the corridor and sprang out to open the door for her. With her round milk-maid's face and anxious smile she was obviously younger than her height at first proclaimed. He signalled to a porter.

'Put the young lady on her way, there's a good lad.'

And the porter, in spite of no luggage and therefore no tip, led Davina down the steps to the roadway, studied the address she showed him on Albert's last letter, and pointed to the road to West Heath. Davina's spirits soared; she liked Birmingham people, they were so kind.

March was gardening when she heard the telephone ringing in the house. It was Chattie's afternoon off and she hurried indoors, pulling off her gloves as she went, already smiling because it would be Albert. He finished early on a Friday and always telephoned her for a 'private' chat. She missed him terribly, but in some ways they were closer now he was away. The constant friction between himself and Fred had scraped raw his relationship with March; now that was gone, and his homesickness had swept away other barriers of embarrassment on his side and innate sharpness on hers. They wrote at length, letters full of humour, not at all typical of their usual exchanges. Already March was planning that their summer holiday would not be like the Christmas one. Albert had left the room when Fred came into it; it had been very difficult. This time she wanted to go away somewhere; to the seaside perhaps; just herself and Albert. She'd have to work on Fred carefully, he wouldn't like it.

She picked up the telephone, laughing already.

'Hello, darling, you're early today.' She surveyed herself in the hall mirror like a young girl, full of vanity. A wiry grey hair sprang from the smooth auburn cap parted so severely in the middle; she caught hold of it firmly and pulled.

A woman's voice said, 'Is that Mrs Luker? Have I got the right number?'

March left her hair and assumed a different expression. 'This is Mrs Luker. Who is that please?'

There was a pause. March could hear the caller breathing very quickly. Then the voice said, 'This is Mrs Adair here, Mrs Luker. I thought you should know something. It's only fair that you should . . .' The voice ran out of steam and there was another panting pause.

March said, 'Yes, Mrs Adair? Are you still there?'

'Your husband and I – we're in love, Mrs Luker. He doesn't want to tell you, but I must. We've been in love . . . it must be nearly three years now. Yes, nearly three years. I know how you must be feeling, Mrs . . . oh, March, I'm sorry if you're hurt but you must have known – guessed! I can't help it anyway, I just love him – are you there – can you understand – can you—'

March hung the receiver very carefully onto its hook and stood still staring at her reflection, feeling the tingle where she had pulled out the grey hair and wondering why she did not faint or scream . . . wondering quite consciously how she ought to react.

She did not doubt Tilly's assertion for one moment, in fact she wondered if the woman was right and she'd guessed at it for a long time. She thought back. Three years ago it had been 1934, the year Fred had bought the land at Tuffley from the Peplows and the Adairs. Yes, of course, the Adair land had belonged to Tilly. It was Leonie Porterman all over again. He would explain away his infidelity as he had done then; he would put it down to expediency and assure her that Tilly Adair meant nothing to him.

March dropped her gaze and looked at her hands. In spite of the gloves they were grimy. She went slowly out to the kitchen and swilled them under the tap. Then she looked in the garage: Fred's Rover was there, he must be using one of the garage's spare cars today. She turned and went back into the house, across the tessellated floor and up the stairs. She packed a case: night things, a change of underwear, cardigan in case the weather changed, another frock. She took the case down to the Rover and put it on the back seat, then she slid beneath the steering wheel and stared through the windscreen at the gravel drive before her, the double gates, the quiet peace of Bedford Close. She had bought this house, it was hers, could she bear to leave it to Fred?

She pulled the self-starter and the car fired immediately. She hardly remembered negotiating it into Barnwood Road. Fred had taught her to drive when she was fourteen and it was second nature to her now. She knew the way to Cheltenham and after that would have to rely on signposts. It should take her no more than two or three hours to drive to West Heath and Albert. She hadn't locked the house and her gardening tools were all over the lawn. She did not care.

Fred went down the road to the telephone kiosk at Winterditch crossroads to contact March. Davie wasn't likely to go to Chichester Street and there was no reply from Bedford Close. 'That could mean she went there this morning to ask March about Albert,' Fred said, desperately trying to find words of comfort for the two grey-faced women and the weeping child. 'March is probably bringing her back home right now.'

April just nodded over Flora's head. Aunt Sylv said yet again, 'I think you ought to get your David 'ome 'ere, April. 'E ought to know what's 'appened.'

'Just another half an hour, Aunt Sylv.' April looked at Fred. 'She might be playing truant for some reason and plan to be back soon. No need to worry David unnecessarily.'

Fred saw the way her mind was working and said strongly, 'Don't be so ridiculous, April! A child her age—' He saw Aunt Sylv's lizard eyes turn on him and he went to the window. 'Look, come and sit here and let Flo keep an eye open for her. It will cheer her up to have a job to do.' He grinned around at all of them. 'She'll be back any minute now. I'll go to Bedford Close and see if there's a message from March.'

April left Flo and drifted with him to the gate. She hugged her arms around her although it was still warm, and stared up and down the lane. Around the bend near the crossroads came a horse and cart. April and Fred watched it tensely; it was a flat cart, a few cabbage leaves revealing what it had carried. Old Man Byard, who managed to raise greens on his run-down small-holding, grinned beerily at them.

'Summer yer at last, missus,' he called.

Fred lifted a hand and the cart was nearly past when April called, 'Have you seen my little girl, Mr Byard? The one who – who plays with your Micky?' Davina was terrified of Micky Byard; he threw stones at her and waited for her on the field path. Might he have spirited her away somewhere?

Old Man Byard pulled in his horse, leaned down and had to have the question repeated. Fred fidgeted.

'En't seen nuthin' of the kiddies today, missis. Went into Eastgate market first thing with me greens. Bin in Saracen's Head since. Look, if any of 'em back 'ome knows aught, we'll send down. 'Ow's that?'

'Thank you, Mr Byard.'

Fred said in a low voice, 'April, try to keep calm. This is nothing to do with you. She's a happy bright child—'

'Don't tell me it's coincidence that I heard that filthy rumour today, that we met each other . . . don't tell me that, Fred. You said yourself – a pattern – everything made a pattern.'

'April, pull yourself together!' Fred remembered the

watching eyes from the window and pulled April in front of the privet hedge. 'If David comes home before Davina you'll be blurting it out to him.' He paused, then took her chin and forced it up. 'You wouldn't, would you?'

'No.' Her voice dragged. 'No, I could never hurt David like that.'

He released her and spoke gently. 'April, you've got me to share the weight. If only you would let me.' But he knew that wasn't her way.

He slid into the car and watched her walk back down the drive, shaking her head as Aunt Sylv and Flora came to the door to meet her.

Albert Tomms walked slowly down the Longbridge road, thankful that summer seemed to have come at last. He could not keep his thoughts from Gloucester, so quite deliberately he forced himself to think of Beryl Langham and whether she'd gone to the cheese-rolling at Cooper's Hill with Victor. It was ten months since he'd walked out of the attic room at Chichester Street where she'd been standing in Victor's arms without a stitch on. Although the boys had made up their rift in the other attic room at Bedford Close, they had never had the opportunity to talk about it. At Christmas there had been a constraint between them, fostered by March who blamed Victor entirely for the last attic incident. Victor wrote often, but he never mentioned Beryl, and Albert did not care to ask after her.

Now, with summer on the way, he let his thoughts become obsessive; it was so much better to think of Beryl than of Davina. Some nights she walked through his dreams stark naked; in the day she came between him and the sheet of paper before him as he tried desperately to write down what was so easy to do when they let him loose in the factory. He deliberately thought of her hair lying on her cheeks, her cigarette in its long holder, her bare buttocks and long, tapered thighs. The sweat smudged the ink as he wrote and the long-suffering tutor suggested again that Albert Tomms needed much application to put practice into theory.

The other students were not unsympathetic. At eighteen their thoughts were almost entirely concerned with the female gender. But unlike Albert, they nearly all had official 'girls' at home who took up their slack by correspondence and frequent visits. Sometimes the rambling club would invite a girl along, but then it was never the same. The young men eyed one another furtively and could not bandy their jokes about freely. To varying degrees they were all sexually frustrated, but Albert was a year older than most of them and was terrified that he was 'unnatural'.

He turned into West Heath Road while he was trying to work out how many hours were in six weeks, six weeks being the time he had left before his summer holidays. Those two precious factory weeks were like a light on the horizon, the last seven days of July, then the glorious August Bank holiday, then the first seven days of August. He and Victor could cycle to Rodley, climb Churchdown Hill where Grandpa had had his rabbit shoot, go out to Newent and visit Awful Aunt Vi. And they could talk again, really talk. If there were 168 hours in one week, then six times that would be one thousand and . . . and . . .

From the small grove of bushes which surrounded

number seventy-eight where he had his digs, a figure erupted. Blue-striped frock, long socks, panama hat; taller than he remembered, but even at a distance of two hundred yards, unmistakably Davina.

He stood still at her shriek, his mind a jumble of questions and doubts and warring emotions. Then he threw them all out and gave a hoarse shout in reply and lifted his arm. The next instant he was running and so was she. His books went flying into the gutter; her hat fell back and jogged from its chin elastic. They met with a thud, winding themselves. Without inhibitions, she encircled him with her arms and hugged him ecstatically. After a moment he put his arms carefully around her and laid his cheek against hers. They did a little jig on the spot; she transferred her arms to his shoulders and turned her head to kiss his cheek. She was laughing with joy.

After a while he held her still and withdrew slightly. 'Davie, why are you here? What has happened?'

'Aren't you pleased to see me? In your last letter to Mother – why do you address your letters to Mother then say "Dear Everyone"? In your last letter you said you were still homesick and you hated Birmingham so I thought as soon as I've saved enough money I'm going up to see Albie. And here I am!'

'But Aunt April, Uncle David – where are they?'

'Silly! I'm on my own.'

'You came all the way on your own? How?'

'On the train. I told you. I saved lots of money then I told my teacher I'd got a pain in my chest and had to go home. And I caught the bus to King's Square and walked round to the station—'

'Don't they *know*? Don't they know you're here?'

231

'Of course not. They wouldn't have let me come so I had to keep it a secret.'

'But Davie, they'll be so worried!'

'Yes, but when I get home they'll stop being worried. And I'll have seen you!' It was the same cool logic she'd used to Victor. The best way to a fait accompli was simply to accompli.

It took Albert's breath away. He was so concerned about her action he forgot that his own feelings were suspect now. She picked up his books for him and urged him along to the house.

'Listen. You always ring Aunt March on Fridays, so you can tell her where I am. It's not your fault, you won't get into trouble. And I don't mind about being in trouble if I can see you.' She hugged his arm. 'Can we go to your digs now, Albie? I'm awfully hungry.'

He was recalled to the fact that she was only eleven and had undergone an enormous adventure. They went on to number seventy-eight and he draped an arm around her shoulders, squashing her hat.

'We'll work it out later then. My landlady leaves me a dinner and I warm it up myself. You can share it.' He hugged her suddenly. 'Nuisance.'

She grinned at him. 'I love you, Albert,' she said. She'd said it often before, but now it meant something more. He tried not to think what it meant. She was here. He was going to enjoy her company while he had it.

Exhausted by her own tears, Flo fell asleep at her post in the bay window and April laid her gently on the sofa and went into the kitchen where Aunt Sylv was making the inevitable tea. The two women moved together laying a tray and cutting bread, silently and without

232

getting in each other's way. When they sat down with the teapot between them, it was Aunt Sylv who spoke.

'David ought to be called, April,' she said again obstinately. 'You ought to have your husband with you at a time like this.'

'Not for a while, Aunt Sylv. I need time. I would rather be with you than anyone else.'

Sylvia flushed at the unexpected compliment.

April said in a monotone, 'I want to tell you something, Aunt. In case . . . in case anything happens . . . I want you to know. Fred thinks he can help me, but he cannot. I cannot be in league with Fred Luker against David. Never.'

Sylvia frowned, uncomprehending, yet knowing April needed some words here.

'You 'gainst your David? 'Twouldn't be possible, little April. Put it out y'r 'ead. 'Tidn't possible and that's that.'

A faint smile lifted April's mouth for an instant, then was gone.

'Thank you, dear Aunt Sylv. You know . . . so much.'

'Aye. Reckon I know a great deal about you Rising girls. An' I know . . .' Sylvia searched her mind for something to reassure this youngest of the trio who was in such obvious distress. 'I know that whatever they does, they does it for love.' She put her horny palm over April's hand. 'Remember what I said to you when you was grieving over your father, my girl? D'you remember?'

Again the smile appeared. 'I remember. You said he wanted the moon but his feet stayed in the cow . . .'

'Cow shite, child.' She patted April's hand. 'S'long as we goes on reaching for that there moon, mebbe our arms will grow long enough one day. Eh?'

April suddenly put her forehead on Sylvia's hand and began to weep. The tears ran onto the table and clogged her throat, but Sylvia could hear and understand her words.

'Davina is Fred Luker's child . . . she could have been David's, but – but – you can see she isn't. David needed a child so desperately – he caught Mannie Stein trying to – to molest me – and he hit Mannie. Then he – he – we had sexual intercourse. Properly. He said it wouldn't work and he didn't want to see me for a while. He hated me then – just for a moment – because I was a constant reminder of his – his – what Mannie Stein called his impotence. So I ran down Westgate Street, I didn't know where I could go . . . the cathedral perhaps. Then Fred was driving down to the Forest and he picked me up and I told him and he said—'

By this time Aunt Sylv had got her bulk around the table and was holding the shaking figure to her substantial shoulder.

'I kin guess, my lamb. You don't need to go no further. I know Fred Luker well enough.'

April turned into the flowered overall that smelled of her mother, and wept anew. 'It wasn't Fred . . . it wasn't his fault, Aunty. He told me a way to make David happy and then he left it to me. It was my choice.'

'Ah lovey. I knows. Your Aunty Sylv knows. Cry it all out. There, there. Carrying such a load all this time. And now our little girl disappeared and thinkin' it were God's punishment.' An off-white handkerchief dealt expertly with April's face, and she saw that, incredibly, Sylvia was smiling. 'You'm forgettin' something, our April. You en't only got God up there now. You got Flo and you got our Will. I don't reckon they'm going to let no 'arm come to any one of us down yer. Do you?'

April stared, hiccupping. It made such wonderful, common, ordinary, everyday sense. And when Sylvia spoke such sense with her smile proclaiming its truth, there was no brushing it aside. April was going to tell her about the Mannie Stein rumour. She was going to explain that Flora's conception and birth had made her 'sacrifice' completely unnecessary; but she did not do so. Mother and Dad knew. And understood.

Aunt Sylvia cuddled her again and felt a resurgence of her old strength because she had a purpose. Flo and Will still had need of her down here. She stared above April's red-gold head at the cream-painted wall of the kitchen, and her smile died. She and Fred Luker were probably the only people in the world to know the whole truth: that Albert Tomms and Davina Daker were brother and sister.

The tall nineteen-year-old and the relatively tall eleven-year-old shared a riotous feast in the house in West Heath Road. Mrs Potter, Albert's landlady, was a widow and out most evenings cleaning offices and schools. The house was one of a dozen constructed of wood with large square tiles on the roof, sharing a garden area liberally dotted with trees and bushes. Because Davina loved it, Albert saw it through new eyes. He showed her round with a proprietorial air. Bounding the small development was a brook which made the whole area sylvan.

'I thought Birmingham would be chimneys, like Gloucester,' she said, squatting on the grass to remove her socks and shoes. 'Come on, Albert, let's paddle.

235

Look, if we made a dam up here, there'd be a deep pool here—' She waded in and immediately began to lug flat stones from the bed of the stream to the side. Albert hesitated for a moment only, then joined her.

'We must go and ring my mother,' he said. 'I don't know what will happen. Mrs Potter hasn't got another bedroom.'

'I'll sleep with you,' she said tranquilly. 'Don't think about it, Albert. Let's be happy.'

Her innocence was infectious. In the face of it he was certain that his own feelings were acceptable at last. He took off his shoes and socks and waded in the stream with her. It was as if some enormous weight had suddenly dropped off him. He splashed her and started to laugh.

An hour later March arrived to find them soaked and happy. Her amazement equalled theirs. They forgot to apologize and asked her how she had known where to look and why wasn't April with her.

She stood on the bank looking down at them and putting two and two together. She thought of her unlocked house in Gloucester, the fact that she had left no note for Fred. Everyone would think she had gone off in search of Davina. She hadn't burnt her boats after all. She could go back. What was more she could go back as a saviour, because April and David must be mad with worry. After all, it *was* her house, why should she give it up? And Fred . . . of course she hated him, but he was rich and if she couldn't have him she wasn't going to give up his money. She would make him pay for what he had done to her this time. Pay and pay again.

She waited while Albert helped Davie out of the

brook, then she said sharply, 'You'd better come into the house and clean up before Mrs Potter gets back.' Then she added in a kinder voice, 'I'm not surprised you came to see Albert, Davie. Where else would you go? You two have always been so close.'

And in spite of everything she smiled as she watched them go barefoot over the grass to the house. They reminded her so much of herself and her brother Albert. Why shouldn't they love each other? Why shouldn't their love grow and develop and be shared later on in marriage?

She had left the house like an automaton, driven out by Fred's betrayal. Nothing could be done about Fred; on the long drive up here she had told herself she no longer cared anyway. But the future might have some meaning after all. Because the future belonged to Albert and Davie.

And Albert took his mother's hand and swung it gratefully. She should have been angry, and she was not. She understood, and her understanding confirmed his own acceptance of the situation. He was entitled to love Davie; it was natural. It was good. He could stop thinking of Beryl Langham's nakedness. He smiled happily at March.

Chapter Nine

The train journey seemed endless. For March and May there were echoes of the first time they had departed for Bristol, when luggage had been piled around April's pram and Will had told them it was like a moonlight flit. Then they had also had to change at the big joint station at Temple Meads, and had been awe and horror struck by its tiled subterranean passage and the endless trains of cattle that had trundled through while they waited for their connection to Bath. Now the subways were discovered with similar amazement by Davina and Flora, and the boys, though so much older than Albert had been, were just as lordly about the whole thing. Both boys were used to train travel and both had their own special excitement to sustain them during the long journey: Albert was to have a whole two weeks with Davina; Victor was going for the painting.

After six weeks of frantic arranging, the three Rising girls were taking their children on a proper summer holiday to Cornwall. In fact they were going to visit the artists' colony in St Ives.

The train, headed by a Castle locomotive no less, was already assembled on platform five as they struggled up the steps with their hand luggage. Steam enveloped it snortingly; it seemed on the point of departure although the luggage-van doors were still open and some mail was being loaded. March, on pins lest they either miss it, lose their luggage or one of the children, called some quick instructions to a grinning Albert, and made for the lift with her odd walking-run to check that the porter would emerge with the three large cases. Albert accompanied the youngsters to the engine itself, ostensibly to let little Flo see the glowing fire that would take them the rest of the way to the seaside, but really to follow March's instructions to make sure that the engine-driver himself knew they were going to St Erth-for-St Ives. March did not trust station porters or even foremen and inspectors. Only the driver knew exactly where his train was going.

April found an empty third-class compartment and began to stack their stuff in the luggage nets. She was still trying to fill the small hole left inside her when the train pulled away from the Gloucester platform, leaving David, Fred and Monty waving somewhat forlornly. Monty was in the middle of cataloguing a library in a mansion just outside Cheltenham which Tolly had planned to start himself at the beginning of the year. After the expense of the Italian holiday David could not afford to accompany them; and Fred . . . Fred had not been asked. It was to escape Fred's presence that March had first suggested the holiday. And she had wanted April to come too so that Albie and Davie could be together. And somewhat reluctantly she had included May and Victor because Albie wanted them, and Victor would be in his seventh heaven among so many artists. And gradually the whole thing had taken shape, and here they were.

She climbed laboriously aboard.

'Where's May?' she asked, glancing around approvingly at April's arrangements. 'Don't tell me she's mucking about with the children when there's work to be done!'

April smiled peaceably and took a large basket from March. 'I think she's gone to the luggage-van to check on the cases,' she said. 'We'll keep this down by my feet, March. We shall need a sandwich soon.'

'She's not at the luggage-van at all. I had to trail down with the stupid porter myself. He obviously expected a tip so May would not have been in sight.'

'Darling, do sit down. You know how short of money May is. Let's have a cup of tea before the train starts, shall we?'

March subsided. 'I thought we said we wouldn't begin on the picnic until Exeter?' She smiled suddenly at April's face. 'Oh, come on then. Serves May right if she misses one of her cups of tea anyway. Let's get the corner seats too. Oh, darling, I can't tell you how glad I am to get away.'

April smiled, beginning to catch a little excitement from somewhere. 'Have we ever been away together?' she asked. 'You and May went to Weymouth of course. And you and I were in Bath when I was expecting Davie.'

March made a face. 'Our London trip to see May's house,' she reminded her sister. 'May and I left Victor and Albie with Mother then. This is much better.'

'Yes. Yes it is.'

April sat back, sipping her tea from the Bakelite cup and staring through the smeary window at the opposite platform. Perhaps it was good to leave David too. Perhaps, as Fred had said in June, she was flying off the handle about the Mannie Stein rumour. Once before when she'd been in a dreadful muddle about her feelings, she had gone away for a while. Now, even though March's arrival that night with Davina had ended her terrible fears and there had been sobbing and laughter and shared relief, she still felt she needed breathing space to accept once again the load of responsibility she knew she must always carry with her.

Outside the compartment and further down the corridor, May and the children began to embark with much noise. April noted March's tightening mouth and grinned at her, shaking her head.

'We're on holiday, March. And we're going to have fun with a capital F.'

March forced herself to relax and smile back at April wryly. April did not know, of course. How could she know and understand March's terrible predilection for unhappiness? April had never sinned in her life, she was good in the way Florence had been good. That kind of people, the 'good' kind, never had much material good fortune, but at least they had their own special kind of peace, which March could never hope to have. But she must count her blessings: she had Albie. And she had this very precious sister and her two little girls; one of whom might well be a daughter-in-law one day. She made herself small in her corner so that there was plenty of room for the children, and lifted her cup to May.

'Help yourself, dear. We've decided to eat when and where we feel like it. After all, we are on holiday.'

May glanced her surprise, but then smiled at Victor who settled himself next to her and tucked his hand in her arm. Yes, they were on holiday; all their problems left behind.

*　　*　　*

It was strange to Sylvia how different she felt now about David. The total love between him and April had always made him acceptable to both Florence and Sylvia, but on his own account they had remained cautious, even wary. Without David Daker, April would not want to live; but David must be very careful to make her happy at all times.

Now, since April's confession, Sylvia saw David in a different light. He was the one to be protected; somehow the pendulum had swung and April's vulnerability had become David's.

She cooked him corned beef hash and summer cabbage, with treacle roly-poly to follow; it was the hottest day of the year.

'Sylvia, you should have gone with the girls. You must be damned lonely here by yourself all day.' David eyed his piled plate with some alarm. 'It's not too late. Let me put you on the train tomorrow.'

'An' 'oo'd look after you?' Sylvia demanded truculently.

'If Monty can look after himself, I'm darned sure I can.'

'Ah well. We'll see about Monty.' Sylvia had no illusions about Monty Gould either. She intended to walk out to Chichester Street regularly during the next fortnight to keep an eye on Monty.

David had to ignore this cryptic remark, so after three sticky mouthfuls, he took another tack.

'Anyway, I could doss down with Fred. March suggested it actually. She said Chattie wouldn't have enough to do.'

Sylvia sighed heavily. How she could spread herself between Winterditch Lane, Chichester Street and

Bedford Close she did not know. But Fred needed watching too.

David thought he might be making headway and said encouragingly, 'Come on, Sylvia. Say you'll go. It would do you good.'

'I'm not leaving Gloucester again. Not even in my box,' Sylvia said repressively. 'An' I want this yer corned beef finished, so 'urry up an' 'ave a second 'elping.'

David grinned wryly. 'Trying to kill me off with over-eating, Sylvia?' he asked. 'I know you don't exactly love me, but I thought we were better friends these days.'

Sylvia recognized she was being teased, even so it was a bit too near the truth for laughter. She replied energetically, 'I wouldn't kill you any ways at all, my lad. You'm more of a son to me than me own two. An' your April's more daughter than Daisy.'

David stopped masticating and stared at her in surprise. Sylvia never spoke without meaning. He put out a hand. 'Oh . . . Sylv . . .' he said.

And even more surprisingly, she said fiercely, 'Don't you go making me cry, David Daker. 'Tis too 'ot to be crying.'

David gripped her hand anyway and smiled at her, and after a while she smiled back. Manfully, he began to eat.

It took eight hours from Bristol what with the wait at St Erth for the branch train, then another wait for a taxi to take them to the top part of the town where they had booked some digs. While David and Sylvia ate their hash, the holidaymakers clambered wearily out of the taxi and surveyed the terraced house with its narrow tiled pathway and burgeoning hydrangea bushes.

Davina said, 'Oh, Mummy – Albie – look. This must be the holy well Daddy read about.'

Behind them, gushing out of a bank and trickling down the steep road, was a clear spring. The taxi driver lifted Flora onto the pavement.

'That there en't no holy well, my 'ansome. That there be draining off the fields. Clear 'nuff if you want to drink it. St Eia's Well be along the nut grove to'ards Lelant.'

Victor listened to the strange accent, entranced. Ten years before, Stanhope Forbes had moved from France to Newlyn just over the spine of the peninsula, and painted real people from real life going about their real work. Victor could see why. The taxi driver's face looked like leather, and his button eyes shone with amusement. Victor couldn't wait to unpack his stuff.

Mrs Noall came out of her front door and surveyed them sardonically. Her hair, scraped on top of her head, seemed to draw her face upwards. She wore a clean apron over a long cotton dress. Beyond the terrace of houses could be seen a jut of land covered in white patches.

Mrs Noall ignored the adults and their polite self introductions, but was moved from her statuesque silence by Flora.

'What's that glittering in your wall, Mrs Noall?' asked the small girl.

Mrs Noall leaned down and picked her up.

'Eh, you're a fine girl, a lovely girl,' she said. 'Fancy you noticing that, eh? Well, that be the crystal in the granite, see. The sun do catch it lovely each evening.

Eh . . .' She turned and walked past people and luggage as if they did not exist. 'You'd best come in and see what Mrs Noall's got for your supper, 'adn't you? Nice bit o' crab – just right for you I reckon. An' some Cornish taties. And some tart and cream to follow.'

'And what are those white patches over the top of the wall, Mrs Noall?'

'Well, my 'ansome, that's the washing a-drying on the island. 'Tedn't no proper island you unnerstand. 'Tis where the sailors' chapel be to. And it do catch every ray of sunshine and every breath o' wind. So the town women and the fishwives do spread out their washing to dry and pin it down at the corners with big rocks.'

Behind her, very close behind her, everyone looked at each other and rolled their eyes. They were very hungry and rather apprehensive.

Victor leaned close to Albert and Davie.

'What's that in your wall, dear Mrs No . . . all,' he whispered. They screwed up their faces against giggles.

'Good old Flo,' Victor said loudly. 'Ambassadress extraordinaire!'

Davie held Albert's hand.

'We're going to have such a lovely, wonderful time here,' she said.

And, leading the way, Mrs Noall smiled.

Fred had never felt tired like this before. It might be the heat or the fact that Tilly Adair seemed to be every-where at once – waiting for him at the garage, hanging around Barnwood Road when he came home, even ringing him at home, though she put the phone down immediately he answered it. He was dreading that these repeated calls would elicit the information that March was away. March was his protection now.

That was the real reason for his tiredness: March's absence. Not only her absence, but her . . . distance . . . during the last two months. She had found endless excuses for avoiding him. She had been worried about April after the Davina escapade, and had insisted on staying at Longmeadow for a couple of nights. She had gone up to Birmingham again, booked herself into a hotel at Barnt Green for a weekend, and she and Albert had 'done the town'. And when she came home she wasn't very well. She complained of headaches and if he went into the bedroom without knocking he would find Chattie brushing her hair.

It had been her excuse for arranging the holiday; he hadn't liked it, he'd wanted a chance to patch up the year-old rift between himself and Albert.

'Albert would rather come with me to the garage, Marcie,' he protested. 'You know all he thinks about is cars.'

She smiled, but not at him. 'Don't be so sure about that. Albert is nineteen now – he's a man.'

'You can't cut the apron strings, can you, Marcie?'

If he hoped to provoke her into a row he was disappointed. Her smile grew. 'Perhaps I won't have to,' she said.

He wanted a row. He wanted her to go for him so that he could grab her and kiss her and make it all right between them. He said, 'He's my son too. Perhaps now is the time to acquaint him with that fact.'

The smile did not disappear. She stared at him, almost objectively. Then she seemed to come to a conclusion and she shook her head. 'You'll never tell him that, Fred. You know it would be the end of anything between you.' She stood up and walked away from him. 'Don't try to frighten me like that, Fred,' she said over her shoulder.

It had been the first time he was conscious of the tiredness. It was as if she no longer needed him. He wondered if her need for him was the source of his energy. But that was absurd; whimsical nonsense; the sort of thing Victor might spout about.

The trouble was that this August Bank holiday gave him time to think about whimsical nonsense of all kinds. They had been at St Ives over a week now and no letter or card from March. They could all be dead; he wondered what he would do without March and Albert. Without April and Davina.

Chattie came into the sitting-room with a meal on a tray. Hard-boiled eggs and salad. It was what he had asked for, but looking at the shining blue-white eggs lying in lettuce, he didn't want them.

'Thank you, Chattie.' He took the tray and put it on the Bechstein. 'You get off now. I'll manage all right. Enjoy your day.'

Chattie hummed and ha'd. Would he be all right? There were clean sheets in the linen cupboard and he had plenty of underclothes. The fridge hummed with food for him, and a man was coming in early tomorrow to do the grass. She'd be back about ten o'clock to give him a cup of tea.

'I'll be at work then, Chattie, anyway. Now get *off*!'

He pretended to go for her and she ran out of the sitting-room giggling. He wondered what he'd have done if she'd let him catch her. She was so plump and fresh. Would it help to seduce her? He remembered he had offered her to Albert once as if she were a trussed chicken. He had done it to shock the boy. Why had he wanted to shock him? God, why was he forever deliberately hurting the people who meant most to him? He had promised April – *promised* her – that he would squash that Mannie Stein rumour, or at any rate make sure David never heard it. How the hell could he do that? Unless he told it to David himself; told him that Adair had made it up to get his hooks into Bridie Hall. He considered that solution, frowning and staring at the two hard-boiled eggs as if they might provide an answer, when the doorbell rang. He almost ran to open it. It was Tilly. He stared at her, not speaking, waiting as if she were some deliverer of tracts, unwelcome.

She said in a low, angry voice, 'You nearly ran me down yesterday. If I hadn't stepped back quickly I think you would have done. I wish you had. I wish I was dead. You'd be put in prison for manslaughter. And I'd come back to haunt you.'

He said nothing, but leaned against the door jamb wearily. All he had behind him were two hard-boiled eggs and an empty day.

She clenched her hands at her sides. 'Well? Lost your tongue? Why don't you throw me into the road like you did last time? Why don't you rip all my clothes off and send me home in some filthy sack from your garage?' She put a hand to the throat of her powder-blue silk dress and pulled hard. Three buttons flew onto the gravel drive and revealed something lacy.

He shifted his position and continued to eye her expressionlessly. But he felt less tired and almost wanted to laugh. It would have been a derisory laugh but better than nothing.

She had shot her bolt and seemed to shrivel a little. Her mouth turned down childishly.

'Freddie. Please. Let me come in and . . . talk.'

He sighed, stepped back into the hall and began to shut the door. 'I'm afraid March wouldn't like it,' he said.

With startling suddenness she screamed. She screamed very loudly indeed and Fred's eyes involuntarily went past her to The Beeches opposite. As soon as his attention was elsewhere she launched herself at him. Her nails went through his poplin shirt and clenched on his chest hairs. She screamed again, and kicked at his shins. Furiously he dragged her inside and slammed the door. Then he tore her away from him, held her at arms' length with one hand and swung at her face.

The scream climbed a register, cut itself off, and was followed by anguished sobs. She fell in a heap on the tiles. He lugged her to her feet.

'Pull yourself together, woman,' he snapped. 'I've told you I won't put up with your behaviour any longer. Do I have to come and ask Charles to restrain you?'

She gasped, 'I know March isn't home. I met your maid waiting for the bus in Barnwood Road. She said March was on holiday and you were here all on your own. Let me stay, Fred. I'll look after you. I won't be a nuisance, I'll—'

'Are you absolutely sure Charles won't mind?' Fred said, heavily sarcastic. 'Or is he meant to walk in on our domestic bliss and challenge me to a duel?'

She made another sudden move, twisting away from him like an eel and diving for the stairs. She was lighter, nimbler than he. He grabbed and grabbed again, but always missed. Ahead of him she flung herself onto the bed in the front room, rolled onto her back, spread her arms wide and gazed up at him, panting. He felt a familiar flare of desire. Well, why not? March was three hundred miles away and hadn't wanted him for months. And he was no celibate, completely different from that damfool Tolly Hall. But, suddenly, he didn't know how to go about it. Before, he had made love to her almost coldly, watching her reactions all the time. His love-making had been for a reason. Now the reason was gone. He hung onto the foot of the bed, getting his breath back, staring down at her. He didn't even hate her.

She said in a small voice, 'Hit me if you want to, Freddie. I don't mind.'

It was despicable, yet he still didn't hate her. Rather he hated himself. He had done this to her. He had reduced her to this stupid lump who would take anything from him rather than be without him.

He raised his hand and hit her with all his might across the face. She screamed again and rolled her head away from him, protecting it with her arm but not attempting to get off the bed. He pulled brutally at her clothes and shoved himself on her like an animal. There was little satisfaction in it; he felt himself slipping further and further into degradation and wanted to scream aloud for March. Afterwards, when he flung himself away from her and lay with closed eyes, she came up under his arm and kissed his chin.

'Oh, darling Freddie. I knew it would be all right. You see, I understand you. I know what you need.' He did groan then, pushing her away and rolling off the bed and kneeling for a moment as if in prayer. But still her complete insensitivity saw nothing wrong. She got off the bed and started pulling at suspenders and knickers and giggling.

'Darling, what have you done to me?' She went to the mirror and stared at herself. 'Just look at my frock! And I'm going to have the biggest shiner in the world!' She turned her back and peered over her shoulder. 'This frock is ruined. Absolutely ruined. Freddie, you are naughty. You are the naughtiest boy in the world!'

He couldn't look at her. He got off his knees and stumbled to the door and along the landing. Down in the hall, looking up, a frown making her more ox-like than ever, was Sylvia Rising.

March, May and April sat in deckchairs outside the canvas beach tent they had hired. April wore a green eyeshade, khaki shorts and a white aertex shirt. March and May wore cotton dresses with deep v-necks and no sleeves. March was bare-headed, May sported a large linen sunhat. The weather had not been all good, but most days had been spent on Porthmeor Beach which was contained within the arm of the laundry-dotted island.

The Rising girls and their children thought they were in heaven, rain or shine. From the cosy cobbled streets to the wild panorama of rocks and sea, everything delighted them. Victor, unwittingly following the footsteps of Nicholson and Wood, had discovered the primitive work of the fisherman Wallis and had mentally discarded all his carefully learned techniques. He was now endeavouring to paint innocently on any material that came to hand. Large flat pebbles were his medium at the present, and the hallway at Mrs Noall's was carefully edged with them, some bearing recognizable views and even people, other insouciantly daubed with an abstract idea. Flo sometimes followed him around, carrying his brushes and palette; at other times she spent hours with Davie and Albert constructing elaborate harbours in the rock pools or sculpting huge beasts from the wet sand. As for Davina and Albert, this was their time. Albert had pushed all thoughts of unnatural love to the back of his mind. He loved his cousin as she loved him, with true innocence.

Today it was August Bank holiday and Mr Johnson, who leased the beach, had brought down two donkeys to amuse the children from Hayle and Camborne and even Plymouth who had come for the day. One donkey was black and one was grey. Flo had already ridden on both of them and preferred the black one. She watched from the edge of the sea, while a rough-looking boy mounted him. April could read her thoughts even at that distance, and when the boy had finished his ride she smiled to see Flo's shoulders go down with relief, and her attention turn to the incoming tide.

May said lazily, 'What are you laughing at, April?'

'Nothing. Flo actually. Is Victor with us today?'

'Not until lunchtime. I told him crab sandwiches at one o'clock, so he'll arrive then.'

March marked the place in her novel with a sandy finger and looked up. 'We shall grow shells the way we're eating crabs,' she commented. April reflected that she had stepped aside from an opportunity of criticizing Victor; the holiday was doing her good.

Then she went on more typically, 'You know, we shouldn't be so lazy. This is the third day running we've spent all day on the beach.'

May groaned theatrically. April said, 'Tell you what. Let's go to St Eia's Well this evening. The girls can be late for once. Flo's keen on seeing it. David told her about it and said it was a wishing well.'

'I know what I shall wish,' March said.

'What?'

'It won't come true if I tell you.'

'That's silly.' May stretched luxuriously. 'I shall wish that Monty and Sibbie can be friends. D'you know, the other afternoon he came in from work, saw she was having tea with me and went straight out again. He didn't come back till it was almost dark. Now if that's not bigoted I don't know what is. We had the most frightful row.'

'You must be an absolute fool if you want Monty and Sibbie to become friends,' March said without rancour. 'Oh well, if it's all right to tell . . . I shall wish that one day Albie and Davie will get married.'

May exclaimed delightedly, and April lifted her eyeshade and stared, then began to smile.

'You really are the most surpising person, Sis,' she said, her tone tinged with admiration. 'Is this because Davie played truant that time and went to see Albert?'

March shrugged. 'Not only that, no. They've always been such friends.'

'Yes but . . . friends.' April smiled still but shook her head warningly. 'They're cousins after all.'

May chipped in. 'Cousins are all right, darling – quite, quite legal. And March isn't trying to fix something up next week. She's just going to wish that some day they will get married. I think it's the most romantic idea in the world. And . . . somehow . . . right.'

April's smile saddened and they all thought of the

first Albert and what he had meant to March. Then she adjusted her eyeshade and leaned her head back against her deckchair. The sun was positively hot and seemed to soak into her bones, replenishing them with new marrow. She knew what she would wish and had no intention of telling. The fact that she intended to wish it at the holy well, made her realize how desperate she was.

Sylvia waited while Fred took Tilly Adair home with a cold compress over one eye. She was not shocked but she was grieved. She remembered the holiday at Weymouth in 1917 when March had found herself pregnant and Fred had been reported missing. They had always been meant for each other and Fred was risking it all . . . messing about.

Sylvia discovered the egg salad on the piano and carried it into the kitchen. She was happier in the kitchen. Even there March's fastidious touch was off-putting, but at least she couldn't do much about the sink and the gas stove. Sylvia skirted the fridge nervously as she laid Fred's place at the table.

One thing she had to say for him, he could face up to anything. She heard the car drive into the garage and half expected him to go upstairs first to compose himself, but no, he came straight through the house looking for her, and sat down at the table, bold as brass. 'There you are,' he said, giving her a strange, twisted smile, then, deliberately, 'I might as well eat this. Dealing with Tilly has given me an appetite.'

She had made tea and brought the pot to the table now without so much as a flicker of shock. She poured two cups; she'd made it strong and when she added the milk it turned into a colour fashionable at the moment, called burnt orange. She sipped appreciatively.

Fred said, 'Well?' He cut one of the eggs in half and the yolk crumbled into the lettuce. He put down his knife. 'Come on. Get it over with. Tell me I should know better after all that's happened. Tell me I'm a swine. Tell me *something*!'

Sylvia replied, 'If you cassn't eat, at least drink your tea. I'm not going to tell you anything. I've come about something else entirely.'

Fred stared at her, then heaved a sigh from his feet and picked up his cup. 'You've seen it all, haven't you, Sylvia? Your own brother, poor old David Daker, me . . . you expect people to be rotten.'

At last Sylvia was shocked. 'I dun't expeck no such thing, Fred. An' the folks 'oo does wrong things sometimes, is often the folks 'oo does good things other times. Will was the kindest 'usband and father as ever was. David the same.'

'And that leaves me. What can you find that's good about me then, Sylvia?'

'I'll tell you, Fred Luker. I'll tell you.' She supped again, looking at him over the rim of her cup. He picked up his cup too and she waited while he drank some of the scalding brew. Then she said gently, 'I knows, Fred. I knows about April. I knows about our little Davie.'

He choked and put the cup down with a clatter.

'Who in God's name told you?' Then he closed his eyes momentarily. 'Of course. April. The day Davina went missing.'

'Ah.' Sylvia put her cup in its saucer with great care. 'Ah, it were that day. The load were too 'eavy for 'er to carry on 'er own.'

255

'She had me,' he said bleakly.

'You'm thick at times, Fred. Cassn't you see that you comes between 'er and David?'

He looked at Sylvia again, this time frowningly and with new respect. For the first time he noticed that her blue Rising eyes had the same kind of depth as April's, and her big shapeless mouth was never pursed as old Gran Rising's had been.

He said in a low voice, 'Yes. Yes, I see that.'

She gave a nodding, congratulatory, grimace. 'Well then . . . it were as well I were there. It might 'ave been David else. 'Er knew that 'erself, that were why 'er din't want 'im sent for.'

He never made excuses, never asked forgiveness, yet he found himself saying, 'It wasn't as bad as it sounds, Sylvia. Not at the time. It seemed sensible—'

'I don't want to know about all that. That's gone and done for. What we got to think about now is Davie.'

'She's happy. She loves David. Strangely enough, if he has a favourite child, it's her.'

'Of course Davie's 'appy. But it's more important than being 'appy, Fred, innit? 'Er and Albert. Your Albert. 'Ave you forgot I knows about Albert too, Fred?'

He was checked. If he'd thought that all this was another roundabout way of ticking him off, he had to think again.

He said slowly, 'Temporarily . . . perhaps. But of course March told me you were the only one who knew.' His eyes went past her and he picked up his cup automatically and drained it. Then he went on. 'So, you think the same as I thought last year. Why do you suppose I sent Albert to Birmingham?'

She nodded. 'I did wonder. But it weren't enough,

were it? Our Davie's got a mind of 'er own. Wherever you send 'im, 'er'll follow 'im now. 'Er's getting older all the time. 'Er'll follow 'im to the ends of the earth if need be.'

'You're worrying unduly, Sylvia. It's just a schoolgirl crush.'

Sylvia leaned forward. 'She's 'alf you and 'alf April Rising. Think it over, Fred, think it over.'

There was a long silence. She got up and refilled the teapot and came back to pour more tea. Absent-mindedly he drank again. At last he nodded.

'You could be right.'

'I'm right,' she came back promptly.

'But what can I do? What else can I do? You don't want me to tell April about Albert, surely?'

'Christamighty no. April's jumpy enough as it is. If she knew that, it would finish 'er. 'Er couldn't look March in the face again. An' what could 'er do about our Davie? Naught.'

'Well then.'

''Tis Albert 'oo will 'ave to bear the pain o' this, Fred. Your son. You must tell 'im as soon as you can. Afore the 'ole thing gets too settled.'

He had already considered that possibility and shook his head definitely.

'Never. He would hate me for good and all. No, I'll never tell Albert I'm his father. At one time . . . not now. Especially not now.'

'That's the least o' your worries. It's when you tell 'im about being Davie's father that the sparks will fly.'

'Christamighty, Sylvia. I could never tell him that. He would hate April. And I think he might try to kill me.'

She was stolidly stubborn. 'There en't no other way, Fred. One of 'em's got to know, and it can't be Davie.' She took her cup to the sink. 'I'd reckon Albert can stand it. 'E 'aven't bin tested nor tried yet, but I'd reckon 'e'll stand it.' She turned and lumbered back for his empty cup. 'Albert's got you and March in 'im. You're strong and March is stiff-necked. So I reckon—'

Fred pushed his chair back viciously. 'You reckon! What do you know about anything? You've been on the edge of everything that happened with the Risings – the edge, not the middle! Albert's never had a proper father. Thinking that dirty old man at Bath was his pa, then putting your stupid brother in his place, then having me foisted on him when he was already twelve years old! What sort of childhood did he have, swinging like a pendulum between Bath and Gloucester? Christ, my poor old dad was drunk most of the time, but at least he was *there*! At least when he gave me the strap I knew it was because he cared one way or another – usually another, but he cared!' He hung onto the edge of the table like a cornered animal and almost spat his words at her. 'You're asking me to take everything away from Albert – everything. He won't respect his mother any more. He's been in love with April since he was a kid – all that will be gone. His grandfather slept with the town whore and now his father . . . Christ, you don't *reckon* anything, Sylvia Rising!'

She looked at him calmly and with compassion. 'My name is Sylvia Turpin, Fred. I 'ad three children on the wrong side o' the bed linen, remember. I reckon . . . yes, I *reckon* I know what Albert is goin' to 'ave to take. An' I reckon it be a good thing you'm thinkin' of 'im and not yourself. An' I reckon . . . yes, I reckon 'im'll take it all right.'

And suddenly Fred Luker, who had shouldered so many sins besides his own, sat down again and buried his head in his arms, scattering salad and plates as he went.

Mrs Noall asked them if they would take with them her brother's son who was nineteen and elevenpence half-penny in the pound. March and April looked doubtful, but Victor clapped Horace on the back and said, 'You'll walk with me, won't you, old chap?' and May smiled beatifically at Mrs Noall and said, 'He'll be all right with my Victor.' Since Victor had started trying to find original innocence, he doted on small children, and Horace was, after all, a large small child.

They wandered along the cliff path to Carbis Bay, strung out in a long line, picking the first of the black-berries and standing to watch the train chuff along the branch line. Horace wasn't that daft, and told them how the Great Western Railway Company had had to stop the engines a-whistling because they fritted the pilchards away.

Victor asked, 'Do you go out with the seiners, Horace?'

'Naw. I'd mend the nets when they'd get 'oles in.' Horace laughed uproariously at this and Davie joined in politely.

Victor was enthusiastic. 'I could paint you doing that if you like,' he suggested hopefully. To paint Horace would be akin to Stanhope Forbes painting the fisher-men of Newlyn. Better; Horace was the complete child of nature.

'Can't stop ee I s'ppose,' Horace agreed un-graciously.

They climbed down onto the white sand of Carbis Bay and up the steep hill on the other side. The foot-path wound along the side of the rocky cliff, protected by leaning hazel trees, then through the dunes by the side of the golf course. Somewhere between was the well of St Eia. By the time they reached it the sun had almost gone and a few dark clouds lay on the sea. The well was surrounded by mud and brambles and when Albert pushed them aside, the glittering black hole looked indecently exposed.

April tried to recapture their sense of excitement.

'Wishing time!' She herded March and May forward. 'I know what you're going to wish, but you'd better keep it secret from the girls and it might come half true!'

March and May played along and stood with closed eyes, incanting mysterious gibberish while Flora watched, round-eyed, and Davie giggled. Then they took it in turns to close eyes and concentrate inwards. Davie wished that Albert would leave Birmingham very soon. Flora wished that they could have a kitten and come back to St Ives again. Victor wished that he could become a famous artist. Albert started to wish some-thing about Davie, then stopped, then backed away from the well. April put her hands in her cardigan pockets, clenched them hard and wished that David would never find out. And Horace would not wish at all.

'I say, it's getting very black,' May said, climbing away from the overhanging foliage and studying the sky. 'I think we'd better make haste back home.'

The darkening sky had an effect on Horace too. He

hurried ahead of them, muttering about thunder and lightning and the tides a-turning. They all stepped it out, but Flora was tired by now and the adults had to slow occasionally for her. They spaced themselves out: Horace and Davie a long way in front, Albert and Victor next, the others far behind.

Victor said, 'God, if I can get some wood – an old door panel or something – I reckon I can make something of Horace. I can just see him bending over those nets on Smeaton's Pier, his eyes seeing the fish, weaving the fish in with his needle—'

'Oh lord. The chap's got no imagination, you idiot. If he's mending a net, he sees the net. Anyone would.' Albert was still confused about his wish. He let Davie run on ahead, wanting to be with Victor and forget the whole of the female sex. 'And why a door panel? What's the matter with paper? Or canvas if you want to use your oils.'

'Too sophisticated. I'm trying to get back to roots, old man. That's why Horace is such a godsend.'

'I see.' Albert spoke with exaggerated sarcasm and glanced sideways to meet Victor's grin. It was not there. Victor was absolutely wrapped up in this stupid art business. How did you earn a living by painting pictures? You only had to look around St Ives, at the state of the many artists there, to see there was no way of making real money with a brush and easel. Now motor cars . . . they were different. Albert pulled himself up, wondering if he was beginning to think like Fred. Surely not? In any case, Davie would always stop him thinking like Fred. Davie was his innocence and his goodness and he ought never to be ashamed to admit it. He lengthened his stride to catch up with her.

She was some way ahead, trying to slow and calm Horace who was by now panic-stricken by the gathering storm.

'It will only be the clouds bumping together,' she tried to reassure him, using the imagery David had always used for her.

But he knew better. He began clambering down a bank to a lower path which looked more sheltered. His foot broke the thin surface of soil and found one of the many underground watercourses which drained the land. He slithered and slipped downward, yelping like a dog and landing on all fours with grazed hands and cut trousers. He put his head down and began to cry.

Davie was horrified. She called back to the others, then deliberately jumped onto the water-chute and shot down to Horace. She must have hurt him more crashing into him, but it seemed to cheer him up a bit. He lifted his ravaged face and laughed, then put an arm around her comfortingly. They were both soaked and muddy. This smaller path, used by the coastguards, had none of the cultivated wildness of the middle one. It was broken in places, and below it the sea seemed to wait with a confident menace for any victims. The water was glass-clear and the shapes of the rocks moved and twisted within it.

Davie tried to sound matter-of-fact. 'Now what exactly frightened you then, Horace? There's nothing to be scared of.'

'Light,' he said and made rapid movements with his free arm. 'Light kin strike you dead. We gotta hide.'

'Lightning?' Davie herself was more cautious of lightning. 'Yes, well. We'd better try and climb back up and hurry home then. Are you hurt? Stand up and let me see you.'

Horace stood obediently, then, grinning, fumbled in his trousers and produced a large, flaccid penis for her inspection.

Davie was appalled. Having no brothers, the male body was completely strange to her. She knew its shape theoretically and had often mentioned to her mother how lucky boys were when it came to the mechanics of passing water, but this sudden presentation shocked and horrified her. Perhaps if she had had time to reason that Horace was nineteen and elevenpence halfpenny in the pound, she might have dealt with the revelation a little better. But there was no warning. One minute it was covered, the next it was not. She screamed.

Albert arrived at the top of the bank while the scream still lingered. He looked down and saw the bizarre cameo just as the first ragged gash of lightning tore at the sky and was swallowed by the sea. He shouted, but it was doubtful whether Horace responded to that or Davie's scream or the lightning. Probably a combination of all three. He stuffed his offending member inside his trousers and began to lumber off. The path was covered with loose stones and broken in many places. Albert shouted again but this time warningly. In any case Horace was possessed of a clumsy kind of sure-footedness and negotiated the first few hazards easily, then rounded a bluff and disappeared from view. Everyone else arrived.

'What on earth— ?'

'Davie – darling – are you hurt?'

'Where's Horace? Has Davie frightened him off?'

Albert addressed the last speaker viciously.

'He's an animal, you damfool! He was exposing himself to Davie! Christ— !' Albert pushed himself over the bank and crashed down to his cousin who had her hands over her face and was sobbing uncontrollably. He gathered her against his shoulder and rocked her.

April called, 'Davie . . . it's all right now. Mummy is just coming—' But then Flora started to weep and she had to take her into her arms and tell her that everything was all right.

March said loudly and sensibly, 'Look, Davie will be fine with Albert, he'll look after her.' She called down, 'Albie, we'll walk along this path and try to find a better place to clamber down. Will you be all right for a few minutes?'

He lifted his face; he looked haggard. 'Yes. Of course. Find that – that brute – just find him.'

Victor said quickly, 'I'll find him. Don't worry, Mother, I'll take him back to Mrs Noall. He doesn't know what he's doing – try to calm Albert down for goodness sake. He'll only make it worse.'

May nodded and Victor galloped off. More lightning tore through the sky, followed by a terrific clap of thunder. Flora sobbed again and April began to move off with her. Down on the lower path, her muddy wetness making her begin to shiver, Davie cowered against Albert.

'Relax, sweetheart.' He spoke right into her ear because his own were still deafened from the thunder. 'They've gone to find a way down, then we can all hold hands and get home again quickly.'

By this time Davie had her nose inside his shirt and the smell of his skin, so familiar and homely, reassured her as nothing else could have done. She held onto him and shut off the picture of poor Horace's penis.

After a while she said, 'I'm sorry, Albie. What a fuss.'

'That swine—'

'No. He didn't understand. I told him to stand up and let me see him. I suppose he thought I meant . . . honestly he didn't know.'

'Oh, Davie.'

She realized he was trembling and tightened her arms around him. He lowered his head and pressed his face against hers. It was wet. But then he too was wet from the watercourse.

'It's all right, Albie. Honestly.'

He muttered, 'It's just that . . . I can't stand it if anything bad happens to you, Davie. That creature – that beast – you're precious. Precious.'

She turned her face and kissed his cheek. She could taste salt. Her own tears started again.

'Oh, Davie . . . darling . . .'

They stood up and clung together with a kind of desperation. She sobbed, 'I love you, Albie – I love you – I want to stay with you always.'

And he kissed her frantically and said, 'I love you too, my darling. My Davie—' and he forgot that she was only eleven, and as the heavens opened he kissed her properly and she was the embodiment of everything he held dear; the vision of his Aunt April, the allure of Beryl Langham, and so much more. The Davieness of Davie. She held his head and returned his kisses without any reserve and with a passion that matched and surpassed his own. She knew nothing of sexual fulfilment, but she knew she wanted to fuse herself with her cousin; she wanted to become him, she wanted him to become her.

So in the tempestuous rain they pressed close as if they could be diluted and run into one while they stood on the Cornish cliff. Davie knew this was her destiny. Albie accepted his for the first time, and with that acceptance his fear of being unnatural died a death. All other loves might well be unnatural for him; with Davie his love was right and good. He pushed his head hard against hers and through their compressed ears heard the drumming of her blood.

Their desperate bid for one-ness might have lasted one or five minutes; they were reminded of reality by a shout from beyond them. It was Victor's voice.

Albert said urgently, 'It doesn't matter. We'll talk tomorrow,' and Davie nodded and they parted slowly and stared at each other for another moment while water dripped from hair and eyebrows. Then Davie turned and began to walk carefully along the perilous path towards Victor's voice. They must not have an accident now; everything was too marvellous and wonderful. They must be here tomorrow and tomorrow and tomorrow and always.

Victor looked like a drowned rat. 'Come on, why are you hanging about here? No sign of Horace. I've sent the others off to try to spot him on the way home. But they won't hurry till they've seen you two. Come *on*!'

Davie laughed foolishly and Albie said in an exuberant voice, 'What's all the hurry? Lovely weather for a walk!' As soon as there was room on the path he splashed madly in a puddle and Davie was convulsed. Victor looked immensely irritable.

'Nothing very funny surely?' He scrambled the last few feet and leaned down to give the others a hand. They both ignored him. 'My God. We've lost Horace, you're both covered in mud, everyone else is soaked to the skin and all you do is laugh like a pair of hyenas.'

He went on ahead while they squelched behind him, not even holding hands but as close as peas in a pod and almost hysterically happy. They caught the others halfway along the Digey and turned up Virgin Street which was like a waterfall, and struggled past the cemetery. Lightning and thunder were almost incessant by this time, conversation hopeless, but in one flash they spotted Horace ahead of them, hands over head, stumbling from one side of the road to the other. He grinned in recognition when they shouted. And in that instant a crooked finger of lightning struck him downwards and nailed him into the earth.

Davie would never quite accept that Horace's bizarre death was not her fault. Mrs Noall herself told her that he had always known that one day the lightning would catch him; she pointed out that it was an easy way to go. 'Could 'a bin the sea what got 'im. Slow like. Or 'is poor addled brain could a' run away wi' 'im. 'E's better a-going like this.' But her macabre comfort fell on deaf ears. Davie knew that if she hadn't screamed Horace wouldn't have run, and if he hadn't run he wouldn't have been in that exact spot on Ayr Terrace when the lightning found him.

Whenever they could get away by themselves, Albert told her he loved her and that was all that mattered. But although she responded, some of her happiness was dimmed.

'It feels wrong now,' she tried to explain. 'As if – as if – it is cursed. I can't explain.'

'Listen.' He tried to jolly her out of her mood by

splashing her unmercifully as they waded in the shallows. 'Listen, little idiot. We love each other. And in six years time . . . no five and a half to be exact . . . no . . .' He calculated rapidly. 'In five years and four months, we will get married. What do you say?'

She gave her wide painful grin. 'Oh, all right.'

He whooped joyously and splashed again. 'That means we're engaged. I'll buy you a ring.' He caught her hands and swung her off her feet, then was serious. 'Oh, Davie. I'll work so hard now. We'll have our own garage and our own house. Shall we have a dog?'

She caught his mood at last. 'Oh yes. And a cat.'

'What about my train set?'

'We must get a house with an attic.' They hugged and laughed. But as they walked back to the others, Davie felt cold again. She could just recall the awful time when her grandfather had died suddenly; she remembered very clearly how ill her mother had been after Grandma Rising went to Jesus. She thought, 'I hate death. I hate it.'

Chapter Ten

Winter came early that year, and by the end of October crisp, frosty days were interspersed with iron-cold murky weather when fogs would boil up around the docks and creep through Bearland and along Westgate Street to the Cross. By three o'clock on those afternoons it was time to light up and run a poker through the banked fire so that it would be red-hot in time for tea. Flora had a picture postcard of the two little princesses sitting before a fire toasting bread on a long fork. Every day after school she liked to carry a plate of bread into the living-room and make toast. She did it importantly, as a ritual, placing a cushion on the hearth and arranging her school skirt so that just her feet and ankles showed. Neither of the girls had a second Christian name, but Flora asked whether she could be known as 'Flora May'. It had the same rhythm as 'Margaret Rose'.

Unconsciously Davina too adopted a similar role and played Princess Elizabeth to her small sister. She became very serious and grown-up and talked of her 'responsibilities'. She went into Gloucester every day now to the Girls' High School in Denmark Road and learned French. Next year she would have a choice between German and Latin.

'Better choose German, little apple,' David advised soberly.

Davie had no intention of listening to one of the discussions her parents often had on the imminence of war, and abandoned her adult pose to say petulantly, 'Daddy, you shouldn't call me little apple any more. I'm *big*!'

David picked her up with difficulty and hugged her. 'Yes, but you're still so edible!' he teased and opened his mouth wide. She screamed and Aunt Sylv shushed and Flora kept on with her toasting. April looked at them all and loved them so much it hurt. When they were at St Ives March had accused May of taking Monty for granted. April wished with all her heart that she could take her happiness for granted.

But Monty, returning home to an empty house and no fire, was fed up with being taken for granted. May was out again, doubtless with Sibbie and her fine friends. Victor was spending the weekend at the Langhams, so Monty was expected to look after himself. He was good at it. After his years on the road he was very adaptable. But May was taking advantage of that fact and he didn't like it.

Moodily he put a match to the carefully laid fire in the sitting-room and went through to the kitchen to make tea. Like his nieces he toasted bread by the fire while he drank his tea, but the flames were new and the results were smoking and grey. The *Citizen* arrived and he flapped it open and looked through it without interest. He refused to become parochial and the *Citizen* was a parochial broadsheet. But there was a small column of news about the war in Spain. He read it more closely than usual. The Italians were helping old Franco . . . well, naturally, they were all Fascists after all. But the Republicans were having a thin time of it by all accounts; at the end of the column there was a short casualty list. No-one from Gloucester. Monty frowned; that did not mean anything of course, there must be hundreds of unidentified bodies and Tolly could have died in the week he went out there. Monty turned the page, not wanting to let any thoughts form about Tolly's possible death. The facts were there all the same whether he thought about them or not: without Tolly life was better for Monty Gould. He ran the book department at Williams' sloppily, but he ran it. Tolly had never overtly criticized Monty's work, but his silences had been hard to bear. And then there had been those blasted letters. Tolly must have known about his liaison – his so brief liaison – with Sibbie. And that had been hateful, simply hateful.

Absently he poked the fire and found a good red cavern of heat; he speared more bread on the fork and began on another slice of toast. It was better this time; it soaked up Mrs Goodrich's butter deliciously and melted in the mouth. Monty leaned back in Florence's old chair which May had had re-covered, and stared up at Victor's painting. If only May hadn't become so friendly with Sibbie again, he might have resumed that liaison now that Tolly was out of the way. It would have made life interesting again to walk down the Bristol road on a Friday night to Sibbie's cosy little bungalow. It had all been curiously innocent once he had given in to her. May had been going through a difficult time and had practically driven him into Sibbie's arms anyway, so he had been able to dispose of his guilt fairly easily; and Sibbie herself had a gift for taking the sin out of it. Perhaps because she laughed so much; perhaps because she went along with his role-playing; perhaps because Will Rising had gone before him, paved the way as it were. Will had successfully loved two women. And lots of people thought he was like Will. But of course Will had managed to keep his two women a long way apart. Now that Sibbie and May had resumed their schoolgirl friendship, it would be impossible to come between them. He frowned again, wondering whether to have another piece of toast, threw the *Citizen* onto the floor with theatrical disgust, and was about to fiddle with the wireless and try to find Henry Hall or the Savoy Orpheans, when the door-knocker sounded loudly out in the hall. His frown disappeared. Any company was better than none. It might be Victor after all and they could play draughts or sit and chat. It might even be May if she'd lost her key.

It was neither of those two. It was Sibbie. And she was smiling like a cat who has just found a saucer of cream.

The *thé dansant* had finished at six and Charles had wanted to take them all out to dinner. However, Sibbie said she simply must get back to poor Edward, and Maurice Foster, who used to dance attendance on Bridie Williams in the old days, had plans of his own. So that left May.

'Another time perhaps,' she said regretfully, because she still adored food and there was only toast for tea back home in Chichester Street. And Charles Adair was so delightfully attentive.

Sibbie encircled her with one arm and Charles with the other. 'Darling May, so Edwardian.' She never lost an opportunity to emphasize May's new image. 'Charles wants you to dine with him, darling. It's perfectly respectable and Monty wouldn't mind in the slightest.'

May blushed. 'I'm afraid he would. I'm sorry, Charles—'

Sibbie kissed her lightly to stop her words, then said with an air of dramatic conspiracy, 'But he need never know! An assignation! May darling, it's absolutely right for you. A dinner engagement with a gentleman admirer—'

'Sibbie, stop it!'

But Charles said gallantly, 'I agree entirely. You need to be just a little clandestine now and then, May. Otherwise you run a great risk of becoming over-frank and too too nineteen-thirties for words!'

Sibbie and he laughed uproariously and May followed suit a second later. She began to feel foolishly prudish.

Sibbie said grandly, like a chaperone, 'Take her to the Bell, Charles dear. I think champagne, don't you? You might even drink it from her slipper.'

'Done!' Charles lifted May's hand to his lips. 'Gracious lady, we will wine and dine and I will return you to your humble abode on the stroke of midnight!'

'Oh, much earlier than that, please, Charles—'

But Sibbie laughed at that, kissed May again and slid away, looking, in her ample furs, rather like a predatory lynx.

It was an evening for the unexpected. In her tall house in Brunswick Square, Bridget sat feeding tiny Tolly and listening, with a little more sympathy than usual, to her mother-in-law, Kitty Hall. Since the birth of her son, Bridie's personality had suffered a sea-change. She no longer justified her adultery with Charles Adair; she no longer vilified Tolly for his desertion; she no longer cried out at the meaninglessness of her life. She fed the baby from a bottle and her love for him was compounded by a terrible sadness. She had discovered too late that the deep satisfaction she had had from bearing her other children and suckling them so un-inhibitedly was almost entirely because they were Tolly's children too. After twelve years of marriage she realized she was in love with her husband.

Kitty said, ' . . . and I've looked at that casualty list ever since they started printing it and there's never been a mention of him . . .'

But Bridget, so certain in June that Tolly had purposely disappeared to punish her, saw things differ-ently now. He might loathe her, but he did not loathe Olga and Natasha and Beatrice and Catherine and Svetlana.

Echoing her thoughts unconsciously, Kitty droned on, 'But if he's alive why doesn't he write? He might at least think of the girls. Poor Olga is distraught and I'm sure her back is getting worse.'

Bridget said strongly, 'Olga's all right, Mother, don't worry about her. She's been doing too much knitting for the Brigade lately, that's all. As soon as I've weaned Barty, I'm going to start Tolly's exercise programme again for her. The club-swinging especially was very beneficial and will do us all good.'

'You're a good girl, Bridie,' Kitty said. 'Little Beattie told me the other day how you persuaded her to do her homework because she might be the first woman prime minister. Tolly always told her that.'

'Tolly took great pains with their education.' Bridie winded Barty expertly and looked sadly past his small shoulder. 'If only he'd tried to educate me as well. But I wouldn't have listened to him then.'

'Oh, Bridie—' Kitty tried to envelop mother and baby in her arms just as the door opened and Mrs Goodson appeared.

'A gentleman caller, madam,' she said repressively. 'A Mister Emmanuel Stein. He seems quite elderly so I've put him in the dining-room.'

As Mrs Goodson usually kept callers waiting on the cold step, this was a real concession. Bridget and Kitty eyed each other sharply.

'Mannie Stein. April's old flame,' Bridie murmured. 'And he met up with Tolly last year in Berlin. What on earth—'

'Tolly didn't like him,' Kitty reminded her. 'And neither did you.'

'Well, I'll have to see him, Mother, nevertheless.' Bridie passed Barty over. 'Elderly? He's David's age surely?'

But when she went into the dining-room, she saw that Mannie Stein looked much older than David. He was dressed all in black and held a black homburg hat on his lap. He reminded Bridget of a crow. And a funeral crow at that. She shivered, took his outstretched hand and went to light the gas fire. It popped and she blew out the match and stayed where she was. He did not speak. She felt panic flutter in her diaphragm. It was something about Tolly. Tolly was dead.

Mannie spoke softly. 'Thank you, Mrs Hall. I feel the cold. Your husband told you perhaps?'

She turned herself and somehow stood up. It *was* about Tolly.

'No. My husband never spoke of that time in Berlin. I knew you joined him there and he accompanied you and your relatives back home. But— ?'

'You did not ask him? Question him?'

April had told her how Mannie could find a weak spot with unerring accuracy.

She spread her hands frankly. 'It was a sore point. I did not ask him anything at all.'

'Ah.' He smiled and nodded. 'You were angry because he went alone. Of course.'

She almost said, 'I was young and silly then.' But she remembered it had only happened just over a year ago. She changed her words. 'You have come to tell me something about my husband? Something that happened in Berlin?'

'No. Although had it not been for Berlin I would not be here now.' He smiled up at her. 'Sit down, Mrs Hall. I have good news. You can afford to relax.'

She sat down very suddenly on a hard dining-chair. Through the two ceilings she could hear Barty starting to cry; she had no idea what Mannie Stein might call 'good news'. Might it be that Tolly had died a hero? Why else would placid Barty begin to wail? As if he knew . . .

Mannie Stein leaned forward and put his hat and gloves on the dining-table and covered her hand with one of his. His hands were long and bony; the finger-nails were scrupulously clean.

'Tolly Hall is alive and well . . . as well as can be expected,' he said quickly. 'Please do not faint, Mrs Hall. He is alive and well, I do assure you.'

Bridie was conscious of the pressure on her wrist and Barty's weeping upstairs. Nothing else.

Mannie stood up and pushed her head down; she resisted momentarily then collapsed like a rag doll. He knelt before her and chafed her hands, then lifted her head and stroked her hair and face as tenderly as any woman.

'There. It is all right, *kindchen*. It is all right.' They were on the chesterfield together; he was cradling her. 'It is no rumour. Two of my . . . cousins . . . joined the Brigade at its inception. They knew your husband. They met him in Berlin and admired him greatly. They told me themselves and I came immediately.'

She recovered quickly from her state of shock, but then tears followed. He dealt with her sensitively, expertly, and she responded to him as she had responded to no-one since Tolly's departure. She began to understand why the rumours about April might have started; he had a way with women. Unlikely Romeo though he looked, he had a way.

At last she said, 'You must tell me everything. Everything. You must explain my husband to me. Oh, Mr Stein, I am so glad – so thankful – to see you—'

'Mannie. Call me Mannie. Everyone does. Tolly did.'

'Mannie then. You are a messenger from the gods. You must stay to supper. Please. And overnight. And talk and talk and talk . . .'

He smiled enigmatically and gave her his handkerchief and she went out to find the disapproving Mrs Goodson and give instructions, then to rescue Barty from Kitty and ask her to make up the spare bed. Tolly was alive. And whatever they said about Mannie Stein, she would love him to the end of her days.

Charles Adair kept up the Edwardian assignation pretence diligently, even to removing one of May's satin danceshoes and pouring a spot of champagne onto the inside of the heel where it would not wet her foot when she replaced it. She couldn't help enjoying it. There was no disloyalty to Monty; in fact this escapade would somehow vindicate all the tea-dances she'd gone to this autumn. She would tell every detail of her 'opera supper' to darling Monty, she would enact it with great exaggeration. They would laugh at Charles's expense. Perhaps it was rather mean of her to laugh at someone who was buying her a slap-up meal, but surely if it put paid to Monty's irritability about Charles, then it was justified? She smiled and fluttered her eyelashes and Charles, somewhat portly these days after looking after so many ladies, scraped back his chair yet again and dropped to his knees before her, causing some concern among the waiters and many veiled smiles from other diners. Somehow May was reminded of the time in London when she and her sisters had gone on the town with three young men who were not their husbands. It had been fun then and it was fun now. And that was all.

But Charles had squired May on and off for a year now, and Sibbie had goaded him only last week that he 'couldn't quite make it any more'. He was a very determined man. He replenished her glass constantly, until he was certain she was on the point of collapse.

'Darling,' he said, fondling her hand across the table. 'I think Charles should take May home now. May is very tired and rather tiddly and Charles does not want to have to carry her all the way down

Northgate Street and get completely lost in the fog.'

May pouted. 'And why not? Is it because May is too heavy perchance?'

'How on earth would Charles know that? Has May ever permitted him to—'

'And May is not tired. And definitely not tipsy. In fact she would like another drinkie please.'

He ordered more champagne and she drank with bravado. Then she stood up.

At once the floor of the dining-room, with all its tables and chairs and palms and string orchestra, tilted up to meet her. She put out both hands to force it down. Her hair came unpinned and fell around her face. Luckily it had grown long enough not to need a full hairpiece, just the curls and fringe in front were not her own.

Charles lifted her hands off the table and put them around his neck.

'Darling May. You look somewhat dishevelled. Let's pop upstairs and put you right, then we can call a taxi.'

'Oh Charles—' She was terrified about the hairpiece. 'Darling Charles. You're so sweet. Is there somewhere upstairs – a powder-room—'

Charles signalled to the waiter and led the way to the stairs. It was as carefully arranged as it had been last year when he and Bridie had so enthusiastically seduced each other at the New County. And May seemed as keen too. Perhaps all these women who had been girls together were the same. So different from wishy-washy Tilly.

The waiter opened the door of the bedroom with a flourish, Charles leaned down and hooked May's knees over his free arm and hoisted her up. She was damned heavy but somehow he staggered over the threshold and practically threw her onto the bed. She clutched at her head.

He closed and locked the door. As he came back to the bed he was already sliding out of his jacket and snapping off his braces. May was fiddling with her hair and groaning.

'Darling Maysie. Have you got a headache? You'll soon forget that, sweetheart.' He sat by her and shuffled off his trousers. Then his underpants. Thank God he hadn't gone into his winter coms yet.

May said, 'No, it's all right, Charles. I haven't got a headache. It's just . . . nothing. Dear Charles, carrying me so carefully. I was a bit groggy downstairs, but I'm all right now. I can drink champers by the bucketful. It's gin that makes me squiffy. I remember when Davie was born I drank half a bottle of gin and I could hardly walk home . . . Charles, what on *earth* d'you think you're doing?'

'Darling, I'm trying to get your damned dress off. I'm absolutely mad about you. Mad. Help me with these buttons before I tear the blasted thing to shreds.'

May sat up and pushed her hair out of her eyes and saw him trouserless, kneeling by her, pulling at her expensive satin dress. She was very nearly unshockable, so she did not recoil or squeak or do anything that would have announced unequivocally to Charles that she was non-cooperative. Instead she said in tones of astonishment and mild reproof, 'Honestly, Charles. I'm ashamed of you.'

He thought this was still the game. 'Oh, I know,' he panted. 'I'm thoroughly ashamed of myself.' And at last succeeded in opening her bodice. He thrust in a hand

and scooped out one of May's large breasts. He kneaded it frantically.

Not only was he hurting her but she objected strongly to seeing so much of herself. Even with Monty she liked the light off these days. Her corset was her second skin. She slapped furiously at Charles's hand and when that had no effect she rolled off the bed, landing with a thump on the rug which immediately skidded on the polished boards and deposited her full length and prone. She was hurt more than ever, she had lost all her dignity and the staff would be investigating the noise at any moment. She sprang up, trying unsuccessfully to stuff herself away again.

'How dare you, Charles! I expected better of you than this – my God, we've been friends for years now and I thought you had a little more respect—'

He advanced grotesquely, first across the bed, then on all fours in his shoes and suspendered socks. The front of his shirt was draped over his erect penis.

'Come to me,' he leered. 'I'll show you plenty of respect. I'll show you—' He stood, grabbed her by the shoulders and bore her down. They crashed to the floor and rolled about clumsily. Then he took hold of a bunch of her hair and immediately she was breathlessly still.

'That's better,' he gasped laughingly. 'I might have guessed this was how you'd like it. You Rising girls are all the same, aren't you? I hear that Jewboy – Mannie whatever his name is – had to force your sister. And Luker must have to rape March every night, she's such a cold fish. And now you—'

May looked into his eyes. She tried to tell him he was a filthy liar, then stopped because to speak would use too much energy. She took a deep breath, sank her teeth into his chin and at the same time raised her knee sharply. He screamed and left her. Then there was an urgent knock on the door.

She left him where he was doubled up on the rug, stood up and adjusted her dress. The knocking grew louder. She scooped her hair expertly on top of her head, found the comb which fastened it to the hairpiece and jammed it in. The knocking was thunderous. She went back to the bed and found her dance-shoes among the rumpled blankets. She slid into them. Charles was trying to be sick. She went to the door and opened it. The porter stared at her wide-eyed, then, as she swept past him, opened his eyes still wider at the sight of the trouserless Charles retching on the bedroom floor. She went on downstairs and asked for her coat and a taxi. The night air was thick with foul fog, but tasted better than the champagne. She breathed deeply as she waited for the cab to appear from the murk.

'Everything all right, miss?' asked the porter anxiously.

'Absolutely tophole,' she said brightly. 'And would you mind telling the gentleman upstairs that he has got the Rising sisters wrong. Completely wrong. And he'd better change his ideas about them, otherwise he might find himself in quite a lot of trouble.'

'Er . . . yes, miss. By all means, miss. The Rising girls. And change his ideas. Else . . .'

The taxi arrived and May stepped into it.

'Else,' she agreed.

She suddenly felt on top of the world. This evening had been positively 'meant'. If she hadn't gone to dinner with the hateful Adair, she would never have known the sort of filth he might broadcast about April.

Yes, the whole thing had been destined. She could tell Monty about it because it was a personal triumph. And Monty could make love to her and it would be like the days at Bushey Park, wonderful and crazy. Monty and May. May and Monty. They were indestructible.

The taxi drew up at Chichester Street and she flung money through the window like they did in the films, let herself in and opened the door of the sitting-room with a flourish.

Monty and Sibbie looked up from the rug in front of the fire. They had no clothes on.

Kitty and Bridget could hardly believe their ears. Tolly, in spite of his schoolboy jaunt to war-torn France, was not the stuff heroes were made of. The thought of him hiding beneath the enormous Olympic stadium, getting hold of two taxi-cabs, bluffing his way past the black uniformed Nazis and the border guards, was incredible. Yet Mannie assured them it was all true.

Bridget breathed, 'He only went over to report to the British Communist Party. He said nothing—'

'The Party would not have approved,' Mannie said gravely. 'To act on impulse is always frowned on. And Tolly acted on impulse. I tried to keep him out of it. He had given me a room, he lent me his respectability. That was enough. But he insisted.'

'And why on earth did your relatives go to Spain to fight almost immediately you had rescued them?' Kitty asked.

Mannie lifted expressive shoulders. 'Franco is a tyrant. They felt they had escaped one tyrant in order to be free to fight another. Also they could not get work in this country. I was not able to place all of them. You can imagine.'

Kitty looked sad, but Bridget said, 'If they had not gone, we should not have known that Tolly was safe.' She leaned forward eagerly. 'Tell us again where and how—'

Mannie smiled. 'You know about the blockade, of course. It was off the coast at Barcelona. There is a regular run from this country, a privately owned vessel stocked by sympathizers. It drops anchor outside the Spanish zone and small boats come to unload . . . Tolly was on one of the small boats. It is very dangerous. Italian fighter planes machine-gun the beach regularly, even in the darkness. But Tolly brought his small boat ashore with my cousins in it.'

The two women listened avidly as Mannie repeated his tale of blockade-running and secret supply lines to Madrid. At the end they sat back, eyes shining, hands clasped.

Bridget said suddenly, 'We'll have a party. Yes. We'll have a wonderful celebration party.' She had been a grass widow since last December; nothing had happened except the bearing of Barty who wasn't even Tolly's child. She had to *do* something. 'Today is Friday. We'll have it tomorrow. We can send the girls round with letters to everyone in the morning. It will be a complete surprise. We won't say a word about you, Mannie. And when everyone has eaten and drunk and chattered away for a couple of hours, we'll produce you like a rabbit from a hat and you can tell us all about Tolly.'

'Really, dear lady, I cannot impose on your hospitality.'

'I insist. It's the least we can do. You must tell them everything. Not only that Tolly is safe, but all this business in Berlin. It's the *only* way to do it. It will be marvellous, absolutely marvellous. My Tolly will be a hero – I'll ask that nice man from the *Citizen* to come.'

Kitty said, 'Are you sure, Bridie? Tolly wouldn't like it, you know. He is so modest.'

'But the time for modesty is past. Oh, Mannie—' she was nearly hysterical. 'You really are Mannie-from-heaven!'

They laughed politely at the joke while she went upstairs to kiss the children good night. But left alone they were silent again until at last Kitty asked quietly, 'How much did your relatives pay you to help them to escape, Mr Stein?'

Mannie stared at her and remembered old Gran Rising and her daughter Sylvia who had seen through him right back in 1919 at April's wedding.

'A great deal of money, Mrs Hall,' he said levelly. 'People will give you everything they have if they think you can save their lives.'

'And what do you think my daughter-in-law will give you for coming here with the news of my son?'

He spread his hands. 'Good will,' he said.

She sighed deeply. 'Yes. Yes, I expect you have great need of that,' she said.

The champagne had caught up with May at last and she went into the grandest attack of hysterics any of them had ever imagined. As she screamed and stamped and clenched her fists, Monty struggled into his clothes and tried to soothe her.

'Baby. Darling. Don't upset yourself. She means

nothing to me. Absolutely nothing. You know yourself she is a professional wh—' May's screams redoubled themselves and he snapped his braces over his vest, left his shirt where it was and tried to take her in his arms. She lashed out with her handbag and blood spouted from his nose.

'Christamighty May, now look what you've done—' He staunched the flow with his shirt. May flung herself onto the chaise longue and went rigid.

Sibbie had slipped into her satin petticoat, but one shoulder strap hung down to her waist and if anything she looked more decadent than ever. She bundled Monty to the door.

'Go away, Monty. Just go. Now. I'll see to this.'

'How can I? Oh my God, my poor May. I love her. What will happen?' Blood dripped from the shirt to his vest. He howled like a dog. May screamed and drummed her heels on the floor.

'She's not going to listen to you. Whatever you say she won't listen. So leave me to it.'

'Don't be crazy! She won't listen to *you*! This is all your fault. You're nothing more than a—'

'Quite. And a whore can talk to a whore. I told you – she's been with Charles Adair tonight. I *told* you. You can see she's drunk and her dress is ripped, and look at her hair. Oh, I can talk to her all right. You go away, Monty. You're not needed here.'

She was actually smiling. She was actually *smiling*. He removed the shirt momentarily and blood gushed forth. He was going to die. They didn't care. He was going to die here and now. He must get to a cold tap and stop this blood. He left, and was not reassured to hear the key turn in the lock.

Sibbie put the key on the mantelpiece and stood looking pensively into the fire. She had thought May would be gone all night, but perhaps this was better. They couldn't go on as they had. Yes, this was better. She smiled again, and May, opening her screwed-up eyes, saw the calm, smiling figure in its clinging petticoat, one beautiful white shoulder bare, and clenched her fists anew. Sibbie was as beautiful as she had been once. The thought of Sibbie and Monty was insupportable. It was, quite simply, insupportable. She screamed. Sibbie did nothing. She did not move, she did not seem to hear the scream or see the writhing figure on the sofa. She continued to smile.

After a very long space of time, May stopped screaming and drumming, and lay very still with her eyes closed. Maudlin tears began to leak from her lids and course down her face. She said something unintelligible. Sibbie asked, 'What?' and she snapped her eyes open furiously and said, 'My husband and my best friend. That's what I said. My husband and my best friend.'

Sibbie controlled a laugh with obvious difficulty and said, 'Oh, May. Darling, darling May. You are so beautiful and I love you so much.'

May's mouth opened slightly and the tears diminished.

'You love me? After what I saw here tonight? You have the sheer nerve to tell me you love me?' She took a deep breath and said with force, 'Hah!'

Sibbie said slowly, 'Don't you see, it's always been because of you? To get close to you? Don't you see that?'

'Frankly, no. I see that you ruined my mother's life. And now—'

'Pardon me, May. I saved your mother's life. It would have been smashed without me. Will – your father – could not have gone on with her if it hadn't been for me. She wouldn't let him sleep with her – touch her even—'

'The doctor said she mustn't have any more children!'

'Oh yes. I remember that one. But later, when she'd finished her periods. What excuse did she have then, May?'

'I refuse to discuss my mother with you.'

'All right. But surely you see—'

'I don't want to see, thank you.'

'Then you must be made to see. It's you I love, May. I loved you when we were children and I've never stopped loving you. I wanted David because he was close to you. I wanted Will for the same reason. And now—'

'Shut up! Shut up and go home!'

'Not until I make you see.' She came and squatted by the sofa. 'Oh, May . . . May. Men are . . . men. You can make them do anything if you lie down with them. But we're different, May. We go on for ever. What ever happens to them – death, unfaithfulness, getting money and losing it – we're still us, May. You and me.'

May stared at the slight figure crouching by her. The drink still befuddled her, but was it the drink that made Sib so persuasive? It was true they'd been inseparable as children, and after every awful thing that had happened they had been able to resume their friendship and become close again. Incredible, but true. Was it really May and Sibbie, not May and Monty? She watched the blue Luker eyes, so like those of the Risings, and felt almost mesmerized.

Sibbie said softly, 'Don't fight it, darling. Please don't fight it any more. Tell me you love me.' She put May's hand to her lips. 'Tell me, May. Please. I cannot live without you any longer. Just tell me you love me.' Those blue eyes filled with unaccustomed tears also, and May could feel the lips trembling against her knuckles.

She whispered obediently, 'I love you, Sibbie.'

Sibbie sobbed a laugh. 'Oh, May. Oh, May. I'm so glad, so thankful.' She put May's hand to her breast. 'Feel my heart, how it is beating. For you.'

May could indeed feel the pounding heart. And the soft breast beneath the slippery satin. Sibbie moved the hand, massaging herself. Suddenly she leaned forward and kissed May full on the mouth. May stayed very still. Sibbie's mouth opened and her tongue forced a way between May's teeth. She moaned.

And then May, the unshockable, was shocked. She stayed for a second longer, telling herself it was not so, praying it was not so. But Sibbie, believing that she had kindled a similar passion in May, was carried away by her own ardour. She pressed her body close and wound her fingers in May's hair.

This time May's scream was more of a screech. She wrenched herself back and at the same time shoved Sibbie from her. The caressing fingers, torn brutally away, still held the finally vanquished hairpiece. They clung pathetically to the only part of May they would ever hold: the false part. May gave a last disgusted, shivering push, and Sibbie fell backwards onto the hearth-rug, her bare legs waving helplessly, the small thatch of wig aloft and somehow obscene. May sprang up and stood over her.

'My God! You're . . . you're *queer*!' she spluttered. She looked down at the frantic sprawl of female limbs and the whole awful evening dissolved into alcoholic laughter. 'My God . . .' She thought of David, of poor Albert's friend, Harry, of her own father Will, of old Alderman Williams . . . and she could not stop the laughter. 'My God, all the time, they all thought . . . scarlet woman indeed . . . femme fatale indeed . . . you're *queer*! You've never really loved a man in your life, have you?' She reeled around the room picking up discarded clothing and throwing it at the satin shape that was now frozen in horror. 'You poor fish, you! You're not a proper woman at all—' She leaned down and took the hairpiece from numb fingers and went to the mirror. 'When that dirty old man started on me tonight—' She gazed blearily at her reflection and began with drunken care to put everything right. 'I realized then that I *was* a proper woman. More than just a woman. A whole human being. All the love I've had and I've given . . .' Her lip trembled and she peered closer through sudden maudlin tears. 'Mother. Dad. Monty. Victor—' The shape on the floor tried to cough a contemptuous laugh, but May whirled on it. 'Oh, don't worry, I saw what you were getting up to with Monty. And at first I thought it was the end. But now . . .' She began to laugh again. 'Now, don't you see? It's really funny. Oh, we'll laugh about it tonight, Monty and I. We'll really laugh. First that ghastly Adair man. And now you. Oh my God, it's so *funny*!' Tears poured down her face. She marched to the mantelpiece, seized the key, unlocked the door and flung it open. Monty almost fell into the room.

Sibbie gathered her clothes to her and hugged them

protectively. 'Monty—' she begged, getting to her knees.

May said confidently, 'Don't worry, darling, I'll deal with this.' She rolled her eyes. 'All this time, she's fooled everyone. I ask you. Queer!'

Monty shrank against the wall as if she'd announced Sibbie had leprosy. May pointed through the hall to the front door.

'Come on. Out.'

Sibbie gasped, 'Let me get dressed – oh, May, please let us talk. You can't be right. It can't be true—'

'Out. You can dress as you go. It'll help to warm you up.'

Sibbie would not have believed May could be so heartless. She protested desperately, but May was adamant. She stalked to the front door, opened it, tore one of Sibbie's garments from her and threw it into the street. She returned for another.

Sibbie was weeping piteously. 'May, it's not like that. Really. Oh God, oh God, oh God, oh God—'

'There's a church just by the taxi rank,' May snapped. 'You can do your praying in there. Then get a taxi and go home to that poor idiot you're married to. I'm afraid you'll have to put up with him in future too, Mrs Williams. Because if I hear of any more hanky-panky, I shall let everyone know that you're a queer. Don't forget, will you?' She caught hold of Sibbie's arm and with a strength she hadn't known she possessed she bundled her out of the sitting-room, along the passage and down the steps. Then she slammed the door.

Monty said, 'This is terrible. Terrible. May, how can you ever forgive me?'

'Oh, darling . . .' May, suddenly euphoric, draped

her arms around Monty. 'There's nothing to forgive now, is there? Perhaps this is what Mother knew all the time and that is why she was so good about Pa. Did you hear what happened?' She kissed him on the nose. 'Don't pretend you weren't listening.'

Monty was astonished. 'Well, yes, I heard. But . . . you're taking it so well. I mean . . . I thought it would be the end of us. All you've had to put up with, now this.'

'I think it might be a new beginning.' She began to tell him about Charles Adair and how she had left him at the Bell. Then she led on to her feelings about Sibbie. Somehow she found words to explain the inexplicable.

'I feel as if I'm free at last,' she said. 'Oh, I know I've enjoyed her company – I'm not that hypocritical, darling. But it was only a stop-gap because you and I . . . we seemed to be drifting apart. Now I see that whatever happens to us – Charles . . . Sibbie . . . losing the Bushey Park house, oh, *everything,* it won't matter. Because we'll always be there. We can weather anything, Monty. We're two halves of a whole. That's so obvious, isn't it? But tonight I know that with my – with my *soul!*' She shivered and pressed closer. 'Is it Charles's champagne, darling? Shall I wake up tomorrow and feel differently?'

He held her tightly. 'Just to know it for a second is enough,' he whispered hoarsely. 'Oh, May, you're magnificent. Magnificent. So strong . . . my darling girl. Don't let me go. Never let me go.'

'I won't, baby. I won't.' She kissed him. 'Come to bed with Mamma, darling.' She led the way upstairs. She hadn't felt this enveloping tenderness for him since . . . since Victor's conception.

And at the big house in Barnwood, Sibbie sobbed her heart out on Edward's chest.

'You see, Edward, Pa was a drunkard – no good to Ma except to father all us kids. And then Ma fell in love – she really fell in love with Will Rising. And just for a little while he loved her too. Made her feel a queen.' She hiccupped like a small girl and he held his handkerchief to her nose and made her blow. She stared at him as if she were indeed drowning.

'Then Sylvia got to know about it and warned him off and he dropped Ma like a hot cake. For ages she was heartbroken. Then she told me to be hard. To get what I could out of life, out of men. And your father took me up. Well, you know the rest. I never loved him. I suppose I loved Will for the wrong reasons – to get some kind of revenge for Ma. I don't know any more. I just don't know, Edward. What is happening to me – am I going mad?'

'Of course not. Don't upset yourself, my darling. It's all so natural. If all the men you knew wanted you for what they could get, then obviously you would prefer women. May especially was your childhood friend—'

'But you weren't like that, Edward. You put up with the disgrace – losing your seat on the council – everything – for me. And yet I still—'

'Darling, listen to me. I knew about Monty Gould. And I guessed about Charles Adair. And perhaps others too. And I knew that you loved me best. It's quite simple, Sibbie. It was a habit—'

She laughed pathetically and buried her head on his shirt front. He stroked her hair.

'Does that sound funny? But that's what it was, really. You couldn't really relax with me. Perhaps you didn't entirely trust me. Perhaps you were simply bored. You had a power over men, and it didn't mean much to you, so you felt no disloyalty to me when you used that power.'

She said in a low voice, 'I did feel disloyalty.'

'Darling, it didn't bother me. Not that much anyway. Because I knew, eventually, you would forget them and come back to me.'

'If May had . . . if May . . . I wouldn't have come back to you then, Edward.'

'I think you would. Eventually.' He stroked her hair and said quietly, 'Did you realize the extent of your feeling for May?'

'No. I've always known I loved her. But I never thought it was . . . like that.' She pressed her forehead hard against him. 'Oh, Edward, I can't live with myself – I can't bear it—'

'Yes you can,' he interrupted firmly. 'You've got me to help you. We can learn to live with it together.'

'But you must hate me.'

'No. I'm thankful in a way. It has brought you back to me as nothing else could have done. And it explains so much.' He kissed her head. 'And the fact that you came home and told me . . . that is the greatest compliment of all.'

But she continued to weep, and he knew that this had beaten her as nothing else in her life had done. He nursed her tenderly as he had nursed Bridget years ago when she had tried to drown herself. And for the first time in his life he thought of the Rising family with dislike.

Chapter Eleven

The party was not to be enormous. The Rising girls and their families, of course. The Adairs and the Peplows and the Langhams. Bridie was very tempted to bury the hatchet and ask her father and his awful wife, but when she went round on Saturday morning to ask May's advice, May was unexpectedly adamant on the subject. 'Certainly not,' she said. 'If your father would come on his own – but who wants that creature?' Bridie was a little huffy. 'You seem to have wanted her over the past year,' she pointed out. 'Not any more.' May laughed and waltzed around the room. 'I'm free, Bridie. Free as air. Monty earns good money now—' She remembered why he earned good money and kissed Bridie contritely. 'Not that I shall mind when Tolly comes home and he has to go back to his old job, darling. Don't think that. Money doesn't matter any more. Monty and I might set up in business together anyway. Or we might go to live abroad.' Bridie smiled secretly, knowing that May did not believe in Tolly's return. She said happily, 'Don't be silly, Daddy would never reduce Monty's salary now. So that's settled. No guests who are proven fornicators—' They both giggled, feeling young and wicked again.

March and Chattie were cleaning Albert's room when Olga arrived with the invitation. Albert was coming home for the weekend and would arrive at any moment.

'Well, of course he can come, Aunt March.' Olga was a thin, stooped child, very earnest. 'Victor is coming. And Davina and Flora. And Robin Adair. And Beryl Langham.'

'Then of course we'd love to come.' March felt a surge of excitement. Life was very dull now that she ostracized Fred. It would be marvellous to go somewhere, and with Albie too. 'Uncle Fred won't want to, I'm afraid, so Albie can take his place. How's that?'

But Fred came in at that moment and acted the benevolent uncle.

'Uncle Fred would simply adore to come!' He waggled his eyebrows and made Olga laugh. Then he gave her a ten-shilling note and told her it was for her trouble.

'It's no trouble, Uncle Fred.' Olga was fiery red; she knew that Fred Luker was a bloated capitalist and she should throw his ten shillings back in his face, but she had a lot of her mother in her.

'Then that's half a quid for no trouble,' he said gravely and saw her to the gate and told her she was going to drive some man demented with love one day soon. She got on her bike and pedalled fast towards Winterditch Lane.

He went back to Albert's room and told Chattie to scat. She left.

He said directly, 'How long is this going on, March?'

'What's that?' She turned the bed down with great care.

'This frozen fish business.'

'Oh don't be silly, Fred. And I wish you wouldn't

talk to Chattie like that. Scat indeed.'

'All right. We'll talk in front of her if you'd prefer.' He went to the door. 'Chattie!' he bawled. 'Come back here!'

'For goodness sake, Fred—'

'Ah, Chattie. I was just asking my wife why she is acting as if I've got a contagious disease. She would prefer you to be here.' He draped an arm across Chattie's shoulders. The girl looked from one to the other with wide eyes. Fred said conversationally, 'She hasn't slept with me since last June, you see. D'you know what conjugal rights are, Chattie? I haven't had mine for a long, long time, and I want to know why.'

Chattie stammered, 'Please, sir. I've got to get clean pyjamas for Master Albert.'

March, white with anger, forced herself to sit on the bed and play Fred at his own game. She even managed a smile in Chattie's direction.

'It's all right, Chattie. You're one of the family now after all. I don't want to sleep with Mr Luker because he has been committing adultery with Mrs Adair. That's what he wants to know. And what he wants you to know.' She stood up and picked up a duster from the chest of drawers. 'You can go now.'

Again Chattie left and as she ran along the landing they both heard her sob.

March said, 'Satisfied now?'

Fred looked at her back as she flicked the duster around the window ledge. He closed his eyes.

'Are you?'

March did not reply and after a while he asked, 'How did you find out this time? My sister again?'

March adjusted the window nets. 'No. She tele-phoned me herself. And of course since then I've seen her. And her bruises. She's rather proud of them, isn't she?' She tinkled a laugh. 'I do hope you will end up in prison, Fred. Yes, I really do hope that.'

He said, 'When did she ring you? Last June?'

'Yes.'

'And you've waited this long. How much longer would you have waited before you told me?'

'For ever.'

He frowned and lifted his head. 'I don't get it. Don't you want a divorce? Don't you want me to go?'

'No.'

'Are you . . . are you going to forgive me? For Albert's sake?'

'No. Never.'

'But . . . we can't go on like this, surely?'

She opened a drawer, moved some hankies, closed it again. 'I don't see why not.'

'Because it's impossible. You. Me. Leading separate existences. Why don't you leave me?'

'Why should I? It's my house.'

He leaned against the wall, understanding. 'Ah.'

She whirled round. 'What is that supposed to mean? D'you blame me? What would I get from a divorce? The law is all on the side of the man even if he is the guilty party. And the disgrace – for Albie as well as me. No. You might have fallen for another woman, but I am your wife. And I am going to stay your wife.'

He stared at her levelly until she turned away from him and sat on the bed again.

'I see. And you're going to make my life miserable. You're going to poison Albie against me. And you're going to . . . what is that American phrase – you're going to take me for every cent I've got.'

Her hands gripped Albert's counterpane and made two pleats across its silken width, but she said nothing. He waited. After what seemed like a very long time, he went out.

Albert went straight from the station to see Davie, so he heard about the party from her. She seemed to have recovered completely from the tragedy at St Ives, but she was different. He watched her as she helped her mother and Aunt Sylv with laying the midday dinner table, and tried to pin it down. The eight weeks at grammar school showed in a new dignity; and she was gentler with Flora in a way that distanced them; for the time being she had left her sister behind. Albert noted her maturity with a thrill of gladness and a tinge of regret. He had loved her all her life, so it was sad to see childhood leaving her; on the other hand he was in love with her now and there was guilt attached to being in love with a girl of eleven. He wanted her to grow up.

She laid an extra place for him and said in a low voice, 'You're staring. They'll notice.' And that confirmed her difference, because last year she wouldn't have cared who noticed. He rejoiced that their cataclysmic discovery on the cliffs of Carbis Bay was still a secret. It was unique; not even Aunt April could understand.

But Aunt April did not notice anything because she was arguing, most unusually, with Aunt Sylv.

Aunt Sylv said stubbornly, 'Look. If they'd a wanted me to come they'd a put my name on the card. An' it en't there.'

'Because Bridie forgot. She'll go berserk if you don't come. You'll spoil it for her.'

'I'll keep the fire in for when you gets 'ome. If it's another frost like last night Flo can undress down yer and get straight into bed with 'er 'ot water bottle.'

April said, 'We shall bank up the fire and put the bottles in the beds before we go.' She clinched things: 'If you don't come, I'm not going.'

Albert's smile widened with pleasure. He wondered why arguments here were so heart-warming, yet at home they chilled him to the soul. He gathered up the cutlery Davie had just placed.

'I can't stop. Honestly. They're expecting me at Bedford Close, and anyway I'll see you tonight at Aunt Bridie's. Walk to the gate and tell me about your posh school.'

Sylvia frowned and said something about the cold but April laughed and told Davie to put her coat on.

'Children don't feel the cold, Aunt Sylv.'

Sylvia said, 'They're not children. Not where each other's concerned.'

April shook her head. 'Even more reason for them to walk out to the gate together.'

Davie said, 'School's not really posh. But it's very hard work. I'm not a bit clever, Albie.'

'You're perfect, that's all.' He led her outside the gate so that the privet sheltered them from the house. 'Don't let them change you, Davie.'

'Oh, Albie . . . is it all right? I mean, do you still . . . you didn't write last week and I wondered . . .'

'You asked me not to write, you darling idiot!' He flung his arms around her and hugged her hard. She was taller than she'd been at St Ives, her hair tickled his nose. He held her away and looked at her, laughing with sheer pleasure. 'You said they'd suspect something if I wrote every week and as I was coming home for the weekend you could manage without a letter.'

She whispered, 'I know. But I love you so and I'm frightened you're going to wake up one morning and realize I'm just Davina Daker. Oh, Albie, do you *really* love me? Really and truly? Like Hedy Lamarr and Charles Boyer?'

He knew he shouldn't but he did. Very lingeringly he kissed her. She became pliant in his arms. It was almost frightening. He glanced around them; the country lane was deserted.

'Davie. Darling.' It was like waking her up. She opened her eyes and smiled right at him. 'Darling, I asked you to walk out here for a special reason. I've bought you something.'

She straightened and moved away from him with obvious difficulty. He put his hand inside his top coat and found the small jeweller's box in his pocket.

'Oh, Albie. Oh, my darling, you shouldn't.'

'I told you I would. I've been saving. It's a real one, Davie. A real diamond engagement ring. When I give you this, it means we're . . .' He wanted a more important word than 'engaged'. He slid the ring onto her third finger; it was slightly loose, but of course she would grow into it. He told her, 'It means we're betrothed.'

She looked at the ring and her eyes filled. She said shakily, 'I plight thee my troth.'

'You've been reading the wedding service.'

'Yes.'

He bent his head and very tenderly kissed the ring

that sat so loosely on her girl's hand. He said, 'And thereto I plight thee my troth.'

They both agreed it must still be a secret, so she wore the ring on a piece of tape around her neck when she went to Aunt Bridie's party. It made everything wonderful. April always said Bridie was a marvellous organizer, and she was in her element organizing all her daughters, her mother-in-law, Mrs Goodson and the catering staff who came in from the Cadena and kept smiling even when she constantly swept through the kitchen giving orders. Mrs Goodson had folded back the doors between dining-room and sitting-room, rolled away the carpet and put down french chalk. Mrs Hall had hung the Chinese lanterns and arranged huge displays of rowan berries, late chrysanths and beech leaves. The girls had pushed the dining-table into the breakfast-room and covered it with newspaper under the cloth. They had cleaned the silver and polished the glass, and if they'd noticed the tall man in black who had drifted about the house occasionally, they'd thought he was another waiter and ignored him. He was now nowhere to be seen.

David, who could not dance because of his leg, was officer in charge of the gramophone. He turned the handle diligently and watched, smiling, as April foxtrotted with Monty, then Albie, then Victor. He noticed that when Fred asked her for a waltz she shook her head and disappeared into the kitchen, where help would not be needed tonight. Fred danced with Bridie instead, smiling down at her and saying something which made her laugh delightedly. Fred was no longer the rough diamond of the family; March had done a good job on him. David looked at March and recognized only too well her tight, determined smile. She might have given Fred a social veneer, but he wondered at what cost to herself. As for Monty and May . . . he grinned to himself, remembering their blatant, flirtatious behaviour at his wedding nearly twenty years ago. They hadn't changed: there'd been ups and downs galore, but they were still at it, staring into each other's eyes like a pair of romantic screen lovers. How May had infuriated him by her superficiality in those days. No longer. He caught her eye and shook his head in mock reproof. She burst out laughing and he knew that she was following his line of thought; it was good to be friends with May again. Then April emerged from the kitchen and made a bee-line for him and he tried to look at her thin beauty objectively and could not. She was not just beautiful, she was . . . everything. His salvation; his pride in living; his joy . . . everything. He thought of their precious, fragile love, and felt terror and triumph in equal proportions. It was the ultimate achievement to love someone better than life itself, but it was very frightening too. If she stopped loving him he couldn't live; but he couldn't die either because of Davie and Flora. What an idiot he was. He looked for Davie and saw her in Albert's arms. His first child, named for him. His little apple. Flora was wonderful, a second miracle. But Davie had been the first, and Davie had saved April for him.

She said, 'I don't think we'd better dance together again, Albie. Everyone will guess.'

'If I can't dance with you I don't want to dance with anyone,' he said, being deliberately childish.

'You danced with Mummy. You danced with Olga. And you ought to dance with Natasha.' She cleared her throat. 'You can dance with Beryl Langham if you like. I don't mind.'

He longed to kiss her. 'Beryl Langham belongs to Victor, I think,' he said. 'Whether he wants her or not.'

She smiled. Then said, 'I think Aunt Sylv saw our engagement ring when I was getting dressed, Albie. But she won't say anything. She understands.'

Fred put one hand on the shoulder of Charles Adair, the other on the arm of his son, Robin. 'I've got some rather special cigars. Let's take a stroll in the garden and smoke them,' he said benignly.

'Right-ho!' Charles let himself be manoeuvred towards the french doors, sensing that Luker wanted to talk business. 'Come on, Rob old man. Stop looking covetously at the Langham girl.' The three men edged into the frosty night and closed the doors behind them. Above, a window slid quietly upwards.

Fred leaned casually on the terrace wall and made no effort to produce the promised cigars. The night was full of stars and he examined them with interest.

'What happened about the girl you made pregnant, Rob old chap?' he asked with obvious insolence. 'She was a Forest girl if I recall, so it must have been an expensive business. They're notoriously stubborn. Independent they call it.'

Charles came to attention, but Robin was not so sharp. He sniggered.

'Cleaned me out, I can tell you. Little slut wanted to marry me! *Marry* me!'

'Oh dear.' Fred sounded concerned. 'Just so long as

she registers the baby in her name and there's no mention of you. Danby was it? Amy Danby?' He turned round and looked at Robin Adair. 'I used to know her old dad.'

There was a long silence. Charles said at last, 'What are you getting at, Luker? Come on, out with it.'

Fred smiled. 'I want something from you, Charles my old fruit. My dear old fruit. A couple of things actually.'

'Well, you need not think you can use that business of Robin's as a lever. The girl promised – his name won't be so much as breathed—'

'I know Danby. And other freeminers of the Royal Forest of Dean. And if I did some talking they'd be up to Gloucester in an hour flat, with picks and shovels and bloodlust.'

'Stop talking melodrama – come on, Rob, let's get back inside.'

Fred said, 'Heard that old story about the Kempley lad who smiled at a Forest girl in the Gaveller's Arms and was shot for his trouble?'

Robin answered. 'It's just a tell tale. To frighten strangers away from their women.'

'He was Grampy Rising's brother. Old Gran Rising went to Mitcheldean herself to pick up the baby when it was born. She brought him up with her own children. He's called Austin Rising.'

There was another silence.

Charles blustered, 'Look here, Luker, what's this all about, for God's sake? If you want a favour why don't you simply ask? Why all these stupid nonsensical threats?'

Fred shrugged. 'I'd like you to know how I stand. Very firmly. Very firmly indeed.' He turned back and looked again at the sky. 'You know about me and Tilly, I expect. It was me who blacked her eye for her in the summer. Did she mention it?'

Charles made a growling sound in his throat and grabbed at Fred's back. Fred side-stepped.

'I didn't think you'd mind. After what you've been up to with my sister. You do *know* that Mrs Edward Williams is my sister?'

'Why you—'

'Quite. And you too it seems. Ah well. Boys will be boys. You. Robin. And me.' Fred sighed sharply and straightened, dusting his hands. 'Well, let me tell you what I want from you. I want your wife off my back. She's broken the golden rule and talked to *my* wife. So that is that.' He looked at Charles Adair. 'And you'd better make sure we're never alone again, Adair, because this time I might easily kill her.' He went to the door and put his hand on the handle. 'And the other thing . . . you've been spreading a false rumour. About my sister-in-law and a man she once knew called Emmanuel Stein. That's got to stop. Do you understand me?'

From the midst of his shock and fury, Charles presented an expression of momentary bewilderment. 'I've already put that right—' He interrupted himself. 'God, you're scum, Fred Luker. You know they call you Filthy Luker? That's what you are. Filthy!' Robin began to make a strange whimpering sound and Charles rounded on him. 'Be quiet, you little runt! If it weren't for you this – this animal – could not talk to me like he has done!'

Fred said levelly, 'Do you understand? Have I made myself clear?'

'Christ. Crystal clear. I'd like to kill you with my bare hands—'

'Then that is all right. As from now, I do not wish to set eyes on your wife again.' He turned the handle and slid into the big room. Robin began to cry. Charles hit him across the face. Above them, the window was closed.

Beryl danced with the palm of her left hand on the back of Victor's neck, her body arched against his arm. She knew their closeness over the past year was largely due to Albert's absence at Birmingham, and occasionally that knowledge made her petulant. She was annoyed with everyone and everything. Annoyed with herself for loving Victor so hopelessly; annoyed with him for being so young, but especially annoyed with him because he remained obstinately unbesotted.

She said now, 'Frankly, darling boy, I'm bored with art with a capital A. Also bored with a capital B. The only decent thing that happened on your painting holiday – the only un-boring thing anyway – was when that poor idiot was electrocuted. If I have to hear anything more about primitive painting I'm practically certain I shall scream.'

'Oh, shut up, Beryl,' said Victor.

'I mean I quite liked the idea of a series of paintings of little me. But when you started putting the paint on with your bloody fingers—'

'Don't swear. It doesn't suit you.'

She smiled angelically. 'Bloody. Bloody. Bugger. Sod,' she said.

'See what I mean?'

'Oh, shut up, Victor.'

'All right.'

He saw Albie dancing with Davina and knew that the holiday at St Ives had been just a temporary bridge between them. The Siamese twin-ship which the two boys had had for so long was gone. Victor felt a twinge in his nasal passage, almost as if he might be going to snivel.

Fred said, 'David, may I have the honor of waltzing your missis around the floor?'

David grinned. There was something rather special about tonight: April's allegiance; Davie and Albert; Flo talking earnestly to Catherine Hall over by the fireplace where Olga was toasting early chestnuts; and now Fred . . . he liked April being called his 'missis'.

'Just this once,' he conceded.

April said, 'I'm a bit done-up, Fred.'

But Fred took her arm and said smoothly, 'Then I shall allow you to float.'

They made a half circle of the large room without speaking.

Fred was an excellent dancer and April tried to forget her disinclination to be seen with him.

He said, 'It would look much odder if I didn't ask you to dance.'

She smiled because he had so accurately read her thoughts. 'Yes. I expect you're right.'

'Anyway I've got some good news and you must hear it. That – er – rumour. I've scotched it for good and all.'

She looked at him sharply. 'How?'

'Can't tell you. Just believe me. You can relax from now on. It's finished.'

She continued to search his face for clues.

'I don't see how you can *stop* rumour. You can deny it, but to dam it up—'

'Listen. Apparently it started from Charles Adair and went to Bridie Hall. You stopped it at that source. I've stopped it at the other.' He whirled her into a reverse turn. 'And believe me, I've had my ear to the ground. If there'd been a breath of it anywhere else, I'd have heard. Now do you believe me?'

'Yes.' She sounded doubtful still. 'But what if Charles Adair wasn't the source? Bridie said one of Mannie Stein's mannequins had told Charles—'

'Is that very likely? Think about it, April. Mannie Stein would hardly tell his girl that he'd been . . . well, you know, he'd hardly mention other conquests.' He could feel her wincing and went into another fierce turn. 'Believe me, Charles Adair would say anything to get what he wanted.'

April forced a smile and nodded.

He said casually, 'By the way, what's this I hear about Davie getting engaged?'

'Engaged?'

'To Albie apparently.'

She started to laugh, then stopped because Bridie was beating the dinner gong. Everyone stopped dancing and David took the gramophone needle off the record. April patted Fred's arm and slid upstairs to the bathroom.

'Thank you – thank you, everyone!' Bridie was flushed and beautiful. She was wearing a low-waisted dress with a huge shawl collar, and her neck looked swanlike. 'Now . . . it's supper-time, but before you go into the breakfast-room to see what those marvellous Cadena people have got for us, I have a surprise.' There were ooh's and ah's and some of the children clapped sporadically. 'Yes. Well, I told you it was a surprise party, didn't I?' She beamed and looked for her mother-in-law. 'Kitty darling, come and join me. And girls, gather round and listen very hard. It's the most wonderful surprise you will ever have in your whole lives!' She clasped her hands beneath her chin. 'Darlings – everyone – Tolly is alive!'

There was a momentary hush, then the two dozen people gathered around her burst into noise. Cheers and clapping and questions bounced back and forth. Kitty Hall began to weep and smile and nod. Olga screamed and flung herself on Albert. Beryl kissed Victor.

'Of course I am certain!' Bridie answered Monty who was nearest. 'Of course I am absolutely certain. Let me tell you – everyone – listen!' Hush fell. 'If Tolly wasn't already a hero before he went to Spain, we might not know now that he is safe. But, unknown and unsung, Tolly *was* a hero!' Everyone was staring at her. Suddenly she was so proud she wanted to weep. She had been such a fool . . . such an idiot. If only he would come home, she would make it all right. She would.

'You see—' Her voice was husky. 'When Tolly went to the Berlin Games, he was instrumental in the escape of seven people. Seven men who were in grave danger of being in – in—'

'Incarcerated, Mama,' Olga prompted clearly.

Bridie smiled mistily. 'Yes, darling. These men were Jewish. They had very good reason to remember Tolly.'

She continued with the tale as Mannie had told it to her, making Tolly's part in the escape perhaps more important than it had been. Her face worked, but she did not falter. Everyone hung on every word.

Monty said incredulously into the final silence, 'How did you know all this, Bridie? If Tolly didn't tell you at the time, I don't see how you can know now.'

Bridget went to the door which led into the hall.

'Last night, the man who went to Germany to organize this escape came to see me. He told me that one of the escapees wanting to continue the fight against oppression —' her voice became sonorous as her speech slipped into the way she had rehearsed it '— had also joined the International Brigade and had actually seen Tolly at Barcelona. Naturally he recognized him instantly as his rescuer and wrote to . . . this gentleman. And this gentleman concerned came straight here to tell me the good news.' She flung open the door. 'He is here now. Many of you know him already – David especially. To the others, may I introduce . . . Mr Emmanuel Stein.'

Looking more like a funeral crow than ever, Mannie entered the room, smiling and nodding. He took Bridie's hand and bent low over it. Babble broke out again. David looked around for April. She had disappeared.

He waited until everyone had dispersed into the breakfast room for food, then went to where Mannie waited for him. The two men eyed one another unsmilingly for a long moment like two antagonists in a fight. Then Mannie spread his hands.

'It is time we talked perhaps.'

David nodded. 'It is why you came.'

Mannie did not deny it, though his eyes flicked sideways to where Bridie was holding court at the loaded table. David smiled slightly and dismissingly and turned to lead the way to Tolly's study. Up to a point they knew each other very well; as chess opponents they might have enjoyed countless matches.

'Well. So here we are again Mannie, eh?' David drew two chairs from the solid mahogany table and sat in one himself. The study was sparsely furnished but lined from floor to ceiling with loaded bookshelves. When the heavy door was closed they were insulated in the small room; no sound reached them. David noted the dust: this room had remained untouched since Tolly's departure. He said conversationally, 'How many years is it? Eleven?'

Mannie Stein returned the smile gently and took his place opposite David. 'Twelve years and seven months. You have changed, David.'

David shrugged. 'Older.'

'And wiser I hope.'

'In some ways, yes. Much wiser.'

Mannie's smile widened. 'I have not changed.'

'No.' David nodded. 'No, I thought not.' He leaned back in his chair and put his hands on the table. They were loose and relaxed. 'So. Why did you come to Gloucester after twelve years and seven months?'

'To see you, of course. And to report to Mrs Hall news of her husband.'

'How did you know that Mrs Hall had not received news of her husband by letter? Are you still eavesdropping, Mannie?'

'Occasionally.' There were no visible signs of resentment but David knew it was there. 'But hardly from London. As a matter of fact Tolly and I became friends in Berlin. He wrote to me to tell of the rift between—'

David flung back his head with a bark of laughter. 'I don't believe you.'

Mannie continued smoothly, 'Also a friend of mine has contact with a Gloucester man—'

David interrupted. 'Ah. Eugenie. And Charles Adair?'

'So naturally when I learned that Tolly was alive and well, my first thought was to inform his wife and family.' He inclined his head. 'And, as you say, it is always good to look up old friends.'

David sat back and looked around him. Tolly's collection of books was prodigious and must be very valuable.

He said musingly, 'Strange. I did once think we were friends. When we met at the hospital in the war, I suppose the fact that we were both Jewish threw us together. And I had no friends. I did not know what friendship meant. It seemed natural to ask you to be the best man at my wedding.'

'I have always been grateful that you did so.'

'Because there you met April?'

Mannie inclined his head again.

'But—' David's hands were still loose but he frowned as if trying to understand a difficult fact. 'But you must know that she loathes you?'

The veins in Mannie's face suddenly filled up and were etched visibly like a contour map. His voice remained very calm and precise. 'What is it the English say? Love is akin to hate?'

'Hatred is a passion. Loathing is . . .' David closed his eyes as if thinking. 'Loathing is a shudder.' He opened his eyes and stared across the table. 'Yes. April usually shudders when your name is mentioned.'

At last Mannie's voice changed; it became tight. 'Do you ever ask yourself why?'

David said deliberately, 'I assume because you are loathsome.'

'You are trying to provoke me.'

'I am trying to make absolutely certain that you will never try to contact my wife. That you will keep out of her life.'

'She shudders because she wants me.'

'Hah!' David's laugh was mirthless.

'You do not believe this? You are stupid. Blind. You don't understand because you are impotent. Oh yes, I know about that. I *eaves*dropped at the bottom of the stairs in the Barton that time. I know about you, David Daker. And I know about April.'

David regarded Mannie carefully; the veins were bright red, the eyes burning, the lower lip shining with spittle. He said quietly, 'I am impotent, am I? What about Davina? What about Flora?'

Mannie was past discretion. 'Davina is mine. I don't know who fathered Flora, but I am sure it was not you.'

David sat up slowly. 'So. At last I know where that filthy rumour started. Oh yes, I've heard it, Mannie, just as you hoped I would. But I wasn't quite certain . . .' He put his hands palm to palm in an attitude of prayer. 'Now, listen to me. I know you are lying – I do not care how often you protest because I *know* you are lying. But lies can still cause distress. I do not want April to hear this lie. Do you understand me? The people to whom you have told this – this fabrication – must be enlightened immediately. And tomorrow you must return to London and not come here again.'

'And if I refuse to obey your orders you will perhaps

314

hit me again? As you did when you found me with April last time?'

David smiled. 'No. It is too stupid . . . and unnecessary. If you do not do as I say, I shall inform Bridie, Charles Adair, your London contact, the press in fact, exactly how much those poor Jews had to pay you for obtaining forged passports and running clothes.'

Mannie stared and the veins subsided. He said tentatively, 'I should deny it, of course.'

David lifted his shoulders. 'You must realize that Tolly left me proof.'

'Ah. So that is how his mother . . .' Mannie sat back on the hard dining-chair. There was another silence. Then he stood up. 'I shall of course scotch any rumours I hear. But I cannot scotch what April knows. And what is inside your head.' He moved to the door, smiling again. 'I know you very well, David. You will never ask April for the truth. So you will never be quite certain. And of course April will never tell you.' He turned the handle and opened the door. Outside April was waiting. She was ashen-faced. Mannie flung the door wide. 'Ah. April. It has been very pleasant to meet you all again. What a pity I must return to London tomorrow.' He raised her hand to his lips, his black eyes never leaving her face, threatening to devour her. There was no sound from behind him and he knew that David was sitting there, watching, doubting. He felt an enormous surge of triumph and power. These people, these small-minded, petty bourgeoisie of Gloucester city, would never forget him. To some he was a hero; to others he hovered like a black cloud coming between them and the sun.

And then, quite definitely, from April's thin body,

through her shoulder, arm, hand and then transmitted to his lips, there came . . . a shudder.

He looked back at David, trying to recapture the sense of omnipotence; he reminded himself of the conversation he had overheard through the open window just now, and thought how he could use that to create more mayhem. But it was too late. This thin, pale woman, who had been an enchanting girl, had robbed him of his moment.

He turned back to her and put his face close to hers. 'I hate you, April Daker,' he said in a low voice. Then he left.

Chapter Twelve

It was strange how Mannie's impact on Gloucester, which, at the party, had seemed like the sudden expulsion of a champagne cork, gradually settled with his equally sudden departure. The champagne became flat, then soured. Not only in the Daker household was this evident; the real disenchantment started at the Brunswick Square house and spread outwards very quickly.

Nobody that night had reached the obvious conclusion that if Tolly Hall was alive and well, however preoccupied he might be, he should be writing home. And if he wasn't writing home, then quite suddenly his foolishly heroic act of joining the International Brigade became desertion.

Bridie had known this all the time, but somehow Mannie Stein's news had put it to the back of her head. As other people began to realize it, it returned very much to the front. Olga, Natasha and Beatrice now knew it. Soon so would the other girls. She was in a worse state than she had been before Mannie arrived. She was glad and thankful that Tolly was alive of course; but in some ways she wished Mannie had stayed away.

Perhaps it was just as unreasonable of the Adairs to blame him for their present discomfort; Fred Luker would doubtless have made an opportunity to put his conditions to Charles anyway, but Tilly, grief-stricken though she was, refused to blame Fred for anything. And Charles had a curious grudging respect for him. It was easier to blame Mannie Stein – that creepy little Jewboy – for the fact that they were now stripped of their pretence, and without some pretence life together was practically unbearable.

April, knowing Mannie only too well, waited for the axe to fall. She had no doubt that Mannie had dripped poison into David's ear during their meeting in the study that night, but exactly which poison she had no idea.

For a few days more, Albert and Davie drank of their own very special champagne and were happy. Davie kept her ring around her neck and wrote to Albie every day. And he wrote back.

Then, just before Christmas, Fred went to Birmingham to apply for an Austin car agency in Gloucester. It was the ideal arrangement. Albert was trained at their Longbridge factory and knew many of the managerial staff. Between them they could corner the Gloucester market; and that part of the business would be Albert's. Fred felt his timing was perfect. He was giving Albert a rich living on a plate; in return he had to break up his sentimental romance with Davie. But after all, once he knew the truth, that would surely die an instant death anyway? The truth would be a shock . . . yes, definitely a shock. But everyone had to put up with shocks throughout life; you learned to absorb them and live with them.

He got Gladys to type the letter about the proposed agency. March wanted him to discuss it during her

Friday evening phone call, but he and Albert rarely conversed these days. He explained to March it was a business arrangement and would have more impact if set out on their headed paper. Gladys tucked her chin into her goitre and typed without comment: '. . . as this side of the business will eventually be entirely yours, we had better present a united front at the meeting. I suggest we lunch together first at my hotel . . .' The public venue would make his task easier. He would be able to talk man-to-man there, show Albert that loyalty and fidelity were always relative. Dammit, what could the boy do about it anyway? It had happened, and that was that.

The restaurant was large and chrome-plated. The head waiter led the way to a table at a safe distance from the orchestra and screened discreetly by potted palms. He drew out the chairs, presented menus and disappeared. Fred looked around him: the place was crowded, which was good, the hum of conversation and clatter of cutlery would cover their own talk and fill the inevitable silences too. Albert looked glum in his best suit with his hair greased slickly down from a centre parting. Fred discovered he was sweating profusely and told himself that all the men here had doubtless fathered illegitimate children and not looked after them and protected them as Fred had done.

He said heartily, 'Well, what's it to be, Albert? Shall we start with soup?'

'All right.' Albert sounded ungracious, to say the least. He glanced around the diners, unwilling even to look at his stepfather.

Fred spoke to the waiter and leaned back with a show of relaxation. 'Plenty of time, old man. Good of you to come with me actually. You know 'em all of course, and anyway we must present a united front. As a firm. Luker and Rising.'

'Don't see it like that. I know a lot of them by sight, but they don't know me from Adam. Anyway my record's not much good.'

'Rubbish.' Fred leaned across the table. 'I know the exam results weren't wonderful, but we had a personal letter from your training manager. You are streets ahead of the others in practical work. That counts. Dammit, it's *all* that counts in the end, man. I want you to be there because it gives you clout, my son.' Fred deliberately used the word 'son' and watched for signs of withdrawal. There were none; Albert continued to look bored. The soup arrived. They drank it in silence and decided on beef to follow. Fred sat back again and dabbed at his mouth with his napkin. He drew a breath.

'By the way, old man, I don't want to open old wounds again, but I hope you see now that this course was a jolly good idea. I know you resented me suggesting it in the first place—' Albert snorted '– well, that's what it was, Albert. A suggestion. You need not have taken it up.' The boy stared up at the ceiling in the most maddening way. Fred said levelly, 'I brought no pressure to bear, Albert. Be honest about that, however much you dislike me.'

Albert lowered his gaze and stared past Fred. 'You made it impossible for me to stay at home. Shall we – can we – be that honest?'

'You sarcastic young bugger!' Fred caught his breath and was silent. He so rarely lost his temper, and today he needed to keep it more than he needed anything else.

He waited until the beef arrived. Then he picked up his fork.

'Victor's last year at the art school, isn't it?' he said casually. 'Your mother tells me he's interested in designing stage scenery.'

'Oh?' Albert cut his beef.

'He hasn't had a chat with you about it? I wondered whether you'd got together at your Aunt Bridie's party.'

'Victor and I don't talk much any more. He takes himself too seriously.'

'He takes his art too seriously, don't you mean?'

Albert shrugged and Fred sighed.

'Look, old man. You think I insulted you last year about Davina, and you've borne a grudge ever since. I've done everything I know to make amends—'

'I didn't realize you wanted thanks for sending me on the course and for pushing me forward this afternoon. I thought you were doing it for the business. But anyway —' Albert raised his brows insolently '– if you want me to thank you. Thank you.'

Fred put down his knife with a click.

'I wasn't so wrong about the situation with Davina, was I? Never mind Victor taking his art too seriously, she takes you much too seriously. And you're encouraging her too, giving her a bloody ring. Christamighty, what have you been saying to the girl – she's not twelve yet—'

Albert put down his cutlery too; his face was suffused with anger.

'Be quiet!' He leaned forward. 'Don't talk about Davina – I don't want to hear you – how you got to know about the ring – our engagement – you've no right – no right to *discuss* my life – no right—'

Fred leaned to meet him and gripped his hand hard. 'I've every right. Stop gibbering, boy, and listen. I've every right to discuss whatever affects you.' He looked straight into the pale blue eyes so like his own. 'Christamighty, Albert, haven't you guessed? You're my son. You're nothing to do with that senile old fool in Bath! I was taken prisoner by the Huns and your mother thought I was dead – she married old Edwin Tomms to protect you. You're mine, and I've a right to know what the hell is going on between you and that – that – child!'

There was a terrible silence. Around them the gentle movement of waiters and trays ebbed and flowed with the lunchtime conversation, but the bubble of silence which held the two men made the outside sounds deafening. As if to emphasize this, a three-piece ensemble began tuning up in an alcove. Soon selections from *The Desert Song* were sieved through the other sounds. Very gradually Fred relaxed his hold on Albert's wrist.

'Have some horseradish. Come on, snap out of it.' Albert jerked away and Fred reached for him again. 'You're to stay here. If you act the coward now, we're lost. You've got to take this on the chin, Albert, for everyone's sake, but mostly for yours. Christ, surely you've *thought* about it before?' Albert half turned in his seat but he made no attempt to stand. He looked sick. 'Doesn't it make it better for you, old man?' Fred persevered. 'Knowing that your mother and I have always been . . .' he used a phrase he hadn't used for years '. . . married in the eyes of God? Doesn't that make a great many things more . . . acceptable?'

Albert lowered his head and studied his meal. At last he spoke. 'It makes no difference. None at all.'

Fred frowned, but took his knife and began to eat again. 'So be it,' he said. After a moment, Albert turned and began to eat too. Fred felt suddenly buoyant. Perhaps he would not have to go further; it hadn't been so hard after all. Perhaps Albert was pleased . . . perhaps one day he would even be proud to have Fred for a father. He finished eating and sat back.

'The furniture eventually arrived for the office,' he said expansively. 'I didn't get that chrome stuff after all. Cheap looking. I thought you'd look good behind solid oak. You're a bit slim for the size of the desk actually, old man – eat up and let's have some of the cabinet pudding.'

Albert pushed aside his plate unfinished.

'No. It makes no difference,' he went on as if there had been no hiatus in the conversation. 'Nothing has changed. I had no intention of being beholden to you for my living anyway. I certainly won't be now. I'll come straight home now, get myself a room somewhere, and find a job. By the time Davina is seventeen, I shall have saved enough to start up on my own—'

'Don't talk rubbish, Albert. Why d'you think I bought those premises in London Road? My interests lie far beyond cars now, my son. I bought that business for you.'

'Davie will understand I can't take it. She'll understand that we must do everything properly. Make our own way, get married and have a family—'

'You might well do all those things. But they won't be with Davie,' Fred said brutally. He'd had enough. He knew now how his own father had felt when he had taken the strap to him. Hatred and love. Hatred and love.

He leaned forward and looked into the closed young face. 'Listen carefully, Albert Luker. You are my son. Davina is my daughter. Got that? D'you understand that? You are brother and sister. You cannot marry, and you certainly cannot have a family. Life is not the simple picnic you obviously imagine. Your mother and I had the war to contend with. You've got something else.'

He stayed where he was, fists clenched on the table, head thrust towards the young man who was his son. And Albert stared, stupidly.

'I don't believe you.'

The trio slid easily into a selection from *Rose Marie*. Fred said, 'Why not?'

'Because . . . you and Aunt April. No.'

'She wanted to give David a child. The marriage was on the rocks. She would have done anything – anything – to save it. I was there.'

'No.'

'You young fool. You don't know April. You don't know . . . anything. They'd been married seven years. He was worse than he is now – almost a cripple. Crazy with jealousy of Mannie Stein. Why do you think April came to Bath to be with you and your mother after old Edwin Tomms died? She need not have stayed all those months, but it suited her. She wanted to make sure she was pregnant. She wanted to get herself sorted out. You think everything is black or white, right or wrong, straightforward or crooked. You've always disapproved of me and my methods, haven't you? Think again, my son. Think again.'

'You . . . bastard.'

'No.' Fred smiled coldly. 'No. Sorry, son. You're the bastard. You and Davina.'

'You bastard. You swine. Christ, how I hate you.'

Fred sat back as if satisfied.

'Right. You hate me. Now let's have some coffee and get along to head office, shall we?'

'Do you think – do you actually think, for one moment, that I can work with you again?'

'Of course you can. You'll hate me for a long time. Then you'll begin to understand. Something will happen that will make you see things from a different angle. And you'll begin to accept the position.'

'You fool.' Albert spoke slowly as if his tongue had swollen. 'Yes. You're the stupid one. You're so stupid you can't see . . .' He took a deep breath. 'She doesn't know, of course. Davina doesn't know, and you won't tell her. I shall marry her anyway. You're the only one who knows, and either you'll keep your mouth shut, or – or—' his voice started to shake '– or I'll kill you.' His mouth worked uncontrollably. 'If you think you can destroy our lives, you'd better think again. Nothing – nothing can come between Davina and me. Nothing.'

Fred narrowed his eyes, and felt what might have been a twinge of admiration for the indomitableness of this offspring.

He said, 'Have some coffee, Albert. I'll pour.' He did so with a steady hand.

Beneath the table, Albert's foot found his and trod down hard. 'I mean it. I'll kill you if you try to come between us.'

Fred refused to move his imprisoned foot, refused to wince at the steadily increasing pressure.

'Will you kill Sylvia Rising too? She was the one who insisted that I should tell you. She is the one who said that you would be able to take it.'

For a long moment the agonizing pain in Fred's foot continued; then Albert pushed his chair back and stood up. The coffee pot went flying. And so did the young man who was Fred Luker's son.

He was desperate. He collected his things from Mrs Potter's and left a note and some money. The first train from Northfield station was to Birmingham. He caught it, waited half an hour at New Street and got on the 4.20 pm to Euston.

There was no-one he could turn to now. No-one at all. Except . . . he remembered Tolly Hall telling him that Grandma Rising had asked Tolly to keep an eye on him. And Tolly had passed that on and reiterated that if ever Albert needed help, he would give it.

And Mannie Stein knew where Tolly was.

Fred had been frightened in the war, but not like this. Afterwards he cursed himself that he had not followed Albert from the hotel and stuck to him like glue, but at the time it had seemed more sensible to go on with their arranged meeting and hope that he would turn up. When he didn't, Fred went back to the West Heath house, expecting him to be sitting sullenly there. Mrs Potter was home by then and showed him Albert's note and the money.

'Looks like he in't coming back no more, Mr Luker,' she said in her nasal twang. 'Good boy he's bine all this toyme. Had a bit of a row, have you?'

The first stirrings of alarm began then. Of course Albert would go home; he would go to see Sylv and Davina. He might even confide in the child. Fred sat on the Gloucester train and wondered if Albert might talk her into eloping immediately. Christ, she wouldn't need persuading. Then what would happen to them both? Fred sweated, imagining Albert in gaol and all the Rising linen washed in the national press.

His car was outside the station and he drove to Winterditch Lane through the first of the winter's snow. It clogged his wipers and he had to stop the car repeatedly and clear the sticky wet slush away. He tried to take his mind away from Albert and Davina and think about the new agency he'd been granted. It had been a formality. He had ordered three enormous enamelled signs which would hang outside the London Road garage. It would be a little gold mine for Albert; he would eventually be happy there too. Fred stopped the car a third time and turned his collar up against the weather as he leaned out again to deal with the snow. He was back to thinking about Albert; every thought led back to the boy. Christamighty, what was going to happen with him?

They welcomed him at Winterditch. They were hanging Christmas decorations in the big living-room; Olga and Natasha had been to tea and David was preparing to drive them home. Fred immediately offered to do so. He took David aside.

'Bit of trouble with Albert.' Fred still loathed the way David Daker raised his eyebrows so superciliously. 'He's gone missing. If he turns up here, keep an eye on him, will you?'

One thing about David though, he didn't ask questions.

'Of course. And he will eventually, don't worry. He and Davie are great pals.'

'Yes. Yes, they are. Righto then.'

He wasn't going to get out of the car at Brunswick Square, then he had second thoughts and went inside just in case Bridget knew something. Obviously she didn't. The girls brushed past her in the hall and she turned to Fred with huge eyes.

'You see how they are? They think I drove their father away. Fred, you simply have no idea how utterly miserable I am—'

Somehow he cut her short and got outside again. The snow was turning to rain as he turned right at the Cross into Northgate. The *Citizen* man stood inside the porch of the church, but his summary of the night's news was tied as usual to the street lamp and Fred could just make out through the running ink something about the Rome Berlin Axis. If there were no murders or other local news, the *Citizen* man invariably tried to catch a few customers by writing up those three evocative nouns. Fred had taken the trouble to look up the word 'axis' and as far as he could make out, it meant an imaginary axle. He knew a lot about axles. Without them a wheel could not rotate. He hoped that the Rome Berlin axis stayed entirely in the imagination.

On another impulse he turned left in London Road and went down Chichester Street in case Albert was with Victor. He wasn't, and, unlike David and April, Monty and May asked a lot of questions in the horrible, interested, curious way they always did. He shut them up and instructed them to keep quiet about it until Albert turned up.

'I'm not having March worried unnecessarily,' he said belligerently.

'No, of course not, Fred,' May replied sweetly as they saw him off. Victor said, 'You will let me know,

Uncle Fred . . . ?' But Fred had already slammed the car door.

Obviously Albert had gone straight home to March and told her everything. And March couldn't hate him more than she already did, so there'd be no extra bones broken. He changed down with a horrible grinding noise to take Wotton Pitch. They'd sort it out somehow. Broken bones could be mended and so could broken hearts.

But Albert was not at home. He put the car away and went in through the kitchen, where Chattie, very subdued these days, was laying a tray with a single cocoa cup and a plate of biscuits.

'Mrs Luker was going to have an early night, sir,' she said before he could ask. 'She's got a bit of a headache and I've been brushing her hair—'

'It's all right, Chattie. I won't bother her tonight.' He sat on a chair and took off his shoes. 'Has Mr Albert telephoned her, d'you know?'

'No, sir. No telephone calls at all tonight. We've been very quiet.'

'That's all right then. I wondered whether he'd let her know about the agency. We've got it, Chattie.'

'Very nice, sir.'

'Yes. Well. Perhaps you'd tell my wife. I think I'll go to bed.' He smiled slightly as he met Chattie's veiled eyes. 'No. You take up the cocoa and tell her the news. I'll sleep in Albert's room. And I'd prefer a whisky.'

It was the first time they'd slept separately, though a shared bed meant little enough any more. As he stripped off his damp clothes and huddled under the cold sheets, he wondered if it was the beginning of the end for them.

*   *   *

The next day he left the house before she was up. The rain had turned again to snow and the roads were full of transparent slush; a car had gone into the ditch along Barnwood Road, and as he negotiated the hill carefully, an Automobile Association's yellow motorbike and sidecar passed him. It would probably mean business for the garage; bad weather meant good business. His father had said that in the days when they had humped coal around the city. How simple life had been then: earn enough money to buy enough food to live another day. It was when you had enough money to buy what you wanted that life became complicated.

At the top of the pitch he turned right and went out to Winterditch Lane again. He caught David getting the car out of what they called the 'motor house'. Fred was brief.

'No sign of Albert. I'm going to spend the day looking for him. March doesn't know yet.'

David frowned. 'You'll have to tell her, Fred. She has a right to know.'

'If necessary April can tell her. But it won't be necessary. I'll bring him home tonight.'

'Look, Fred. He's twenty years old. You can't bring him home if he doesn't want to come. He had a night on the tiles and he's back at the factory today. That's all it is.'

Fred got back into the car. 'He's paid off his digs, taken all his stuff. He won't go back there. He might turn up here. If so, can you deal with it?'

He didn't wait for an answer. He was fairly sure that Albert would not try to run off with Davie now. That sort of action had to be done immediately or not at all.

He drove to the railway station and examined the train timetables with great care. Albert had left the hotel just before two o'clock. Half an hour to get back to West Heath. Half an hour to pack his bags and clear out. There was a local train to the city at three twenty. Fred flipped the pages of the timetable frantically, then had to ask for the one covering the London, Midland and Scottish services. When he had that, he discovered there was a train leaving Birmingham New Street for Euston at twenty past four. At half-past four there was a train to Newcastle. Fred closed the book and stared unseeingly at the gas lamp above the head of the waiting booking clerk. And he knew that Albert would not have gone to Newcastle.

'A third-class return to Paddington,' he said curtly, pushing the timetable through to the clerk.

He had half an hour to wait. He found a telephone box and rang March. David was right as he so often was. She would have to know.

'Listen,' he said brusquely when she answered the ring. 'Albert did not come with me to the meeting yesterday after all. He was upset about something. He's taken all his stuff and gone off somewhere. I think he might have gone to London. I'm going to look for him.'

He waited. She started to stammer something accusatory and he cut her short.

'I might be a couple of days. Don't worry.' He put down the phone. Obviously she must know it was something to do with him, and something awful, otherwise he'd be leaving Albert to stew in his own juice. As David pointed out, the boy was twenty years old.

The train rolled in from Cheltenham. Fred found an

empty compartment and settled down to three hours of trying not to think.

He was gone for a week.

March thought she would lose her mind. During that time May was strangely ill and spent nearly all day languidly in bed. Aunt Sylv went back to see to things at Chichester Street, which meant that April was tied to Longmeadow more than usual. She had to take and meet Flora from school because the short cut across the fields was under deep snow, and though she came to see March each day, there were still a great many hours of the day when March and Chattie were alone. March hardly dared leave the house in case the phone rang. Each morning early and late, then again in the afternoon, she grabbed the post frantically. Her only real comfort was when Davie called in on her way home from the grammar school. The child was as anxious as March herself and they would sit and worry together in a way April did not permit. April, in spite of a heavy cold and sore throat, insisted on behaving as if nothing at all was wrong. Since Bridie's party in October, she had seemed very bright indeed.

When school broke up for Christmas on 21 December, the Dakers spent all day at Bedford Close. The large, comfortable house had never known such busy-ness. Every room was hung with paper chains and April decreed that the enormous Christmas tree in the livingroom must be decorated with home-made trimmings only. The table in the breakfast-room was covered with newspapers, and the four females sat around it, cutting, pasting, and painting each morning. In the afternoons they took it in turns to go for walks or to shop. On Christmas Eve, March asked David if he, April and the girls would consider spending the next day with her. She was relieved when he said yes. Chattie was delighted. The mince pies which had been put in a tin for April to take back home with her were produced, and the sherry bottle was brought from the sitting-room cabinet to the table. They drank solemnly, even Davie and Flora sipping at a drop in the bottom of a real wine glass.

'We'll be round as soon as the girls have dealt with their stockings,' April promised. 'Try not to think. Take an aspirin and just—'

There was a piercing yell from the kitchen and the next minute Chattie appeared.

'It's him. It's Mr Luker. The car's just druv into the garage!'

It was indeed Fred. He looked different. His skin had the shrivelled look that comes from the cold, and his chin sprouted stubble. When he took off his hat there was a hard line around his forehead from the rim; his eyes were deeper in their sockets. Some of the strength, some of the power, had gone out of him.

April, David and Flo crowded round him, helping him with his coat, gloves and hat, ushering him to the fire. David poured a sherry and he shook his head and asked for whisky. He looked past Flora to where March and Davie stood very still by the table.

He said, 'He's all right. I haven't seen him, but I know on good authority that he's all right.'

March sat down suddenly. Davie came closer.

'Where is he, Uncle Fred? Why did he leave Birmingham? What's the matter?'

'He's gone away for a while. There was a fuss at the

factory. I don't know all the ins and outs, but it obviously took Albert very hard. He needed to get away on his own. But he's all right.'

'But – where *is* he? It's Christmas tomorrow! Is he coming home for Christmas?'

David brought the whisky and Fred tossed it down like medicine.

'No. No, he won't be home for a while.' He looked around the room slowly as if he'd never seen it before. 'He's gone to Spain.'

Chattie came in carrying a pan of coals from the kitchen fire.

'I'm going to put a fire in the bedroom, Mrs Luker,' she said. 'And do some hot bottles. He's not well.'

No-one seemed to hear her words. They were staring at Fred. March whispered, 'He's too young. It's not our war.'

'No, it's not. But he's old enough to fight in it. He's joined the Brigade and gone out to find Tolly.'

'I don't understand.' March looked at Davie.

'It's nothing to do with anything at home,' Fred said, intercepting the look. 'It's some trouble at the factory.' He tossed off another drink and stood up swayingly. 'You'll have to be satisfied with that. I can't find out anything else. You'll have to learn to accept it. Like I have.' He grabbed at the table edge and hung his head between his arms. 'It could be worse, I assure you. I've seen some things . . . people . . . this past week . . .'

'But money, Uncle Fred. He's got no money.' Davie was beginning to hiccup, a sure sign that tears were on the way.

'Mannie Stein lent him money. And I've paid Mannie

Stein.' Fred laughed horribly. 'I've paid him all right. He's probably still in hospital.'

'Mannie *Stein*?' March shrieked. 'What has Mannie Stein got to do with Albert?'

David took Fred's arm and helped him upright.

'If Albert wanted to know where to find Tolly, Mannie Stein was the person to ask,' he answered March. 'Now let's get Fred upstairs, shall we? I think he's had enough. We can ask all the questions we want in the morning.' He began to propel Fred towards the door. Chattie appeared and took his other arm.

March said, 'But Albert – oh my God—'

Davie sat down at the table and buried her head in her arms. Flora quavered, 'Mummy? Are you all right?' And April seemed to wake from a daydream and enfolded Davie and March in her arms. 'Of course I'm all right,' she said cheerfully. 'My goodness, look at us. We've just heard that Albert is well and coming home soon, and we're acting as if the world is collapsing. Now come on, Davie – he hasn't had an accident or anything, he's just gone to find Uncle Tolly, and when he does he'll bring him home. March, why don't you make a hot drink for Fred? And perhaps a sandwich? As soon as David comes down we'll get off and see you in the morning as arranged.' She patted Davie's back. 'Come on, young lady. You go and get all the coats and hats and scarves in the hall and we'll start getting ready. Now, March, I'll bring a piece of ham for tomorrow. And the pudding of course. Flora and Davie made the pudding, so you'll enjoy that.'

She galvanized them into action by constant movement and adjuration. By the time David came downstairs she had the children in the car and was waiting with David's top coat held ready. She did not stop talking all the way home. Tomorrow they would build a snowman and they could have a proper snowball fight. Maybe on Boxing Day they could drive over to Cheltenham to watch the Cotswold Hunt assemble outside the Queens Hotel. Then they might go to Robinswood Hill to toboggan. It was going to be a wonderful Christmas. Really wonderful.

The next day when they assembled for their shared Christmas, Fred could tell them little else. He had spent four days traipsing around London. The police could do nothing to help; Albert was adult, there was no reason to suspect foul play. The Salvation Army had taken him around some of their doss houses and he had seen sights which he did not attempt to describe. One of the helpers at a YMCA hostel had unwittingly given him a lead.

'I suppose he wasn't one of your political jack-me-lads, was he?' came the question. 'If he was, he might have joined up and gone to fight in Spain.'

Fred had gone back to his boarding house in Sussex Gardens and thought about that. Albert was not a political animal, but he had been desperate. Fred decided it might bear investigation, and Mannie Stein was his first contact.

'Not that long since Stein came to tell us about Tolly,' he explained. 'And Albert was there. It was a long shot, but I was doing anything, going anywhere by this time.'

March, sitting by Davie, tried not to look at the lined, tired face. Nobody here knew, of course. Nobody realized that Fred had been searching for his own son. She stared into the fire.

Fred sighed deeply and looked at his hands.

'Stein is . . . twisted in some way. He sees this as some kind of triumph – revenge – I don't know – against us all in Gloucester. Apparently he listened at the window during Bridie's party and heard some . . . some gossip . . . about the Adairs.' He glanced at March and their eyes met for an instant. 'He was gloating about that. He wouldn't tell me about Albert for a long time, but I knew he had some information.' Fred sighed again. 'You won't approve, David, but I hit him.'

David snorted. 'I hit him myself once. It's not something one approves or disapproves. It just happens. Like breathing.'

Everyone forced a laugh except April.

Fred resumed. 'Eventually he told me that Albert had turned up on his doorstep – he lives in Pimlico – that same day. The Friday he left Birmingham. Sorry, I've lost count of the days, I can't remember how long ago that was. But Albert must have planned it because Stein lies fairly low – he goes under the name of Manuel. That's his trade name and he's got a chain of dress shops . . . anyway, Albert found him somehow that same night. Stein put him up for the night, talked to him.' He glanced again at March. 'Albert didn't tell him anything, I'd have got that out of Stein. All he said was, he needed to see Tolly.' Fred leaned back. 'Stein told him where to go, fixed him up with a passage on one of the boats which run the blockade, got him a passport . . . he was delighted to do all this. He knew it would hurt us here. That seems to be one of his objectives in life.'

David said flatly, 'Yes.'

Flora quavered, 'But Albie might get killed.'

Davina said nothing; like March she stared, dazzle-eyed, into the fire. Chattie could be heard sniffing. April said briskly, 'Of course he won't be killed. He'll probably go in with the Red Cross. And once he's found Tolly they'll look after each other.'

'Why Tolly?' March burst out suddenly. 'If he's in trouble, why not me? We've always been so close.'

April put an arm on her sister's shoulder. 'D'you remember that Sunday when we all went to see Mother – the Sunday she died? She asked specially if she could see Tolly. She loved and trusted Tolly. And Albert was close to Mother, so he obviously loves Tolly especially. Maybe in his mind he puts Tolly in poor Edwin's place and thinks of him as a father. Try not to worry. No harm will come to Albert Frederick.'

Suddenly March turned her head into April's neck and let herself weep. Davie stood up and went to the window. David stared at her for a moment, then turned to Chattie.

'Come on. Let's go and wheel in the goodies. A glass of sherry or ginger wine, a mince pie and we can open the presents.'

April watched him leave the room and wondered why he hadn't gone to Davie, standing alone by the bay window. She said determinedly, 'Everything's going to be perfectly all right. Just all of you wait and see. That's a promise!'

March snuffled a damp laugh and Fred looked past Flora and grinned tightly.

'You're a bloody marvel, April,' he commented. And no-one reprimanded him for swearing in front of the children.

338

Chapter Thirteen

On New Year's Day 1938, Davina Daker became twelve years old. The open, rosy, milkmaid's face, which had given her the nickname of 'little apple' had narrowed and become reserved. As winter gave way reluctantly to spring and there was no word from either Albert or Tolly, she seemed to withdraw more into herself. Her school work suffered badly. She brought home a special report in March suggesting extra tuition in maths and French. David said it was a fuss about nothing, but April made an appointment and went to see the headmistress.

Dr Moore was distantly gracious.

'I expect her obvious talent blinds you to the other deficiencies, Mrs Daker,' she said, sifting through papers in front of her. 'We feel that we must give our girls a good all-round education. They can specialize later.'

'Talent?' April had no illusions about Davina. She was sweet-natured and intelligent enough, but she had always been a practical child, not academic.

'Her voice.' Dr Moore lifted bushy brows. 'She has an exquisite voice, I grant you. And Miss Cyril is – of course – encouraging her, training her. Nevertheless as I pointed out in my report to you, other subjects are definitely . . .'

April frowned. Davina sang around the house of

course, and yes, she did have a sweet, lark-like voice; but was it that special?

'Music and maths often go together, Mrs Daker. We feel that if music is to be Davina's life, she should . . .'

Of course, the first Albert had had a good voice. April just remembered him singing in the Cathedral. Hadn't he been the bishop's page at one time?

'. . . six girls who come in on Saturday mornings for special coaching with Miss Dewhurst. The fee is minimal and the results excellent. Perhaps you and your husband . . .'

'Of course. And thank you, Dr Moore. Thank you so much.' They shook hands, mutually impressed. April went into the big square foyer where no girl trod save in disgrace, and caught a glimpse through the open door of the galleried hall where Davina stood every day for morning prayers. She felt a pang of guilt that she'd had no real idea that her small daughter had any special talent. And she must notice everything about Davina now that Albert was no longer here. She went into the front garden of the school. The May tree was in full blossom: the school emblem. She stared at it. David had not come with her today, nor on Davina's first day here.

That evening Davie sang for them with some reluctance.

'It's not important, singing,' she said. 'Not like proper lessons. Anyone can sing.'

'No. They can't actually.' April sat at the upright piano which so rarely was played these days. 'Come on, darling. We'd love to hear you sing. What shall it be?'

Davie looked through the sheet music on the stand; she seemed uninterested to the point of being bored.

340

Flora did not look up from her book. 'I don't want to hear Davie sing. I want peace and quiet.'

'There, you see?' Davie walked away from the piano. 'And Daddy certainly doesn't want me caterwauling away when he's doing the books.' She hesitated and when David did not immediately reply she said, '*Do you, Daddy?*'

David said absently, 'Oh, come on Davie, give us a tune.'

April struck some chords. 'There, you see? Now come on. How about "Who is Sylvia".' She played the long introduction, and Davie drifted back to the piano. She began to sing. It was in a high key yet her small voice rose effortlessly to it, held the notes, never wavered, was clear and true. April felt on the verge of tears.

David said, 'That was very nice. Well done, little apple.' Flora said, 'Now can I finish this book in peace?'

It was left to April to say quietly, 'You do have a voice, Davie. It's beautiful, like your Uncle Albert's. I think you're going to be a singer.'

'Was Uncle Albert a singer? Albie was named for him, wasn't he? Tell me about Uncle Albert, Mummy.'

April told her. And Flora and David continued to pore over their separate books at the table.

Fred and March occupied separate rooms as a matter of course now, and there was never any need for Chattie to brush March's hair. Fred had a permanent line on his forehead which did not disappear even when he started wearing his soft summer cap. And at last March's hair showed grey threads; she wore it pulled back very severely from her forehead so that it resembled a helmet. She had taken to smoking, too, and had a way of narrowing her eyes against the smoke that made her look cold and rather calculating.

But that spring she and Fred found they were agreed on something; it was unusual. They rarely conversed, let alone discovered a mutual enthusiasm. But they were very keen indeed on getting special singing lessons for Davie. The closeness between March and her niece had continued since Albert's disappearance; Davie called into Bedford Close two or three times every week to see if there was a letter from him, although March had promised that she would drive out to Winterditch Lane the minute she had any news. March looked forward to these visits: they were the highlights of her week. Beneath the surface veneer she was lonely and often afraid. When April confided to her that Dr Moore had said Davie 'had a voice', she thought about it constantly for twenty-four hours. Then she broached the subject with Fred.

'I'm talking about my money, you understand. The money I've always kept separate . . . the money from poor Edwin. But I suppose, legally . . . anyway, I want to use some of it. I'm simply telling you so that you won't accuse me of being underhand.'

Fred said wearily, 'I've never accused you of that, March. And, as you say, it's your money. Do as you please with it.'

'Aren't you curious about what I want to do with it?'

He looked up from the newspaper and eyed her. She was smoking a Turkish cigarette, drawing on it in small fierce inhalations and exhaling almost immediately. He remembered how April had luxur-iated in her smoking, making a ritual of relaxation from each cigarette. March was not like that.

'You want me to be curious so that you can tell me it's none of my business?' he asked in the same disinterested monotone.

She threw her cigarette into the fire and tugged down her jumper. She had taken to wearing jumpers and tweed skirts, a single string of pearls around her neck. It made her look 'county'.

'No. I'd like your backing, actually. I expect to have to face some arguments about this.'

'Oh?' He put the newspaper onto his knees. March's voice was as frigid as ever, but her words were reasonable enough.

'April tells me that the High School think Davie has a very good singing voice. I know she would like to have it trained, but for some odd reason she won't ask David to pay for lessons. Perhaps David is in difficulties at the shop.' March paused, looked at Fred and inserted sharply, 'Have you heard anything about David's financial affairs?'

'No. I imagine he's all right.'

'Really? April seemed most unwilling . . . anyway, I thought I would like to do something for Davie. But you know how difficult April can be. David more so. If they think we have discussed it and are making the suggestion together, it might stand a better chance.'

Fred said, 'I would very much like to help, myself.'

'You would?' March leaned on the mantelpiece and stared down at him in surprise. 'Then let it be on a fifty-fifty basis. And when I broach the subject, for goodness sake back me up.'

Fred nodded. 'All right. But let me pay. Keep your money in case . . . in case things become unbearable here.'

She stayed where she was but he could see her become tense. She said quietly, 'I told you last October. I'll never give you a divorce. So if that's what you mean, you can forget it.'

'I don't mean that. I don't want a divorce for my sake.'

'I see. You want a divorce for *my* sake. How selfless of you, Fred.' She laughed shortly. 'Is Tilly Adair badgering you? Why don't you black her eyes again?'

He took a deep breath and let it go slowly.

'Ah, March . . .' He stood up and went to the door. 'I told Charles Adair at Bridget Hall's party to keep Tilly away from me. Actually, I blackmailed him.' He looked around with a kind of amusement. 'It worked too. I haven't set eyes on her since then.'

She stared at him. He had employed the same tactics to get rid of another mistress, Leonie Porterman. And two years later, her husband, Marcus Porterman, had hung himself. It might not have had any connection with Fred, but on the other hand, it might.

She said, 'Aren't you . . . sometimes . . . aren't you afraid, Fred?'

'Yes. Not sometimes, all the time.' He began to close the door, then he called through from the hall, 'Why don't you have the Dakers round for a proper family lunch on Sunday? We can suggest it then?'

He closed the door, not waiting for an answer, and March stared at the elegantly white-painted wood and wondered. Wondered about Fred and how he could live so successfully on one level, when underneath he knew the burden of the guilt he carried and had just admitted to fear of it. Then she wondered about herself, and if there might come a time when she would ask for a divorce and try to start life afresh. Before the thought could take root in her mind she turned fiercely back to the mantelpiece and reached for the cigarette lighter. She *would* stick it out, she wouldn't lose the little she now had, she would make Fred pay for his betrayals. She would.

The Dakers and the Goulds came to Sunday lunch and because it had been March's birthday the previous week, they brought presents and dressed in their best. March smiled and kissed the children, even Victor, and opened various parcels containing stockings, a blouse, a perfume bottle shaped like a cat, and a necklace from Woolworth's Bazaar. There had been no card from Albert, but March ignored the pain in her chest and throat, and toasted him smilingly in the vin ordinaire brought by Monty. Fred carved the beef and Chattie passed the vegetable dishes and asked Flora if she'd like a piece of gravy-bread, and Monty scurried around with a tea-towel over his arm talking with a French accent. May laughed a great deal and ate even more; she was putting on weight again. After the castle pudding Fred opened the door for the ladies and March, May, April, Davie and Flo trooped into the sitting-room where Chattie had laid the coffee tray. 'All real and proper,' Flo commented delightedly, remembering other 'real and proper' repasts provided by Chattie. Then she also remembered that on those occasions, Albert had been present, and she stopped talking.

March went to the piano. 'Come on, Davie. I want Aunt May and your mother to hear that piece we've been practising.' She turned to April. 'Pour the coffee, darling, and listen. I'm hopeless, of course, but the second part isn't important.'

April did as she was bid. The duet was a plaintive 'sunset' piece, very popular at the time. Davie's voice soared above March's on the last stanza. 'The rooks go westward, calling as they fly.' The female audience sighed their satisfaction. Flo said, 'I can just see that. That's better than "Who is Sylvia".'

March closed the lid of the piano carefully.

'Now. How about this. I . . . we . . . Uncle Fred and I would like to give you a present, Davie darling. We want to send you to special singing classes. What do you think?'

Davie looked at her mother. 'It's expensive, Aunt March. Mother enquired.'

'Did you? You never told me.' March looked across at her sister. 'No, don't tell me how much. It doesn't matter. We want to do it and you know we can afford it. And if Davie has a talent like her Uncle Albert's, it should be properly trained. He never made the most of his.'

'Ah, March . . .' May sighed sentimentally.

March said defiantly, 'Yes, all right. I shall be doing it for Albert. I cannot help my son Albert, but I can help Davie. Surely it makes sense?'

April got up and hugged her sister.

'You are sweet and kind, darling. I'm really touched. And I'm sure Davie is overwhelmed.'

'It's ever so kind of you, Aunt March.' Davie's face was bright. 'It would be . . . nice.'

April's heart leapt at this unusual enthusiasm. Perhaps this was what Davie needed to help her see life without Albert. She said cautiously, 'We must wait and see what Daddy says first, darling. Honestly, March, it's so generous of you I hardly know what to say.'

May was too indolent to get up from her chair.

'Consider yourselves hugged soundly, both of you,' she said, her face wreathed in smiles. 'And now, prepare yourselves. I've got some news. At least, Monty and Victor and I have some news. We were going to explode it after we'd eaten, then we decided to wait until tea-time. But I simply cannot wait any longer, I must tell you.' She leaned forward and pulled one of March's velvet covered hassocks into position with some difficulty, then extended her long elegant legs onto it.

'Well, come on, get on with it,' March said with her usual impatience where May was concerned. She badly wanted to call the men in and put her plan to David. It would be impossible for him to refuse in the face of Davie's keenness. She had planned this very carefully and did not want to be delayed by anything May might have to say.

May lifted one leg and pointed her toe.

'Ankles still slim,' she commented ambiguously.

Flora said, 'You've got beautiful feet, Aunt May. Doreen Byard who lives up the lane said she wished she had beautiful feet like you because they are a sign of a lady.'

'Did she?' May laughed and reached for Flora's hand. 'Oh, darling, I do hope the baby will be like you. You're so sweet.' She looked around. 'Yes, I'm forty-four, girls. And I'm having another baby! What do you think of that?'

For a moment no-one voiced their thoughts, if they had any. Then March said indignantly, 'In front of the children, May – honestly, you're the giddy limit!' And April said simultaneously, 'Darling, are you sure? It would be marvellous . . . but are you certain sure?' And Flora chipped in, 'A real baby, Aunt May? A real proper baby?' And Davie just looked.

'Yes, a real proper baby, Flo. A little girl I hope. And yes, April, I am certain sure. Young Dr Green examined me just after Christmas because I felt so tired and odd and sick all the time. Then he came again last week and told me what it was. And there's no reason why the girls shouldn't know, March, for goodness sake. They're going to have a share, after all. I shall need lots of help with this one.' She looked utterly complacent and repeated, 'After all, I am forty-four.'

'You and Monty, you're incorrigible,' March said, exasperated even as she went to kiss May's hairpiece. 'One minute you're dancing every week with that awful Adair man, then—'

'Darling, that was *ages* ago. And it was because of him in a way. I didn't tell you, did I? He made the most awful pass at me and then I went home . . . oh, I can't explain. But Monty and I laughed and laughed and—'

'Don't go any further, May, please,' begged March.

April said, 'I knew there was something special on the night of Bridie's party.'

May crowed, 'Did you? Well, we think that's when it *happened*! Though of course it could have been almost any night since.'

April and March shrieked in unison and the door opened to admit the men of the party. By the time David and Fred had been told of the happy event and Monty suitably ribbed, March's offer had been robbed of its importance. Singing lessons for Davie seemed almost boring now.

David barely took it seriously. He smiled perfunctory gratitude at March and took his coffee cup from April without looking at her.

'Oh, I don't think so, March. But it's awfully kind of you. Perhaps later.'

'But, David, the school thinks she is really good.'

'She's doing extra maths and French, you know, March. I don't want to overburden the child. There's plenty of time.' David pecked her cheek and turned to Victor. 'And what do you think of having a baby in the house, old man?'

March glanced at Fred and saw him watching David with narrowed eyes. She moved towards him. 'Say something,' she commanded.

Victor was like a cat at the cream. 'Not bad, is it? Considering they're almost drawing their pension—'

Monty jumped his son and they wrestled as they'd done in the old days, laughing inanely. They knocked against the piano and sheet music scattered from its polished surface.

'Honestly, Monty. You're worse than Victor.' March moved in, tidying around their heels as they continued to brawl. Fred looked across at April, met her eyes and said nothing. March slapped at Victor and pushed Monty into a chair by the coffee tray. 'Help yourself. Idiot.' She turned to David. 'You can't leave it at that, David. This is your daughter's future we're talking about. If you've got any pride – any—'

April said, 'March, you haven't had any coffee yourself. Come and sit down and have one of your birthday cigarettes. Perhaps I'll try one too. It's aeons since I smoked.' She pressed March into a chair and said in a low voice, 'Not now, darling. Please.'

March accepted the cigarette box, but for once did

not immediately light up. She sat there with a cigarette between her fingers and watched April frowningly. She had seen all this before: at Christmas time. April being the life and soul of the party. Jollying Monty and May. And before that too; years before; when April and David had lived in the flat over the shop and April had led Gloucester's fashionable world. Something was wrong.

Luckily Flora's attention had been completely diverted by the prospect of another baby in the family, and during her bedtime routine she babbled a list of possible names and asked awkward questions about where the baby was now, until April had to tell her to be quiet and go to sleep. Davie, as was usual now, said very little, and nothing at all about March's offer of singing lessons. April saw her take something from her neck and slip it onto her finger before she knelt to pray. She had no doubt it was some ring she'd got from Albert out of a Christmas cracker or similar. At least Davie still had Albert. If only he was safe and well – whatever disgrace he was in back in Birmingham did not matter – he would come home one day and marry Davie just as March had wished that day at St Ives. At least she would have someone who cared for her more than anyone else on earth.

April went downstairs with dragging steps. Like March she wondered about the future. It was obvious now that David knew Davina was Fred's daughter and was going to say nothing. But could they live for always with such knowledge suppressed between them? She shuddered as she went into the living-room.

'Cold, darling?' David moved towards the fire but Aunt Sylv anticipated him and got to the poker first.

David was notorious for poking a fire in instead of up and out. Sylvia produced a red glow from the banked up coals and drew up a chair for April.

'March is a treacherous month,' she remarked. 'I reckon we'll have more snow before this winter's gone.'

David leafed through the Sunday post and found an air-letter. 'Henry and Miranda. Good. I wrote to them three weeks ago, not bad, eh?' He flipped through the close scrawl. 'Yes, this is in reply to mine.'

April said, '*You* wrote to them?' He usually added a postscript to her epistles.

'Yes. I had something special to ask.' He went over to the bureau, pulled down the writing-flap and spread the flimsy paper flat. 'The answer is yes. I thought it would be. They're good people, Henry and Miranda.' He continued to read and Sylvia settled herself again on the sofa. April spread her hands to the fire and waited.

David folded the letter.

'Darling. Did you mind that I turned down March's offer for Davie?'

'Well . . . no, not really.' April turned to Sylvia and told her about the singing lessons. She already knew that May and Monty were expecting a baby; Flora had entered the house shouting the news to the rooftops. 'David thinks Davie is too busy now with her extra school lessons. But wasn't it marvellous of March?'

'Ah.' Sylvia let her lizard eyes flick towards David for an instant. 'Ah. March is very fond of our little maids.'

'She is. And since Albert went off to look for Tolly she's found a lot of comfort from Davie.'

'I wondered whether Davie might be hurt.' David picked up the letter and tapped it on the bureau. 'But I knew this was on the way and there was no point in making other plans until we were certain what was happening.'

April and Sylvia looked at him, April with apprehension. David shook his head at her. 'You won't like it at first, darling. But please try to understand.' He sighed. 'There's going to be a war, April. It's going to be worse than the last one. Civilians are going to be involved. Remember the Movietone news at the Hippodrome last week? The bombing of Madrid? That's how it will be. Herr Hitler knows about the Gloucester Aircraft Company. He knows about the factories at Staverton. And down the Bristol road. Gloucester will be one of his targets.'

'David, don't be pessimistic. Mr Chamberlain won't let it come to that. And Hitler himself – he's not an idiot—'

'April. It's going to happen.'

Unexpectedly Sylvia offered her support. 'I reckon he's right, April. I reckon no-one can stop that madman now.'

David drew another breath. 'D'you remember Miranda's suggestion when we were in Venice? About the children going to live with them if there was another war in Europe?' April nodded dumbly. David went on, 'I wrote to her about it. I've been putting money aside for your fares. I want to send you over soon, darling. Before it all blows up in our faces. Quite literally.'

He waited, obviously expecting protests and arguments. After a while she said softly, 'Me and the girls? Not you? Davie, Flora and me?'

'Darling, I'd keep the shop going. Somehow. Maybe do some war work too. Try to keep a home for all of us. For after.' He tried to grin. 'Aunt Sylv will look after me. She won't go with you. She tells me she won't leave Gloucester, not even in her coffin.'

There was another silence. April continued to stare at him. She knew now how he was going to cope with the knowledge that Davie was not his child. He was going to send them all away.

She said through stiff lips, 'If you think it's best, David, then that is what we will do.'

There was yet another silence, then David said quietly, 'Thank you, my darling.'

Aunt Sylv stood up abruptly. 'I kin hear that Flora still going on about babies. I'll go and tuck her in. What our May and Monty are thinking about I don't know. At their age too . . .' She left the room.

David said, 'Darling, are you sure? I know how you must feel.'

April said steadily, 'I want to do what you want to do, David. I love you better than anything – anyone.'

He turned away suddenly so that she could not see his face. She spread her hands to the fire but she could not stop shivering.

Victor was first into the house that evening, so he gathered up the Sunday post from the mat, saw Albert's handwriting on a thick envelope, noted it was addressed to him personally, and slipped it inside his coat before he turned with the rest.

'Bills.' Monty made a face. 'Lady Day last week so I suppose . . . golly, it smells cold in here. Wait while I light the fire, Mummy. Victor, coal—' He passed the hod as he knelt down before the empty grate.

May subsided into the chaise longue.

'Wasn't it marvellous to see their faces? Honestly, I can't wait to hear what Aunt Sylv says.' She blew a kiss to Victor as he disappeared in the direction of the cellar. 'Wish I could tell Bridie, but I'm going to leave that to April. Poor Bridie.'

'Don't you wish you could tell Sibbie?' Monty asked slyly. He swivelled on his knees and began to kiss her with pseudo-passion. 'Don't you wish you could see her face when she hears that you and I have done it again!'

They both laughed and left it to Victor to lay kindling and small coal and light the fire. Then they were repentant.

'Darling, how do you put up with us?' May reached out an arm to include him in their embrace. 'It must be such a bore for you, all this baby talk. Are you as pleased as you say you are?'

With his usual grace he crouched before the chaise longue and engulfed them both in a bear-hug.

'I'm pleased and I'm proud and I'm just slightly incredulous. I thought you two were going to be just friends from now on!' He grinned at them and thought of the anonymous letters and wished he could share the joke. But in some ways he was much older than his nineteen years.

'But won't it be rather embarrassing when I make you push the pram into town?' May asked archly.

'Not really. Anyway . . . my old dears . . . this is as good a time as any to tell you, I suppose. I probably won't be here.' He released his father and held up a hand as the protests threatened. 'Nothing at all to do with the baby. One of the reasons I'm so delighted is that I feel this new Gould will let the old Gould cut his apron strings.' He pecked at May. 'Mummy, d'you mind me saying that? I'm nearly twenty. And there's theatre work in London, and you know that's what I want more than anything.'

'Oh, Victor.' Easy tears flowed. 'Oh, darling, a dozen babies couldn't make you less special. Our first. I'll never forget that night in Manchester when you were born and your poor father—'

'Yes. Well.' Monty cut short that particular reminiscence and clapped Victor on the back. 'He's right of course, Mummy. If he wants to work in the theatre, then London's the place to go. And with his diploma he ought to be able to find something without too much difficulty. Perhaps he could stay with Maud Davenport. I've still got contacts, you know, old boy. I'll write a few letters and see what I can do.'

'Golly. Thanks, Dad,' Victor replied dutifully. He stood up, timing his exit perfectly. 'Look, I'm all in. This excitement's too much for me. I'm going upstairs to leave you two lovebirds in peace. Don't do anything I wouldn't do.'

Monty said jovially, 'From all I hear about you and Beryl Langham, that leaves us plenty of scope.'

May said, 'Darling, put your gas fire on. It'll be cold upstairs.'

Victor said, 'Dad, I've told you a dozen times there's nothing between me and Beryl Langham.'

Monty, laughing again, spluttered, 'Then you'd better sit down and write a letter telling her so, old man. I don't think she knows.'

Victor picked the cushion from behind his mother's head and threw it accurately. He left. The letter was thick and hard against his chest.

May said, 'Darling, I'm so happy I don't know what to do with myself.'

Monty said, 'Darling, I'm so happy, but I know exactly what to do with myself.' He kissed her lingeringly. 'Who is a clever Mummy. Who is the best Mummy in the whole wide world.'

'Oh, Monty, I do love you. But it's awfully cold upstairs. And afterwards I shall be desperately hungry.'

'Well, let's stay here in front of the fire, darling. Then afterwards Monty will make Mummy a lovely supper and bring it in on a tray and we'll be so cosy, just the two of us.'

'But, darling . . . Victor.'

Monty stood up, took the chair on which Florence had so often sat as she button-holed suits for Will, and put the back beneath the door handle.

'Monty, darling. Put out the light. The fire is so romantic.'

He did so and she removed her hairpiece carefully and tucked it discreetly beneath a cushion. Then she began on the long row of buttons over her bust. She sighed with happiness and wondered what Monty would produce for supper.

'Dear Victor. This is like nothing we've ever imagined or talked about. When we see it on the newsreel at the Hippo it's two minutes then we go into the sun or watch the main film. Here it's all the time. The Comintern Brigade are fighting for the people, but the people are frightened and bar themselves in their houses when we go into the villages. They think we are going to steal their food and rape their women. And usually that's what we do. Not me and Tolly of course, but most of the others. Only two in this regiment speak English besides me and Tolly. I don't think many of them are here for their ideals either, it's for the money and excitement – yes, they think it's exciting. They like war. It's already taken me three days to write this. Every time I start we have to advance or retreat – I don't know which way we're going but sometimes it's forwards and sometimes it's back. I found Tolly three weeks ago and he told me I must write to someone back home to tell them what has happened. You are the only one. He thinks he might be killed and then no-one would know. Aunt Sylv knows, but she is old and he says it's important that someone else knows too. You must not tell anyone, Victor. No-one at all. If I get killed too, no-one must ever know what I am going to tell you. If I don't get killed, if I come back home, we won't talk about it together either. In spite of Tolly I wouldn't be telling you at all except for one thing. I want you to look after Davie. I don't know how. You'll have to think of something, old man. But do something for her. Something. At first I wanted to get killed, I thought it would be the best thing for everyone. But Tolly talked me out of that. Besides, I don't want to any more. I'm frightened of dying. That Emmanuel Stein got me here somehow. He gave me an envelope with some papers inside and a friend of his took me on a boat down the Thames to Tilbury. There was a bigger boat there with half a dozen blokes in it. We all of us rowed, some old lighterman was at the tiller and seemed to know where we were heading. We ended up in the middle of the night on some little shingly beach, I don't know where it was but when the sun went down I worked out we were going north-east. Anyway there was a bigger boat there, proper cargo boat, it was being loaded with tinned food. We had to help, about twenty trips we made. We had to get through the blockade at Barcelona. That was hair-raising. Then a chap put me on a bus to Tarragona where the headquarters of the Brigade was supposed to be. Sorry, Victor, I wrote that last week. We had to move then because some Fascist planes came at us out of the sun. They're called the Condors. They come screaming in and drop their bombs right on target, then finish off with machine guns, so you've got to get out of the way fast. Tolly says I'd better hurry up. The thing is, old man, you won't believe this but it's true, Fred Luker says I'm his son. And so is Davie. His daughter I mean. You can see why I can't talk to my mother or Aunt April about this. Fred Luker reckoned that Aunt April was desperate because David couldn't have kids – something to do with his war wound, and Fred was around at the time so she agreed to it as a sort of business arrangement. It sounds mad, doesn't it? I've thought about it so much I can't think any more. Tolly says he thinks it's true so I suppose it is. The thing is, Davie and I are quite fond of each other. We were going to get married actually. I gave her a ring – she wears it round her neck. What she is thinking I don't know. She is probably quite upset at me dashing off. Could you have a word, old chap? Sorry to be a nuisance. I'd better close now, sure to have another raid soon. God knows when you will get this. All the best. Albert.'

Victor crouched before his gas fire, staring at nothing. Then, with great care, he read the letter again. Then he stared. Below, he could hear his mother laughing and there came the clink of Florence's white china cups. He suddenly craved a cup of tea. He swallowed his own saliva and looked again at the fire. After a while he leaned forward and turned it out. Within five minutes the room was very cold. He stood up, folded the letter flat and put it with his painting things. Then, shivering and thirsty, he got into bed. At the moment it was all he could do for his cousin. He considered going without sheets and blankets and huddling in the eiderdown, but then he decided against it. Tomorrow he would see Davie. He would have to do it tomorrow. He lay sleepless, thinking about it and hearing her voice saying, 'I love you, Victor, but I am in love with Albert.'

Long after his parents had come upstairs, he lay wide eyed, staring into the darkness and wondering what to do. Then as the clock from St Nicholas struck two, he sat up in bed. It was so obvious. He would try to make Davie fall in love with him instead of Albert. It would take years, probably; but that didn't matter because it would be his mission in life.

He went to sleep. In the morning, his tongue thick, his throat dry, he remembered that he had planned to go to London this summer. He wondered for a moment or two whether he should give up his plans as part of his Albert-effort, then decided against it. He could write to her and make her interested in his new life.

March, her voice heavy with sarcasm, said, 'Thank you so much for your promised support. I don't quite know what I should have done without it.'

Fred continued to stack glasses onto the trolley. It looked as if he found them very heavy.

'Sorry. I was going to say something. Then, I wasn't

sure. I had a feeling that something was up.'

March frowned again but said nothing, mainly because she hated to agree with Fred. She watched him narrowly and wondered whether he might be ill. His hair did not show the grey like hers did because it was so colourless to begin with, but beneath the new standard lamp she could see he was almost white. He was forty-seven, getting on for fifty after all. It was only natural he should be showing signs of age; but he had seemed unchanged until Albert's departure. Since then, only three months ago, time had caught up with him.

He turned and saw her staring.

'I'm going to bed,' he said abruptly. 'I'll get my suit out of the wardrobe for the morning.'

'That's all right. I'll help Chattie with the glasses and lock up. I'll be a while.' It was ridiculous. He slept in Albert's room but kept his clothes in the wardrobe in the front room, and never went in there to get them without mentioning it; as if he was asking her permission. And she never entered the room when he was fetching his things. Yes, it was simply ridiculous.

She took the glasses into the kitchen and rinsed them carefully, glorying in the fact of the constant hot water. Chattie was 'doing the rounds', putting guards in front of the two fires, wrapping rubbish into neat parcels, locking up. March left her to it and went upstairs, trying not to think of Albert and where he might be and what he might be doing. Since Fred had come home with the news of him on Christmas Eve, she had tried to keep him in a locked cupboard of her mind. There were so many unanswered questions and so many painful conclusions. Surely nothing . . . *nothing* he might have done in Birmingham could have been serious enough to send him away from her. But . . . she knew he would come back safely. She knew that. And it was all that mattered.

She went quietly along the landing and was almost at the door of her room when she heard a sound. It was so like the squeak of the mice at Chichester Street when she was a small girl, that she instinctively looked around her for a mop or a broom or similar weapon. Then she knew it couldn't possibly be vermin, not in her house. She crept on and looked into the big front room. Fred knelt by the bed, her nightgown crumpled in his clenched fists, his head in its satin folds. He was weeping.

For a moment she stayed where she was, paralysed with a mixture of feelings: embarrassment, shock, curiosity and a terrible, agonizing pity. Then she moved forward and sat on the end of the bed. Immediately he checked himself, held his shoulders rigid, and stopped sobbing. His head stayed down, his hands whitened on the flimsy material of her nightgown.

She waited and when he made no move and did not speak, she asked matter-of-factly, 'Well? What is it? What's the matter?' He let his breath go in a gigantic gasp that could have been sob or laughter, and she repeated almost irritably, 'Well?'

He turned his head sideways and she saw his face, mottled, nearly bruised.

'My God, March,' he said thickly. 'My God. You . . . you're marvellous, aren't you? Bloody marvellous.'

'Never mind me. What's the matter with you?'

'Don't you know? Aren't you gloating about it? I've come to the end, March. I've come to the bloody end.'

'The end? What d'you mean? Has the business collapsed?'

This time it was a laugh. 'No. No, the business is thriving. So we're all right. You don't have to panic. The money is still rolling in.'

She said tightly, 'I assumed that was what would reduce you to . . . this. After all, your business has always come before Albert and me and every other human being in the world. Why should things be different now?'

There was a long pause. He opened his eyes wide and seemed to be trying to analyse the weave of the satin. Then he replied, in a monotone, 'I wonder if you're right. I said I did it for you . . . I always said that, didn't I? Getting you away from Edwin . . . taking you back there – selling you to him really. Then Leonie Porterman. I hated Marcus Porterman but I didn't want him dead. And Tilly Adair – I still thought I was doing it for you and Albert. I wonder if I was kidding myself all the time. Was I, March? Do you really think the business meant more to me than anything else?'

The words 'nervous breakdown' flitted into March's mind. She said uncomfortably, 'I don't know. It doesn't matter now anyway. Forget about it – go to bed. It'll seem better in the morning.'

'It won't, it'll seem worse. It seems worse every morning. And every night. I've lost Albert. And if I've lost Albert I've lost you.' He moved his face against the satin. 'I thought I might get a little satisfaction from helping Davie . . . and you know what happened there. I suppose it was David turning you down out of hand that made me know I'd come to the end.'

She said in a poor imitation of her usual brisk voice, 'You'd lost me before Albert went. And Albert going had nothing to do with you.' There was another pause and she asked sharply, 'Did it?'

He said dully, 'Don't you know? Haven't you guessed, March? That day in Birmingham, I told him.'

'You told him?'

'Oh, for God's sake, March, isn't it obvious? I told him he was my son!'

'You . . . what?' She was aghast. Her detachment left her and she clasped her hands and put them to her chin. 'Oh no . . . oh my God . . . oh no, *no*!'

'He was defying me about something and asked me what right I had to . . . well, I told him what right I had. He hated me so much he couldn't take it. The thought that I was his father was so awful he had to get away. That's why he went, March.'

She stared at him, her eyes almost bulging.

'You fool. Is that what you think? He's disliked you ever since we got married – and that's my fault because I poisoned his mind against you!' She put her hands over her face. 'Oh, Fred . . . Fred . . . he hasn't run from you! He's run from me! Don't you see? He loved and respected me – if that hadn't changed he'd have come home. But he didn't. Oh God. You shouldn't have told him. You shouldn't.'

He said in the same wooden voice, 'Well, I did. So it's my fault. Like everything else. But I can't carry the load any more, March. I can't do it.'

'The load?' She was too shocked for tears. Through her fingers she looked at him sprawled on her night-dress, clutching hopelessly at it. Fred Luker, the indomitable Fred Luker, beaten at last. She repeated stupidly, 'The load? You mean the guilt, Fred? The guilt you carried for me?'

The half of his mouth which was exposed lifted slightly. 'Guilt? That's what Tilly said. I'd carry the guilt.'

She whispered, 'Oh, Fred . . . even *her* . . .'

'I shouldn't have mentioned her name. But I can't be cunning Fred Luker any more, March. He said he didn't want to see me any more. He said—'

'You've got to go on, Fred. You've got to forget that and go on. If you don't, what will happen? You cannot give up now.'

'Why?'

There was a pause. Then, without apparent volition, she suddenly slid off the bed and onto her knees. She took his shoulders in her hands, pressed her cheek against his ear and held him fiercely.

'Because I'm telling you to. Because there's nothing else to do. Because, even if we've lost Albert, we've still got each other.'

She felt his amusement like a tremor against her face.

His voice, muffled, came to her from beneath her own mouth. 'Oh, March, we haven't had each other for a long time now.'

Her grip did not loosen.

She said, 'Oh yes we have. We've hated, we've despised, we've loathed . . . but we've been together. If we go to hell, Fred, we go together. There have been so many things . . . Edwin, Leonie, Tilly . . . lies and deception, they're the cement that hold us, Fred. And now they're cleared away – brought into the open – and it's still not the end of us. We're still here, Fred – *here*!' Her voice rose again with her need to convince him and herself. She repeated, 'We're here, don't you understand that? We need each other more than ever now, because Albert has gone. He'll never come back to us. Oh, he might come back home, but we shall never have him again as we did before. So we've got to . . .' She raised her head and twisted his face to make him look at her. 'You said to me before, Fred, that we deserved each other. That's still true.' She stared down into his blue eyes and felt the pity in her melt the hardness. 'Oh, Fred, it'll be all the same in a hundred years. Don't give up. Stay with me, Fred. Don't go . . . don't go . . .'

Tears ran down his face again; he seemed unable to lift his head from her nightdress. She put her head by his and let her own tears run freely. She hardly ever wept, and Fred never. After a long time they crept under the sheets, fully clothed, and lay in foetal positions facing each other.

And when the sky beyond the curtains began to pale into dawn, March drew herself higher onto the pillow and took Fred's head on her shoulder and nursed him until she knew he was asleep. She remembered holding her brother Albert like this when they were children and he was frightened and lost. Albert, Fred, and Albert-Frederick, who symbolized them both. She hardly knew the difference any more.

Chapter Fourteen

It was May's birthday. She was 'the size of a house', Monty boasted proudly; Victor, helping her into Fred's big Rover, amended gloomily, 'You mean two houses don't you, Dad?' May crossed her still-slim ankles and gave a smug smile. 'Make it Buckingham Palace, why don't you?'

March was driving.

'Now behave yourselves, you Goulds,' she said with unusual equanimity. 'Fred wasn't terribly keen on coming to your birthday treat as it was, May. I don't want the racket to put him off entirely.'

'He loves it really,' May said comfortably. 'Don't you remember that time at Rodley?' She tried to make more room for Victor. 'And why on earth Fred has to work on Whit Monday I'll never know.'

'He's mending the small charabanc.'

'Yes, but he's got mechanics to do that sort of thing now, surely?'

March said steadily, 'He enjoys working with his hands again. It's good for him.'

They stopped at London Road and Fred came out of the garage, still drying his hands on some cotton waste. He slid in beside March. Monty asked, surprised, 'Are you going to let the little woman drive, old man?'

Fred looked round and smiled slightly but said simply, 'Yes.'

May sighed dramatically. 'Monty won't let me do a thing. He's going to bribe Aunt Sylv to come back when the baby is born so that I can lead a life of luxury.'

March's mouth tightened for a moment, then relaxed. She said, 'I thought you told me that when Monty had his rise, you'd be moving out to Longford?'

Monty put his arm round May's ample shoulders.

'Well . . . we thought of it, March. But we're used to the old place. And if Aunt Sylv comes to us she'll be happier in Chichester Street.'

Fred said unexpectedly, 'That's true. If April and the girls are really going to America, Sylvia will love returning to Chichester Street. And perhaps David will come and lodge with us.'

Victor, who had studiously not looked at Fred, nor spoken since he entered the car, frowned at the newly installed traffic lights at the top of the pitch and wondered whether he might mention this dialogue to Albert in his next letter. He had written nine times since he had got the official address of the Brigade's sorting-office, but had heard nothing more.

March drew up at Longmeadow and waved to David who was just opening the doors of the motor house. Aunt Sylv and April emerged from the kitchen, each lugging picnic baskets. Flora was already in the car, waving through the back window; Davina waited by the privet hedge, her hand at her throat in what had become a very typical waiting pose. Victor sprang out of the Rover and joined her.

'I'll come in your car if that's all right.'

April nodded. 'Of course. How is May?'

'Mother's fine. Everyone is fine.' Victor took

Davina's hand and swung it. 'Yes. Everyone is fine. Aren't they?'

She gave him her quiet, adult smile. 'Dear Victor. Of course they are.'

They drove sedately in convoy to Down Hatherley and the bluebell woods. April, sitting alongside David, listening to Flora's chatter from the back seat, Victor's amused replies, Davina's silence, could hardly believe they were on the brink of another summer. The piercing beauty of the new beech leaves and the creamy cow parsley was too much. She thought of their last picnic there . . . three years ago? No, it must be four because Davie had been eight and already aware that she was different. Yet they had been happy then. Flora had been still such a baby; Davina had been David's favourite and Albert's very special cousin; David had been blessedly ignorant. And April herself . . . April had learned to live with her own guilt. She stared out of the window as the village pump went past, and wondered if it were possible to damage the heart physically with a weight of grief. After all, it was only a pump like the one out there, and pumps could be overworked.

Flora said, 'I *know* the new baby will be my cousin, Victor. But it will be years and years younger than me, so I don't see why it can't call me Aunt Flora.'

Victor replied, 'I know. Why don't you let the baby call you Grandma? After all, you're such an old lady—'

'Well, I shall be when we come back from America,' Flora interpolated. 'It might as well call me Grandma as anything else.'

April glanced over her shoulder and saw Davina staring through the window, hand at throat. The child was probably holding on to a ring or something Albert had given her.

April said brightly, 'Now stop that, Flora. Most people would give their eyeteeth to have an adventure like we're having, and all you do is grumble.'

'That wasn't a grumble,' Flora argued. 'It was a – a remark.'

'An inaccurate one, darling.' April smiled at Davina, though speaking to Flora. 'If there is a war it will last about two months. You'll hardly be an old lady by then.'

Victor said, 'I'm not so sure, Aunt April. She's getting older by the minute. Is that a grey hair—?' There was a scuffle and a squeal and Davina raised her eyebrows at her mother.

David said, 'Back to normal, darling. Well done.'

April kept smiling but her heart still ached as if over-worked. Two months – obviously a war couldn't last longer than that. But would David ever want them back again?

They picked their flowers and emerged into the sunshine of the wilderness for the picnic. Mackintoshes were spread against possible dampness, and a steamer chair produced for May. She had brought no food, but Chattie and Aunt Sylv had made up for that. Chattie's sandwiches were two inches square with no crusts, bedded in lettuce and cress with a delightful variety of fillings. Sylvia had boiled four enormous gammon hocks and torn a cottage loaf into chunks; she had made two of her weighty fruit cakes and brought a pot of gooseberry jam which had not quite jelled. She suggested they dip pieces of cake into it. 'It's the best birthday cake I've ever tasted, Aunt Sylv,' May sighed, replete with food and happiness. 'I did not really appreciate your cooking before, but I can assure you that if you come back to us, I'll never leave anything on my plate again!' Sylvia smiled, well pleased. It constantly amazed her how Will and Flo, up there somewhere with all the others who had gone on, kept finding work for her capable hands.

March passed a sandwich of tongue and lettuce to Davina. She said in a low voice, 'I've got something to show you. Everyone can see it afterwards, but I thought you'd like to be the first.' She delved in her calf leather handbag and passed an envelope. Davina took a short deep breath as she saw the handwriting. March said, 'It was for my birthday, but it has taken this long to reach me.'

Davina slid out the card. It was a postcard of a church, heavy, Gothic, completely foreign. On the other side was printed, 'No birthday cards in English, so this must do. Many happy returns. Love, Albert.' She put it back inside the envelope; her throat was working uncontrollably. She stood up. 'Very nice. Thank you, Aunt March.' She wandered off among the gorse bushes, and after a few minutes Victor followed her. The card was passed around; everyone was excited. May said what with that and the cake, she thought she might burst with happiness. April began to clear away the picnic; Aunt Sylv snored suddenly and everyone smothered laughter and then settled back to snooze themselves. Flora sat cross-legged, bunching her bluebells and singing softly.

Victor said, 'What's up?'

Davina shook her head. 'Nothing.'

'I should have thought you'd be relieved to hear from Albert.'

'I didn't hear from him. It was Aunt March's card.'

'Ah, I see.'

She walked on, clothed in that maddening silence of hers, pulling off a gorse blossom now and then and never catching her fingers on the thorns.

He said, 'Jealous, are you?'

'I don't know.'

'Well, I'll tell you then. You're jealous.'

Again she retreated into her private silence. He wanted to shake her. He had made opportunities to see her alone half a dozen times since Albie's letter, and each time she had blocked all his efforts by simply shutting up. He wasn't used to it. His parents talked all the time, even when they were furious with each other or gooey with love; and Beryl Langham could talk even when she was being kissed. His dream of making Davie transfer her schoolgirl crush from Albie to him was getting absolutely nowhere.

He said deliberately, 'Davie, do you know the facts of life?'

'Of course.' Her hand went to her throat.

He said, 'Then what if Albie had got a girl into trouble? Hasn't it occurred to you that that is the logical explanation of him suddenly clearing off?'

She shook her head dumbly, her hand clutching at the neck of her cotton frock.

He caught her arm and made her stand still. She was shaking like a leaf. He said, 'Look . . . Davie. It's not the end of the world. There are other people who love you just as much as Albie.'

She said chokingly, 'He's written to you about it,

hasn't he? That's why you keep seeing me and trying to be nice and kind. Does he want his ring back?'

'No. No, he doesn't want that back. And he still loves you, Davie. But . . .'

'But not in a grown-up way.' She hung her head. 'When I was a kid, he loved me then. Daddy loved me then, too. Now I'm grown up, he's gone, and Daddy is sending me away.'

Victor could feel his objectivity melting away like ice in the sun. He put his arms around her juddering shoulders.

'Your father is sending you away *because* he loves you. Idiot. And maybe Albie cleared off because he loved you too. And there's me. I love you.'

She tried to laugh. 'And you're going to London in the autumn.'

'Not so far as Detroit.'

She shivered again and he tightened his arms.

She whispered, 'Will you write to me, Victor? Please?'

'Of course.'

'Yes, but proper letters. Not just jokey ones.'

'Proper ones. I promise.'

She stayed very still within his clasp, and he wondered whether she was relaxing slightly. Then she said, 'You *did* have a letter from Albie, didn't you?'

He breathed carefully. 'Yes.'

'Was he all right?'

'No.' He felt her jerk and said, 'You wanted the truth. He's in a helluva state. But he's alive and he's found Tolly, and like Fred told us at Christmas, Tolly will look after him.'

'Will he come home one day, Victor?'

'He might. I don't think so. Sorry, darling, but I'm trying not to be jokey. I don't think he'll ever come back to live with Fred and March in Gloucester.'

'What about me?'

Victor tightened his arms again and suddenly she put her hands around his waist and pressed her face into his neck.

He said into her ear, 'Davie . . . darling Davie . . . he won't come back to you. I'm sorry, so sorry. But he won't.'

She gave one huge sob and then was still, hanging onto him for dear life. He was frightened, wondering whether she might be rigid with a convulsion, or even having a heart attack. From somewhere behind them, Flora's voice sang, 'In and out the bluebell windows, count your lovers on your fingers, is it one or is it hundreds, out . . . goes . . . you . . .'

He said urgently, 'It wasn't his fault, Davie. He still loves you. It wasn't his fault. And it's not yours, either. You must try to forgive him.'

At last her voice, pitiful and small, came to him. 'I don't understand.'

'You will. When you're older he'll talk to you and explain and you will understand.'

'How much older? How much older must I be to understand?'

'I'm not sure about that, Davie. It depends.'

'What does Albie want me to do until then?'

'He wants you to . . .' Victor's mind felt as if it were whirring as it tried to find something real to say. He had not concentrated so hard in his life before. 'He wants you to try to think of him as a brother, Davie. Really. A brother. If only you can do that it will be all right.'

She felt slightly less rigid.

'Well, I already do that. But he's not – not my brother, I mean. So I thought if we got married then it would be next best to being a brother.'

'Yes. Well. I suppose you were right in one way. But now, what Albert wants, is that you forget the marrying part and just concentrate on the brother and sister part.'

'Because of this other girl?'

'Other girl?' He had forgotten his previous allusion and felt his heart skipping. Then he wondered whether to deny it. But after all, it was the simplest way of 'doing something' and he had promised Albert in that first letter that he would 'do something'. So he said simply, 'Yes.'

'Will he marry the other girl?'

'No. I don't think he'll get married at all, Davie. He just wants you to be his sister and he wants to be your brother. Are you beginning to understand?'

'I think so. He doesn't hate me?'

He pulled her away and looked at her face and said solemnly, 'He doesn't hate you. Neither does your father. Nobody hates you.' He wondered whether to kiss her. It was terribly tempting. Albert must have kissed her often.

She said quickly, 'Then I'll keep our ring, always. And I'll never marry anyone else either. And when we're grown-up – really grown-up and quite old I mean – we'll live together in a country cottage. Lots of brothers and sisters do that. Will that be all right, Victor?'

He knew he couldn't kiss her. He said gently, 'That

will be marvellous, Davie. Albert will be so happy if you can do that.'

'Can I write to him?'

'I . . . I don't know. Let me write first. Let me tell him that you understand about not getting married. Do you mind?'

She minded very much, he could tell. But she gave her wide smile and took his arm to walk back to the others. And she did not pick at the gorse flowers, nor put her hand to her throat. Victor sighed. He had done the very best he could; she would never fall in love with him and if he were sensible he should be glad. The responsibility of her sort of love was too great. But . . . it was also very precious. It had little to do with the crush Beryl Langham had on him. It had a lot to do with Grandma Florence Rising, who had let her husband be happy in his own inimitable way. Victor felt his head throb; it was all too difficult. He thought of London and the sheer pure joy of paints and canvas. Not much longer . . . not much longer at all.

April watched Flora plait her bluebell stalks into a pattern of nodding blooms, incanting her strange doggerel as she did so. The rhyme and action seemed to grow more significant each time it was repeated. '. . . count your lovers on your fingers . . .' Was that in fact what life boiled down to? Tripping haphazardly along its various paths, meeting, mating, to beget the next generation who would go in and out the bluebell windows all over again? She glanced around and saw that the others were either asleep or resting with closed eyes. She stood up and walked away from them, away from where Davie and Victor had gone, away. It crossed her mind for a fleeting second that if she kept walking, she could leave it all behind her. Forget it. 'Self-induced amnesia' . . . where had she read about that? Could she induce amnesia and begin another life with no David, no Davina, no Flora? She knew she could not. She was a prisoner, clinging to her own chains.

She came to a five-barred gate and leaned on it with a small gasp of bitter amusement. She really was such a fool. Nothing very awful had happened after all. If David knew anything, he obviously wasn't going to speak about it. He was sending them away; that was a small price to pay to retain a shred of their happiness, surely? All she had to do was to play the game his way: pretend they were being evacuated to Harry and Miranda, make it an exciting adventure for the girls, hope and pray that they could all soon return home and pick up the threads again. Some of the threads at any rate. Surely – *surely* – she could do that?

She heard David's step in the grass behind her, and would have known he was there anyway. She did not turn.

'Hello, darling. Bluebells in the wood, but just look at those buttercups.' She noticed them as she spoke. Brilliant, eye-aching gold.

He stood by her, leaning gratefully on the gate.

'You can't rest, can you? Even March has unwound and is fast asleep with her head on Fred's shoulder.'

'Yes, they've become very close. Perhaps since Albert's disappearance. Fred certainly went through a terrible time in London and I expect March is grateful.' She did not want to talk about Fred. 'I felt like a stroll, that's all.'

He was silent, gazing ahead of him, not touching her. She began to feel her nerves tighten inexorably. The silence went on and on.

She said brightly, 'Flora certainly cannot sing like Davie. That awful rhyme—' Through the tangled gorse came a thread of verse.

She could not continue to talk through it and was forced to listen to the end. There was a pause and it started again. April thought she might scream.

'Shall we go back?' She sounded normal enough. 'There is some tea left in the thermos and plenty of lemonade.'

He said very quietly, 'Not yet. I want to say something.'

Her heart leapt with sheer terror. She dug her nails into the top bar of the gate.

'No need for . . . explanations, David.' Somehow she had to stop him. Her voice was high-pitched, very gay. 'I really don't mind about America. Well, of course I *mind,* but I understand. And when we come back everything will be all right again and—'

'Be quiet, April.'

She cut herself off with a small gasping scream and stood with bowed head, looking at the grain in the wood and praying in a silent gabble for she knew not what.

David said, 'Listen. Please listen to me, darling. You haven't listened for a long time now. If you had, I wouldn't have to say this. You would already know . . . you *should* already know.' He turned his shoulder so that he was facing away from her. 'I won't look at you. I don't want you to have to put on any act for me. I just want you to hear.' He waited perhaps three long seconds, then drew a breath. 'Sometimes, April, we can talk. And sometimes we can't. And about this, I think we can't. That's why I've said nothing, and you've said nothing. But I cannot watch you tear yourself to shreds any longer. Let me be quite blunt, my darling. If Davie belongs to Mannie Stein, it makes no difference to me at all. Do you understand that? No, don't speak, don't touch me. Just *hear*!' He took a step away from her, though she had made no movement at all but was frozen to the top of the gate. He said, 'That time all those years ago, Primrose . . . I know you wouldn't have permitted . . . permitted . . . anything. I don't want to know what happened. It's finished and over. But it makes no difference. It makes me love you more. It makes me want to protect you more. Now . . . that's what I had to say. I tried to tell you a long time ago, before we went to Italy. But you wouldn't hear. Please hear now.'

She stayed where she was and closed her eyes against the brilliance of the buttercups. At last she parted her dry lips.

'You're sending us away.'

His shoulders sagged. 'Ah. Is that how you see it? Darling . . . Primrose . . . to risk the lives of you and Davie and Flo, is – is—'

'Davie too?' she interrupted.

He was still again. 'I don't understand that question,' he said slowly.

'You said just now you still loved me. But Davie – what about Davie? If you think she is another man's child—'

He whirled around, wincing as he pulled his leg muscles, his eyes black holes of sudden anger.

'How dare you, April? How dare you question my love for Davie? Would I punish her for my own inadequacies? My God, Davie is mine – mine in His sight – and she is our first-born. How can you doubt – how can you think—'

She said, 'You did not mention Davie. Only me. And I have never, ever doubted your love for me, David. Even if you hated me you would still love me.' She made a gesture at such a paradox, then flattened her hand as if to keep him at bay. 'I have not really doubted your love for me. But you have ignored Davie. You – you—'

He said levelly, 'If that is really so, then it has been in an effort not to smother her with a love which could become possessive. I did not wish to come between her and Albert. And I did not want to burden her with my stupid pride in her singing voice.' He said, as if taking an oath, 'I love both my daughters, but Davie especially because you went through hell to have her, my darling.'

She closed her eyes again and took a deep slow breath. It was as if she could see into the future and choose which way to go. The sun was hot on her closed lids as she spoke. 'If you mean that, if you mean all you have said now, then prove it.'

'How?'

'Do not send us to America.'

'April, that has nothing to do with this. I assure you that my motives in suggesting—'

'I know. But families – real families – stick together in danger. There is more danger in separating us than there is in keeping us together throughout whatever might happen.'

She waited. After a while she opened her eyes. He

was staring at her, searching, and as she met that stare, he smiled, surrendering.

'We will stay together, April. You, me, Davie and Flo. We will stay together. It was what I wanted most in the world, which made it a selfish wish. That was why I repudiated it.'

She let her breath go.

'Then I will tell you, David. Mannie Stein did not touch me. Not ever. And that is the truth.'

He went on staring and she met his stare and let him see into her soul. She had no need to think of anything else except that one statement. He had agreed to keep them together, and in return she had told him that Davie was not Mannie Stein's daughter. There was no need to go further.

After a very long time he said, 'It wouldn't have made any difference, April. That I promise you. But for your sake, darling . . .' He held out his arms. 'I am so very thankful.'

She went into his embrace and they held each other without passion, in a long moment of gratitude. He asked no more questions, though there were many more to be asked. And she offered no other explanations because God had given her David again, whole and happy, and she was not going to risk that for the joy of personal absolution. He had told her it did not matter, and she had told him Mannie Stein was nothing to do with it. She had chosen her path and she had chosen his too.

After a while his hold on her tightened, and for a moment they clung, two shipwrecks. Then he released her, cupped her face and said, 'I knew you loved me. I never doubted that.'

She nodded. 'And I knew you loved me. If you had not, it might have been easier to bear.'

'Shall we go and find her? Tell her?'

She nodded. 'Flo will be pleased too.'

They walked back through the rough grass, arm in arm, companions more than lovers. They knew that they were battle-scarred and that they could do nothing about each other's injuries except respect them.

Davie and Victor were crouching by Flo, watching her plait her bluebells and listening carefully to something she was saying. Davie looked up and met her father's eyes directly for the first time since he had turned down March's offer of singing lessons.

She said, 'Daddy?'

He held out a hand. 'Your mother has talked me out of America. She thinks we should go to war together.'

'*Daddy!*' She took his hand and swung it high. 'Oh, Daddy, I want to stay with you so much!'

Above her flaxen head, David's eyes met April's. 'You are my precious, precious bane,' he said.

'And me, Daddy. And me!' Flora clamoured, bluebells forgotten in the excitement.

Victor's eyes went to Fred Luker and surprised for an instant on that waking face a smile of . . . could it be contentment? How could he possibly be content? And how could Aunt March lean over and kiss him as if she really loved him?

Victor plonked himself down by his own parents who might shout and yell and throw things at times, but who had conceived him in wedlock and were satisfyingly together again – with a little help from their wonderful son, of course.

'For goodness sake, Victor, you missed the baby by

an inch!' protested May, heaving herself upright and reaching for the picnic basket.

'Such a fuss about nothing anyway,' Monty was saying to the capering foursome in front of him. 'Take it from me, there won't be a war this time. Neville will let that painter fellow do what he likes in Europe. Surely we learned our lesson last time trying to protect Belgium – and what thanks did we get? No, we're nothing to do with Europe. Let them get on with it. This sceptred isle . . . this England . . .' He lumbered to his feet and began to declaim Shakespeare with suitable gestures.

Fred's smile crescendoed into a laugh. Victor joined him and David chuckled, shaking his head despairingly. March slapped May's hand away from the midday leftovers which had to do for tea, and April encircled her family with her long arms and looked across their heads at Aunt Sylv.

And Aunt Sylv, who had taken out her teeth, chewed on her gums like a cow at cud, and lifted her head to the dazzling blue and white sky. Where, surely, Florence and Will Rising were watching and smiling too.

THE END